I0785689

Forrestine C. Hooker

The Long Dim Trail

OK Publishing 2021

*Forrestine C. Hooker*

# The Long Dim Trail

A Suspenseful Tale of Adventure and Intrigue in the Wild West (From the Author of Star, Prince Jan St. Bernard and Child of the Fighting Tenth)

Published by

## MUSAICUM

Books

- Advanced Digital Solutions & High-Quality book Formatting -

musaicumbooks@okpublishing.info

2021 OK Publishing

ISBN 978-80-272-7576-2

# Contents

# Part One

# Chapter One

"Everything all right, Limber?" asked Allan Traynor, boss of the Diamond H ranch, as a cowboy with jingling spurs reined his pony before the closed gates of the corral.

Doctor Powell, standing beside Traynor, scrutinized the rider, whose broad-brimmed Stetson, caught by the wind, flapped from his face, exposing the sun-brown skin, firm chin and grey eyes. It needed no student of psychology to decide that Limber was not a man who would flinch when facing a six-shooter held by a rustler.

The cowboy nodded answer to Traynor's query. Limber's eyes scanned the herd, then, satisfied, he leaned across the neck of his pinto pony, and said, "Paddy Lafferty wants to sell out."

"Who told you?" Traynor spoke with undisguised surprise.

"Dillon. Paddy tol' him he was gettin' too old, that the rheumatiz is botherin' again, an' he's goin' to quit because he won't trust no one to run his herd when he can't get 'round to it hisself."

"Did Paddy say how much he wanted?"

"Nope," was the laconic reply. "I'll find out. It's a mighty good bunch of stuff. Lots of three-year steers, an' thar ain't many three-year-olds left in these parts, now."

"It's worth looking up," commented Traynor. "I'm glad you spoke of it. How soon will you be ready to hit the trail?"

"'Bout ten minutes."

"Keep the boys out of mischief this trip, if you can."

There was a twinkle in Traynor's eyes that was reflected in the grey ones of the cowboy, who said soberly, "I'll do my best. But when they get to mixin' in things they're slipperier than a bunch of quicksilver. You think you got hold of it and you find you ain't."

Limber turned his pony toward the corrals, twisting in his saddle as Traynor called after him, "Tell some one to saddle my pony and Doctor Powell's. We'll ride out with you."

As the cowboy disappeared, Traynor said, "It will give you a faint idea of the work. You'll find it mighty different from the cowpuncher's life of moving pictures."

The doctor laughed. "I feel like a small boy about to wriggle under the canvas of a circus tent. I never dreamed that Arizona was such a wonderland."

The eyes of the two men swept across the Sulphur Spring Valley that undulated twenty miles from the Galiuro Mountains on the west to the Grahams on the east; starting sixty miles north of the Diamond H in the narrow Aravaipa Cañon, it gradually broadened into a great plain that terminated at the Mexican border.

"Of course," continued the doctor, "I had a vague idea of its mineral wealth and cattle interests, but I must confess that until I reached here the name of Arizona conjured visions of burning desert, Gila monsters, rattlesnakes, horn-toads and Apaches. Even when I stepped from the train and met you, the impression of a 'No-Man's Land' was strong upon me. Yet now that I have been here a month I feel as though I shall never want to leave it."

"You can make sure of that," retorted Traynor, "if you will go to the Hasayampa River, kneel on the brink and drink of the water. You must be very careful, though, to kneel above the crossing. This will keep you from ever wishing to leave Arizona and you will receive the gift of absolute truthfulness; but, should you drink while kneeling below the crossing, truth and you will be divorced the balance of your life."

"Did you drink below the crossing or above?" challenged the doctor with an amused smile.

"There is only one case on record where a man acknowledged that he drank the water below the crossing. His name was Hasayampa Bill. He died a year ago. Hasayampa Bill was a victim of circumstances, not intention. He said that he was drinking above the crossing when he lost his balance and fell into the stream which carried him far below. Though Hasayampa swore solemnly that he kept his mouth shut-for the first time on record-his reputation was thoroughly established. A letter addressed to the 'Biggest Liar in Arizona' was accorded him by popular vote."

The doctor was about to reply, when the air was filled with ear-splitting whistles and staccato cries. Then the big gates of the corral swung open, and an avalanche of cattle tumbled madly through and headed in a wild rush down the road that led south toward Willcox-excited bellows and plaintive lowing of calves seeking their mothers, mingled with the voices of invisible men, completely obliterated by the clouds of alkali dust.

Traynor led the way into the stable where two saddled ponies twisted nervously. The men looked at each other and smiled as the doctor approached the pinto pony. Its eyes showed whites, its ears went back. It sheered nervously, but Powell gained the saddle and, with Traynor close beside him, they reached the moving herd.

Through the haze of dust a shadowy rider would loom momentarily, then disappear. Traynor rode on the outer edge of the herd. Doctor Powell became aware that Limber had materialized at his side, and forgot everything else in his admiration of the cowpuncher's unconscious grace as his lithe, swaying figure adjusted itself to each movement of the wiry, dancing pony.

"Head off that buckskin," shouted Limber, rising in his stirrups and waving his quirt at a cow that was making a wild dash for freedom.

Bronco's pony emerged from the haze and tore madly after the cow, reaching her side just as she made up her bovine mind that she had no intention of deserting. Her expression of injured innocence as she ambled quietly back roused Doctor Powell's mirth and Bronco's ire.

The cowpuncher reined his pony beside Powell's, muttering imprecations that finally ended in a verbal explosion.

"Durn her! Whenever you turn an old buckskin cow like that loose in the herd it's as bad as sickin' a mother-in-law on a happy family. She won't rest till she gets 'em millin' and stampedes everything in sight, and then she picks up her knittin' and looks innercent and says she never allowed to start nothin' noways! Gee! I wish I could strike a ranch where there warn't nothin' but steers. The minute you mix up with a female critter, cow or petticoats, you're roundin' up trouble for yourself and lots of others."

He paused long enough, to jerk out a sack of tobacco and cigarette papers, letting the reins fall on his pony's neck as he glared at the cow. She was slowly dropping to the rear of the herd, but Bronco and his pony did not relax their vigilance.

"Mebbe you thought I didn't know you, you old buckskin bag o' bones," apostrophized Bronco. "I'd know that derned twisted horn if I was dead twenty years!"

Holy Dick galloped up, grinning broadly.

"Hello, Bronc! Ain't that your ol' buckskin friend?"

Bronco snorted. "Yep! An' you bet she's goin' to keep movin' until she's loaded in the car and headed for trouble somewhar else. Arizona ain't big enough to hold her an' me."

Holy rode off, turning in his saddle and screaming in a shrill nasal whine that he fondly imagined was singing:

> "'Tis ye-a-a-rs since las-s-s-st we-e-ee met
> An' we ma-a-aa-ay not me-ee-et agin.
> I stru-ug-gle to-o-oo forgit
> But I stru-ug-g-g-gg-g-ll-l-ll-le aa-aal in va-aa a-in."

Holy's pony contributed to the tremolo effect by its short, nervous trot.

"I'm glad she's a gittin' offen the range," soliloquized Bronco, "but I'll always be sorry we didn't butcher her on the ranch so's I could help chaw her up. If ever I get to Heaven all I'll ask is to eat buckskin cows for everlastin'."

As he uttered the last words Bronco raced ahead, leaving Doctor Powell at liberty to laugh and wonder what the mystery of the buckskin hoodoo might be. Then his eyes wandered from the dust-cloud ahead of him to the purple-blue peaks that reached thousands of feet upward as if striving to pierce the brilliant sky; across the valley clumps of greyish brown saccaton grass, slender tufts of waving gietta interspersed by tall spikes of Spanish Dagger formed a typical Arizona landscape.

"Well, what do you think of it?" asked Traynor, riding up to him.

Powell's eyes sparkled with enthusiasm. "It's a wonderful country! How far away is Hasayampa River? I'm ready to start now for that drink!"

They laughed together as their ponies' heads were reined toward the ranch, but Powell could not resist a backward glance at the herd which had now settled down to a steady amble. The sunlight filtering through the dust formed a golden mist in which the cowpunchers and their ponies were dimly silhouetted.

"Of course there are annoyances, unpleasant people to encounter at times, bad seasons to offset the good ones," —Traynor deftly rolled a cigarette with his right hand as he spoke, his left resting lightly on the high pommel of his saddle. "Taking it all in all, though, when I ride across the valley or reach a high peak and look down where thousands of cattle graze undisturbed by the in-roads of civilization, I feel it is a royal heritage. Do you think I would barter it, like Esau, even though my menu might read, 'Pottage a la champagne and truffles'?"

"Is the role of Prodigal Son necessary to qualify for a fatted calf in Arizona?" queried Powell. "I'm as hungry as the proverbial bear. Oh, that reminds me. Bronco was bewailing the fact that a certain buckskin cow had not been butchered at the ranch. He seems a bit sensitive regarding buckskins. What's the trouble?"

Traynor's mouth twitched as he answered, "Ask him. It's too good a story for any one else to spoil in the telling."

They reached the stables and left the ponies with the Mexican stableman. As they entered the large court-yard which formed the center of the house, they were greeted by the welcome sound of the lunch bell and Fong, in immaculate white and with neatly coiled queue, smiled amiably from the dining room door.

After lunch the two men sat smoking and chatting in the deep porch between the dining room and living room, where easy chairs, a hammock, a table littered with newspapers and magazines, tempted one to loiter. The stable boy interrupted them, speaking in Mexican, and Traynor explained that there was some trouble with the acetelyn plant.

"I always take care of that myself, and unless I do so we will have to resort to coal-oil lamps. I'll be back shortly. Make yourself comfortable."

Powell leaned back lazily in his chair, trying to reconcile Traynor who had just spoken with the Traynor he once knew; a young chap fresh from college, unlucky enough to lose his last remaining relative at the same time he inherited a fairly good-sized fortune.

It had been the usual story of "wild oats." Then Traynor's revulsion had been complete, though not in time to avoid a quarrel with the girl to whom he was engaged. Exaggerated stories of various episodes, exploited by a Sunday paper, caused her to return his ring and refuse absolutely to see him or listen to his explanations.

Traynor thrashed the reporter, paid a heavy fine for that privilege and started on a trip West with no definite idea except to get as far as possible from a place filled with bitter memories.

During the journey he met a young army officer returning from leave of absence, and the lieutenant's invitation to visit Fort Grant had been accepted by Traynor. Some months later Traynor, disposing of all his Eastern interests, had purchased the Diamond H ranch, the owner of which had recently died.

In the seven years after this purchase, Cuthbert Powell was the only one of Traynor's former acquaintances who ever heard from the young rancher. Powell had promised to visit the ranch, but not until now had that promise been fulfilled. It was not easy to recognize the tanned, alert chap who grasped his hands as he alighted from the Pullman. As days went by, it was a constant source of surprise to the doctor to note that the mental change in his friend was more marked than the physical. It was as though the breadth and strength of the country had been absorbed by the owner of the "Diamond H."

Traynor returned and slipped into the chair he had vacated.

"You see, on a ranch one becomes blacksmith, veterinarian, doctor, cowpuncher, carpenter, farmer —. In fact, a veritable jack of all trades. No one cares what your family is, how much money you own or what your social status elsewhere, past, present or future, may be. It is yourself that is judged. There is no court of appeal if you are condemned. You've got to look a man in the eyes, grip his hand as a comrade, shoot as quickly as the other chap, roll in your blanket and take any weather that comes, without growling. If you can do these things the life will suit you and the vastness of the place sinks into your soul. It mends one's broken faith in humanity."

Powell, watching his friend, saw the lines about his mouth harden and knew that the memory of the past was burning like a corroding acid. Then the mood passed and Traynor turned with a half-smile.

"Well, what do you think of your first experience as a cowhand?"

"I'm thankful that I knew how to ride before I came here," laughed Powell. "That was rather a gay little nag I had this morning."

"That animal's name is Hot Tamale. The boys wanted to try you out a bit. I knew you could take care of yourself, so did not say anything. The joke is on them now; but you have won their respect and will be free from other pranks."

"I think I'll insist on riding Hot Tamale hereafter," asserted Powell. "By the way, when Limber spoke to you about that bunch of cattle, I thought I would like to buy them, provided you, yourself, did not intend to do so. Of course, I realize that I am a tenderfoot, ignorant of the first rudiments of the cattle business, but what would you advise about my locating in this section?"

"It would be a good move," responded Traynor. "Paddy's range lies between my own and the Hot Springs country across the Galiuros. He has permanent water, which is a gold mine, especially during a dry season. The mountains between here and Hot Springs are rich in feed, so Paddy's cattle work that way." He puffed silently on his cigar for a few seconds, then turned suddenly to Powell. "Look here, Cuthbert, if you are really serious about locating in this section, why don't you get in touch with Doctor King who owns the Hot Springs? The place would interest you professionally, for the water comes out of solid rock at a temperature of 140 degrees and is the purest water I have ever tasted. It is noted in the Territory as a cure for various complaints."

"I would certainly like to see it," answered the doctor enthusiastically, "if you can arrange it for me."

"King only held Squatter's Right until recently. Under that, the possessor loses title unless he stays on the ground. It is not under government survey yet, so could not be patented like surveyed land. I advised King to patent it under Indian Script and make his title secure. He has just done this. King has been hoping to erect a sanitarium at the Springs, but lack of funds, and his flat refusal to consider anyone as a partner except a resident physician able to finance the plans, has blocked his scheme."

"It might appeal to him to let me carry out my own idea of establishing a sanitarium for tubercular children in Arizona. I don't mean wealthy invalids, attended by a retinue of nurses and other impedimenta, but poor children who otherwise would have no hope of health. The climate, altitude and all conditions would be simply ideal. I should like to talk to him myself."

"Do you know that you are setting forth the very ideas that King discussed with me the last time I saw him? That was, a place for poor, tubercular children. He loves every child that he sees. His own boy died at the age of six. The mother died soon after. King gave me no details, and I doubt whether anyone else besides myself, knows this much. I fancy his thought was to make the place a memorial to the boy he lost."

"It would be a splendid idea to carry out with such a man!" exclaimed Powell, deeply moved. "How soon do you think it could be arranged for me to meet him?"

"It's a waste of time to write. No one but King and a family named Glendon live in that section. Mail lies at the Willcox post-office until one or the other happens to be in town. It's thirty-five miles from Willcox to Hot Springs, and twenty-four across the Galiuro trail from here. When Limber gets back, you and he could ride over the mountains, have a look at the Springs and talk it over with Doctor King. I feel very confident that you might join forces."

"Fine!" ejaculated Powell. "Now, what about that cattle deal?"

"You are determined to 'jump in with both feet' as the boys would say," laughed Traynor. "However, it would be wise to take that matter up as soon as possible. Paddy is a queer character, so you had better stay out of the deal until I get it arranged with him. If you make the buy and at any time wish to sell out, I will take the herd and ranch at the same price you pay for it, so you will not run any risk of being tied up here if you wish to leave."

"I asked you to tell me how far it is to the Hasayampa River?" reminded the doctor. "Even if I do not indulge in a drink from that historic stream, I am here to stay."

"You'll make good," asserted Traynor, heartily. "The man who is a real man wins out here in the end, if he lets whiskey and cards alone. Living on ranches, miles away from civilization, one does not have the problem of women. 'Cherchez la femme' does not apply to this section of the country, thank the good Lord! That's why this place appealed most strongly to me. Unless I go to Willcox I can forget there is such a creature as woman in the universe."

"All women are not the same, Allan," protested Powell, placing his hand on Traynor's arm and looking at him earnestly. "I hope the right one will come into your life some day. One who can appreciate you as you deserve, and who will be big enough and fine enough to be a wife in the best sense of the word. Why, man! Think of the pride and pleasure you would have in this place, knowing that it was the heritage of your son!"

Traynor rose hastily, turned abruptly from his friend and stood staring through the open door of the porch across the wide pastures. His face was white when he confronted Powell.

"What would you do if you found that the patient upon whom you are operating has not succumbed to the anaesthetic, Cuthbert? Cut without pity?"

"Yes," answered Powell, "if it meant life or death to waver or hesitate a second."

"I thought I was numb; that it would not hurt any more; but when you spoke of—a son-it cut into my heart. I've tried to forget-it's like burying something that is alive. In the night I hear its voice; I see its shadow even in the darkness."

He rose and moved restlessly; his face white. "No one knows what it meant to give her up. She believed those damned reports and gave me no chance to prove the truth, and I—, why-it would not have mattered of what she was accused; the blackest charges proved against her, —I would have held her and fought the world for her, innocent or guilty. I believed she loved me as I loved her-she refused to hear my story."

"Did she never know the truth?" asked Powell.

"Returned my ring, asked me to spare her the humiliation of talking to me. Yet, after I came here, I wrote telling her that the man in my automobile with that woman, was not myself. You remember the newspapers spared the woman's name. She had a husband and child-eloping with that cad, Brunton. Cheap machine broke down at two o'clock in the night. I recognized them. Put 'em in my machine and told her to get back home before it was too late. Oh, she was ready enough then to be decent. Brunton took her to her door, then he went to his place, but that fool reporter saw the number of the machine, and wrote the story. You know it. Woman's name kept out, my name not mentioned outright, but description sufficient to identify me beyond doubt. Couldn't sue the paper, my lawyer said, and Brunton lit out for Europe. Rotten mess all around.

"I wrote the full truth to Nell, begged a word from her as a man dying of thirst begs for a drop of water. She never answered the letter. A year later I wrote again, and that one was returned unclaimed."

"You say that the second letter came back unclaimed," spoke Powell, "but, you have no proof that the first one ever reached her. Had you thought of that?"

"Yes. Both letters had my Arizona address on the envelope as well as inside. When I did not hear in reply to the first letter, and it was not returned to me, I communicated with the Dead

Letter Office, but no such letter had been turned over to that department. The only logical conclusion was that she did not wish to answer."

The doctor made no comment. Traynor's reasoning was too convincing for suggestions.

"Yet, I made a second effort," went on the boss of the Diamond H. "After that, there was nothing more to do but accept the situation. Now you know the truth, Cuthbert. No other woman will ever fill her place in my life, —but, I cannot keep her out of my thoughts, day or night."

"I'm sorry I spoke, old man," answered the doctor.

"I'm glad you did," replied Traynor. "Now, you understand."

As the shadows lengthened on the prairie the two friends smoked and spoke of other things. And yet-both Traynor and Powell-and many another-had read with the careless glance of the unscathed, the account of a train wreck in Kansas, in which the loss of life had been appalling, and the loss of mail had not been mentioned.

# Chapter Two

The cattle that Powell and Traynor had watched starting from the Diamond H, constituted the first shipment of the season, contracted to an Eastern buyer. Official inspection by the Live Stock Sanitary Board was exacted, not only regarding the health of shipped cattle, but also to protect cattlemen from rustlers on the miles of open range.

After reaching Willcox, the boys of the Diamond H drove the herd into the shipping pens beside the railroad track, locked the gates and turned with joyous expectation toward the main street of town. Limber parted from the others a short distance from the corrals.

"I'll tell the inspector we'll be ready tomorrow mornin' soon as the cars get in," he said, and without waiting reply rode toward the part of town where the more pretentious houses were bunched.

Like schoolboys out for a holiday, Bronco, Holy and Roarer raced their ponies to the Cowboys' Rest Corral. Here they were greeted vociferously by Buckboard Bill, who had retired from driving a skeleton stage and established the only place where horses or vehicles might be hired.

A few minutes elapsed before the three cowpunchers, afoot, made their way along the street. Ponies standing with dangling reins and hoofs buried fetlock deep in the fine, white alkali sand in front of the stores, told that many other cowpunchers from other ranches were in town. The Diamond H boys quickly identified the owner of each pony by its brand.

A row of irregular buildings, consisting of three stores, a Chinese restaurant, several saloons and a hotel, formed the principal street of Willcox. Facing the stores across the dusty expanse, lay the Southern Pacific depot which was the heart of the town, while radiating from it east and west, like great arteries, ran the steel tracks of the railroad. Pack burros, loaded with miners' supplies, shuffled out on the road to Dos Cabezas. Many of these tiny animals were animated woodpiles-only legs and wagging ears visible from beneath a canopy of split wood destined for a camp where fuel was not procurable, otherwise. The only break in the grey monotone of the landscape was the few cottonwood trees, planted by optimistic souls around their dwelling places.

It was a typical frontier town of three hundred people, two-thirds of whom were Mexicans speaking no English. If, by chance, a stranger alighted from the "passenger" train, the arrival of which was the most important event of each day, the town, like a naughty child with dirty face and torn clothes, looked the new-comer over critically. If he met the inspection squarely, it held out a friendly hand, and as long as he "played fair" that hand was ready to fight for him and his.

The boys from the Diamond H sauntered leisurely along the street, exchanging greetings with those they knew, until, under their usual pretext of expecting mail, they reached the combination store and post-office. It was an important duty to ascertain beyond doubt whether any letters were waiting to be claimed by Peter N. Hewland, Dick Reynolds and Henry Jackson, who were thus able to keep their legal identification. At all other times they were known as Bronco Pete, Holy Dick, whose vocabulary of cuss-words held the Arizona record, and Hell-roarer Jack, with a gentle falsetto voice which under stress of emotion became a tiny squeak. Convenience had curtailed these names to Bronc, Holy and Roarer.

Having digested the information that no mail awaited them, they entered into conversation. One could learn the news of territory, county and nation in the post-office, besides ascertaining what outfits were in town. Additional attractions were found in the posters to be read, notices of round-up work, advertisements of stolen horses or stray cattle.

It was while browsing on such literature that Bronco halted with mouth half-open and disbelieving eyes. He read the hand-written notice deliberately to the end twice before he turned to where Roarer and Holy were inspecting silver-mounted spurs-which they did not need, but intended to buy because they had to spend their money someway.

"Say, boys, thar's goin' to be a ice-cream festival tonight!"

"Shucks!" squeaked Roarer. "Try something else, Bronc. You all know that thar ain't no ice any nearer than Tucson. And nobody's fool enough to send ninety miles and pay cut-throat rates for ice just to make ice-cream, except a regular ijit."

The grin on Roarer's face and the faces of other by-standers recalled Bronco's exploit of ordering ice from Tucson, and reaching the Diamond H with nothing but a wet blanket in the wagon.

Succumbing to the alluring display in a mail order catalogue, Bronco had bought an ice-cream freezer, declaring he was going to get filled up on that delicacy for once in his life-if it took three months' pay. The episode became historic, and the freezer kindling wood.

"If you don't believe me," challenged Bronco, "come and see for yourself! What's more, it says here, it's goin' to be free with cake throwed in," he finished triumphantly.

Holy edged beside Bronco and peered over his shoulder. "Derned if it ain't so," he acknowledged at last. "But, mebbe that air paper's lyin'."

"What do you think of that?" ruminated Bronco, his mouth watering in anticipation. "Ice-cream —and cake throwed in free gratis for nothin'. Looks like some one's struck it rich-turnin' all that loose on the range for everybody to corral."

"I don't believe it," gloomily asserted Holy, who had acted as escort for Bronco and the ice that failed. "You can't get ice from Tucson so's thar'd be anything left unless you order a whole carload at onct."

"Well," retorted Bronco in self-defence, "it depends on who's cartin' the ice. You would keep on cussin' all the way to the ranch that time, Holy, an it's no wonder the ice was all melted up. But, this yer ice is goin' to be in the church and won't have its constitution tried so hard."

Holy and Roarer looked at each other uncertainly. They hungered for that ice-cream and cake; but the necessity of treading consecrated board floors made the matter serious.

"I wonder if you've got to have 'em deal you a ticket if you don't belong in the pasture?" speculated Bronco, unable to tear himself from the vicinity of the poster. "Say, Larry," he called to the store-keeper, "how about this here ice-scream layout? Is it a bluff, or sure enough free-for-all?"

"Sure enough," answered Larry. "There's a new minister come to town and the women-folks have pitched in and fixed this up so he can get acquainted with people. You boys had better take it in. Every one's going to be there. We're shutting up the stores at seven o'clock tonight, so everybody can go."

"Say, Larry, did they sure enough get the ice here all right?" questioned Holy doubtfully.

"They sure did! And that ice-cream and cake is way up in G. Home-made, every bit of it. What's more, the ladies went to the saloon-keepers and got them all to promise to shut up the saloons from seven till eleven tonight. So every one's got to go to the Festival or else go home to bed."

"I guess we're headed for the ice-scream, boys," announced Bronco, and the others nodded acquiescence.

They filed out of the store and, after registering on the empty page of the hotel book, received a key and mounted the protesting stairs that ascended outside the hotel to the upper rooms.

While they were engaged in splashing soapy water over faces and hands, brushing dusty coats and plastering down anarchistic locks, Limber joined them and was informed of the evening plans.

"Well, I'll see you over there," he promised. "I'm goin' to supper now. Then I've got to have a talk with Paddy Lafferty and find out what he's holdin' his herd at."

He reached the door, paused and looked back quizzically. "I reckon you boys'll be all right tonight, seein' as how you'll all be in church. So long."

After supper the three cowboys joined a stream of people moving toward the church, where open doors emitted rays of welcoming light. It was a medley of humanity possible only in a frontier town. Women had resurrected dresses more or less old in style, from the depths of swaddling sheets necessary to keep them from the dust of sandstorms penetrating chests and trunks. Husbands, whose "best suits" smelled of camphor, helped shoo small girls in stiffly starched white dresses, tied with varied-coloured sashes, and boys who twisted and squirmed uneasily under the galling yoke of white collars and shirts.

Fortified with promises of ice-cream and cake, the youngsters were distributed on a double row of chairs back of the minister and facing the audience, where they had a full view of the other victims. Many miners had wandered into town for their usual Saturday-night and Sunday recreation, only to face the unprecedented situation of the closed stores and saloons-learning that there was no "balm in Gilead" from seven till eleven, for the first time on record in the Territory, they headed voluntarily for the church. Mexicans, whose own Catholic church was only opened twice a year, when the Padre came to marry and baptize wholesale-and frequently married the parents when he baptized the infant-rubbed elbows with clerks from the stores, bartenders and prospectors.

Holy, Bronco and Roarer, with amiable, though uneasy grins, faced the pretty school-teacher, Miss Gordon, a recent importation from San Francisco. She smiled sweetly at them and held out a small, white hand, which Bronco took hold of as gingerly as though it were a hot branding-iron, and let it drop as quickly. Holy, not to be outdone, extended his own horny hand, but Miss Gordon said, "I have to ask for your pistols, please, until you are ready to go. There are so many people here tonight we had to make this rule."

In consternation that was almost paralysis, they stared at her outstretched hand, then looked at her wheedling smile. Reluctantly, half-bewildered, each man slowly drew his beloved gun from the holster in which it reposed, and helpless, watched her add it to the stack on a table behind her. Then they looked at each other forlornly. Still under the influence of that dazzling smile, they made no resistance as Miss Gordon drove them forward. They were as embarrassed as though stripped of more conventional apparel than six-shooters, but they hoped the contortions of their faces might be classed as happy smiles when they saw they were expected to shake hands with the long, rigid line of the Committee of Ladies which flanked the minister.

As Limber entered the church, he saw his outfit run the gauntlet of introductions, then they turned precipitately with relieved countenances and slipped into chairs at the centre of the room. Bronco advised this location. "Ice-cream might give out if we get too fur back. Thar's a lot of people here tonight."

A program followed in which the school children sang a song, pitched in as many keys as there were voices. A recitation by a boy of fourteen, starting in a megaphone voice, and after the fifth line lapsing into a whisper, a gasp, silence —a bobbing head-and ending in hasty exit.

Next a five-year old carefully starched youngster galloped breathlessly without a pause through a couple of verses, exploiting her knowledge that she knew the audience would be surprised that "one my age should speak in public on the stage." The applause had hardly died when a buxom lady with white kid slippers three sizes too small, appropriated the piano. She arranged her toes on the pedals, then wiggled her feet until the heels slid out. An expression of beatitude adorned her face, her chubby hands were lifted and came down on the tinkling keys.

The assaulted, helpless piano responded with the familiar "Maiden's Prayer," while an apparition in a white lace curtain materialized at the back door of the room, flopping and twisting toward the spell-bound spectators. The number had been announced as an "Interpretative dance," and Holy whispered cautiously to Bronco, "Is it an Apache dance, or has she just tooken carbolic acid?"

"Search me," was the response. "Looks like a mixture of both of 'em."

The dancer was agile and angular. She had the distinction of being the only old maid in the county. Her bare, thin arms waved, gyrated, supplicated; her knees cracked audibly several times, but her mind was far away. She was mentally repeating the instructions she had studied so carefully from a book entitled, "The Art of Classic Dancing without a Teacher." Then with a last squirm, a convulsive shudder, she flopped to the floor, and ended the agony with one or two feeble kicks.

"It was a fit!" decided Bronco. "But it's the wust one I ever seed anything have."

The last number on the program was a little, weazened man with brilliant red hair, lighter red beard, faded blue eyes, who had brought a small talking machine. With stupendous dignity he wound it up, then stood with a new record ready to immediately replace the one being scratched out by the needle. The pile of records was formidable and he was apparently determined to skip none, until the head committee lady gently, but firmly and diplomatically, came to the rescue.

He bowed his appreciation of the tumulutous applause, assuming it was intended for him. It continued unabated. He opened his mouth wide, to express his gratification at the ovation accorded. The muscles of his face twitched, his eyes stared wildly and as the audience leaned forward anxiously, a terrific sneeze smote the air and a set of false teeth catapulted like a meteor in the midst of the audience.

A suppressed titter, a bobbing of bodies in the vicinity of the teeth, and then one of the children, groping on the floor, located the lost property and rose with a triumphant squeal.

"I got 'em!"

The red-haired individual grasped the rescued property with a smile that proved Nature may abhor a vacuum but sometimes permits it to exist. The owner of the touring teeth surveyed them, then nonchalantly popped them into their accustomed place before he gathered up his records, machine, and resumed his seat in the front row of the audience, which directed its attention to the minister.

He was a tall, raw-boned man in long-tailed coat and the white muslin tie needed a woman's touch, for one end had escaped and hung like the tail of a kite, as he advanced to the table on which stood a white pitcher, decorated with brilliantly coloured flowers; a part of the china set loaned by one of the ladies, whose artistic soul scorned such trifles as proportion, perspective or the mere "holding the mirror up to Nature."

In a few words the minister expressed his delight at this large gathering when he had expected a small one, and thanked the dear ladies who had arranged the beautiful program. Then he beamed graciously at the wiggling children.

"I know these little ones are growing impatient, so will only hold you long enough to relate an incident that returned to my memory as I sat here tonight.

"Many years ago I was travelling through an unsettled Southern district, and passing a high, board fence heard a child's voice praying. I stood up in my buggy and looked over. I saw a little girl, a dog, a cat and a small Jersey calf. I waited till her prayer ended, then asked, 'My dear, what are you doing?'

"'I'm playing Sunday school,' she replied. 'Kitty and Ponto and the calf are my Sunday-school scholars, and I'm the preacher.'

"A few more words and I went on my way, meditating upon the beauty of the child's devotion. I did not happen to return for nearly a year, but when I approached the fence I paused and peered over. The child was there alone.

"'How is your Sunday-school getting along?' I asked. She broke into sobs.

"'Kitty and Ponto got to fighting something awful,' she answered, 'and —'

"'And where is the calf?' I said.

"'He got too big to come-unless I had a box of grain for him to eat!'

"The story came back to me and I wondered how many of you who are here tonight will get 'too big to come' to services tomorrow morning?"

There were amused titters from many, guilty faces and sidelong glances, but the tension was relieved by the next words of the minister; "Now, we will enjoy the refreshments so generously provided by our dear sisters!"

At the back of the room were three immense ice-cream freezers. The committee, armed with heaping plates of the frozen delicacy, flanked by generous slices of chocolate layer cake, moved swiftly among the audience. Miss Jenkins carried a large tray to the group formed by Holy, Bronco and Roarer.

Their eyes appraised the huge heaps of tri-coloured cream-chocolate, vanilla and strawberry, without a doubt. Their hands were reaching to appropriate the plates when Miss Jenkins, who had danced the Maiden's Prayer, lisped affectedly, "Won't you boys help me a tiny, tiny bit, peath?"

She held out the tray and rolled her eyes pathetically. "It's awfully heavy for poor little me, and there are so many people to wait on. Won't you, peath, path it around and when it's all gone I'll have some more ready for you to therve."

Appalled they stared at her, as she continued her baby appeal and kept the tray in front of them so there was no possible retreat. The three reached out simultaneously. By some slip the tray lowered a bit and Holy's hand went into a cold, wet mess. With a half-choked oath he jerked back-and the tray crashed to the floor. A scream rose from the lady who had lent her hand-painted plates, and in the confusion that followed the three cowpunchers slipped out of the church obsessed with visions of a tri-coloured milky way that wended between gobs of squashed chocolate cake and hand-painted flowers.

Down the street they moved. It was no time for mere words. Even Holy's vocabulary was inadequate to express their feelings. Everything was dark, every place was closed. It was not later than eight o'clock and there was no place to go except to their room in the hotel.

In gloomy silence they mounted the stairs and sought refuge in the little room. Through the window they had a view of the church and the moving silhouettes within. The iron entered more deeply.

Roarer went to the window, and like the prophet of old contemplated the Promised Land that his feet were not to tread. Suddenly his gentle, falsetto voice pierced the silence.

"I hope that ice-scream will choke that outfit, especially that lace-curtain female critter! Why didn't she let us alone, anyhow? We was gettin' along all right until she went and butted in!"

There was no response, and he continued forlornly, "Gosh! There was strawberry and chocolate and vanilly all on the same plate, and that hunk of cake was as big as my fists! And every one in town's eatin' it exceptin' us!"

They lighted the tiny coal oil lamp and tried to reconcile themselves to the inevitable. As the smoke from their cigarettes filled the room their effervescent spirits reasserted themselves. Holy minced over to one of the narrow beds and robbed it of a sheet which he proceeded to pull over his shoulders and twist about his wrists while the other two watched him curiously. Then the empty corridors and rooms rang with shouts of laughter as Holy twisted, cavorted and gyrated, waved his long arms and extended supplicating hands in an amusingly accurate imitation of the dance of the Maiden's Prayer. It was their revenge for the loss of the cream.

An unexpected climax was reached when the sheet slipped and precipitated Holy full-length on the floor, but the sounds that rose on the air could never be confused with the words of any Maiden's Prayer.

Bronco leaned forward listening intently, and as silence reigned once more, he announced, "Say, Holy, that was the best you ever done yet. I counted sixteen new cuss words that I never heerd you use before. That was the best Maiden's Swear I ever listened to!"

Roarer looked up suddenly. "Say, did you notice them freezers was right along side the back door? Mebbe we kin slip over and corral one of 'em without being cotched. I'm powerful thirsty and there ain't no place to get nothin' till eleven o'clock except the church."

"We could make a try at it," responded the others hopefully.

They slipped down the stairs. At the bottom, Bronco suggested they get spoons from the hotel kitchen. It was a matter of generalship to boost Roarer through the window, where his collision with pots and pans was no impediment to his triumphal return with a soup ladle and two large spoons. In the darkness Roarer was able to retain the ladle for himself, handing the spoons to the other boys. Thus equipped they sneaked to the rear of the church and crawled cautiously to the open door. One of the cans was within easy reach-the other two some distance from the door. Conversation was in full swing and every one's attention was directed toward the minister at the front part of the room.

"Slip her quick," whispered Bronco, "and then we kin pack her out on the prairie and eat all we want."

The plan was carried out successfully. Roarer and Bronco slid the freezer until it was outside the door. Swiftly they lifted the tin can from the tub of ice and hastened away with their prize, while Holy kept pace with them.

At a safe distance from the church, they paused and removed the cover. Roarer thrust his dipper down, but had to reach further than he expected. Deeper he scooped without reward. Once more he tried. It was too dark to see inside of the can.

"Say, are you tryin' to hog it all yourself?" protested Bronco.

"Nope, Take your turn now."

Bronco wasted no time, and the other two listened to the click of his spoon against the tin can. After a few seconds, he raised up, saying, "All right, Holy. You're next!"

"How is it?" asked Holy as he leaned over the can.

"Fine as silk," was Bronco's recommendation.

"Best ice-scream I ever et," asserted Roarer.

Holy's spoon tattooed on the tin; it scraped forlornly, then there was breathless silence, a grunt, followed by the sound of an empty ice-cream freezer receiving several vigorous kicks accompanied by a terrific volley of cuss-words.

"You darn chumps," he gasped at last, "what made you go and take the one that hadn't northin' in it!"

"Oh, darn it all. What's the use," piped Roarer's gentle voice. "Let's go back and go to bed. Thar ain't nothin' else to do in this yere town."

They were settled in their beds when Limber opened the door and peered into the room.

"Hello! I been lookin' all over for you," he announced. "When did you get back? I was up here a while ago and none of you was in."

"Oh, we was just walkin' around town a piece," was Bronco's answer.

"Well, I got your guns for you. You all went off in sech a hurry from the church that you forgot 'em. It's too bad you boys didn't stay for the feed. It was fine."

"Oh, we knowed we had a hard day's work ahead of us," drawled Bronco, "so we figured we'd better come home and git to bed."

"Some one stole one of the freezers," continued Limber, soberly. "But whoever done it got the empty one."

"Served the derned galoots right," pronounced Bronco virtuously.

"That's what I say," endorsed Roarer, while Holy expressed his sentiments more forcibly.

Limber struck a match which he held to his cigarette, but his eyes regarded the grave faces of the boys. The match flickered out and the room was again in darkness, but not before they had seen the ghost of a twinkle in Limber's grey eyes.

"They got the freezer all right," he continued in the darkness.

"Who found it?" asked Bronco carelessly, pretending to smother a yawn.

"I done it," said Limber. "I was just a walkin' around town a piece, like you all was doin', and I come across it accidental like."

Silence was the only comment.

"The Inspector will be ready for us at eleven o'clock. Agent says the cars will be here by that time, so we can load out and get back to the ranch by supper."

"All right," chorused three voices in the dark, and Limber went to his own room. As he lighted the lamp there was a broad grin on his face, and his eyes danced with laughter, while he reiterated Bronco's denunciation, "Served the darned galoots right!"

Willcox slept late Sunday morning, so no one noticed shadowy figures dismount from three cowponies two hours before daylight. A struggling calf was making a heroic fight for freedom, but found itself propelled toward the picket fence surrounding the church and thrust through the gate. The mysterious men hitched the animal firmly inside the fence, then two placards of pasteboard, tied loosely together, were thrown across the calf's back and secured like a pack-saddle by strong cord. This accomplished, the three men mounted their ponies and disappeared in the starlight.

Willcox woke, rubbed its eyes and remembered a minister was to hold Divine Services that day of the year. Ten o'clock arrived. The first youngsters and their adult family connections approached the church gate. They congregated in animated groups, were joined by others, and finally spectators across the street, realizing that something interesting was detaining the congregation from entering the church, sauntered over. These inquirers hastened back to town and circulated news that caused a veritable stampede.

By the time the minister reached the scene the crowd composed the entire population of the town-men, women, children and dogs, several of the latter adding to the excitement by proceeding to settle feuds of long standing.

The Reverend Silas Hunter passed through the gate and his eyes swept the crowd, then rested on the centre of attraction —a husky, white-faced calf tethered to the fence by a rope. The animal had been lying down, in no way disturbed by the people or dog-fights, but as the Dominie scrutinized it, it rose and bellowed loudly into his face amid shouts of laughter. Across the calf's back swung the placards on which, printed in irregular letters, were the words;

I AM NOT TO BIG TO KUM
BUT FOR GODS SAKE HEAD
OF THE PROJIGUL SON.

"Oh!" ejaculated the Reverend Hunter, beaming upon the assemblage. "I see we have a donation. We will keep the calf, sell it and apply the proceeds to our Church Funds. Now," he addressed two half-grown lads, "you boys sit close to the door during services and see that the calf does not get away. Some unprincipled person might try to steal it, you know. We will find a place to care for it after services."

Across the street Bronco, Roarer and Holy stood in consultation. They had hovered on the edge of the crowd when the minister made his announcement, and they realized there was to be no opportunity to get possession of that calf in order to turn it loose-as they had planned.

"Say, he sure called our hands," said Holy despondently. "He's too derned smart to be a minister. What the devil are we goin' to do about it?"

"Let him keep the doggone calf and we'll have to put up a jackpot for the feller that owns it," advised Bronco.

"It ain't marked," squeaked Roarer excitedly. "Did any of you see the brand on the cow it was with?"

None of them had noticed such a trifle in their desire to capture the calf and accomplish the trick without discovery.

"Well, I guess we'll have to own up," asserted Holy, as they dropped side by side on the wooden bench in front of the hotel, and stared hopelessly across at the calf and the widely-opened church door.

"We sure got a hoodoo on us this trip," said Bronco. "First we got buncoed out of the ice-scream by that female window-curtain, then we goes and steals an empty ice-cream freezer and now we're stuck about that air calf. It'd be easy enough, to pay for it if we knowed the mother's brand, but seein' as we didn't pay attention to that, we've just got to buck up and go to that gospel-shark and tell him we done it. There's no tellin' what he'll do about it, let alone the feller that owns the calf. Darn it all, why didn't Limber stick along with us all the time and keep us from gettin' into this mix-up?"

"Looks to me like Limber can't do nothin' more'n he's done, except he chloroforms us the next time we get in town," replied Holy emphatically.

Then the unexpected happened. The restless calf, working against the stiff, new rope, untied it. Before any one in the church had observed it, the animal was down the railroad track and pushing its way among numbers of cattle that always congregated near the inspection chutes. It moved to and fro, searching for its mother. The watching cowboys could see the two placards still firmly in place.

"Gee! If we could just get them pasteboards off'n her, nobody would know what calf it is"; Bronco said breathlessly.

"Come along!"

It was Holy who spoke and led the way to where their ponies stood tied and saddled ready for work when Limber and the Inspector arrived.

"We kin ride down there and scoop it off in no time."

The ponies dashed forward in a cloud of dust, but as they neared the group, a long-horned buckskin cow turned angrily as the calf pushed against it, and with a sidesweep of her horn she caught the string that held the placards. The string broke, but the placards snapped over the cow's eyes, twisted lightly to her horn, and with a frightened bellow she dashed down the railroad track, past the emerging congregation, with the pasteboards banging and flapping across her face until she disappeared.

"That's the fust decent buckskin cow I ever seed," said Bronco. "She may have a yeller hide but she's a thoroughbred Hereford inside, you bet!"

Then Limber and the Inspector came toward them, and joined in the ride to the corrals. As they passed the group of cattle they saw the calf contentedly taking nourishment from a cow that was evidently its mother. Bronco, Holy and Roarer cast surreptitious glances at the ear-marks and brand of the cow. Their eyes met. Idiotic grins spread over each face. The cow was branded Diamond H. None of them spoke.

The cattle were inspected and loaded without any untoward incident, and Limber breathed more easily as the time approached for him to head his men toward the ranch. It was only during leisure hours in town that mischief hatched, and the foreman could never tell what might develope in a very short time.

It was with a feeling of relief from responsibility that Limber tucked the certified check in his pocket, but as they started homeward the boys were as glad as he. Bronco's ear-splitting whistles, "Home, sweet home," found sympathetic response in the breasts of the other men. It had been a strenuous trip. The ranch loomed like a haven of rest.

The next morning Powell and Traynor discussed Paddy's proposition with Limber, as they sat in the court-yard of the ranch, after Limber had started the men for their day's work.

"Thirty-five thousand in gold coin is what he wants," said the foreman, "and his bunch of stuff is worth every cent of it with the ranch throwed in. He won't count anything under six months old, if you want to tally the herd out, and tail 'em."

"It's a good buy," Traynor replied. Then turned to Powell. "Paddy is unique. He is seventy-six years old and has toiled many years to accumulate a herd. He cannot read or write a word, and carries every item of his accounts in his memory. The storekeepers say that Paddy never makes an error when their statements for six months are read to him, no matter whether the mistake is to his advantage or not. He lives alone. Refuses to accept silver or paper money and insists on gold for all sales. He buries his money secretly, as he has no faith in banks. He is a joke in the corrals, but no joke, however, when he is roused. A bunch of rustlers found that out to their sorrow."

Limber's eyes twinkled, as Traynor added, "Tell the doctor what happened. You were there, I wasn't."

"Well, the rustlers rounded up a band of fine horses and cattle and was makin' for the Mexican border. Pretty near got thar when ol' Paddy run into them alone. Him and me had just parted trails, and when I heerd shootin' I hurried to him. The rustlers was back of some rocks on the hill-slope, Paddy a lyin' down in back of a bit of brush not big enough to hide a good-sized jack-rabbit. His head was hid and all the rest of him in plain sight, and those rustlers was pumpin' lead as fast as they could. So was Paddy, but they had the advantage of him every way. Four of 'em back of the rocks. Paddy had shot two of their horses from under them, and they let the stolen stock run whilst they hunted shelter afoot. Jest as I got near enough to help him, he got a cartridge jammed in his Winchester, and couldn't get it out. He worked and cussed around, then got right up on his feet and walked around that hillside, as if he was prospectin' for a mine, takin' his time to find something to pry out that cartridge. And those rustlers kept popping away at him. Every time the dust kicked up close, Paddy'd squint at the rocks and cuss harder. Then jest as I got into the game, he got that gun fixed, and derned if he didn't jest walk slow up the hill, and fust thing, the rustlers come a humping out from the rocks in every direction, and all of 'em-four men-with their hands helt up over their heads, and Paddy back of 'em."

"That was one of the times Paddy did not whisper," laughed Traynor. "Well, I'll see Paddy for you, and now, Limber, Doctor Powell wants to go see the Hot Springs and talk with Doctor King."

"Doctor Powell could cut across the Galiuros the day the boys start from here with the herd," said Limber, "or, if Doctor Powell wanted to stay at the Springs a couple of days with King, I could take him there and then go on to Willcox to attend to the loadin', and go back to the Springs. Anyway suits me that suits him and you."

"That would be the best," commented Traynor. "You and Doctor Powell can leave here the same day that the herd starts to Willcox. Then let the doctor wait at Hot Springs until you get back there after the shipment."

"It would suit me perfectly," was Powell's hearty reply. "That is if I will not be imposing unwarrantedly on Doctor King's hospitality."

"If you knew him you would not say that," Traynor spoke earnestly. "He is one of the biggest-hearted men I have ever known. You and he will find many topics of mutual interest apart from your profession. I am pretty sure he will be delighted with your idea of sanitarium for children as he loves children dearly. He has not an enemy in Arizona. Every one likes him."

So the matter was settled, and four days later Limber and Doctor Powell started just after daylight breakfast for their ride of twenty-six miles across the Galiuro Mountains to the Hot Springs.

# Chapter Three

Katherine Glendon stood outside the door of the Circle Cross ranch house. On every side the view was blocked by the tall Galiuro Mountains above which loomed a sky of intense, glaring blue without a cloud to soften it —a sky as hard and defiant as the mountains that stared back at it; a masculine sky —a masculine country.

For eight years she had called four crude adobe rooms home. Other women had attempted to live in the Hot Springs Cañon. But the isolation was too oppressive, and one by one the squatters drifted away, leaving deserted ranches to testify to their defeat, until only the Glendons and old Doctor King, three miles distant, remained.

The morning meal was over, and Juan led a saddled pony from the stable to a hitching-post in front of the house. A tall, heavily set man slouched out, and the Mexican paused to ask; "Shall I saddle my pony, señor?"

"Not now," Glendon replied. "I want you to mend the fence in the lower pasture. When you get done you can follow me."

"Bueno, señor!" The man tied the pony and went back to the barn, and Glendon dropped on the steps of the porch, scowling at the ground. Accustomed to these spells of moodiness, his wife made no attempt to rouse him, knowing it would only increase his surliness.

A child appeared at the side of the house; glanced quickly from the man to the woman and then, seeing his mother smile, made his way quietly to her side as she seated herself on the steps. He held a book in his hand, and as he leaned against her knee, with her arm about his shoulder, turned the pages slowly, looking at her occasionally but uttering no word.

The sound of hoofs on the road caused the three to start curiously, for it was not very often that a visitor passed the Circle Cross. Only on a few occasions during the past eight years had anyone except a cowboy or a prospector entered the house. Once Doctor King had ridden down at intervals, but Glendon's aggressive disposition made these calls unpleasant for all of them.

Katherine, knowing her husband was in one of his ugliest tempers, was sorry when she recognized the white-haired old doctor, who loped his grey pony up to the gate, smiling as he dismounted and slipped his reins over the post.

"Hello, everybody!" he called cheerily. "A day like this makes a man glad to be alive, even if he is old enough to die."

Glendon stared at the ground, making no response. Doctor King, with a comprehensive look, passed him by and smilingly held out his hand to Katherine, who came down the steps while Donnie ran ahead of her, holding up his book.

"It's about Sir Galahad and the Holy Grail," the child began eagerly, "and there's a picture —"

"His mother is always filling his head with a lot of trash," growled Glendon, and the boy shrank back, the happy light dying from his little face; but the doctor smiled down at him as he took the book and turned over the pages.

"It's just the right kind of a story for Donnie to read," asserted the old man warmly. "This world would be a happier, better place if we all had the strength to live up to our Vision."

Turning to Mrs. Glendon, he continued: "I can only say 'howdy and good-bye' today. I'm on my way to see a couple of sick people on the San Pedro River, but will stop when I come back in three or four days. By the way," he said to Glendon, "when I was in town last week, there was a telegram from Fort Apache to Fort Grant saying that old Geronimo and about a hundred and twenty-five Chiricahua Apaches have jumped the reservation and the troops are out after them."

"Do you suppose there is any real danger?" asked Katherine, who had lived too long in Arizona to be frightened at rumors.

"No one can count on an Apache. He's a twin-brother to Mark Twain's jack-rabbit —'Here he comes-there he goes!' He knows that Army officers are tangled with red tape and unable to use their own judgment in pursuing him and takes advantage of that fact. However, you know there is one safe place in Arizona and that is the Hot Springs; because the Apaches are superstitious about the water. The house is safer than any fortress for that reason. I've lived there twenty-five years and never been bothered by them. Even Indians employed as Government scouts have the fear, and will not camp within a mile of the Springs, I've been told by officers and interpreters. I wish you folks lived a bit closer to me."

He rose as he spoke. "Well, I'll stop on my way back, Mrs. Glendon. It's hardly neighbourly, rushing off this way, but you know a doctor is not his own master. Take my advice, young man," he added to Donnie, "never be a doctor, whatever you may do. Why, just think how ungrateful people are! You get them well, or try to help them, and when they see you they stick out their tongues at you!"

Donnie laughed, and King continued: "I don't believe those people on the San Pedro would mind if I took time to give you a ride. You see, a little bird told me that today was your birthday, and we haven't had a ride for a long time."

Placing the book in his mother's hand, the boy hastened to the old grey horse and was lifted up in front of the saddle. Doctor King mounted and slipped his arm about the little fellow as the pony started at an easy lope down the road towards Hot Springs lying south of the Circle Cross in the opposite direction from the San Pedro River.

"So you are six years old today?" quizzed the Doctor. "Getting a big boy now, and it won't take many birthdays for you to be a man."

"Marmee gave me a book." Donnie spoke freely, now that he was not in the vicinity of his father. "She made a cake for me with white icing and six little red candles; and Juan bought a mouthorgan for me when he was in Willcox, and he is going to show me how to play on it when Daddy isn't home, so the noise won't make him nervous. Daddy is going to Jackson Flats, and Marmee and I are going to read the book tonight. We lit the candles and cut the cake this morning, so Daddy and Juan could see it and have some in their lunch. I'll give you a piece of it when we get back home. It was awful pretty."

The doctor's hand reached over the boy's shoulder. "You can't guess what I have in it," he challenged, and Donnie shook his head slowly.

"Open my hand, and findings shall be keepings," bade the old man.

After several futile attempts, the fingers relaxed and Donnie gave a cry of delight. It was a penknife with four bright blades —a real penknife like those men carried-the first knife he had ever owned in his life.

"Oh!" the child's surprise could find no other word for a few seconds, as he surveyed his treasure; then he lifted his happy face. "I always kiss Marmee when she 'sprises me," he said shyly, "but Daddy says men don't slobber."

The grey horse came to a halt and began nibbling contentedly at the bunch grass between the rocks. He was accustomed to these halts when Donnie and the doctor rode and talked of many things. When one is young in the world it is easy to clasp hands with those who are nearing the border of another world. Together they see life in the same light. Youth has not learned to place a false value on imitations and age has turned from them in disgust. So the child and the old man understood each other.

"Once upon a time, Donnie, many years ago, I had a little boy, and when he was six years old I gave him that knife, and when I gave it to him, he kissed me. Then, afterward, we made a wonderful boat with sails. When I come back from the River, you and I will make a boat like it to sail in the big pond at the Springs."

The child looked up, then his arms went about the neck of the old man and their lips met.

As the grey horse turned back toward the Circle Cross, Donnie was silent for a few minutes, then asked, "Where is your little boy, now?"

King's face bent over the child's curls, his chin rested on his chest, his eyes were dim with recollection, as he answered gently, "He went away from me, Donnie."

"Did he die?"

"Yes; and that was when he gave his knife for them to give to me when I got back home."

They neared the porch where Katherine stood talking earnestly to her husband. Doctor King let the child slip from the saddle without himself dismounting. Donnie ran to show his new gift.

"What a perfectly splendid knife!" exclaimed his mother, opening the blades. "Why! It has four blades!"

Gratified, the child turned uncertainly to his father, holding out the knife for his inspection and approval. "See, Daddy!"

Glendon impatiently brushed away the hand and knife. Katherine's eyes dimmed with sudden tears at the crestfallen face of the boy and she held out her hand again for the knife. King's eyes flashed angrily, and he checked the horse he was riding away.

"Marmee, can't I give doctor a piece of my birthday cake?" begged the child, and Katherine with hearty assent went into the house, followed by the boy. In a few seconds they emerged, Donnie proudly bearing a bit of cake crudely decorated with white icing and a tiny red candle that had burnt low. No words had been exchanged between the two men in the interval.

Doctor King regarded the cake with admiration; ate it and was loud in his praise as the finest birthday cake he had ever tasted, and Donnie's face lighted up once more.

Glendon paid no attention to this episode and moved to the hitching-post where his pony waited. He unfastened the tie-rope without uttering a word. Doctor King studied the sullen face.

"Which way are you going?" he asked pleasantly as Glendon swung on the pony and dug spurs into the animal's sides, yanking viciously at the cruel Spanish bit as the pony started.

"Jackson Flats," was the curt answer.

"Do you think it wise? This report is reliable."

"Back tomorrow afternoon."

"I'll ride as far as the forks of the trail with you," said King, ignoring the surliness of the other man and congratulating himself upon having an opportunity to broach a topic that had occupied his thoughts for many months.

Glendon's look was not inviting, but side by side, the two men rode into the Hot Springs Cañon toward the San Pedro River. The wagon road terminated at the stable of the Circle Cross, and from there merged into a narrow, rocky trail which twisted zig-zag at the bottom of the cañon for five miles, then divided. One fork of the trail struck up the side of the mountain and led to Jackson Flats, twenty odd miles distant; the other followed the bed of the dry creek to the San Pedro River, fifteen miles away. In the rainy season the sandy cañon became a raging mountain stream that was impassable.

The two men carried on a perfunctory conversation at intervals, the doctor trying to find a suitable opening that he might not antagonize the other and so defeat his purpose; while Glendon, submerged in his mood, replied in monosyllables. King looked at the younger man in disgusted anger; but remembering the woman and child, restrained the bitter words that burned on his tongue.

"I wish it were not necessary for me to make this trip just now," the doctor said, assuming a casual tone, "but I cannot put it off any longer. I was thinking this morning, Glendon, that it might be wise to have Mrs. Glendon and Donnie stay in Willcox until things are more settled."

"If I kept them there till rumours of Apaches are settled, they would never come home at all," retorted Glendon. "You know as well as I do there is less danger when the Indians are reported off the reservation than when it is supposed they are quiet. Besides, they will be in too much of a hurry just now, trying to get across the Mexican border before the Tenth Cavalry catches them. They won't be up to any deviltry for a while."

King could not help acknowledging the truth in Glendon's words, but a sense of uneasiness oppressed him.

They reached the parting of the trails. "So long!" muttered Glendon, but King laid a detaining hand on his shoulder. Glendon turned his bloodshot eyes on the old man and hitched his shoulder from the wrinkled hand.

"Glendon, there's something I have wanted to say to you for a long time. I'm an old man, and being a doctor gives me many privileges, you know."

Glendon's lips tightened. He made no reply as he slouched in his saddle, slapping his leather 'chaps' with his quirt. King hesitated a second and then went on speaking in his kindly voice.

"My life has been long, Glendon, and my trail has led over many rough places. I'm almost at the end of it now. When one looks back, one can see more clearly. You are just starting life. It is easy to avoid the places where others have stumbled, if someone points them out. You have a splendid wife and a fine boy; the future holds many possibilities for you-possibilities that I and many other men envy. Glendon, don't sell your birthright for a mess of pottage."

The other man scowled, but was silent, and King hoped that his words were reaching the man's heart.

"Let me help you," pleaded the doctor eagerly. "I understand what a struggle it is to overcome one's self. Years ago I threw away my chances, and I know the cost. I saw friends avoid me, and I did not care. My patients deserted me, because I was not to be relied upon; my wife and boy were taken from me while I was too drunk to know they were dead. My father pleaded with me and I cursed him. Then I became a tramp, drifting from place to place, my only ambition in life to get whiskey. The train crew threw me off a freight car one day and I wandered around in Arizona, penniless and friendless, until I was able to conquer myself and find my lost manhood. Thirty years ago!" His head sunk and his voice trembled as he added, "Nothing can ever give back the things I threw away, nor can I undo the suffering I caused those who loved me best. I saw the Vision, but had not the strength to follow it."

Glendon laughed sneeringly; "So, like most reformed characters, who have had their own fling to their heart's content, you want to drag everyone by the hair of the head into the particular straight and narrow path you select for him. Thank you for your interesting sermon, King. I prefer stumbling alone. I'm perfectly able to look out for myself. By your own admission I couldn't place much confidence in your assistance. Hereafter, mind your own business and keep away from me and my family!" He jerked his pony toward the upper trail, and kicked it with his spurred heels. As it snorted and jumped, Glendon sawed its mouth with the reins.

Doctor King watched this unnecessary brutality, then moved his pony beside Glendon's. The man's eyes gleamed with fury, but the old man made one more appeal.

"Glendon, think of your wife and boy, just a moment! You are crushing all the happiness from their lives. It is taking advantage of their helplessness. Only a coward would do that!"

King had said more than he intended; but now that he had spoken his true thoughts he gazed steadily into Glendon's bloodshot eyes. He did not flinch as Glendon wheeled his horse against the grey pony. Leaning over the doctor, the other man volleyed a stream of oaths. The doctor's face expressed only pity. Glendon realized it, and his fury broke all bounds. He lifted the heavy leather whip that hung on his wrist and struck viciously at King's face. The grey pony leaped in fright, so the blow glanced to the old man's shoulder. Glendon raised the whip a second time, then let it fall by his side. There was no resentment in the doctor's face, only infinite pity as he held out his hand.

"Glendon, I understand. I struck and cursed the man who tried to wake me. It was my own father."

"You mind your own business after this," snarled Glendon. "I'm sick of your meddling, posing and preaching. I won't let you, Katherine, or anyone else dictate to me about what I shall do. Damn the whole bunch of you, anyhow!"

His pony scrambled up the steep trail under the sharp prods of the spurs and the lashing of Glendon's whip. Doctor King looked after him, sadly.

"The same old road-each one stumbling over the same rough places-learning only from his own bruises and wounds. God pity the broken hearts of those who commit no sin save loving."

The peculiar foreboding that had oppressed him all day, returned more strongly. King wondered whether he had better retrace the trail and put off his trip till tomorrow. Then, recalling that Juan was at the Circle Cross with Katherine and Donnie, and that Glendon would return the next evening, while Leon's sick baby needed sorely the doctor's care, he finally headed the grey pony toward the San Pedro determined to make the trip as quickly as possible.

# Chapter Four

The shadows on the ground told Katherine's practised eyes that it was nearly ten o'clock when she closed the book she had been reading to Donnie.

"We'll finish it this afternoon," she said, "and now the bread has to be worked, you know."

"I wish I could be like Sir Galahad, Marmee," answered the child wistfully. "Do knights hunt for the Sangreal any more?"

"Not in suits of armour, my dear; but we all can be like Sir Galahad, even today. The Vision of Right and Wrong comes to everyone. Then the true knight puts on his invisible armour and takes the oath of the Round Table; —never to wrong rich or poor; never to be cruel; to show mercy to those that ask it; always to be true; to take no part in wrongful quarrel, but to help the weak and helpless and serve the King loyally."

"Can't I be a knight? I'm six years old and Doctor King said I would soon be a real man."

His mother looked down at the eager face, then said tenderly, "Yes, dear. You can be mother's little Knight. Kneel down, like Sir Galahad and take the oath."

Slowly and solemnly the childish voice repeated the words of the Round Table oath, while the distant yelp of a coyote quivered faintly in the air and the hooting of an owl sounded like derisive laughter for the woman and child alone in the wild cañon. Neither of them heard the sounds. Lightly the child's mother touched him on the shoulder. Her eyes were misty as she gazed down at the little knight who must someday go out alone against the hordes of invisible foes. Would he have the strength to live up to the Vision? A leering face with bloodshot eyes seemed to confront her, and the child's father drew the boy away, saying, "He is mine as well as yours." She put the thought from her.

"Rise, Sir Knight! Defender of the weak and helpless!" she said, while her hand rested on the boy's shoulder.

The child rose with serious eyes, then remembering what the book had said, he knelt and kissed his mother's hand, looking up as he said, "Marmee, now I'm your knight really and truly and I'm going to take care of you all the time."

Katherine caught him in her arms, and the newly-made knight forgot the dignity just conferred, to nestle against her breast and talk of the wonderful things he was going to do for her when he was a big man; but not once did he speak the name of his father.

As they talked, Katherine's eyes glanced at the high edge of the cañon, where the trail led to Jackson Flats; she was surprised at seeing something that moved along the trail toward the house. Two horsemen were distinctly silhouetted against the sky, then a turn in the trail hid them from view.

She rose hastily, speaking to the child. "Your father and Juan are coming back," she said. "So, if you will run and get some dry wood, I'll start the stove."

Donnie laid his book on the front room table and hurried out the back door, but Katherine, knowing the riders would reappear at another turn of the trail, took a pair of field glasses from a nail, and focused them on the point. She wondered if her imagination tricked her when she saw several other figures in the gap where the first two had appeared. Three, this time; then more followed, a fourth group loomed for a few minutes, then they, too, vanished like wraiths.

Her breath fluttered, her heart pounded heavily, for she knew too well what that line of riders meant. The glasses crashed from her nerveless hands, and Donnie came running to her side. She looked at him, paralyzed by the knowledge that those coming down the trail toward the little home, were Geronimo, the grim, blood-thirsty Medicine Man of the Apaches, and his band of bronco Indians.

Stories of the hideous fates that had befallen women and children at various times of the Apache outbreaks, flashed across her brain. Then she recalled Doctor King's words, "You can't get an Indian within a mile of my place." To remain in her home and barricade herself was hopeless, but she could try to reach the protection of the Hot Springs with her boy.

Donnie asked no questions when she went into the house and returned at once, buckling a belt of cartridges about her waist. A pistol swung in the holster. The field glasses had not been broken in the fall; she lifted them and looked once more at the gap of the trail. There was nothing to be seen. The Indians could not make fast time down from that point, she knew, nor could they see the ranch or cañon until almost upon the little corral back of the house.

"Come, dear," she said, as she seized the child's hand, and together they hurried down the steps through the dense mesquite and shrubbery, on the road to Hot Springs.

The child could not keep pace with her nerve-driven feet. She felt him lag, and looked down into his white face and tear-filled eyes, and realized that he understood their danger. She stopped and clasped him in her arms.

"Don't be afraid, dear. They won't find us."

He tried to smile, but his lips quivered. In her desperation a thought was born. It would be impossible to reach the Springs, but up on the side of the cañon was a large cave. She and the child had often gone there pretending they were explorers. The entrance was concealed by heavy brush and surrounded by huge boulders. It had been a place of refuge many times for the child when his father's irascible temper awakened.

"We'll go to our cave," she said, "and you know we're the only ones who can find it."

Donnie's hand gripped hers tightly, and with a sharp survey of the trail to Jackson, she started the climb up the steep cañon side, always keeping in the thickest part of the mesquite. Down the cañon they had to cross the bed of the dry creek, but once that was passed the boulders stood thickly. Slowly they made their way, for the rarefied Arizona air, the sharp pitch of the incline, the almost dead weight of the stumbling child, the fear of those who rode back of them made the climb doubly hard.

At last they reached the entrance of the cave, and sinking to her knees, she half-pushed, half-dragged the terrified child into their place of refuge. With her arm about the boy, she sat huddled against the side of the cave, but through the brush at the mouth, she could discern the Indians riding down the trail that ended at the corral. They circled cautiously about the ranch, then growing bolder broke into three bunches. Two groups approached the house from front and rear, while the third party dashed into the corral where the milk calf was kept, and in a few minutes it was dead. The Apaches, apparently in frenzied haste, slaughtered and quartered the calf, not taking time to skin the carcass which was tied in sections to the ponies. Others chased and captured all the chickens possible, wringing their necks and adding them to other plunder, until the leader, whom Katherine recognized as Geronimo, gave a command which was reluctantly obeyed. The entire cavalcade mounted and dashed down the cañon, following the road toward the Hot Springs ranch.

Katherine knew that the real danger now confronted her. Though the cañon was a mass of rocks, the roadbed where she had crossed was sandy, making it possible that her footprints might be discovered by the sharp-eyed hostiles, who were constantly on the alert for signs. A short distance from the spot which might betray her steps, several of the Indians halted suddenly, whirling their ponies and gesticulating to the others. The woman in the cave gripped the revolver more tightly.

"They will have to come up single file," she thought, then wondered why she no longer feared.

Carefully she calculated her chances, grateful for the obstructing brush, the gloom of the cave and its projecting sides which would protect her so long as her ammunition held out. One by one, she counted the cartridges in the belt, without taking her eyes from the figures in the cañon below. The distance across the cañon was so narrow, that the call of a quail on the other side of the Apaches could be distinctly heard by the woman.

"Six, seven, eight," the pitifully few cartridges slipped through her hands until the last two lay in her upturned palm.

She looked at them, then her eyes travelled to the child, and she knew that she would not flinch at the last moment. It was the only thing for a mother to do in Arizona, miles away from any living being except 'bronco' Apaches.

Donnie's eyes met hers, but he asked no question with his lips. The Indians were becoming more excited. Their voices reached the place where the mother and boy had found refuge. Katherine peered through the bushes. Geronimo was speaking, the others listened, and in obedience to his gesture, wheeled their ponies and rode up the side of the cañon opposite the cave. They reached the ridge, halted a few minutes in consultation, then turned their ponies' south-east along the backbone of the elevation until they vanished like a hideous nightmare.

"They are gone," she spoke with white-lipped tenseness, as she held the trembling boy in her arms, and the full realization of their narrow escape swept over her.

Immediate danger was past, but it would not be safe to venture from the cave. Stragglers might arrive at any moment. Familiar with Apache superstition which prevents raids or fighting during night, she decided to remain in the cave until it was dark, then creep to the house and obtain food and water. Sunrise was the favourite time with Apaches in making attacks. She dared not further attempt to reach the Hot Springs. Then she wondered if her husband and Juan had escaped the Indians or not.

# Chapter Five

It was almost noon when Katherine saw two horsemen coming along the road that led from Hot Springs, and her fears returned. But as the riders approached more closely, a look of almost incredulous relief showed on her pale face. Hastening from the cave, she stood on the slope of the cañon, holding out her arms.

"Limber! Limber!" she called, half-laughing, half-sobbing.

The men jerked their ponies suddenly, stared up and exchanged a few hasty words, then sprang from their saddles and hurried toward her.

"What is the matter, Mrs. Glendon?" Limber was the first to reach her, and his face was almost as white as hers, as she swayed slightly. Her outstretched hands were caught in his firm grasp and the touch steadied her. She tried to smile into his eyes.

"I'm all right now," she said, making a brave effort to control her faltering voice, "but, you see, the Indians passed here this morning. Donnie and I hid in the cave. I thought they were coming back when I saw you."

"Whar's Glendon?" demanded Limber sharply, his eyes narrowing as he spoke.

"At Jackson Flats with Juan. They will be home tonight."

"He had no business leavin' you alone;" the cowboy's voice was angry. "He knowed the Indians was restless. I warned him last week when I seen him down in town, and he promised me he wouldn't take no chances with you and Donnie."

"Doctor King told us this morning, but we did not think there was any immediate danger, Limber," she said. The man understood the gentle reproof.

"I didn't mean to knock Glendon, but it was takin' a heap of chances, jest the same, and Glen hadn't orter done it when he knowed Geronimo had jumped the Reservation an' your ranch right on the old Indian trail to Mexico."

He turned to Powell who had been observing the woman.

"This is Doctor Powell, Mrs. Glendon. We rid across from the Diamond H to see Doctor King. He ain't home today, though."

Powell clasped the extended hand and felt the quivering nerves, but before he could speak, Donnie appeared at the entrance of the cave, his darkly-circled eyes telling the hours of fear.

"Hello, Donnie!" called Limber cheerfully, placing a calloused hand gently on the lad's shoulder. "You fooled ol' Geronimo that time, all right. We've got the laugh on him, haven't we?"

A faint smiled rewarded the cowboy, whose glance now rested on the little pile of cartridges and the pistol. Limber said nothing, but stooped for the gun and ammunition, then he saw the two cartridges lying apart from the others. The muscles of his jaws twitched. As he picked up the last two, he hesitated and looked closely at the ground. His eyes travelled toward the rear of the cave then past the brushy entrance. Katherine and Powell were making their way down the side of the cañon and Donnie's hand was held by the doctor. Limber followed them, lifted the child to Peanut's back, and with a nod at Powell, mounted the other pony and rode slowly toward the ranch house, while the doctor and Katherine talking earnestly together, took a shorter cut.

They found the kitchen of the ranch in chaos. It had been rifled of all provisions, but owing to the haste of Geronimo nothing but blankets and some Navajo rugs had been taken from the rest of the house. Limber, hearing the milk cow bawling at the corral, left Powell, Donnie and Katherine in the house taking inventory while he announced his intention of milking the cow.

When the cowboy opened the corral gate, Beauty, the cow, rushed into the corral and sniffed the ground suspiciously. She caught the scent of fresh blood and lifted her head, her eyes rolling wildly as she bellowed rapidly and shrilly, sucking her breath audibly between her cries, like terrible sobs.

"You may be only a cow, but you know enough to have it hurt you jest like humans," said Limber pityingly, as he offered feed which she refused to touch. Gently he stroked her heaving sides, and she paused in her cries, looking at him with eager, appealing eyes. Then, as though understanding he could not help her, she resumed her shrill grief.

Limber tied her to the fence, milked her and carried the bucket to the kitchen. He put it on the table, glanced at the empty wood-box and left the room. In a few minutes the sound of splitting wood mingled with Donnie's chatter and Powell's occasional remarks to Limber. From the kitchen they heard the cheerful clatter of pans and the hum of an egg-beater.

The little dining-room into which Powell was summoned half an hour later, showed no traces of the hurried visit of the Apaches. The table was spread with fresh linen and decorated with a bowl of wild flowers. Despite the raid on her larder, Katherine had managed to provide a luncheon to tempt even a jaded palate.

"You must have Aladdin's lamp hidden somewhere," Powell remarked admiringly as he took the place opposite Limber.

Katherine glanced up smiling, as she served a dainty omelette.

"Nothing so magical as that," she said. "The truth is that the Indians overlooked the spring-house where we keep surplus stores. Limber helped more than Aladdin, for he milked the cow, found a few eggs and chopped the wood. With that much accomplished, any woman could manage a meal."

"We must agree to disagree," dissented Powell, but the conventional compliment was sincere. He was filled with admiration for the woman, who within twenty-four hours had gone through such experiences, yet retained her poise. "I wish some of my hysterical women patients could meet you, Mrs. Glendon."

Her surprise was not assumed. "Don't give me credit that I do not deserve," she answered simply. "When circumstances conspire against one, there is no time to plan or think. You just do things instinctively. Then, too, women living on ranches learn to adapt themselves to many things that would seem hardships to other women. Beside, you and Limber reached me just as I was beginning to quake. So I don't feel entitled to any praise."

"I am thankful that we happened to come when you needed us most," the doctor responded heartily. "We wanted to see Doctor King; but, finding him away from the ranch, Limber suggested that we ride down here and possibly find out when he might return."

"Leon's baby was sick," she explained, and Limber nodded. "He'll be back in a couple of days, he said."

"I want to find out whether the doctor will consider a proposition of mine regarding building a sanitarium at the Springs," Powell went on. "Mr. Traynor said King had such an idea, himself, and needed a partner-physician. That was how Limber and I came this way today."

"You know our Arizona custom—our homes are the homes of our friends. You are royally welcome to the best we have until Doctor King returns."

The two men exchanged sudden glances, and Limber hastened to say, "I've got to get to Willcox this evening, for the boys are on the road with a shipment of stock. But, Doctor Powell could wait here till King gets back. I was thinkin' I had better ride down to Leon's and head King back this way. Then he and Doctor Powell could talk together, whilst I kin go to Willcox by the San Pedro road instead of comin' back here."

"Don't change any plans on my account," the woman said quickly, sensing their thoughts. "My husband and Juan will be home tonight, so there is no occasion for anxiety."

"We'll wait till they come," Powell's voice was decided. "After they reach here, Limber and I can follow Doctor King. We have a new moon tonight and Limber says the trail is plain." Then Powell changed the conversation by asking Donnie if he spoke Spanish, and the child nodded assent.

"Marmee and I talk with Juan in Spanish all the time."

The doctor continued, "I used to live in South America, so I learned it down there. It varies a bit, but I have been able to understand and make myself understood, so far."

Luncheon over, the doctor went on the porch with mother and child, and Limber sauntered back to the stables to water their ponies. He was holding the halter-ropes of the animals while they stood by the water-trough, when he saw Glendon and Juan riding down the trail back of the house.

"Hello, Limber!" called Glendon as he swung from his saddle.

Limber regarded him with angry eyes. "Well, Glen, you sure kept your word to me in fine shape," he said in open disgust.

The other man shrugged his shoulders. "There's no danger. I can't sit around the place all the time holding a gun because some fool rumour is started about the Indians."

He was unfastening the double cinches of his saddle, but the leather straps fell from his fingers when Limber said slowly and meaningly; "No. Thar ain't no danger now! The whole bunch headed by ol' Geronimo passed here today. That's all!"

Glendon's face paled; "Katherine —"

Limber relented. "Mrs. Glendon seen 'em in time to get away, or else the Apaches would of got her and Donnie. She hid in a cave, and when we found her thar was two cartridges put one side. You know what that means. 'Tain't a pleasant thing for any woman to be alone and get to a point where she has to save two cartridges. No man has any right to ast her to take such chances-and if he is skunk enough to expect it, he ain't wuth doin' it for."

"How did you happen to find her?" asked Glendon, fingering the hanging strap of the cinch, and avoiding the other man's eyes.

"I come over with Doctor Powell. He's a friend of Mr. Traynor's and been at the Diamond H over a month. We come to see Doc King and rid down here to trail him up. He wasn't at the Springs. That's how we found Mrs. Glendon, and it made me hot all the way through."

"Oh, she's able to take care of herself. I guess there wasn't so much danger. Katherine always exaggerates things. She's too melodramatic. I'm used to her ways, you aren't."

Limber's eyes flashed and he grasped Glendon's arm roughly, compelling the man to face him.

"Look here, Glen! I've stood by you when every other decent man has throwed you down for a yellow cur. I done it because I thought mebbe thar was a white streak in you that didn't show on top, but the bunch you're getting mixed with ain't goin' to do you no good, and you've got to pull up mighty quick. Best thing you kin do, and what you'd oughter done without any one telling you, is quit this country. If you ain't man enough to do it for your own sake, do it for their'n;" Limber's head jerked toward the house.

"You've been a true friend, Limber, or else I wouldn't let you talk to me that way. I can't leave here now, but I will pull out as soon as I can arrange it. I give you my word of honour."

Limber gripped the outstretched hand, "I'm durned glad you told me," he said earnestly. "I'll do anything I know how for you and Mrs. Glendon any time you call on me."

Juan approached and removed the bridle from Glendon's pony, replacing a halter on it he was turning away, when Limber spoke, "Thar's fresh lion tracks leadin' to that cave whar Mrs. Glendon and Donnie hid this mornin'. I didn't tell 'em, but they'd better keep away from the cave. *Lucky the lion wasn't thar.* You lay for it, Juan."

"Si, Señor," the Mexican's promise was emphatic, and Glendon, too, declared he would "run the brute down."

"I've been having a lot of bad luck lately," Glendon said as he and Limber walked to the house. "This rough range is hard to work and cattle so wild you can't round 'em up without running all the fat off their bones. By the time they are driven thirty-five miles to Willcox, no butcher wants 'em. The longer I stay here the worse off I will be. I've written the old man and asked him to give me a chance somewhere else. He may not answer my letter, but it won't be any worse than now, if he doesn't. I didn't have enough money when I started to pay expenses."

They reached the house where Glendon welcomed Doctor Powell effusively. Something of the charm that had attracted friends in other days, still was apparent when Glendon was not drinking. Powell's keen eyes observed the handsome face marred by lines of weakness and self-indulgence.

"Glad to meet you," Glendon's voice sounded sincere and he grasped Doctor Powell's hand warmly. "We don't have very many visitors around here, but from what Limber tells me, it's been a regular reception day at the ranch. I wouldn't have gone away from the house if I had thought there was any real danger."

Powell, remembering that Limber had warned Glendon previously about the Indians, and that Mrs. Glendon had spoken of Doctor King's warning them, knew Glendon was lying, and Powell hated a liar. Glendon's eyes shifted under the steady gaze of the doctor, and he hastened to say, "I don't suppose Katherine offered you a drink. Lucky I don't keep it in the closet or Geronimo would have it by this time."

He started to get the liquor, but Powell prevented it by rising from his chair and holding out his hand to Mrs. Glendon.

"Now that you are not alone, I think Limber and I had better be on our way, trailing Doctor King. I am anxious to meet him as soon as possible."

Katherine and Donnie bade him farewell. Glendon kept talking volubly. "I'm glad we know the Apaches have passed here. No danger when you have a line on their whereabouts, but when you don't know, they always bob up. They hike for the Mexican border when the soldiers make it too hot for 'em in Arizona." Limber now led the ponies to the gate, and Glendon held out his hand to Powell, saying, "Glad to have met you, Doctor, and let me know if there is anyway in which I can show my appreciation for what you have done for Mrs. Glendon and Donnie."

Katherine smiled her gratitude, then Powell and Limber rode down the trail to the San Pedro River, followed by the eyes of husband and wife who stood on the porch of the Circle Cross ranch.

As the turn of the trail back of the stables hid the riders from view, Glendon said to his wife, "I wonder what they want to see King about. Looks urgent, chasing him that way."

"Doctor Powell said that he and Doctor King might form a partnership to build a Sanitarium at the Springs. You know that has been Doctor King's dream for many years; but he never has found any one who could qualify as physician and also have sufficient capital. I hope they may carry out the plan. It is such a splendid idea!"

"Oh, you do, eh?" Glendon snarled the words as he scowled at his wife. "Well, you may be interested in knowing that I'm figuring on getting the Springs myself. I've written father about the place. The only hitch would be that it is on unsurveyed ground, and no one can get a title except Squatter's Rights."

"But Doctor King won't sell to any one except a physician who will live there with him and establish a Sanitarium," Katherine asserted. "I've heard him say that so many times. He also told me that Mr. Traynor had made a good offer for the place, but it was refused for those reasons. Maybe Mr. Traynor wrote Doctor Powell about it. You see, Doctor Powell could qualify as a physician, and if he has not the money to finance the buildings, Mr. Traynor could supply that, or interest other capital."

Glendon did not answer, but sat on the lower step of the porch, staring moodily down the cañon trail toward San Pedro. His wife, learning from Juan that they had not eaten the lunch in their saddle bags, busied herself preparing an early dinner, for the hands of the clock announced four. She arranged the table then came to the front door and spoke quietly. Glendon did not hear her.

She moved to his side and touched him lightly on the shoulder, saying, "Dinner is ready, Jim. Juan said you had not eaten lunch."

He leaped violently to his feet uttering an oath and glaring at her.

"What are you doing? Spying on me?" he demanded furiously, and brushed past her, knocking against her shoulder as she stood in the doorway.

Her face paled. She made no answer, but turned to the dining-room where Juan was at the table. Glendon fortified his ragged nerves with a generous drink of whiskey and slumped into his chair, only to grumble at everything before him and finally push away his untasted food. Then he rose so suddenly that his chair fell backward with a crash. He started, glanced at the chair, gave it a kick and with another oath, flung himself from the house. Through the window Katherine saw him again mount his pony.

She sat with trembling lips, tears slowly forcing themselves from the drooping eyelids and wetting her white cheeks. Juan's face was filled with pity, but he knew he could do nothing-say nothing, and he rose softly and slipped away that she might be alone with her misery. Donnie's hand touched her cheek, and she opened her eyes and smiled at him, thankful that the child was safe. Nothing else mattered, after all. So while she removed and washed the dishes, she talked cheerfully to Donnie.

Back in the front room again, the boy moved to and fro, and at last turned his anxious face to his mother.

"I can't find my book, Marmee. Do you think the Indians took it?"

"Why, no, dear," she replied, looking at the table. She had noticed the book where Donnie had left it. It had been there when she called Glendon from the porch for dinner. No one had passed through the room since then but Glendon.

Carefully she and Donnie searched the room, but no trace of the book could be found. She stood staring down the front walk to the gate, unwilling to acknowledge her suspicions against the father of her child. Then on the walk she saw something that caused her to hurry out.

The wind carried a torn page to her feet. She stooped and picked up the fluttering, tell-tale bit of paper, and as she held it in her trembling hand, the words caught her eyes, "and he shall be a better man than his father." On the upper part of the page rode Sir Galahad.

"Donnie, dear," she called and the boy came quickly to her side. "Come and help me look out here for the book. Maybe we can find it in the bushes, somewhere. See, here is a page, and the rest of it must be close by."

They found it torn, soiled, the covers broken and cracked, and the child's sobs came unchecked as his mother's arms went about him; the ache in her heart was too great for tears.

"Donnie, we can mend it so it will be almost as good as ever," she cheered him, and the child's sobs were choked though the quiet tears rolled down his cheeks, as he went back to the house with his mother, the mutilated book held in his little hands.

# Chapter Six

In the meantime Powell and Limber were riding down the cañon, immersed in deep thought until Limber said, "Thar was fresh lion tracks leadin' into that cave."

Powell jerked about, "Good Lord!" he ejaculated, realizing what it would have meant had the brute been there when the woman and child sought the place of refuge.

"I told Glendon and Juan, and they're layin' for it, and Juan'll tell Mrs. Glendon to keep away from the cave. He won't forget it."

"Well," Powell commented, "I'm glad you told the Mexican. That fellow Glendon thinks of no one but himself. I was watching the child when his father came on the porch, and I'd hate to have any child or animal look at me with such abject fear. It made me sick with fury. How can that woman stand such a life!"

"Glen really does think a heap of her, in his own way," Limber replied slowly, "But when he gets the smell of the cork of a whiskey bottle, he goes plum loco. That's what made the row between him and his folks back East. His father has heaps of money, but won't have nothin' to do with Glen. Leastways, that's what Glen tole me hisself, onct. He said today that he's goin' to pull up stakes as soon as he kin fix it to move, and take his fambly where the Apaches can't run 'em like they done today."

"I'll give him credit for some decent instincts when he moves them to a half-civilized place; but I wouldn't take his word for anything. He's a natural liar, I think. I'm sorry for that wife of his, and for the child."

"She's one of the finest women that ever drawed breath," answered Limber. "She's stood a lot, and she'll stand a heap more."

Conversation ceased until the cowboy pointed to a high peak.

"See that peak up yonder? An ol' fellow lived thar fifteen years prospectin' for gold. Stayed all alone. He was always cocksure he was goin' to find a big mine someday. Some one called him Monty Cristy, and the name stuck to him like a cockle-burr in a horse's mane. One day I was deer-huntin' and run into his camp. He had a dugout in the side of the mountain and a tunnel whar he'd been prospectin'. I went into the tunnel to look at the ore, and found him sittin' thar against the side wall. His pick was across his knees and a piece of ore in his hand, but he had been dead over a week. I buried him up thar."

"Was the mine ever developed?"

"Twarn't nothin' to develope. The bit of rock in his hand was like all the stuff on the dump outside the tunnel. Plum worthless. Chock full of iron pyrites-not worth a damn. 'Fools' Gold' is what the miners calls it."

The cowboy leaned over and petted his pony's neck gently, then straightened up in the saddle and went on; "I've often wondered whether ol' Monty knowed at the last that it was only 'Fools' Gold.' Thar's a heap of people besides ol' Monty that keeps on diggin', hopin' for a strike and gettin' nothin' but 'Fools' Gold.' Tain't no use talkin' to them. It's the lucky ones what don't find out the truth, after they've put in the best of their lives workin' on a false lead."

Powell's thoughts went back to the woman at the Circle Cross, and he answered soberly, "You are right, Limber."

A number of buzzards circled in the cañon a short distance ahead of them, but not directly on the trail. Limber called the doctor's attention to them, and added, "We'd better go over and see what it is that interests them. Maybe only a dead cow; but when the Indians is out, you never know what you're running into. You learn not to pass anythin' by when you find buzzards."

They left the trail, worked through the dense underbrush that was matted with dead grass and other debris from past heavy floods. Buzzards flew up thickly at their approach. Then they sat looking down at a grey horse huddled in the rocks. Saddle and bridle were gone. A few feet away was the body of an old man, his white hair clotted with blood from a bullet wound in the left temple; his sightless grey eyes upturned to the blue skies, as though in mute questioning.

"God!" ejaculated Limber, as he leaped from his horse. "It's ol' Doctor King! Damn them Apaches!"

Powell's shock was not less than the cowboy's, and he knelt beside the body of the man whom he had hoped to work with at the Springs. He did not think of the annihilation of his own plans, but the things he had heard of the kindly old man. Death had been instantaneous. The bullet had entered the left temple, ranged downward and out behind the right ear. The two men looked at each other, then Powell's eyes went up to the broken side of the cañon. From back of one of those rocks had sped the messenger of death, with no warning to the old doctor who was on his errand of mercy to a little Mexican baby.

"Why didn't the Indians take the horse?" was Powell's question.

"Because it's grey. They ain't got no use for a grey or white horse, specially when they're out for trouble."

Limber studied the ground about the horse and its dead owner.

"Too rocky to show any trail," he commented at last.

"He's been dead over night," Powell asserted as he finished examining the body.

"The Apaches have been hangin' about for several nights in the Graham range. Thar's two bunches. I seen 'em signalling three nights ago right back of Fort Grant where the soldiers couldn't catch sight of their fires. They keep lookouts on the high peaks and hold a blanket in front of the fire. Beats a telegraph office. Thar ain't nothin' smarter 'n an Apache, unless it's two Apaches. You can't trust one unless he's dead. Chances is that the two bunches figure to come together at Point of Mountains, seven miles north of Willcox. Then when it's dark they'll jump across the valley to Cochise Stronghold and work into Mexico."

"But, the soldiers could head them off," Powell interposed.

Limber snorted. "Sounds that way all right. But, if you jest look at these mountains and cañons, you'll pretty soon see that the soldiers has jest as much chanct against them Apaches as an elephant would have if you set him in a hayfield to kill a flea by trompin' on it. When they're tired of killin' people and want a vacation and no hard work, they come in and give themselves up and go home to the Reservation."

"There's nothing to be done here now, except to notify the proper authorities at Willcox, I suppose," Powell resumed. "We found him-but it's a different ending from the way we thought."

Limber unstrapped a Navajo blanket from the back of his saddle, and together they wrapped the stiffened form of the old doctor.

"Thar's heaps of people goin' to miss him," the cowpuncher said slowly, as they stood looking down. "Nobody ever called him that he didn't go, rain or shine. He never took one cent for what he done. Jest tol' 'em to feed him an' his ol' grey horse and that was all the pay he wanted. He was sure a good man;" both heads were uncovered in silent homage.

"I'll stay here," continued Limber, "if you'll ride back to Glendon's and get his spring wagon, so we kin take the body to Willcox. It'll be hard gettin' the wagon in the cañon, but I guess we kin make it. We'll lead our ponies behind the wagon."

Powell was already mounting his horse, as Limber added, " 'Twon't take a Coroner's jury long to bring in a verdict. I'm doggone glad, though, we ain't a packin' Mrs. Glendon and Donnie along with Doctor King. They sure had a close call this mornin'. If Geronimo hadn't been in a hurry to get across to that other bunch, they'd sure trailed Mrs. Glendon to that cave."

"It is no place for any woman to live," Powell's voice vibrated with indignation. "I can't understand how any man could bring a woman like her to such surroundings. I'm glad he intends to move his family away. Any place would be better than this, for her."

Limber watched his companion ride off, then busied himself with a second examination of the ground in the vicinity of the dead man and horse. Satisfied at last that he had overlooked no trace, he dropped on a boulder and rolled a cigarette, but as he shook the tobacco from the sack into the brown paper, a portion of it fell to the ground unnoticed. Limber was staring into space, an expression of doubt lurking in his grey eyes.

"Derned if I kin understand why they took so much trouble hidin' their trail, Peanut," he spoke to the little pinto pony at his side. "The main bunch must of rid higher up and one of 'em come down for the bridle and saddle after King was shot; but, thar ain't a moccasin or any other track nowhars. It beats me."

When Powell returned he was accompanied by Glendon, who climbed into the driver's seat and picked up the reins after they placed King's body in the wagon. Limber, leading Powell's pony, followed the wagon, mounted on Peanut. The vehicle bumped and jerked over large rocks of a trail that never before had been traversed by wagon wheels.

Powell was not inclined to talk, but Glendon forced conversation, though it savoured of a monologue.

"King told us he had no one belonging to him," Glendon's voice broke the silence of the cañon, while the team headed for the Circle Cross. "Katherine said you expected to form a partnership with him and establish a sanitarium at the Springs. I suppose his death will alter your plans. All this part of the country, you know, is unsurveyed ground and title held by possession only. I'd have bought the Springs myself if there had been a regular title. Hesitated at it because I only could acquire Squatter's Rights, you know. However, I took the matter up recently with my father, and am now waiting his reply. I don't understand why King didn't let you know I was figuring on it. Did he give you any option?"

"No;" answered the Doctor, wondering at the statement which conflicted with what Limber had just said regarding Glendon's plans to leave the cañon. Then he recalled that Traynor had asserted King would not sell to any one except a physician who would co-operate with him in his plans. He knew the man beside him was lying for some reason, but what that reason was, Powell could not decide. "I have not even broached the matter to Doctor King. I came over today to look at the place and if it suited me, to make a proposition to him. I never met him and I don't believe he ever heard of me."

"Of course," Glendon went on, as Powell stopped abruptly wondering if Glendon had no sense of decency to keep talking while the dead man lay in the wagon they were driving, "I had no written agreement with King. Out here, a verbal contract is all we ask of a man. So I ought to have prior right because of our understanding. I don't suppose he made any will, as he had no heirs, and could not will the Springs, anyway, without a legal title to it himself. In that case, the estate would revert to the Territory. A Government Patent would have made less complication."

He glanced furtively at Powell, who made no reply, as they had reached the corral of the Circle Cross. Katherine Glendon stood on the porch, her eyes blinded with tears, her lips quivering.

Glendon climbed heavily from the driver's seat, and Powell saw that his steps were uncertain. Limber tied his pony, Peanut, and the doctor's horse to the back axle of the wagon. A few quiet words were spoken by the two men to Mrs. Glendon, then they went on their way with their tragic burden, and each man was busy with his own thoughts.

It was past sunset when they reached Willcox. After reporting the tragedy and turning the body over to the authorities, there was nothing more they could do, and Powell went to the Willcox Hotel where he obtained a room. Limber parted from him at the door.

"I guess I'd better hunt up the boys and see how things is goin' along with the cattle."

Though neither spoke of it, the uppermost thoughts in the minds of the two men was the woman at the Circle Cross, alone with a man whose indifference to her danger had almost cost her life and that of her boy's.

Back in the lonely cañon a coyote skulked past the empty house at the Hot Springs. Further down the road a woman stood at the door of her home staring into the darkness.

When she had made her final visit to see if Donnie were all right for the night, and leaned over to press a kiss on the child's cheek, something slipped from his relaxed hand. Wondering which of his toys he had smuggled to bed with him, she stooped and saw the pen-knife that old Doctor King had treasured through his long, lonely years. A wave of realization overwhelmed her. There would be no more visits from this loyal old friend, now. The future loomed ahead of her as black as the night that wrapped the cañon.

## Chapter Seven

The second shipment of the Diamond H cattle had reached Willcox a little after noon, and Holy lingered at the Cowboys' Rest with Buckboard Bill, while Bronco and Roarer proceeded up the street. They were not visible when Holy, hastening through the corral gate, encountered Montgomery Walton. The latter's manner was so cordial that Holy halted in surprise.

Montgomery Walton, the most unpopular man in Southern Arizona, was almost seventy years old, though as alert as a man of forty. His white, flowing hair and patriarchal beard were contradicted emphatically by ferret-like face and shifty eyes, while his oily smile exposed yellowed tusks. He owned a fairly good-sized herd of cattle that were preternaturally prolific, as his cows were very often seen with twin calves following them. Walton discouraged calls from other cattle men, and lived alone except for a half-witted Mexican-Loco.

To the disgust as well as amazement of Holy, Walton ambled along at his side, and finally, tugging at the cowboy's blue flannel sleeve, drew him to a bench on the edge of the sidewalk. Then he produced a letter, extracted a small photograph and handed it to Holy.

"What do you think about her?" asked Walton with a smirk, as he pressed more confidentially towards the cowpuncher.

Holy studied the picture of a sweet-faced girl.

"Why!" he ejaculated enthusiastically, "She's a regular peacherina. Who is she?"

Walton replaced the picture as he said, "She's coming on the west-bound train today and we're going to be married at once."

"Gee! You sly old dog!" commented Holy jocularly, while he wondered if the picture really looked like the girl, and if so, why she was going to marry a man like old Walton. Then an inspiration dawned upon him, and he turned to Walton, clapping him heartily on the shoulder.

"Well! Why shouldn't you get married, I'd like to know?" he demanded as though that privileged had been questioned by some invisible individual. "A man's age ain't to be reckoned by his years. No, sirree! I've seed some men who was ready to die of old age when they was twenty-five, and I've seed others that was young when they'd past eighty. Now, no one would ever think you was a day over forty, Walton, if it wasn't for that air white hair and beard of yourn."

Walton preened foolishly and tried to look incredulous, as he replied, "Do you really think so, Holy?"

"Sure thing!" asserted the other.

He looked contemplatively at Walton, then leaned closer and whispered, "Say, Walton, why don't you get Dunning to dye your hair and beard before the girl gets here. It'll make a difference of thirty years in your looks."

Walton hesitated. "Maybe I will," he temporized. "You see, I sent her a picture of myself, but it was taken when I was about twenty-five. So I was a bit worried how she would act when she found I was not so young as she expected. I hadn't thought of getting my hair dyed, though. It's a good suggestion, I think."

"You bet it is!" Holy waxed enthusiastic. "Women is queer critters, an' a young and pretty woman likes the man she marries to be somewhar near her own age. She don't want to risk other women thinkin' that she had to go to an Ol' Man's Home and kidnap a husband. You jest take my advice, Walton, an' have a heart to heart talk with Dunning right away."

"I'll think about it," evaded Walton, as Holy with congratulations, parted from him, knowing Bronco and Roarer could be located behind the swinging doors that led to the bar-room of the Willcox Hotel.

Holy's smile expanded to a broad grin as he recognized his friends at the end of the room and made his way to them.

"Thar's somethin' interestin' goin' to be cut loose if you fellows will chip in," he announced confidentially. "Now, don't waste time talkin' or askin' fool questions. You jest come along with me down to Dunning's and fix it up with him. We ain't got no time to lose."

Before he had finished speaking, he was half-way to the door-the other two close at his heels. Holy vouchsafed no explanations for his mysterious actions. Hurrying down the street they entered a small barber-shop which was unoccupied save for the owner. Dunning was the only barber in Willcox. He was an autocrat.

A chair, facing the wall on which was a fly-specked mirror, a row of wooden seats, and a conspicuous placard bearing the pleasant, but misleading fiction, "Fresh towel for each customer," constituted the furnishings of the place. Dunning's hair shone glossy brown; his moustache curled tightly as a pug dog's tail, a gorgeous red four-in hand, tight, grey trousers with broad black stripes made him brilliantly conspicuous among the citizens of Willcox. Between shaves and haircuts the barber delved into sentimental fiction.

With reluctance he put aside a yellow-backed novel and rose leisurely to his feet. His speculative survey was interrupted by Holy.

"Say, Dunning, you know ol' man Walton," he began.

"Lived round here fifteen years, never had his hair nor beard cut onct;" catalogued Dunning. "So derned stingy that he'd skin a flea to get its hide and tallow!"

"Mebbe you'll git a chanct at him today;" encouraged Holy. "He's goin' to git married!"

The others snorted in surprise, and Bronco announced contemptuously, "There ain't a bunch of calico in Arizona that would let him near enough to rope her, let alone carry his brand."

"Oh, you make me tired," Holy retorted. "Who said he was workin' any Arizona range? The girl's comin' from the East on today's train. He showed me her picture. I give him a fill about his white hair makin' him look old, and said he'd oughter get Dunning to fix him up. Say! —he swallered it like a rattlesnake swallers a gopher."

"She must be locoed," growled Bronco, suspiciously.

"I own I ain't been dazzled by the charm that draws her," acknowledged Holy, "but what interests me is that the Diamond H owes ol' Walton for a heap of things he ain't done. Say, Dunning, there's twenty-five pesoes for you, if you fix him good and proper. I got an idee-but you may have to go out of town for a few days."

"That's all right. Business ain't pressing. I figured on goin' out prospecting for a couple of weeks, anyhow. If any of the boys wants a hair-cut they can wait till I get back."

"Say Dunning, stay away three weeks," begged Bronco. "I'll make it thirty dollars if you do."

It was not solicitude for Dunning's safety that prompted this request, but Bronco, remembering that Dunning was the only barber, had a vision of the entire male population of Willcox sporting Rip Van Winklish hair, unless their flowing locks were mutilated by connubial scissors during Dunning's absence.

"Thirty goes," agreed Dunning. "Now, what is it you boys want done?"

Holy explained, interrupted by bursts of laughter from Bronco and Roarer, and finally, Dunning, with a grin, ended the consultation by saying, "You fellers get him in here and I'll earn that thirty."

## Chapter Eight

Walton left Soto's store after giving orders that his purchases be ready when he came with his wagon at four o'clock, then he walked slowly down the street, weighing Holy's suggestion. Vanity struggled with parsimony.

He reached Dunning's shop and paused uncertainly, without suspicioning three pairs of eyes that peered from a small window in the hotel. Dunning, inside the shop, was seemingly oblivious to the man on the sidewalk but looked up with a professional smile when Walton entered the door.

"Well, Walton," Dunning's attitude was almost affectionate, "What can I do for you? Shave? Hair trimmed a leetle bit? I don't wonder you kept away from me all this time, and I'm just artist enough to say if you want me to cut off your beard or hair, I won't do it for you or nobody else. But a leetle bit of trimming would improve it lots."

"I —Do you ever dye hair or whiskers, Dunning?"

"Sure;" was the answer. "I guarantee my work and mix my own dyes, and you'd be surprised if I told you the names of people I've fixed up. But, my work is confidential. My customers trust me and I never betray them."

"Well, do you think you could fix mine?" asked Walton with an uneasy smile.

"Bet your boots! Nothing would please me better. Now, I suppose you'd want it dark, wouldn't you?"

"Black. That's what it used to be," Walton replied. "But how long will it take?"

The barber cocked his head sideways, squinted an eye critically, then walked solemnly around Walton several times, and finally slipped his fingers through the beard and hair.

"It's a fine growth," he announced. "I can finish it in an hour."

"How much will it cost?" Walton paused in front of the chair which Dunning was adjusting for him.

"Well, I usually charge fifteen dollars for such a job, but I'm willing to do it for five, if you promise not to let any one else know I cut the price to you."

"I won't give over three," asserted Walton firmly, moving to the door.

Dunning, fearing flight and the attendant loss of the thirty dollars, followed Walton humbly.

"Now, see here, Walton, why can't we split the difference? If I come down a dollar, you can sure raise one. I'll do a first-class job for four dollars. My regular price is fifteen. Why, man! It will make you look twenty years younger!"

Impervious to flattery, Walton kept edging nearer the door.

"Three and a half," compromised Dunning desperately.

"Three dollars;" declared Walton, reaching for the knob, but watching Dunning sharply.

"All right," consented the barber. "Three dollars. But don't you fool yourself into believing you are going to get an everyday, ordinary dye. It's my own invention. Guaranteed permanent or money cheerfully refunded. Results astonish everybody."

"Sure you will get it done by train time?" asked Walton anxiously, as Dunning led him to the chair and deftly pinned a sheet about his neck.

Dunning glanced at the clock, "Just time to do it fine," he assured Walton, who stretched out luxuriously, determined to get his three dollars' worth as far as possible. Dunning was engaged in mixing various liquids.

"Going on a trip?" he asked, standing with his back to Walton while he stirred vigorously.

"Not exactly. I'm going to be married. The young lady will arrive on the west bound train, and we're to be married at once and go out to the ranch."

"Well, you did the right thing in coming to me," announced Dunning, as he finished manipulating the concoction. "That white hair did make you look old, Walton, and I often wondered why you didn't touch it up a bit. I bet when I get you fixed up, that she won't ask how old you are. Say, I'll stake ten dollars on that bet."

"Will it stay black, or have to be done over again?"

"Guaranteed permanent. Only way to remove or change the colour after it is once on, is keep the hair shaved close to the roots for six months."

Walton twisted nervously. "I wish you'd draw down that shade and lock the door. I don't want any one hanging around while you are busy."

"That's what I figured on doing," agreed the barber, acting as he spoke; but winking at the boys of the Diamond H who were sauntering past as the shade was lowered.

Walton sank back with a sigh of relief. The silence of the dimly lighted room and the movement of the barber's hands, had a soporific effect on the customer, who closed his eyes and snored peacefully, while Dunning kept a wary eye on the clock until he heard the whistle of the approaching train from the East.

"Better hurry, Walton! Train's pretty near the depot, now. I just got done in time."

Walton waked with a start as the sheet was jerked off, and Dunning's voice sounded jubilantly in his ears, "Job's done fine. I'm proud of you!"

With a hasty glance at the small mirror in the dimly-lighted room, Walton's blinking eyes saw a dark flowing beard, a mass of dark hair. The noise of the train warned that time was precious and fleeting. Thrusting the three dollars into Dunning's palm, he grabbed his hat and ran across the street to the depot, where the train was puffing to a stop.

Walton scanned the rows of windows with passengers looking aimlessly at the town. Their bored faces suddenly became animated with smiles. Walton found the tourist sleeper, where he saw a girl in a grey suit on the platform of the car descend the steps, while the porter helped a delicate-looking boy.

The bridegroom-elect moved more swiftly, and reached the girl just as the porter shook hands with the child and said, "You'll be a big cowboy before long, Ah reckon;" then the train went on its way, leaving the girl looking about nervously.

Among the loiterers at the depot, Bronco, Holy and Roarer glanced at each other in consternation.

"Good Lord!" "Holy, that ain't the girl, is it?"

Holy did not answer. The enjoyable flavour of the joke had evaporated, like a dose of castor oil in orange-juice, and a decidedly disagreeable taste remained. Holy acknowledged to himself only, that his preconceived idea of the picture as a fake, sent to old man Walton by an unattractive, elderly woman, was without any foundation. This girl was much prettier than the photograph. Any doubt as to the identity was dispelled when Walton sallied up to the girl and took off his hat with an elaborate flourish.

She started back, her frightened eyes travelling slowly over Walton's hair and beard. Meeting that prolonged glance, he attributed it to his fascinating appearance, and smirked and preened consciously.

"I'm Montgomery Walton," he said unctuously. "Everything is arranged so we can be married without delay and get out to the ranch tonight. The Justice of Peace is waiting for us."

The girl's pretty colour faded suddenly as she saw him pick up her valise with an air of proprietorship. She looked at the child, took a step toward Walton-stopped, then cried out, "No! No! I can't do it!"

Walton scowled, but controlled himself and said, "You are tired from your long trip just now, I know. It won't take long to get started for the ranch after we are married."

He beamed on the child, "Come along, Sonny."

The boy shrank back, clung to the girl, who clutched the thin little hand and looked about her desperately. Her eyes swept over strange faces, rough-looking men, then, like an animal at bay, she ran to the waiting-room with the child, and slammed the door violently. Walton stared at the closed door, then at the valise in his hand.

The listeners outside heard hysterical sobs, and the soothing voice of Mrs. Green, the agent's wife. Walton, pale with rage, glared at the grinning faces about him, drew himself up, entered the waiting-room and closed the door behind him with a bang. The mingled sounds of a girl's sobs, a woman's angry tones, Walton's voice in *crescendo* notes, then the door opened and he dashed out, scattering those who obstructed his wildly waving arms, and stopping at the door of Dunning's shop. It was closed. A notice hung on the door. "OUT OF TOWN."

Walton hurried to the bar-room of the Willcox Hotel. His face was aflame with rage; the hand he rested on the bar was shaking as though with palsy. The occupants of the room grinned at him.

"Them the latest style in whiskers?" joked the bartender, winking at another man.

"Mind your own affairs and give me a glass," ordered Walton.

Purposely misunderstanding him, the barkeeper held out a glass of liquor and said, "You seem a leetle nervous, Walton."

The glass was struck to the counter. Walton screamed in maniacal fury, "A looking-glass is what I want, you doggone idiot! I want to gaze on my 'seraphic countenance' that seems to paralyze everybody. Look like the 'green fields of Virginia,' do I? 'Rent me out during a drouth,' will they? Where's a glass?"

"Keep calm, Walton, here's one;" the bartender handed out a small mirror.

Silently Walton gazed at hair and beard of vivid emerald green. The venomous glitter of his eyes was like that of an angry rattlesnake. He laid the glass down and spoke with a voice that was quiet, but deadly.

"Some one put Dunning up to this, and I'll find out who it was, before I get through." He flung out of the place and the men in the room glanced at one another. They knew that some day, somebody would pay. Walton was a man whose debts of personal animus, never outlawed by time, were sure to be settled in full with compound interest.

# Chapter Nine

"The boys don't mean no harm, but it jest seems they can't come to town without things happenin' when they mix in," Limber had said when he parted from Powell.

The cowpuncher went to the corral, mounted his pony and rode down the railroad track to the shipping pens. The cattle were in good shape, gates fastened securely. No matter what the short-comings of the boys of the Diamond H, they never slighted any detail of the work; but Limber felt the responsibility of it all.

When Peanut was properly cared for, his master ambled carelessly along the street until he reached the swinging doors of the bar-room of the Willcox Hotel.

"Any of my outfit here?" he asked the man behind the bar. "I jest got in from Hot Springs with Doctor Powell."

A number of men in the place called to him, others came nearer Limber and held out hands, and he was the centre of a small group when he uttered his next words.

"The Apaches killed ol' Doctor King last night in the Hot Springs Cañon below the Circle Cross. We jest brung in his body for the Coroner."

Exclamations of sincere regret were voiced by his hearers, for each of them could recall little acts of kindliness to himself or to some one he knew. Limber was plied with questions, and gave the meagre details, but he did not speak of the narrow escape of Mrs. Glendon and her child.

Comments were interrupted as the doors swung back once more. Bronco, Holy and Roarer stood bunched together and surveyed the assemblage with brooding eyes. Then, they saw Limber. Their solemn countenances lightened, and Bronco grasped the foreman's arm, leading him to a table at the rear of the room, where they all slumped into chairs. Limber studied each face.

"Well, what have you done this time?" he asked in a resigned voice.

"Say, Limber, we're in a hell of a mess," confessed Bronco abjectly. The other two punchers confirmed the assertion by silence. "We was waitin' for you to get us straightened out, someway."

Limber made no comment until the situation had been fully explained, but his eyes were anxious and his lips harboured no smile.

"It ain't a question now of how we got into it," he finally said, assuming the onus of the episode with the culprits, as a matter of course.

They had slept side by side in their blankets, bunkhouse and range; had shared chuck and tobacco, storms and fair weather, and, if necessary, each would have used his last cartridge in defense of the others. "The wust of it was that we all promised the Boss not to stir up trouble this time. It's all right about Walton; he don't count in this deal, but it's damn tough on the woman. I don't know what to do about it."

"Gosh! Limber, we've got to fix it up-someway," Bronco's tones were desperate. "If we don't, the whole bunch of women in this yer town will be on the war-path after our scalps, and the Diamond H outfit will be huntin' new ranges. You kin lick a man if he gits fresh and sassy, but when a petticoat goes on the rampage, the only thing a feller kin do is cut and run."

"It's because a woman is mixed in it that I'm bothered," Limber went on. "You boys know the Boss will stand for pretty near anythin', so long's thar ain't women in it. He's been pretty plain about that, and it's the one thing he'll fire the whole bunch for. It's the worst mix-up we ever got into."

The foreman looked at the floor, and the other men looked at him. Limber knew he must either tell the truth and clear himself in the eyes of Traynor, or remain silent and take the blame with the others; even though this might mean losing his job as foreman of the Diamond H. His admiration for Traynor was deep and sincere. It hurt to lose Traynor's faith in him.

"We're sure all down and out," Holy's voice was lugubrious, and he let the cigarette he had made, fall unlighted on the table.

"I jest felt that if you were turned loose on the range today that you would stampede. I didn't figure you'd get here so quick with the cattle, and, the trouble about King kept me back.

I wisht I'd got here sooner, so's to round you up before any damage was done. What started you, anyway, Holy?"

"I thought it was a fake picter Walton showed me, until I seen the woman get off'n the train," responded Holy feebly. "Thar's a Kid, too. 'Bout five or six years old. Kinder peaked and sickly and scarey."

A long, low whistle was Limber's only comment on this additional complication.

"She looks young to have a Kid that big," Bronco put in, "But, then you can't look inter a woman's mouth to tell her age, like it was a horse."

Limber's meditations covered many moments, but neither Bronco, Roarer nor Holy interrupted his thoughts. At last he looked up, and they leaned across the table hopefully.

"Thar don't seem anythin' to do exceptin' ask Mrs. Green to help us figure it out," was his decision.

"Gee! That's just the medicine!" agreed the rest with alacrity, nodding at each other in happy approval. "You kin sure fix it up with her, Limber," was Holy's verdict. Limber's grey eyes were sombre as he contemplated the relieved faces.

"Yep!" he said positively, rising as he spoke, "It's the only thing to do. Come along."

Consternation eclipsed the smiles; none of them got up from their chairs. Limber looked at them, then said, "Come along."

Slowly the chairs were pushed back with a loud rasping noise; slowly the sombreros were transferred from wooden pegs above the table to the heads of the three cowpunchers; slowly the spurred feet moved toward the door, passed draggingly through it, and trailed meekly behind Limber until he reached the rooms above the depot, occupied by the Agent and his wife. Limber knocked. The cowboys' hearts were thumping more loudly than Limber's knuckles, it seemed to them.

The door opened, they did not look up, but the feminine voice that bade them enter, sounded ominous. With eyes still downcast, and hats in hands, they followed Limber's heels. They saw nothing else in that room except the rugs on the floor. Then Limber's voice broke the deadly silence.

"The boys say they've got into more trouble on the range, Mrs. Green," Limber said soberly.

"I should say they have," she retorted vehemently. "They ought to be ashamed of themselves, putting a woman in such a position in a strange place! Making her the laughing stock of the whole country! She's been crying her eyes out, ever since she got here. And, you almost frightened the boy to death with your idiot ideas of fun! It takes a big brain to do those things!" she paused breathlessly to look at them with flashing eyes.

Not one of the Diamond H boys would have hesitated at any danger, but now, their one desire was to scurry ignominiously down stairs and hit the home trail without delay. They cast longing eyes at the door that led to freedom and safety. It was closed. Between them and it stood an angry woman.

"We came to you because we all are stampeded, Mrs. Green," pleaded Limber, and the men, hearing the incriminating pronoun, swore allegiance to Limber for the rest of their lives. "Can't you get us headed right, somehow?"

Mollified, she answered, "What had you thought of doing?"

No one had thought of anything, but they were all loathe to admit it, so each one cudgelled his brains vigorously.

"Say, so long as we busted up the weddin'," gasped Bronco, "we'll chip in and refund her fare-ship her back in a box car —I mean-pay her way to whar she come from. Won't we, boys?"

"Sure!" was the chorus.

Now that the ice had been broken, the situation was less strained.

"Derned-hanged —! Oh, say, Mrs. Green! We'll do any damned thing you say, to put an end to this yer doggone millin';" floundered Holy, struggling to be intelligible without profanity. "We never figgered it would buffalo no one but ol' Walton, and to Hell-Oh, shucks! I mean he don't count noways!"

Holy paused and wiped his perspiring face with a red cotton handkerchief that was not more vivid than his own complexion. His effort had been heroic. Mrs. Green recognized it, and her smile refused to be suppressed longer. A dimple sneaked into her cheek. The boys breathed more freely. Dimples didn't frighten them very badly, unless one of them was alone with it.

"Sit down," suggested Mrs. Green, "and let's talk it over together. Maybe we can work out the trouble." Roarer, Bronco and Holy deposited themselves cautiously on edges of chairs, their huge hands hanging pathetically helpless between their leather-clad knees. Their hats decorated the floor and they were conscious of tousled heads.

"You see it all came through the child being delicate. Lung trouble, the doctor said, and Arizona the only hope."

"He sure does look peaked," Bronco hastened to agree. If Mrs. Green had said the King of England was hiding in the kitchen pantry at that moment, Bronco would have backed that statement with his very life.

"Her folks are all dead," continued the Agent's wife, "and she has been supporting the child. It took all the money she had saved, to get here."

"That's tough luck," commented Roarer with a squeak of emotion. Then startled at the sound of his own voice, he subsided.

"She has got to stay in Arizona on account of the child's health," Mrs. Green explained. "Walton answered her advertisement asking for a place where she could work in return for board for herself and the child. Nobody else answered her. Then he proposed marriage, and she agreed. She says the boy means more to her than her own life."

"Well, if she wants to marry Walton," Limber volunteered, "we'll rope him and get her brand on him before you can wink, and you tell her so for us. But, I don't know but we'd be handin' her a worse deal than the fust time."

"I told her what kind of a man he was. She never wants to see him again." Mrs. Green's voice was sharp, hope seemed to die in the breasts of the four men.

"Well," Roarer's tones rose shrilly in his excitement and nervousness, "Do you think any of us'd do in place of ol' Walton? Seems to be up to one of us to make good. Of course, Limber ain't in on this deal; but the rest of us is, ain't we, boys?"

Weakly the rest assented. With deliberate cruelty Mrs. Green critically surveyed each candidate for matrimonial honours. Her eyes roved slowly from their heads to their boots, while their ears grew red, feet shuffled uneasily and mouths were compressed grimly. Cost what it might, the boys of the Diamond H were going to see the trouble straightened out. The clock measured two minutes, but it seemed two hours to those under inspection.

"I don't believe that would be the remedy," she concluded. The men sighed with unconcealed relief, and each registered a vow to get even with Roarer later on. It had been a close shave. The agony would never be forgotten.

"I think she had better stay with me until she finds work," offered the Agent's wife. "She can help me about the place, and I've got some sewing I want to finish up. Then, you know, I have to help Jack a good bit down in the office. Meantime, she could be prospecting for a place that would suit her. She understands house-keeping, cooking and has been employed in office work. So it won't be long before some one will snap her up, out here."

Limber nodded and said gratefully, "We sure are much obliged to you, Mrs. Green," then his hand was thrust into a hip pocket. Had Mrs. Green been a man, she might have been alarmed at the movement, but the hand came out clutching crumpled greenbacks. "It's up to the Diamond H outfit to look out for her till she gets on her feet good and square, and we'll sure be proud to do it."

With hasty awkwardness Holy, Roarer and Bronco added to the donation Limber laid on the table, glad there was something at last that could be done.

"I'm sure we can get things straightened out before long, some way, and I'll do all I can to help her and you, too;" promised the woman.

"I'll talk it over with the Boss when we get home," suggested Limber.

The other men looked at him quickly, but after they said "good-bye" to Mrs. Green, Limber parted from them. They sat side by side on a wooden, backless bench in front of the Willcox Hotel, and discussed the situation with its new angles.

"Limber ain't to blame, and we're goin' to let the Boss know it, too-and then we'll take our medicine like little men," was Bronco's ultimatum, which was endorsed by Holy and Roarer; but their hearts were heavy at the prospect of being "fired" by the Boss of the Diamond H. No other ranch, or Boss, or foreman would ever be the same to them.

# Chapter Ten

Limber started the boys to the ranch at dawn, to make sure they would be safe while he and Doctor Powell attended the inquest over King's body.

Holy, Bronco and Roarer reached the Diamond H without adventure, and after caring for their ponies, grouped in the office at the end of the court-yard, waiting Traynor's advent.

One comprehensive glance told him that something had happened. "Trouble" was written in capital letters across each face. The Boss seated himself at his desk, looked up and said, "What's the matter, boys? Been fined for shooting up the town again?"

"Gee! I wisht it was that," groaned Bronco, as he dropped astride a chair with his arms draped over the back.

"Any of you killed any one?" the voice was more serious now.

"Nope! It's our funeral this time," squeaked Roarer's falsetto.

Traynor twisted about and looked apprehensively at them all. "Great guns! You haven't all gone and gotten married, have you?"

"It's worser'n that," Holy's sepulchral accents boomed, "This yer damn fool outfit has been an' busted up a weddin'! That's all we done this time!"

The worst was over. The men relaxed and waited the effect of their news.

"Well, go ahead. Tell the rest," ordered Traynor curtly, with knit eyebrows.

Interspersed with interruptions, interjections and gestures, the three managed to acquaint the Boss with the situation. When their story ended, he said very sternly, "You boys know that I am always ready to stand by you, but I gave you all fair warning when I hired you, that if you got into any trouble or mix-up with a woman, it would mean your time. I certainly never anticipated such a scrape as this. I'm disgusted with you all!"

"We knowed that before you said it," Bronco agreed meekly, "but what we want to make plain is-we don't want Limber to get any blame for what we done. He wasn't in town when we busted loose. But Limber's liable to tell you jest as if he was right thar hisself."

"You say the woman is looking for ranch work?"

"That's what Mrs. Green told us," was Bronco's reply, reinforced by nods from the other two men. "Says she can cook an' keep house and sew an' work in a orfice, an' Mrs. Green says she can stay thar until they find work for her, somewhars."

Traynor sat looking thoughtfully at the paper-knife he held in his hand. The eyes of the cowpunchers also stared at the paper-knife, as though hoping it would solve their problem. The knife dropped on the desk and Traynor looked up.

"I'll write to Mrs. Green and tell her that if the woman wants to bring her child and come here to supervise the house, I will pay her seventy-five dollars and board her and the boy. Fong is kicking because he doesn't like the housework, and if I get a Mexican woman to come, there's got to be some one to oversee her. This is the only daylight I can see in the muddle you have made of things."

"Say, Mr. Traynor," Bronco leaned over the desk and spoke earnestly, "You tell her to say we're ready to lay down in the corral and let her put her iron on us without a squeal."

"An' we're all halter-broke, gentle and trained to feed from the hand," piped Roarer over Bronco's shoulder. Holy joined them. "If she don't find things pan out like she wants 'em, anytime, all she's got to do is chaw the rag and cuss, an' you bet your sweet life this yer outfit will see that she gets things her own way."

Bronco and Roarer nodded vehemently, and Holy waxed more eloquent. "Tell Mrs. Green if she acts like she's goin' to buck, to talk her into tryin' us out. You know, we're a Hell of a sight better'n we look or act, Mr. Traynor. I'll promise to put hobbles on the damn cuss words the minute she gits here."

"All right, boys. I'll do what I can," promised Traynor. With hopeful expressions they trailed through the door, but halted as he called, "What's her name?"

"Mrs. — — Mrs. — —," began Bronco confidently, then as he saw the shaking heads, he finished, "Derned if we know. None of us ever ast. We'd make fine cowpasture! We're so fresh and green!" his confession wound up in disgust.

Left alone, Traynor wrote briefly to the wife of the Station Agent at Willcox.

Dear Mrs. Green:

I understand that the lady who is with you is looking for employment on a ranch. I would be glad to have her assume charge of the house-keeping at the Diamond H.

There will be no menial labour. A Chinaman does the cooking and washing, and I will employ a Mexican woman for the housework. A little assistance on the ranch books would be of great value to me.

I will pay seventy-five dollars a month, with room and board for her and the child.

If satisfactory, will you write me by next stage, and I will send down for her and her baggage.

Kindly state that I regret the pranks of the boys, and hope it has not caused any serious annoyance to you or her. They wish to make amends in any manner possible. Their contrition is sincere, and so are my apologies.

Very truly yours,
The Unfortunate Boss of the Diamond H.

Traynor smiled as he signed the letter, knowing that Mrs. Green and her husband would appreciate the humour of the situation that forced the Boss of the Diamond H to employ a woman for the first time on the ranch. He also sighed, as he realized it would mean readjustment in many ways. But, he was resigned, and the men could not kick at conditions for which they were responsible. It would be a relief, though, to have some one else arrange the list of provisions when necessary, plan menus, and order new sheets and towels as needed.

The letter was delivered to the stage-driver Monday, and an answer could be expected on Thursday when the stage returned from Willcox. So when Limber and Powell reached the ranch that evening, the dark cloud had a lovely silver edge that promised a similar lining.

Thursday morning Traynor and Doctor Powell rode to the Cienega Ranch, four miles north of the Diamond H. The Cienega, named because of the marsh formed by under ground water, was one of the many smaller watering places belonging to the Diamond H. A man usually stayed at these points to see that the ponds and troughs were kept in shape for cattle to water. The idea of using gasoline engines instead of the orthodox Perkins windmills, was an innovation of Traynor's.

Limber and the boys were working on the pasture fences near the ranch house, when the stage from Willcox passed. They looked at it speculatively from the other side of the field.

"Wonder if she's wrote that she'll come?" Bronco's audible question voiced the thoughts of the others; but only the return of the Boss could answer that query.

At noon the men dismounted in the stable just as the bell that hung outside the door of the men's kitchen rang loud and long. No time was lost in responding to the summons. It was music in their ears after a long morning in the invigourating air, augmented by hard work. Fong's cooking was famous throughout Southern Arizona. Lunch over, they sat peacefully side by side on the wooden bench against the wall of the stable, enjoying the inevitable wheat straw and Durham cigarette, as necessary as a pony to any Arizona puncher. Fong appeared at the door of the men's kitchen, looked across at the group, then ambled over and addressed the foreman.

"Bloss no clome home for lunch, maybe. I clatchee lunch in Bloss's dining-loom or I clatchee lunch in chuck-house for lady and lily bloy?"

The men started.

"What lady?" demanded Limber, with dire foreboding.

"Lady clome on stage. Lily bloy clome, allee samee. Glo in parlour."

"Good Lord!" ejaculated Bronco. "She ain't writ, she come! An' yer's the Boss and Doctor Powell gone off and left us all alone!"

Fong's grin of comprehension was irritating, and Limber ordered, "Fix lunch in the Boss's dining-room, and fix a good one while you're about it, too."

The Chinaman hurried to obey. He had made a scientific study of Limber's face and voice. Fong liked the work at the Diamond H; he also like the generous wages and not having to skimp in any way.

Limber turned to the rest. "Well, I guess it's up to us to go in and squar things with her," he announced. "She's been sitting thar for two hours now, an' nobody gone near her. Darn that Chink, anyway! Come along, boys."

Anxious to make amends for their many sins of commission and omission, they clanked with spurred heels along the cement walk of the court and followed Limber into the living-room of the ranch. Then they stopped, bunched in the doorway.

A slender figure, with rippling brown hair, was huddled forlornly in a big chair, asleep. The flushed cheeks bore traces of recent tears. Hat, gloves and a child's cap were in her lap, a suit-case on the floor beside the chair, as though in readiness for departure. On the couch was the boy; but his eyes were wide open.

As he saw the four cowpunchers in the doorway, he shrank back timidly and reached out his thin hand. The girl woke instantly. She did not see the men until, as they advanced into the room, Holy's foot collided with the leg of a chair, and he suppressed an ejaculation. The girl flushed with embarrassment as she faced the four cowpunchers of the Diamond H.

None of them spoke. She rose to her feet and looked from one to the other, uncertain whom to address, as she said, "Mrs. Green told me of your generous offer. I did not wait to write, but came up on the stage this morning;" her voice was low and tremulous. "I thank you with all my heart. It means so much-to me. I —will do-my very best to please you all," her last words came with a rush.

No answer was made by the four ominous figures confronting her. An expression of fear crept into the blue eyes that dimmed with tears. Her hands went out in appeal.

"Please, please, don't say that I won't suit you. I am a great deal stronger than I look, and I'm not afraid of hard work. Jamie," her arm went about the child at her side, "won't bother any one," the pitiful catch in her voice seemed to grip the throat of each man, and the words they wanted to utter refused to make a sound. The girl read the pity in Limber's grey eyes, then the foreman smiled at her and said in his quiet, kindly voice; "Thar ain't no reason for you to worry. We was jest scairt that you wouldn't want to stay. That's all. We didn't know you was here till Fong told us jest now. He's fixin' lunch for you. I'm jest Limber, the foreman." He turned and indicated the other punchers who were trying to smile naturally, but making a terrible contortion of facial muscles. "This is Bronco, and Roarer an' Holy, and we're the Diamond H outfit."

Awkwardly the men advanced and held out calloused hands, but the grip was a pledge of fealty, and the girl looked gratefully into their eyes.

Then Limber happened to note Traynor standing in the open doorway back of the girl, and relief shown plainly in the foreman's face as he said, "Thar's the Boss, now."

She whirled sharply, like a tormented creature at bay, sensing a new enemy. Traynor's face was drawn and white through its tan. Unmindful of the men, his hands reached out. The girl stared incredulously. Then the tension was broken by their two voices:

"Nell!"

"Allan!"

The cowpunchers' jaws fell in astonishment, their eyes popped, then with one accord they fled precipitately, jostling each other through the doorway. Limber was the last one to leave the room. He lost no time, but he saw the arms of the Boss of the Diamond H holding a sobbing girl. When Limber reached the stables there was only a cloud of dust to show that the boys were anxious to finish up very important work away from the vicinity of the ranch house.

They did not know of the consultation between Traynor and Limber an hour later, nor that Limber had driven down to Eureka Springs, eight miles away, and returned accompanied by Mrs. Burns, wife of the owner of that ranch.

Just before supper the foreman found the men in the bunk-house. They looked up at him with hopeless faces, as he surveyed them and remarked, "Well, you sure mixed things up good and plenty that time!"

"Oh, you don't have ter tell us that," retorted Bronco, despairingly. "We all knowed it without anyone's help!"

"I wisht someone'd put me in a lunitic asylum for the rest of my life," was Holy's disgusted announcement. He stared at the whitewashed wall of the bunkroom, visioning his possible future domicile.

"We figgered we'd got it all fixed up fine, an' you know it was, Limber, till the Boss butted in. How'd we know that he knowed her, anyway? Well, now things is millin' worser'n ever." Bronco's voice was almost unrecognizable in its woe. "Say, Limber, are we all fired?"

Limber seated himself, took out his sack of tobacco and papers, rolled a cigarette and lighted it, without one word. His face was serious. Six mournful eyes watched him. They read their fate in his silence. There was no appeal. In a corner of the bunk-room three rolls of blankets were stacked. Limber looked at them, but said nothing. Three hands went to hip pockets. In dead silence three cigarettes were made and lighted. It was a cowboy wake. Five minutes went by. They smoked and sank more deeply in gloom.

"Of course, we kin get jobs somewhar," Bronco spoke at last. "That ain't what's troublin' me. But it's how we went and made such a mix-up for the Boss, when he's always been so white to us all. I can't figger how he's goin' to get it straight for hisself, now!"

Limber studied the cigarette in his hand. "He said thar's only one thing left that you all kin do, now."

"We knowed we was fired, Limber," Roarer's voice was a higher pitch than ever before, "You don't have to tell us. Thar warn't anythin' left for him to do but fire the whole bunch of us. We bin an' got our war-bags all packed up and ready."

"But, we're derned sorry we made this mess for you and him and the lady," Holy was now on his feet, picking up a roll of blankets from the corner. He slung it over his shoulder and held out his hand to the foreman. "It hurts like Hell to go."

Bronco and Roarer with their own rolls, lined beside Holy.

"Tell the Boss 'so long' for us," was Bronco's request. "And, we're damned sorry for it all."

Limber looked at the three outstretched hands, the three dejected figures with the rolls of blankets across their shoulder, then said, "He told me that the only way you boys kin squar things is for the whole outfit to meet him tomorrow night at Mrs. Green's place at eight o'clock."

"What fur?" they three inquired in startled tones, as their hands fell weakly at their sides.

"Well," drawled Limber, as a twinkle lit up his eyes and his mouth twitched with a smile, "Thar's goin' to be a weddin'! The Boss says that the only thing left for him to do with you boys, is to let the little Lady run this yer outfit and keep it straight! He owns up it's too much of a job for him to handle!"

Three rolls of blankets dropped with dull thuds to the bare floor. Three wild yells broke the quiet air, then with arms intertwined about each other's shoulders, they formed a circle and indulged in an Apache war-dance. A smile that was almost paternal illuminated Limber's face as he watched them.

When the exuberance had subsided a bit, and they had finished ejaculating and slapping each other on the back, Bronco turned to Limber.

"Say, Limber, this is the wust mix-up of all! Here we go and stampeded the heifer what Walton figgered on ropin' for hisself, and she turns an busts into the home corral with the Diamond H brand on her! Can you beat it?"

No one answered.

The clamour of the supper bell brought them to their feet once more, and they hurried to the chuck-house, talking as fast as they could. All talked at once; no one replied or listened, but it was a happy bunch of cowpunchers that slid along the wooden bench at the supper-table that night.

Back on the floor of the bunk-house lay three rolls of blankets waiting for the men to stumble over them in the dark.

## Chapter Eleven

Unusual excitement was evident in the Willcox Hotel, as the cowpunchers of the Diamond H rushed in with mysterious packages which afterwards developed into conventional attire. They had ridden to town early in the afternoon, Saturday, the day the wedding of the Boss was to take place.

Confusion reigned in their small room. Roarer danced around, struggling to fasten a collar, his face becoming apoplectic; while Holy, with his entire vocabulary and muscular strength, was coaxing his feet into patent leather shoes a size too small. When his frantic efforts culminated in a broken loop-strap, it left him, for once in his life, speechless.

Before a bilious mirror, Limber plastered his hair down rigidly with a stick of barber's cosmetique, recommended by the bar-tender; and Bronco stood ruefully contemplating four enormous pairs of white kid gloves reposing in a long row on the bed.

"I don't balk at toggin' up swell for the Boss's weddin'," came in a gasp from Roarer as he clutched at his throat, "but derned if I see why the feller what invented collar-buttons and biled shirts wasn't lynched for his fust offense. Doggone the beastly little contraption, anyhow!"

The others regarded him sympathetically, for they, too, had struggled, as the numerous twisted, soiled collars about the room testified; even those now decorating their brown throats showed marks of desperate fray.

"I've spiled seven collars and busted five collar buttons already," groaned Roarer, pausing in his struggle. "Oh, Lord! Where did that thing go. Any one see it? It's wusser'n a flea the way it lit out."

They grasped his meaning. Each had recently been on a voyage of discovery for other collar buttons.

"Mebbe it's under the bed," suggested Holy, trying to balance himself and walk in the tight shoes. He paused, standing like a gigantic stork on one foot. "Mine rolled under the bed."

Roarer fell to his knees and groped without avail, then crawled out on all fours, gazing up disconsolately into the faces of the other men. "Not a hair nor a hide of it," he puffed, still on his knees. "That's the last one we had, and what's wust, thar ain't no more collar-buttons in the whole blamed town. Everyone's been buyin' 'em this afternoon."

"Well, it couldn't get outen the room;" consoled Limber, whose toilet was finished before the others, because he had had the foresight to enlist the services of a clerk in Soto's store, and after buying a shirt, collar and tie, the two had retired to a small back room. Hence, Limber had emerged victorious and unruffled, but his sympathies were with the other punchers.

"They say collar-buttons take to a bureau if the bed don't suit 'em," he suggested. "Suppose you start a round-up on that range, Roarer. I'd like to help you out, but this collar checks me up too high."

Inspired by the idea, Roarer assumed his devotional attitude and clawed wildly. Something gave way, and he emerged precipitately.

"I got her," he triumphed, "but something busted-What was it?" he supplemented with an anxious glance over his shoulder.

The others surrounded him.

"Suspender," reported Limber. "Button's busted off'n your trousers."

"Much damage?" he inquired of the investigating committee, which continued looking him over.

"Nothin' but what can be fixed up with a pin," was Bronco's decision. "Any one got a pin?"

They shook their heads. It was a pinless crowd, but a brilliant idea struck Holy, who delved into the pockets of his discarded leather chaps and produced a horse-shoe nail. Drawing a piece of the trouser cloth through the button-hole of the suspended flap, he thrust the nail in dexterously.

"Thar you are," he pronounced cheerfully.

"Say, Holy, you're a wonder!" flattered Roarer obsequiously.

Holy grinned at him and demanded, "What do you want me to do for *you*?"

Roarer's childish accents pleaded, "Can't you help me get into this collar? It's the only one we got left that's fitten to put on, and it ain't big enough for this shirt, nor me, neither, but I've got to get into it somehow."

Holy inspected the dilemma. "I'll go see if I kin find something," he said vaguely as he left the room. In a few minutes he returned.

"I got a button-hook off'n the chambermaid. We can fix it up now!"

Surrounded by an admiring group, he grasped the collar band of Roarer's shirt, thrust the button-hook through the button-hole of the collar and gave a vigorous twist.

An agonized squeal, like a dying pig, assaulted the air and Roarer retreated rapidly with the button-hook hanging to the collar, while he rubbed the prominent bone in his throat that had interfered with the adjustment.

"What in thunder do you think you're doin'?" he piped, glaring at Holy. "Looks like you was figgerin' to make cider outen my Adam's apple, the way you squoze."

"Well, I done the best I knowed how," defended Holy. "That's the way things goes. I pulled an ol' Bar Z cow outen the mud, and the fust thing the durned cow done was to make a bee-line for me whilst I had my back to her a cinchin' my saddle. She spiled the only pair of trousers I owned, and then went back into the mudhole and died. Thar's a heap of human nature in cows, and heaps of cow nature in humans! Here's the button-hook." Holy rescued it from the floor where it had dropped as Roarer massaged his throat. "You dig yourself outen your own mud-hold. I'm done!"

He limped painfully across the room and dropped into a chair, the picture of disgust, and watched with fishy eye as Roarer plied the button-hook until the collar succumbed.

The agony was almost over, but the four pairs of gloves promised further trouble.

"Say, Bronc," insinuated Roarer as he contemplated the bed, "Couldn't a feller go without wearin' these derned things? Suppose we just put 'em in the outside pockets of our coats and let the fingers hang out, to show we got 'em?"

"No, sirree!" vetoed Bronco emphatically, in the self-assumed role of social adviser. "There ain't nothin' too good for the Boss; and the boys down to the store told me that white kid gloves has got to be wore at weddin's. So them gloves has got to go on, if it busts us flat!"

With looks of grim determination and the spirit that inspired the 'noble Six Hundred,' they swooped down on the gloves. Appropriating a pair, each man settled himself on a chair. The room was silent. Moments passed unheeded. Four struggling cowpunchers sat in four creaking chairs and laboured until four pairs of huge hands were encased in bedraggled white kid gloves, which the owners surveyed with triumph.

"They squinch," announced Holy, closing his hand convulsively, "but they'll stretch if you work 'em a bit."

There was an ominous sound, and a look of consternation on Holy's face as he gazed at the split glove on his left hand.

"Now, you'll have to get another pair," commanded Bronco.

"Hanged if I will," retorted Holy, rebelling at the prospect of repeating his experience.

"Then you got to remember to keep your hand shet up," compromised Bronco. "Lucky it's the left hand, because we all got to shake hands with the bride and the minister you know."

"Say, Bronc, are you sure about the minister?" asked Limber dubiously.

"You bet! You see it's this way," elucidated Bronco. "The groom is in luck to get the girl, ain't he? So you shake hands with him. The girl's lucky to get married, ain't she, stead of dyin' an old maid? So you shake hands with her; and the minister is the luckiest one of the bunch, because he gets paid for marryin' them and he don't take no chances on havin' trouble afterwards. That's why you have to shake hands with the minister."

No one disputed the logic.

"People makes me think of flies in cold weather when it comes to gettin' married," reflected Limber audibly. "The flies that's outside the window keep tryin' to get in, and them that's inside keep workin' for all they're wuth to get out. Looks like they're just bound to be miserable either way."

"I knowed a feller down in Texas had two dogs named David and Jonathan," said Bronco. "Wherever you seen one dog the other was right along side of him, like his shadder. You jest couldn't keep 'em apart. One day some smart geezer seen 'em sleepin' peaceful an' ca'm, side by each, and tied one of David's hind legs to one of Jonathan's, and when them dogs woke up they blamed each other, and from cussin' something awful in dog lingo, they lit in and chawed hair and hide till they was pried apart. Ever since then the minute they see each other, it's just a signal for them to start a free-for-all to a finish. The way them two dogs has soured on each other is a caution."

"What's that got to do with gettin' married?" demanded Holy with a snort.

Bronco gazed at him a few seconds before he answered, "Well there's lots of folks that would be good friends all their lives if they didn't hunt up a minister to marry 'em and give 'em the right to scrap till they die. When David and Jonathan got too serious, somebody got a club. But if you find a man and his wife scrappin' and you try to ca'm them, they both turn and pitch into you for meddlin' with their family pleasures."

Limber took out his watch and announced it was time to start, and Bronco, after a final survey of his charges, led the procession from the chamber of torture. They crossed the street, holding their hands stiffly at their sides, while each gloved finger stood out separately, like an individual Declaration of Independence.

As they ascended the stairs leading to Mrs. Green's rooms, Bronco whispered his last instructions, "Don't forget to shake hands with the whole outfit; and you be careful Holy, to keep your left hand shet."

Holy, leading the procession, halted suddenly and called back to Bronco, "I thought you said we was only to shake hands with the Boss and the Little Lady and the gospel-shark," but as the door opened in front of them, Bronco made no reply.

The room was filled with guests, and after the first wave of bashfulness had receded, the Diamond H boys bunched together like a herd of scared cattle. Doctor Powell crossed the room and joined them, then Mrs. Green entered with Jamie, the little brother of the bride. Powell smiled and the child shyly edged closer, until he was lifted to the doctor's knee. There was a slight confusion. Traynor stepped to a space in front of the minister, and the doctor, rising, consigned the child to Limber, then advanced to his place beside Traynor.

The cowboys of the Diamond H fidgeted nervously, and wondered at the Boss's calm appearance, noting with proprietary pride how handsome he looked and how high he held his head. There was a tender smile on his lips and his eyes were fixed on the door leading to the hallway.

Bronco leaned closer to Holy, whispering, "I bet he don't even know he's got a collar on. Ain't some men lucky?"

"Shet up," boomed Holy's voice treacherously, and many heads turned toward them, while Holy tried to efface himself behind Roarer and Bronco.

The door leading to the hall opened and Jack Green came in with Nell on his arm. The women's eyes became moist as they looked at the girl, and the men silently voted Allan Traynor a lucky chap. Mrs. Green had dressed the girl in a pretty white gown, and the real wedding veil that floated about the slender form was the one that had been worn ten years previous by the agent's kind-hearted wife.

Outside, a mocking bird sang in the wonderful Arizona moonlight, as though it understood and sent its benison of love while the solemn words were spoken. Traynor stooped and kissed the girl, whose eyes looked into his with a dazzling light that shone through tears, like the sun breaking through a mist.

"Till Death us do part," he repeated unsteadily.

Then Jamie was beside them, holding up his thin arms to his sister, who kissed him tenderly. The boy turned uncertainly to Traynor, looked up at him, and laughed gayly as he was caught by the man's strong hands and held up a second, while Traynor said, "You've got a grown-up brother, now, old man."

Beaming, Jamie slipped his hand into Nell's and stood beside them as the guests showered congratulations on the couple.

Bronco marshalled the Diamond H boys in line and Traynor suppressed his inclination to laugh at the unaccustomed regalia of store clothes, 'biled shirts' and white kid gloves, when the men held out their hands to the bride and groom.

Holy, recalling Bronco's final instructions on the stairway, forgot the damaged glove in his exuberance, and shook hands vigorously with everyone he could reach. Then with the consciousness of duty nobly done, he sought a corner and mopped his moist forehead with a Lilliputian sheet that he considered a handkerchief. Bronco edged up to him, and a sudden light gleamed in Holy's eyes.

"Say, Bronc, what the devil did you keep kickin' me an' trompin' on my feet for?" he demanded indignantly. "You acted like a cayuse with the stringhalt."

"Stringhalt!" grunted Bronco, "If you'd had any hoss sense whatsoever, you'd knowed I was doin' my durndest to get you to shet that big fist of your'n."

Holy looked down at the tattered glove that dangled in dingy strings from the offending hand, then he pulled it off in sections. "I hope some one will shoot the top of my head off if I ever wear them damned things again. Not on your life-even if the Boss was to get married every day in the year for the rest of his life!"

He jerked off the other glove, wadded them together in a compact ball, and deftly tossed it out the open window.

The wedding party adjourned to a feast spread in the dining room of the Willcox Hotel, where toasts were given and merriment continued unabated till the west-bound 'Flyer' stopped at the signal, and Traynor and his bride left for a couple of weeks in California, leaving Jamie with Mrs. Green.

Powell boarded the train at the same time, as he had to go to Tucson on business connected with his intention to bid for the Hot Springs Ranch.

Bonfires had been lighted near the track, and the boys fired a salute to the Boss and his bride. The coloured porter darted back to the platform of the train, and looked at the men with wild eyes.

"You ain't got no call to be scairt," reassured Bronco, "We're jest seein' a bridal couple off, that's all."

Then the whites of the porter's eyes disappeared entirely, and in the black face shone a row of gleaming teeth.

The tail-light of the train disappeared in the distance, the bonfires died away, and the boys of the Diamond H. feeling they had done things up 'good and proper,' sought their beds in the hotel.

"Gosh! I'm glad the Boss ain't a Mormon!" sighed Bronco, as he dropped to sleep. The only response to his remark was a chorus of snores in which he soon joined.

Out in the dusty road was a tiny ball that had once been a pair of white kid gloves.

## Chapter Twelve

The weekly stage from Willcox to Aravaipa Cañon, which stopped at the ranch on Mondays, brought a letter to Limber from Allan Traynor, instructing the foreman to meet himself and his wife upon their arrival from California on Thursday. There was also a note from Doctor Powell, who was still in Tucson, saying that he would return to the ranch on Wednesday.

The men had just eaten lunch and were grouped about the stables when Limber imparted the news to them, adding, "The Boss says to slick up the big room on the front porch, and we've got to hustle to get it done in time. They'll be here in three days."

"Say, Limber," interrupted Bronco, who was usually the ruling spirit, "Don't you think we'd oughter get a weddin' present for 'em?"

"I sure do!" endorsed Limber, "But, what kin we get? If we'd had any sense among us we'd of sent off long ago for somethin' proper. Mrs. Green would of knowed, but it's too late now."

"Let's chip in and get some big Navajo blankets like Mrs. Green's," suggested Holy. "Looked a heap prettier'n carpets on her floor."

"Gee! Holy, you do get an idee onct in a while," jeered Bronco, whose chief delight in life was to tease Holy, and, like tourists who throw stones into the crater of a volcano, stand by in admiration of the eruption that followed.

"Now, see here," admonished Limber, "don't you and Holy get to millin'. Thar ain't no time for it."

Holy glared at Bronco, who grinned back at him and murmured, "Fust blood."

Limber reverted to the letter. "It says that Mrs. Traynor will have the little room off'n the big room for her'n, and we'd better whitewash it."

He broke off and looked at the others, as he said, "Have we got a whitewash brush that is fitten to use?"

"Whitewash your grandmother!" retorted Bronco contemptuously. "We'd oughter paper it. I seen some dandy paper with pink roses stampeding all over it at the Headquarter Store. White-wash is all O.K. for cowpunchers and bronco busters, but girls likes paper and-and-them sorter things," he concluded hastily.

"We don't know how to do it," objected Limber, "and thar ain't no paperhanger in Willcox."

"Shucks! Tain't no trick noway," responded Bronco airily. "I'll show you. All you got ter do is get the paper an' do what I tell you."

Impressed by his convincing air the quartette engaged in making a list of the things Bronco considered necessary, the principal items being the paper with pink roses and three of 'the biggest, highest priced and reddest Navajo blankets in town.'

After watching Bronco start on his mission, Limber and the others saddled their ponies for the daily routine work on the range, as they knew that Bronco could not get home before late that night.

It was nearly midnight when Bronco rode into the stables, but the entire bunch of men met him with a volley of questions as he dismounted from his pony. Bursting with importance, he unrolled the Navajo blankets which had been tied to the back of his saddle; while the paper, carefully packed in gunny-sacks, was swung across the front horn.

The men grasped the purchases and carried them to the bunkhouse where they opened the sacks eagerly. The blankets had been fully endorsed and admired; but when Bronco, imitating the storekeeper, unrolled a sample of the paper and held it up with a flourish, no words were left to express their delight.

"Now, we'll get up early tomorrow so's to tackle the job and get it over," said Limber, after they had disposed of the packages in the room they contemplated papering. Filled with joyful anticipations they tumbled into their bunks.

Bronco was the first to waken, and he roused the others before daylight, despite their protests.

Roarer sat up and blinked stupidly at the lamp which Bronco was lighting.

"I ain't had no sleep that was any good," he quavered in his thin voice. "I was chasin' pink roses all night-they had horns and tails and four legs, jest like cows, and I was tryin' to rope 'em. I'm plumb played out."

His tale of woe was unheard by the others as they hurriedly adjusted clothes and tumbled out of the bunkhouse to the ranch kitchen for breakfast. Fong, the cook, was in no amiable mood because he had to serve breakfast an hour earlier than usual; but when he learned that they expected to take possession of his kitchen and sundry utensils, his wrath was expressed in a wordy battle in 'pidgin English. He only succumbed to superior numbers when he retreated to the back porch. His mutterings could be heard distinctly by those in the kitchen, and Bronco cocked his head on one side and listened attentively to the angry cook.

"Say, Holy, I don't savvy what that year Chink is sayin', but it sounds a heap worse'n anything I ever heerd you say. He's got you beat to a frazzle. Why don't you learn Chinee? Then when your stock of cuss words gets stale you can start on a new lot."

Holy's retort was cut short by Limber, who paused in rolling a cigarette and observed, "You're captain of this round-up, Bronco. How do you start her?"

They all gathered about Bronco as he explained the process unhesitatingly. He did not divulge that he had asked information at the store, regarding the preparation of paper, making paste and other necessary details of paperhanging. It had seemed so simple that he was sure he could remember everything.

"Well, fust you cut the edges off'n the paper, then you make a biscuit dough and thin her out and stick the paper up, and thar you are! Easy as rollin' off'n a log!"

"That's all right so long as the log ain't pinted into a mudhole whar thar's a buckskin cow," murmured Holy, with a side glance at Bronco. The innuendo was loftily ignored, and Holy tried other tactics.

"Whar' did you learn to paper, anyhow?" he demanded suspiciously. "You never let on you knowed how until last night."

"Think I'm Hasayampering?" Bronco answered indignantly. "I seed them paper a room down to Eureka Springs three years ago. I helped them do it." He reserved the elucidation that he had helped carry in a galvanized tub, nothing more. "Mebbe you don't believe me, but if any of you fellers thinks he knows more'n I do about it, I'm willin' to lay back in harness and let him take the lead, and yours truly won't do no kickin' over the traces, neither."

As no one was disposed to dispute his authority, he continued in a mollified voice:

"Roarer, you go get all the flour you kin find and bring it here."

Roarer looked dubiously toward the back porch and scratched his head, then he tiptoed to the door, peeped through it, and discovering Fong had deserted the place, started on his search, while Bronco issued his commands to the others.

"Limber, you kin chase that new whitewash brush I left in the bunkhouse, and Holy can trim the edges off'n the paper. Then you kin all help mix the paste when I get ready."

"Does anybody know whar the shears is?" queried Holy, knowing from experience that a needle in a haystack could be located twenty times before the one pair of shears on the ranch was generally found by the searcher. "Bronc, you had them scissors three weeks ago cuttin' Limber's hair. I seed you. Whar are they?"

Bronco looked nonplussed, then asserted, "Roarer took 'em away from us before the job was done, and then he disremembered whar he'd put 'em. Limber had to go to town with one side his hair cut and Dunning finished up the job."

Limber appeared with the whitewash brush, and at his heels came Roarer dragging two sacks of flour.

"This is all I kin find," said Roarer. "Reckon it will be enough?"

Bronco was non-committal, "I'll use it up and see how fur it'll go."

"Say, Roarer, you got to find the scissors. You was the last one that had 'em. Where are they?" called Holy accusingly.

Roarer stared blankly, then whirled out the door. Holy sat swearing until Roarer re-appeared and exhibited the lost shears, explaining, "I just happened to think that I couldn't find the wire-nippers that day when you was cuttin' Limber's hair, and that was why I got 'em from you. I left 'em in the blacksmith shop, but I disremembered it till you spoke about 'em. They may cut paper, but they ain't no good for cuttin' wire."

He handed the badly damaged shears to Holy who seated himself on the floor. Selecting a roll of paper from the pile before him, Holy opened and contemplated it in perplexity, finally appealing to Bronco:

"Say, Bronc, there's two white edges. Shall I trim 'em both?"

Bronco stood gazing down at the paper. "Durned if I know," he confessed. "But thar ain't no use shirkin' the job since we tackled it. Pitch in, Holy. Let 'er go, and cut 'em both off," he directed recklessly before he was attracted by the struggles of Roarer and Limber, who dragged in a galvanized tub.

Behind them came Fong, protesting wildly, "No clatchee more flouler. No makee biscuits tomollow."

"Well, give us crackers," commanded Bronco. "This year room has got to be papered today. Go chase yourself, Fong."

The Chinaman disappeared jabbering and shaking his head, but no one paid attention to Fong's worries. Each was immersed in his own troubles.

Holy struggled heroically with spirals of paper, and volcanic outbursts of his pet expressions floated from his part of the room as he endeavoured to extricate himself from the enveloping coils. Bronco hovered over the tub, directing Limber and Roarer, who dumped a sack and a half of flour into it.

"You gotter put salt in, next," said Bronco, and the two cowpunchers darted to a cupboard where each captured a small bag of salt.

"What next?" they demanded, becoming imbued with enthusiasm as the salt mingled with the tub of flour.

"And-er-and —" floundered Bronco hopelessly. "There's something else. What the devil is it?" he implored the others.

"Water," prompted Holy from his corner, his head and arms protruding from the paper making him resemble a huge turtle. "I knowed you'd forget that."

Bronco's ire found vent in a few words borrowed from Holy's vocabulary, and Limber, mounted on a box, turned from inspecting the cupboard to say: "If we're goin' to paper this room, you two quit scrapin' and get down to business. If you ain't, jest say so, and I'll set Manuel to whitewashin' it."

His threat had the desired effect. Bronco appealed to Limber, "Larry told me to mix it like biscuit dough and thin it out with water. There was somethin' else but I've plumb forgot it, Limber."

"Well, try lard, then," suggested Limber, poking his head back in the cupboard and scanning the contents hoping to find the missing article, even though it were necessary to add everything on the shelves. "How about some niggerfoot molasses?"

"Lard's all right," replied Bronco, "but niggerfoot don't go in biscuits."

"Well, it goes on top of 'em pretty slick, and it's good and sticky, so it oughter be a good thing to put in," persisted Limber, holding out the can. "Mebbe Larry forgot to tell you to use it."

"Jest a leetle bit," conceded Bronco, wishing heartily that Limber would insist upon whitewashing the room; but not brave enough to suggest it himself. It had taken him two years to live down the episode of the buckskin cow, and he knew that Holy and Roarer would make life a burden if he confessed his inability to finish the work he had so recklessly undertaken.

He watched the black molasses trickle into the contents of the tub until the last drop had fallen. Limber ascended the box again.

"Thar's another can of niggerfoot. Don't be stingy with it Bronc," admonished Limber.

Bronco had not the courage to negative any suggestion, but he groped mentally, "It was a short word," he told Limber with a faint gleam of hope.

"Dam!" exploded Holy. "Jest look at this dod-ratted, twistin' paper, will you? Talk about your Hopi snake-dancers, they ain't in it with me! Where am I at?" he demanded from a labyrinth of paper coils.

Bronco was glad of the chance to assume knowledge that he did not possess, much as a small boy bolsters up his ebbing courage in a dark lane by whistling loudly.

"I told you to cut the edges straight," he announced oracularly, "and these year look like a cross-eyed maverick had been usin' a circular saw to cut wall-paper for a merry-go-round. Why that paper would give a minister a jag to look at it!"

"If one of you fellers would hog-tie that end whilst I get a diamond-hitch on this'n, I mought have some show," defended Holy feebly.

Roarer went to the rescue and gripped one end of a roll while Holy conscientiously proceeded to mutilate the edges and succeeded in making the scallops a trifle smaller. Limber and Bronco resumed their consultation.

"I bet it was yeast," jubilated Limber. "We all forgot about that, and it's a short word, sure enough."

"I guess you're right," Bronco agreed with desperate haste, and without delay he dumped a large can of baking powder into the tub. "Now, all we got to do is thin her out and then she's ready to start work."

Limber helped him carry the tub into the front room, escorted by Roarer and Holy, who trailed yards of paper which had escaped from their encircling arms.

"We need a board and two saw-horses to stand on," said Bronco cheerfully, believing the worst of the trouble was over. "Holy, you and Roarer paste the paper with the whitewash brush, whilst Limber helps me stic'er up. We got to have system if we want to get anything done right."

The first strip was duly prepared, and they viewed it with feelings akin to the emotions of Columbus and his crew when they sighted land. Bronco climbed on the plank that rested on the saw-horses. As he reached down for the wet strip which Limber held up to him, the board tipped suddenly. Bronco slid, clawing wildly at space until he enveloped Limber in a pasty embrace. The impact caused them both to fall across Holy and Roarer who were engaged in spreading paste on another strip. The latter proved no obstacle in the mad career of Limber and Bronco, which ended ignominiously in a sea of paste from the overturned tub.

When the confusion had subsided sufficiently, the men surveyed the wreck with voiceless disgust, until Holy spoke sarcastically.

"I suppose you'll say this belongs in the deal, Bronc. What's next? You sure seem to be the movin' spirit. But, one thing I'm stackin' my chips on, is that I'll know better the next time I start to paper a room and won't do it."

"You can quit if you want to. I ain't no quitter. Thar's half a sack of flour left," Bronco challenged over his shoulder as he started for the door to the back porch where he had deposited the surplus flour. The half-sack of flour had disappeared.

"I bet that Chink got it," asserted Bronco wrathfully, but there was no sign of Fong in answer to their calls. Then Limber pointed to a couple of burros that were demolishing the last shreds of a flour sack.

"That settles it," grunted Bronco, blissfully ignorant that while they had been occupied, Fong had slipped slyly through the screen door of the porch, clutched the half sack of flour, retreated successfully and after dumping the contents of the sack into another sack, which had been washed, the Chinaman with a leer of triumph, tossed the original sack to the burros. Then, complacently he began mixing the dough for the next day's baking; but at intervals he peered at the fast vanishing flour sack, and saw that his ruse was successful when the cowboys discovered the two burros.

"Gosh, all we got to show is a nice mess that's got to be cleaned up, and a bill down to the Headquarters for paper with pink roses. Ain't it a shame? Just when we was getting along so fine, too." Bronco's tones were lugubrious, and they all looked regretfully at the coils of paper that cumbered the room. Like mourners at a funeral they gathered around the coils. The pink roses grew more alluring. Bronco lifted one strip and held it against the wall.

"Whitewash makes me sick," he affirmed.

"Suppose I go over to Eureka and ask Mrs. Burns to lend us enough flour to finish up the job?" Limber made the suggestion and the idea was accepted enthusiastically.

While he was gone the others scraped up the paste and collected the scattered rolls of paper, then went to the bunkhouse and waited Limber's return, unaware that almost half a sack of flour reposed in a corner of Fong's tin trunk, while a batch of bread was rising beautifully in the dishpan hidden beneath Fong's bed. Had any of the boys suspicioned the true facts there would have been a badly-frightened Chinaman in Arizona.

When Limber returned he was accompanied by Mrs. Burns in her buggy, while Peanut, Limber's pony, trotted at the back of the rig, hitched to the axle.

"You boys have certainly run into a bunch of trouble," she laughed as she nimbly climbed from the rig. "I told Limber that I might be able to help you, for I've done all my own papering, you know."

Limber extricated a sack that held flour, and joined the procession to the room they were now sure would be decorated with pink roses.

Mrs. Burns looked at the remnant of paste in the tub before she asked, "What on earth did you use?"

"Everything we could find," confessed Bronco humbly. "We did leave out eggs, sugar and pepper."

"All you need is flour, hot water and a little thin glue water," she laughed.

"Glue!" they echoed.

"I told you Larry said it was a short word," triumphed Bronco. "Why didn't some of you muttonheads think of glue?"

"You said he told you to make a thin biscuit dough, an thar ain't no glue in that," retorted Holy, but further argument was avoided as Mrs. Burns began issuing business-like orders.

By the time the sun was setting the papered room was pronounced a thorough success, and Mrs. Burns made her way to the stables followed by four cowboys whose hair and clothes spattered with dry paste, testified to an honest day's labour.

Mrs. Burns surveyed them as she picked up the reins, ready to start home, while Limber mounted Peanut to accompany her. It was eight miles to Eureka Springs.

"I've heard of lost prospectors eating their boots," she said, "but if you boys ate your clothes, you would need anti-fat. Tell the Boss I will be over soon to call on the bride. Adios!" and with a flourish of the whip she drove away, followed by the gratitude of the paste-daubed, tired group.

It required numerous trips to the kitchen for buckets of hot water before the boys removed the greater part of the concoction that clung tenaciously to faces, hands and hair; then began a more vigorous attack on their boots and clothes.

"It's durned lucky that Bronc disremembered about the glue," congratulated Roarer. "We'd a never got that off."

Bronco slumped into a rickety chair, tipping it against the wall to ease its weakest leg, "It takes a woman to round up a stampede like our'n and get the bunch headed right when it gets to millin'. I'm derned glad the Boss is married, for this outfit needs female purtection."

"I never worked so hard in my life," sighed Holy, flopping on his bunk.

Bronco grinned across the room. "Ain't you forgot the time you wrote a letter to Bill Johnson's sister? You sure worked that time-Set around the bunkhouse till daylight tearin' up paper."

"Well, she asked all of us to write her," snapped Holy, "but none of you fellers had the nerve to do it, and when you bet I couldn't, I called your bluff and won out, didn't I?"

"You sure did," agreed the others, recalling the historic missive which had been read aloud and duly admired before it was mailed.

as I hav northin mutch to do I wil rite you a few lines we are al wel hear but my
pony has a soar back and we hope you are the same


as i have northin mutch to say i wil now clos
yours truly
Holy.

None of the Diamond H knew that Holy's letter, neatly framed, hung in Miss Johnson's
room at a fashionable girls' school, where it was the centre of attraction; and a valued souvenir
of her summer visit to her brother's ranch, which included the episode of a dance at Willcox.
    The silence of the prairie brooded over the Diamond H ranch. Inside the bunkhouse four
cowpunchers slept serenely unconscious of the odour of freshly baking bread that drifted from
the ranch kitchen.

# Chapter Thirteen

Jamie was tucked comfortably between his sister and the big, new brother, and as they drove swiftly along the smooth prairie road behind the high-headed trotters, the boy forgot his shyness in constant wonder.

"This is a prairie-dog town," explained Traynor to the child, but Nell was equally interested. "Those holes are where they live, and when a rain is coming they all get busy heaping up the earth to prevent water going down into their homes and drowning them out. They are good weather prophets."

"Oh, look! It's sitting up!" cried the child in delight, pointing at a tiny brown-furred animal squatted on its hind legs and barking shrilly.

"Watch him when we get nearer," suggested Traynor. "See, they are stationed at regular intervals, just like soldiers. They are the sentinels who warn the others of approaching enemies." The prairie-dog nearest the carriage, gave a final bark of defiance, wiggled its short tail and dodged into the hole. The next nearest dog then took up the warning bark.

"What bright little things they are!" Nell smiled at the yapping little animal that shouted pigmy challenge twenty feet distant.

"If they had long tails," Jamie hastened to say, "they'd be like the squirrels we used to feed in the Park."

"We'll get Limber to trap one for you," promised Traynor. "You won't have to keep it in a cage after it knows you, for it will dig a hole close to the house and never leave."

Jamie's shining eyes met Nell's and he gave an ecstatic sigh as he settled against her shoulder. But in an instant he was alert, watching a cotton-tail rabbit dash across the road. It halted by a mesquite bush.

"Maybe I can catch it." Traynor handed the reins to his wife and stepped cautiously until he reached down and picked the cowering creature by its ears. Jamie uttered a cry of delight as his hands closed gently over the rabbit.

"Once in a while you can do that," commented the man as he took the reins again. "The Apaches often catch them that way, but I'd hate to have my dinner depend on the success of getting a rabbit by this method."

The child was holding the quivering captive against his cheek. Its eyes were bright with terror, and when Jamie looked up at Traynor, his eyes held something of the same bright, frightened appeal. "Won't you please let it go home now? I'm afraid it will be lonesome tonight, like I used to be when Nell was away working all day in New York."

Traynor lifted the tiny prisoner and let it slip to the ground. They laughed together as it scurried and leaped across the prairie until it was lost to sight.

"He knew the right way home," said Jamie, clapping his hands, "and it has gone to tell its little boys and girls about the giants that caught it and how it got away. They will be awful glad to see him come home, won't they?" Nell nodded, and the boy went on, "Sometimes I used to think maybe a giant would catch Nell so she couldn't come home to me when it got dark, and it made my throat hurt. But you always did come," he finished with a smile at his sister, who thus learned for the first time of his childish fear.

Her arm went about him suddenly and she held him close as she answered, "And the giants didn't catch me, you see. Instead, you and I ran away to a wonderful, new country, where the Prince came and found us, and now he is taking us home to live with him."

"And we won't have to go back again, ever, will we Nell?" he asked in sudden anxiety.

"No, dear," she answered. "It's going to be just like the story books. Don't you remember? 'And they all lived happily for ever afterward!'"

The child leaned back with a contented sigh, and his closed eyes did not see the look that passed between Nell and Traynor. The horses had slowed down to a walk and Traynor's right hand held the reins loosely, but his left hand closed over the girl's ungloved one with its new golden band on the slender finger. He smiled at her, and then her eyes filled with quick tears, as he leaned over to kiss her tenderly.

"Tears, Nell?"

"Tears of happiness," she answered tremulously. "The tears that come when one's heart is too happy for laughter."

Nell had a distinct recollection of her first view of the ranch when she had seen it from the stage coach, but the thought now that this was her home and Allan's lent a different interest to the little village of cream-coloured buildings with red roofs, surrounded by cottonwood and willow trees. Here and there poked windmills that supplied the troughs and ponds with water. That other ride had been filled with anxious uncertainty as to what lay before her, but now, the whole world was a wonderful dream of happiness and love. This was her home.

The carriage entered the big driveway into the main stable, where the men and Fong were waiting to meet them. A pack of greyhounds lying on the floor, leaped and began to yelp in excitement. From the box-stalls sleek heads of handsome horses peered curiously, then they whinnied a welcome home to the team that pawed the floor impatiently.

Nell scarcely had time to note it all when Doctor Powell came from the court-yard of the house and helped her from the carriage.

"I got back yesterday," he said, after they had all exchanged words of welcome. His eyes rested on Jamie, "Well, I believe Arizona is fattening you up already," he exclaimed, taking the child's hand in his own. "You and I must be chums, Jamie, for we're both tenderfeet, and have lots to learn. Limber picked out a fine little pony for you to ride, and I found a saddle in Tucson that is just your size. We'll both learn to be cowboys, now. Won't that be fine?"

The child's smile told that Powell had won a loyal follower. The doctor's love for children was a magnet that drew them to him at once. Now he looked down at the child, measuring the battle to be fought, and knew the victory would not be easily won, for the child's vitality had been deeply sapped.

Nell paused in the court-yard. It was eighty feet square, with deep porches on all four sides. Triangular flowerbeds were in each corner, and over a pergola climbing roses in full bloom mingled with honeysuckle and flowering syringa, which recklessly distilled their combined fragrance. Even the windmill in the centre of the court was completely hidden by vines.

She followed her husband into the low-ceilinged living room, and with a little smile she dropped into the same big chair that had held her in sleep when the cowboys discovered her that unforgettable day.

"Come see this view," called Allan, and she went to the long French window and stood beside him. "Those mountains are the most wonderful sermons in the world," he said. "It took me a long time to understand them. Limber helped me. When I was discouraged, he did not say anything, but just saddled his little pinto pony, Peanut, and my own horse, Chinati, and we rode silently for hours through long, dim trails, until I found courage and peace. Then we came home again. You and I will ride those trails together dear. They have known my dark hours, and now I want them to share our happiness."

He turned, and with his arm about her waist, led her to a door that connected the living-room with an adjoining one.

"I told the boys to slick up this room for you, and you can select your furniture from the catalogue. That is how we shop when we live on a ranch, you know."

As he threw open the door, the pink roses and red Navajo rugs shrieked discordant welcome, and Traynor started in surprise.

"Well!" he exclaimed. "I told them to whitewash it! This certainly is a transformation. I wonder how on earth they managed it? If you don't care for the paper, Nell, it can be changed. It's a trifle gaudy, I must confess."

"It's the sweetest room I ever had!" she answered warmly. "I just love every one of those awful pink roses, and I'm going out now to tell the men how I love it!"

She darted from the room and found the men in the main stable. They looked at her with evident embarrassment, but she held out her hand, smiling as she cried impulsively, "I want to shake hands with each one of you, and thank you for taking such trouble to make my room so pretty! It is the nicest room I have ever had in my whole life!"

They took her hand awkwardly in turn, then each waited for one of the others to answer. Silence gripped them.

Holy finally made a heroic effort and distinguished himself by exploding, "Oh, Hell! That warn't northin'! 'Tweren't no trouble whatsomever!"

Unable to control the corners of her mouth, Nell retreated to the house, where she sank on a couch and shook with laughter as she related to Allan the result of her appreciation.

As soon as her skirt had vanished through the court-yard the men turned wrathfully on Holy.

"Say, Holy," Bronco said fiercely, "what the devil do you suppose she will think of this outfit with you cussin' at her that way?"

Holy looked abashed and scratched his head, "Damned if I know how I come to say it! But, if one of you fellers had of said somethin' I wouldn't got no chanct to cuss. You all jest made me do it!" He stalked away in offended dignity, while the other men looked after him.

"Well, what d'ye think of that?" Bronco demanded of Limber and Roarer, who only shook their heads. Holy's logic was too much for them to pass upon.

The day's surprises did not end with the elaborate dinner upon which Fong had lavished his best efforts. In the evening, as Nell, Jamie, Traynor and Powell sat in the living-room, Fong entered bearing what appeared to be a Chinese pagoda of delicate carved ivory.

Beaming, he deposited it upon the center-table, and as they drew near, they saw it was a cake with white icing that loomed almost two feet high. It was a lace-work Eiffel tower from which swung fairy-like bridges to the outer base, and this foundation was a mass of intricate designs in pure white icing. Along the edge of the cake, in rose pink letters, was written "Mary Crixmas," for Fong's previous attempts in such lines had been confined to Christmas festivals, and the spelling of the words had slipped from his memory through long disuse.

The Chinaman presented a sharp knife to Neil, as he said, "Your clake. You cuttee him."

"It's a shame to cut it," she protested, as she took the knife. Then she turned to her husband, "I want the men to see it first, and we'll give them each a piece of it, Allan, if you don't mind."

He hurried out of the room to marshal the boys before him. The cake was duly admired and Fong's pride satiated. Then the knife did its deadly work, and the fairy bridges toppled, bit by bit, until the whole outfit had received a generous portion of Fong's masterpiece.

"Hold on," said Traynor. "Fong, you get some glasses, and bring one for yourself, too."

While Fong obeyed the order, Traynor disappeared to return with several bottles of champagne, which he opened.

Thus they drank to the health and happiness of the Boss of the Diamond H and his bride, and in those glasses was pledged an unspoken devotion that would count no sacrifice too great to make for the Boss and the little lady.

It was long past midnight before the men settled in their bunks and the light was turned out. For quite a while nothing disturbed the silence, then Roarer's voice pierced the darkness shrilly, "Say, where did Fong get the flour to make that cake? We all seen them burros eatin' the flour sack, didn't we? An' that's all the flour thar was on the ranch?"

"Shet up!" responded Holy fiercely. "I don't know whar he got it an' what's more I don't care. It was damned good cake, anyhow!"

# Part Two

# Chapter Fourteen

The life of the ranch was like a series of fairy tales to Nell and Jamie in these first days of their homecoming to the Diamond H. Not the least wonderful and delightful of their new experiences were the riding lessons. A couple of gentle, easy-gaited ponies were saddled for the boy and his sister, and accompanied by Traynor and Doctor Powell they rode to the various outlying ranches that formed a part of the immense Diamond H range. Often Limber rode with them. Always the riders were preceded by the pack of greyhounds that darted yelping after jackrabbits or an occasional coyote.

Doctor Powell had been waiting the outcome of King's will, which had been written out by hand with no witnesses. As there were no heirs, and Allan Traynor, the executor, had been appointed in the will without bonds, he was given full power to sell the property in conformance with the terms of the will. This stipulated positively that the property was only to be sold to a physician who would establish a sanitarium upon the place without undue delay; and the Probate Court ordered that these terms be carried out.

Until after the will was made public, only Traynor and a few Land Office people were aware that King had patented the land. Glendon expressed his disappointment vehemently. There were many who wished to bid for the Springs, but Powell was the only eligible purchaser, and was ready with the cash. After complying with all legal formalities, he was given immediate possession of the Hot Springs ranch.

All proceeds of the sale, according to the will, were to be turned over to the executor until such time as the sanitarium was completed, when this entire fund was to be applied to the maintenance of the place. Thus, Doctor King, unable to live and see the realization of his dream, was assisting in carrying out his plans. It was a partnership between the dead and living owners of the Hot Springs, which Powell felt a sacred obligation. He wished heartily that the old doctor could have lived so they might have worked together; but, he resolved that so far as he was able the undertaking should embody the ideals which the dead doctor had not lived to see fulfilled.

Limber was commissioned to find a man to occupy the ranch house at the Springs until the doctor's plans were completed. The search resulted in the hiring of a Mexican dwarf, whose own name, long forgotten, found a substitute in "Chappo," or "Little Chap." When living near any settlement he was unable to resist his fondness for stimulants, yet he was honest and faithful to the core, as Limber knew. The plan of sending him to the place would be an advantage to him as well as to Powell.

The doctor spent much of his time at the Diamond H, while awaiting replies to his communications with various architects and managers of sanitaria, in Europe as well as America.

Entering the dining-room for breakfast one morning, Nell, with cheeks flushing and eyes sparkling, and every movement radiating happiness, glanced out the window across the wide valley toward Fort Grant.

"Isn't this a wonderful place!" she exclaimed turning from the window and dropping into her chair at the table. "It is good just to be alive in this big, free country!"

"I am having two hundred cows branded for you, Nell," spoke Traynor as she handed him his coffee. "It's your pin-money, and Jamie will start his herd with fifty cows. Limber is fixing up a special brand for each of you."

"Allan! You darling!" gasped Nell, then she darted around the table to where her husband sat and dropped a swift kiss on his forehead when he looked up at her with laughing eyes. Fong, who had just entered with a plate of famous pop-overs, grinned sentimentally, and Nell, blushing furiously, resumed her vacated chair.

"I'm beginning to 'act up,' as Bronco calls it. But now I understand why cowpunchers race their ponies and shoot their guns. I'd like to 'whooper up' myself, this morning," she finished with a little laugh.

"Dangerous condition," pronounced the doctor gravely. "I'd prescribe a good, hard ride as the only hope for improvement."

"All right," responded Traynor with twinkling eyes. "Get your togs on, Nell. We'll all go to the big rodeo at Box Springs. You'll get a faint idea of range work, and now that you have your own herd, you should learn how to run it."

"Limber is showing me how to throw a rope," Jamie broke in eagerly, and he scrambled from his chair, clutching his new sombrero that he had deposited on the floor by his chair, the way he noticed the cowboys all did. "Yesterday I mounted my pony all alone. I can saddle him, too-but Limber has to pull the cinches tight." With this final declaration, he hurried through the door, his tiny spurs clicking importantly on the cement walk.

The greyhound pack yelped shrill protests at being left behind when they saw Nell and Jamie were in the party. Then Traynor and Powell mounted their own horses and the four swung along the road in a steady lope toward the Galiuro mountains, west of the ranch.

When they reached Box Springs, Nell's first impression was a dense cloud of dust stirred up by the restless hoofs of thousands of cattle. Then she saw the chuck-wagon, where the camp cook was busy with his pots and pans over a fire of smouldering oak logs. Near the mountains four or five thousand head of bawling cattle, with cowpunchers dashing to and fro among them, gave the appearance of wildest confusion. Yet, to the initiated, the system was perfect. Part of the cattle were bunched and herded by certain men, while others rode through the weaving, tossing mass of horns, deftly picking their way and 'cutting out' some particular animal.

Nell watched it all with frank delight and curiosity, and appealed to her husband from time to time. "What are they doing in that bunch where Limber is riding?"

"'Cutting,'" was the answer. "Watch Limber. See how he picks a cow and follows it up? Peanut is a wonderful 'cutting pony.' He seems to know just what Limber is thinking, and once Peanut points the right cow, he never lets it get away from him till it is out of the bunch and where it belongs. He's the champion cutting pony of Arizona. Limber can use a light cord instead of reins. No one but Limber ever rides Peanut. He turns so quickly he would throw any other man. Watch him, Nell!"

Powell and Nell lost no movement of the pinto pony and its master, now following a big, bald-faced steer. The animal, knowing it was being singled out, twisted and dodged adroitly from side to side. Then, finding its attempts to escape in vain, it made a sudden dash from the herd and tore wildly toward the mountains back of the camp. Peanut, his little pinto body hugging low to the ground, his hoofs tossing clods of dirt, kept close behind the steer. Limber, leaning slightly forward in his saddle held a coiled rope in his hand.

Only a few feet separated them, when the steer's hoof struck a prairie-dog hole, and it went down with a crash. Those who watched gave an involuntary cry. Peanut, too near to stop or turn aside, reached the fallen steer just as it started to rise.

Without a second's hesitation, the gallant little pony leaped over the steer, whirled and raced after it as it scurried in the opposite direction.

A yell of admiration sounded from all the cowboys; they knew how close had been the danger to pony and rider. Nell gasped in terror and amazement.

"That's the finest bit of riding I've ever seen!" Traynor enthused. "Why, no one but Limber and Peanut could have done it! The steer was almost on his forefeet when the pony jumped. If the horse had missed, or waited an instant, it might have meant a broken neck for both man and horse!"

"It was magnificent!" Powell exclaimed in accents of hearty admiration. "But, I suppose Limber counts it all in the day's work and nothing more."

"That's just it," was the answer from the Boss of the Diamond H. "It's a game of chance each day when you ride the open range."

Limber had succeeded in driving the recalcitrant steer into a band of stock herded away from the other cattle.

"Why did he have to put it there?" Nell motioned with her whip.

"That's the 'stray herd,'" Traynor explained. "You see, Arizona being all open range, cattle mix indiscriminately. Twice a year there is a general round-up, or rodeo. Then notice is sent to all ranchers informing them of the itinerary of the work, which extends over certain sections."

They were riding closer to the stray herd as he spoke, and halted the horses a little distance away.

"Each rodeo has its Captain, who is general manager for the territory covered by a number of ranches. All ranches contribute their pro rata of men, horses and chuck, making the work co-operative."

"That's rather fair toward the small cattle owner," Powell interrupted; "but, that is the spirit of the country here. A square deal for all."

Traynor nodded assent. "Frequently cattle are located a hundred miles or more from their 'home range.' We cut these into the stray herd and hold them till the owner drives them back to his place. If he is not represented at the rodeo, he is notified and arranges to get the animals. So, the stray herd is an important item in the round-up work, you see."

They had ridden around the herd until reaching the spot where a fire of glowing coals was tended by a couple of cowpunchers, Traynor said, "This is the branding place. Look at Bronco!"

He pointed the galloping horse that carried Bronco. "You'll see some pretty work now. Bronco won the championship for roping at the last Territorial contest."

"What is it?" demanded Nell. "It's all Greek to me."

"A steer is turned loose on the open, then the cowpuncher takes after it, when it has a certain start. He must rope it, throw it and tie it so it cannot rise. Then he lifts his hands in the air. The time taken from the start of the steer to the second the man raises his hands, is what decides the championship roping."

Leaning forward eagerly Powell and Nell watched Bronco's arm move swiftly. The coiled riata in his hand shot out like an immense, writhing snake. The big loop dropped over the calf, slipped almost imperceptibly, then jerked taut as Bronco's pony squatted down on its haunches and the calf fell with a heavy thud. A quick turn of the wrist, and Bronco had the end of his rope twisted firmly about the high horn of his saddle. Depending on the pony, with its braced feet, and alert eyes, moving backward and holding the rope from slacking, Bronco snatched a red-hot iron from the fire.

A curl of smoke, bellow of pain, two quick slashes of a knife. The calf scrambled up, a freshly burnt brand on its hip, and its bleeding ears, showing the mark of its owner. The animal stood bewildered, snorted, and rushed with a loud bawl to the cow's side. She had been watching anxiously. Now she sniffed at her calf, licked its face in sympathy; then with one accord they scurried away, free to go where they pleased, for they were on their home range and their troubles were over.

"It seems cruel," Nell protested warmly.

"It's the only way to handle range cattle," Traynor replied. "Formerly," he was speaking to the doctor, "the brands were made as large as possible-now we make them as small as legible. Once in a while we still run across an animal with three immense letters-JIM or HUE-across the entire side of the brute. They were two brothers who determined there should be no dispute over their respective ownerships. It ruined the hide and knocked off a good sum on the sale of the animal. Most brands are on the hip or hind quarter. It's an interesting study once you get into it."

"Well, so long as they brand the cattle, why cut the ears, too? Is it necessary?" Nell's sympathy was still with the calf.

"It settles ownership where a brand is indistinct or disputed for any reason? Branding is done when the flies are not troublesome, and calves still follow their mothers. Should a calf escape branding at the proper time, through oversight, it soon becomes large enough to leave its mother, and thus is hard to identify the next rodeo. So, if a cowboy on the range sees a large calf with uncropped ears, he investigates at once."

"Of course," Powell asserted, "I can see the sense of it now that you have explained it."

"Well, even that does not settle a dispute. The long-eared, motherless calves are called mavericks, or in Arizona, where the Mexican language is used, orajanos. The unwritten law of the range gives an unmarked calf to the fellow who catches it, so long as it is not with its mother, you see. Naturally, the man on whose range it is found, is supposed to have a stronger claim. A long-eared calf is a temptation for 'sleepering.'"

"In the name of goodness, Allan," said Nell in despair, "what is 'sleepering'? I just get a glimmer of understanding when something new comes up and I'm floundering worse than ever. I don't see how any one ever learns all those terms."

"Well," laughed Traynor, "now you can understand how hard it was for me, to learn it all. I didn't dare ask questions, you see. Had to pretend I knew it all. On the range, naturally, the ear-mark shows very plainly at a distance, for the animal will face any rider. If a cowpuncher sees the calf, standing by its mother, bears the same ear-mark, he does not inspect to see if it is branded, unless he has cause for suspicion. The rustler knowing this, ear-marks a calf and takes chances on its being discovered the calf has no brand. The ear-mark of calf tallies with that of the mother, you see. When the calf is old enough to be driven away from the mother, the rustler finishes his work by driving it away, then changes the ear-mark and puts on his brand."

"That's what I should class as scientific cattle stealing," Powell decided, and Nell agreed with him, but before they could ask further questions they turned startled faces in the direction of an unclassified noise.

The Boss of the Diamond H laughed, and pointed to the camp cook, who held a dishpan and was banging vigorously on it with a huge iron spoon. Far and near, the cowpunchers lifted their voices in the gleeful shout, "Chuck's ready!"

Part of the outfit remained on guard over the cattle, while the others raced their ponies pell-mell to the wagon near which the noon-day meal was spread.

"I'm hungry," announced Nell, and without further ceremony she led the way on her pony to join the group of men among whom she recognized Limber and Bronco.

## Chapter Fifteen

As Nell approached the chuck-wagon, the eyes of the cowpunchers of the many ranches represented, looked at her with open approval, not unmixed with curiosity, for they all had heard the episode of Walton's green whiskers, and the romantic meeting of the Boss, of the Diamond H and the girl to whom he had been engaged in the East.

Bronco helped her down from her pony, and escorted her to a seat of honour-an empty box that had formerly held canned tomatoes. The men sat tailor-fashion around the canvas that did duty as a table-cloth.

Nell's eyes scanned the table. Granite pans full of boiled potatoes, frijoles-the small red bean grown by Mexicans, which forms the principal article of diet on any Arizona ranch-an enormous dish held a stew made of "jerky," which Nell recognized, for she was becoming initiated into many things that were strange. She had seen Fong pounding strips of sun-dried meat, and watched it transformed to a savory stew, while he explained that the cowboys carried it in their pockets and ate it without cooking.

She sniffed with appreciation the coffee, and accepted the big tin cup with a smile, then added condensed milk from the can Bronco passed to her.

"What lovely biscuit!" she exclaimed, as a white cloth was deposited in front her, and the golden tan biscuit, steaming hot were uncovered. "I don't see how it can be done without a real stove!" The camp cook grinned his approval of a woman of such intelligence.

The clatter of tin plates, iron knives and forks, was broken with laughter or jokes by the punchers at each other's expense. Life during the rodeo was a combined circus and school-day vacation when off duty with the herd. Then, it was grim, hard work. The feeling of restraint at first noticeable when Nell sat on her improvised throne, gradually evaporated as she joined in the laughter. It vanished completely when she slipped from the box to the ground, to be "nearer the biscuit," she laughed as she reached out and appropriated one.

Jamie, seated between Bronco and Limber, was silent but happy, as they acclaimed him "one of the Diamond H outfit," and a "regular puncher, now."

The first relay moved away, some taking their places with the herd to allow the other men their turn at the chuck, but many of them were off duty for a time, and these loafed and talked together, the smoke of their cigarettes forming tiny clouds about their heads. Nell rose and made her way to a fallen log, on which she dropped with a smile at Bronco who had followed her and Jamie from the table.

While she admired Limber, there was a boyish irrepressibility about Bronco that made a little bond between them. He reached into the breast-pocket of his blue flannel shirt and withdrew the hand, partly closed. Jamie looked at it curiously as he saw it was extended to him. Bronco's fingers opened, and Nell and the child stared at a strange thing blinking sleepily.

"What is it?" they asked simultaneously.

"Horn-toad," Bronco replied. "Caught him this mornin' and I was pretty sure you hadn't seen one, so I kept him."

"Won't he bite?" Jamie's tones were doubtful.

"Not on your life," answered the cowboy.

They regarded the little creature as Bronco put it on the ground and dragged a bit of string from his pocket. He tied this about the toad's hind legs close to the body.

"Look at him," was the command, as Bronco slid his finger over the rough, tiny-horned back from tail to head.

With a wild scurry of legs, the toad raced to the end of the string and struggled to escape; but, Bronco's finger touched its head and moved gently toward the jerking tail. The toad's eyes closed, his head drooped toward the ground, the legs and tail became motionless. Jamie gave a little squeal of delight, and cried, "He's gone to sleep!"

"Hang onto the string a minit."

Jamie clutched it, while Bronco held a consultation with the cook at the tail-board of the chuck-wagon. Soon he returned with a small, empty match-box.

"This'll make a fine wagon," he announced, tying the match-box to the end of the string. "Now, thar we are! All you gotter do to make him move lively is run your finger 'long his back like I done, and contrarywise, from his head to his tail, if you want him to stop. When I was a kid in Texas, me an' my little brother uster catch 'em and have races this way."

A grin spread over his face and he looked up at Nell, "Say, Mrs. Traynor, Maw hated horn-toads. Bill an' me rounded-up twenty of 'em once, and hid 'em in a closet in a box. The box got upsot someways in the night, and when Maw got up to start breakfast you never heerd such a whoop! She put her foot on one of 'em. It didn't hurt the toad for she took her foot off too quick, but Bill an me never brung any more into the house after that mornin'. You see, when she put down her other foot, she hit another toad, an' that room was jest naturally alive with 'em. We rounded-up the whole herd, twenty of 'em, but Maw said she knewed thar was a thousand and the rest of 'em got away."

"I'm rather inclined to sympathize with your mother, Bronco," was Nell's laughing comment. She shuddered, "Those little sharp horns are bad enough to step on with a bare foot, but to feel the horns moving would be rather upsetting, I should think."

"It was," Bronco rejoined soberly. "But Maw wasn't so upsot as we kids was-afterwards."

Jamie devoted himself to his new pet, and Nell's eyes wandered to her husband and Doctor Powell who were talking with another man, not far away. She saw this man had a grizzly beard that seemed never to have been cropped or shaven. The dry skin of neck and throat was wrinkled and the texture and colour of a piece of Arizona jerky from long exposure to the sun and wind. On his head, an old straw hat was guiltless of a crown, but flaunted two dilapidated turkey quills. Tufts of unkempt hair peered inquisitively over the broken edges above the ragged brim. A grim mouth made a repository for a corn-cob pipe, and suspicious grey eyes squinted from Powell's face to that of the Boss of the Diamond H.

Bronco saw her interest, and explained, "That's Paddy Lafferty, owns the PL ranch and herd, that the doctor figgers on buyin'," then Nell recalled the many stories she had already heard of this eccentric character. Paddy's eyes caught hers, and she flushed guiltily as she glanced away quickly.

"It's a dandy rodeo," she heard Bronco's voice beside her, as he sat on the ground, knees drawn up, his muscular hands busy rolling a cigarette.

"I suppose I'll get used to wild cattle after a while," Nell hazarded, "but, honestly, Bronco, I'm afraid of them. Their horns are so big and sharp."

"Why!" the cowpuncher's amazement was undisguised. "These is short-horns! We ain't got no long-horns on the range. You'd oughter seen some of the ol' Texas long-horns we uster have. Lots of times the horns was so wide we couldn't get a steer loaded into a box-car till we'd sawed off the horns. And wild —" he paused for adequate words before he finished, "Say, they was a cross between a deer an' a mountain-lion, so fur as disposition counts!"

"Well, I never feel safe except on my pony."

"Say, Mrs. Traynor, you're dead safe anywheres in Arizona," the cowboy assured her earnestly. "Why, if you was to walk over to that air herd, you'd stampede it quick as a wink!"

Nell turned on him with dancing eyes, "For gracious' sakes, Bronco! Am I such a scarecrow as all that?"

Bronco's face and ears grew red. "Oh, shucks! I didn't mean to say it that way. But-you see-range stock is uster seein' men, foot or horseback —a woman in petticoats is a new critter to 'em and plumb paralyzes a herd. Thar was one time, though," he continued mournfully, "I wisht so hard I was a woman that I derned nigh prayed for petticoats."

He was immersed in deep thought for a few seconds, and then he demanded suddenly, "Did the Boss ever tell you about the time I fooled myself into thinkin' I was a bull-fighter?"

"No," was the reply, "but please tell me, won't you?"

"I don't mind it so much, now," Bronco grinned, "but thar was a time when it sure made me sore to talk about it. You see, I been to Mexico and seed a Mex bull-fighter. The feller what fit the bull belt a red handkerchee out in front of him, and when the bull lit out for him, he jest stepped one side and the bull went runnin' past with the handkerchee hangin' over his eyes, like a widder's veil. Then the feller stuck a bunch of ribbons on the bull and made it madder'n a hornet, an' you can't blame a bull for gettin' mad at being laughed at that way. It looked so easy that I thought it wasn't no trick noways-and I made up my mind I'd do it myself, sometime." Nell faced him expectantly.

"Well, one day I was ridin' over from Hot Springs by the Mud Springs trail, and it was near supper time, when the sun went down. I had twelve miles to ride and we had a cranky cook at the ranch, an' I hadn't et anythin' since five o'clock, sun-up. So, when I seen smoke comin' from the camphouse at Mud Springs, you kin bet I humped along pretty lively.

"A feller from the east was stayin' thar fer his health. He was all alone, an' glad to have some one call on him fer a change. I made myself as entertainin' as I knowed how, hopin' fer an invite to chuck. He cooked over a campfire, and said he wanted to get as near to Nature as he could; but I couldn't see any sense in what he said. Whilst he kept on cookin' supper an' not sayin' anythin' about expectin' me to stay, I kept playin' fer time.

"Thar was an ol' buckskin cow standin' near in the brush, and I tol' him about the bull-fight. He got interested, and I begin to see some chance of chawin' that grub before long. Then I got smart and offered to show him how they done it. He said I'd better not try it. Of course, I was only bluffin' at first, but when he said that, it called my bluff. I ambled over to thet ol' buckskin bag o' bones and guv her a crack over the ridge-pole with my riata, but she never even looked at me. She was thet ol' thet she must of been one of the great-grandmothers' of the herd, and when I seen that I got brash." Bronco stared across space, his hands dropping limp between his knees.

"I caught holt of her tail and twisted it, then I slapped her jaw. She woke up some, an' I danced in front of her like a locoed ijit, wavin' my red handkerchee an' yellin' like an Apache on the war-path. She guv one beller, put her nose to the ground and come at me in dead earnest to make me understand that a lady cow her age can't be trifled with.

"The tenderfoot yelled, 'Look out!' and made for a walnut tree and shinnied up it, and thar he set peepin' out like a skeered chipmunk. I wisht I was up thar longside of him, but had to get busy doin' what the bull-fighter done. So, I stood thar and helt that durned handkerchee out in front of me, jest like I seed him do, but, honest Injun! I'd ruther hed a solid adobe wall in front of me just then. Well, that doggone animile got five feet away, and then I seen that she had both eyes wide open, instead of shettin' her eyes like a bull does when he charges.

"It paralyzed me so I fergot to move thet piece of red calicer and jest stood thar holdin' it in front of me, whilst that damned tenderfoot was whoopin' and screechin' his head off, 'She's a comin'! She's a comin'!' Jest as if I didn't know it a heap sight better'n he did! Thar wasn't any chanct left to run, and that ol' cow sure did come.

"She hit me squar and knocked the wind plum outen me, and I went down an' chawed adobe dirt. She made holes all over my clothes, tromped me from head to foot, rolled me over and over like I was a chunk of biscuit dough, then she guv a snort and went off in the brush." Nell's eyes were dancing and she leaned forward eagerly.

"I picked myself up," his voice was mournful, "just as the tenderfoot clumb down from his perch. Neither one of us said a word. He was too scairt to talk and I was too mad. The coffee pot was upset, the dinner burnt to a cinder. I got on my horse and hit the trail for home. I tol' the boys that my pony slid down the side of a cañon with me, and they'd never knowed the difference if that damned tenderfoot hadn't come a humpin' down the next day to see if I was hurt very bad." He heaved a sigh, and kicked at a stone beside his foot.

"I got even with thet ol' cow, though. She was in the last bunch we shipped for Kansas City, and I seen to it that she didn't get cut outen the herd. But, I'll never forget her so long as thar is a buckskin cow in Arizona Territory. The boys won't give me a chanct;" he paused, gazed reflectively across the Valley, then added dolefully, "I'll never be happy until I see some bigger fool than myself, buyin' all the ol' buckskin cows in Arizona to ship 'em down to Mexico for bull fights."

Nell's laughter reached Powell, Traynor and Paddy as they approached where she sat.

"This is Paddy Lafferty, Nell," said Traynor. "He has given an option on his ranch and cattle to Doctor Powell."

She looked up at a tall, gaunt old man with stooping shoulders and joints that seemed to be held together by loose wires, like a jointed doll subjected to much handling.

Paddy regarded Nell sharply from under his ragged eyebrows, but as she rose and held out her hand, smiling into his face, she unconsciously won a loyal friend.

He squatted down on the ground beside her and listened to her merry comments on the cattle business. Limber and Bronco, a short distance away on their ponies, noted the episode.

"She's sure a thoroughbred prize-winner! Ain't she, Limber?" observed Bronco admiringly.

"You bet! She gets her brand on every cowpuncher that comes on her range, and the Kid is jest the same."

"Oh, say! Loco's here. Lookin' for a job. Green Whiskers sol' out last week. Went back to Utah, Loco says. He's sure aching to get married," grinned Bronco. "It's kept him busy shavin' and cuttin' his hair, lately."

"Loco's a good roper. Of course, he gets them crazy fits, but he's never harmed any one round here. We'll need some extra hands, now, with Doctor Powell buyin' Paddy's herd. We'll have to tail 'em in, so I'll see the Boss about hirin' Loco whilst we got a chanct to get him."

Bronco nodded, for tailing a herd meant extra work, as each animal had to be caught, the long hair on its tail cut off, and thus a tally of numbers was made without rebranding. It was only done when an entire herd was sold and the brand included in the sale.

"Tell him about that mix-up in the strays," called Bronco after Limber, as the foreman rode toward Traynor.

While Limber's pony rubbed noses with Traynor's horse, Limber suggested employing Loco. Traynor assented readily. Then Limber continued, "I don't know just how to figger it out, but some one's tryin' to make trouble for the Diamond H."

"How's that?" demanded Traynor, quickly.

"Well, two weeks ago Bronco seen a Diamond H calf, new-branded, following a Bar 77 cow. He thought it was just a mistake, so vented it. Then a few days later me and Holy run into two calves with the Diamond H and one was followin' a Flyin' V cow, and the other was suckin' a Three Moon. We straightened that out, and since then we've come across six calves marked with the Diamond H and every durned one of 'em is suckin' a cow with a different brand. We got to stop it quick."

Traynor's eyebrows knit angrily, "Any of them here?"

"Four in the stray herd," Limber replied, and without further conversation they rode to the strays, where several neighbouring ranchers and a few cowpunchers sat on their ponies. They looked curiously at Traynor and his men, who met the looks steadily.

"Limber has just reported to me about these calves with the Diamond H brand," he scanned each face for sign of disbelief. "I don't think it is necessary for me to say that not one of the men belonging to the Diamond H ranch branded those calves. A single instance might occur to any one, as you all know, but this is being done systematically, and evidently with the intention of causing hard feelings. If any of you hear or see any more of this work, let me know at once, and help me find out who is at the bottom of it. I'll pay five hundred dollars for proof against the man who is putting my brand on these calves. I will report this to the Live Stock Sanitary Board at once, and advertise my offer of reward."

He turned to Limber and Bronco, saying, "Cut out those calves and vent them at once, boys," and they hastened to obey.

"None of us laid the blame on the Diamond H," said Jones, who owned the Flying V Bar. "None of us knew about this work until Limber told us and pointed out the calves in the stray herd. The fellow who is doing this would treat any of us the same way, and it's things like this that start real trouble. We've got to work together to catch him. When we do, we'll run him out of the country."

"Better keep him in the country, under six feet of earth," growled Holy with a few complimentary remarks, then he glanced around quickly to see whether Nell were within earshot.

And as a result of this episode, a week later Traynor advertised offering five hundred dollars reward for detection of the trouble-maker, while an additional five hundred dollars was offered by the combined other cattlemen whose calves had been misbranded; but from that time on there was no cause for further complaint. The matter remained a mystery.

# Chapter Sixteen

"I think I will go over to the Springs in the morning," said Powell to Traynor a week after the rodeo, as they sat in the court enjoying after-dinner cigars.

"Oh, by the way," Traynor interjected, "I had a talk with Paddy yesterday. He wants the privilege of staying at the PL ranch house for a month after the cattle are tallied in. I rather believe the old fellow hates to leave the place."

"How about arranging to have him stay permanently?" suggested Powell. "Limber says some one would have to be there to look after the windmill and water."

"I think Paddy would be glad to do it. He hates mountain work, but he's good anywhere on the flats, and he's as honest as the sun. With Limber at the Springs working across the backbone of the Galiuros, we would consolidate the work of both ranges, and our relative expenses could be adjusted without difficulty. I believe Paddy would be glad to take a small sum monthly, and have his grub provided, and feed for that scarecrow of a horse that he thinks so much of."

"Won't you need Limber here?" protested Powell.

"I can arrange the work with him so that he can stay part of each week at the Springs. So you need not hesitate on that account. We have to ride in the Hot Springs section every few weeks. Many of our cattle drift over there. It's a wild range, and unless the men ride among the stock at frequent intervals, the cattle become too wild to be handled to an advantage. There are five and six year old steers back in the mountains there, that will never be caught except with a bullet-and even then you would have to have the wind in your favour to get in range. They are worse than deer."

"Suppose I talk to Limber? I don't want him to go unless he wishes it."

"He's taken a liking to you," was Traynor's reply, "and I'm sure the plan will suit him. But, decide that for yourselves. If he doesn't want to go, Bronco or Holy would do, but Limber would be more congenial, I thought."

"Limber is one of the finest characters I have ever met," was Powell's remark as he rose and moved toward the entrance of the court leading to the bunk-house. "I'll have a talk with him, now."

A light streamed from the open door of the bunk-house where the cowpunchers sat smoking and talking. Bronco, at a small table, was immersed in the pages of a gigantic mail order catalogue. A sheet of paper and bottle of ink portended a purchase. Powell sauntered in, found a seat on an iron cot, lit a cigarette and glanced around at them all. It was a delicate compliment that no one greeted his entrance formally. It proved that he was "one of the bunch."

Bronco's face was contorted as he began writing on the printed order sheet of the merchant enterprising enough to send out catalogues broadcast. It was good business strategy, for when the long winter evenings held forth, the big catalogue was the center of attraction on many ranches, and thus articles were ordered with sublime disregard as to utility or cost.

"What you sendin' fer this time, Bronc?" questioned Holy, curiously.

"Accorjon," the reply was punctuated with scratching pen that spluttered ink over the order list. "Thar's a book goes with it, tellin' you how to play in two hours."

"Say," Roarer leaned forward with interest, "why don't you get a talkin' machine like the feller that spit his teeth out. Look 'em up. We could chip in and get one, maybe. It'd be easier on you-an' us, too."

With Powell's aid a small talking-machine was decided upon, and Bronco conscientiously inked out the previous order and substituted the latest one. Then each man insisted that the record of his favourite "tune" be included-Golindrina, Over the Waves, Where is my Wandering Boy Tonight, Home, sweet Home, and My Bonnie lies over the Ocean-exhausted their repertoire.

"Six," announced Bronco, "say that ain't enough. Why, we kin sing all them without any talkin-machine. We want somethin' we don't sing ourselves when we're punchin' cows."

Powell came to the rescue, and with his aid a list was completed, including some really good music. He vetoed the command to pick out "about twenty-five or thirty dollars' worth."

"That's a heap sight more sensible than gettin' a cobbler's outfit, like we done the other time," Limber commented with a smile.

In answer to Powell's evident desire, he continued, "Bronc and Holy seen it in the catalogue, an' it told how much money you could save by mendin' your own shoes. It was unhandy havin' to pack our boots to Willcox all the time. Mostly we'd forgot to take 'em, or else forgot to bring 'em home. We all rounded up our boots and Bronco figgered that by mendin' 'em, we'd save pretty near two weeks pay each."

"Well, it would of," defended Bronco, "But you fellers wouldn't wear 'em after I fixed 'em all up, and blacked 'em too."

"We'd a wore 'em," retorted Roarer indignantly, "if we could of got into 'em, but you'd made 'em all so tight that no one could get a foot into them shoes. The wust of it was that you went an' put extra soles on our good shoes and spiled 'em along with the rest."

"Well, you seen me throw mine out the same time you fellers chucked yours into the dump heap, didn't you?"

Limber's mouth twitched and his eyes twinkled as he turned to Powell, adding the climax, "Say Doc, thar wasn't a pair of boots or shoes that one of us could get into, and the day after Bronc finished up his work, we all got in the spring wagon and druv to Willcox in our socks an' bought shoes for the outfit before we could get to work."

"If you'd a guv me another chanct," protested Bronco, "I'd knowed better what to do, but anyway, it was a dandy cobbler's outfit, and wuth the money we guv for it."

"What became of it?" demanded Powell when his laughter subsided.

"Thar was a Missionary come past here, gettin' money for the heathens in Africa, and we donated the outfit to him. He shore seemed pleased with it, but we always had a sneakin' notion the heathens wasn't the ones that used it. That Missionary was like a billy-goat, ready to take anything you guv him, from a gold-mine to a empty tin tomato can. Last we seen of him he was prospectin' for Hasayampa Bill's lost mine, but nobody ain't heerd of his findin' it, so fur."

"How did Hasayampa lose the mine?" Powell interrupted. "Or did he really ever own one?"

"We seen the beginning of it," Limber began, and Powell scenting a story, settled with delighted anticipation.

"It started this way. We was workin' the rodeo back of Dos Cabezas when we come across a seven-year ol' black horse that was an outlaw. He belonged to the Bar X Bar outfit, but they'd guv up tryin' to break him. For three years the Boss of the Bar X Bar hed offered each Fourth of July to give the horse to any man what'd ride him to a finish. Thar was lots that tried it. He was a good horse and worth considerable if he was busted.

"Hasayampa was workin' with us. He'd been havin' a streak of hard luck. His only pony was lame and he couldn't raise cash to buy another. You see, Hasayampa had tried to teach a tenderfoot how to play Stud poker, and that's about the poorest way I know to invest your money, especially when the tenderfoot is dressed like a minister-Hasayampa oughter knowed better.

"Howsomever, Hasayampa bet his lame pony that he could ride that black horse, and of course, everybody took him up.

"He roped and throwed it without any trouble, and got the saddle on its back; then he jumped inter the saddle. Up to then it was easy work, but afterwards-Say, Doc, every one knows that a horse has only got four feet, but thar wasn't a man watchin' that wasn't ready to bet it was a centipede Hasayampa was tryin' to gentle. The horse was called Black Devil, for thar wasn't a white hair on him, and he sure deserved the rest of the name.

"Hasayampa stayed with him, all right, and what's more we all seen him do it, an' I tell you we whooped like Injuns! The next day Hasayampa quit work and left camp, riding his new horse and leadin' the lame pony, and that was the last we seen of him for over six months.

"Then he blew in at the Diamond H, riding his old bay pony, but he hadn't mutch to say-Seemed sorter down-hearted like.

"Then some one ast him what he done with Black Devil and this is what he tol' us.

"When Hasayampa was ridin' Black Devil that day he busted him, the horse seemed to favour one hind foot-acted like he'd sprained it. When Hasayampa started doctorin' it, he pretty near died with suprise, for thar was a nice little nugget of gold smashed on the bottom of Devil's foot, just like a corn. Well Hasayampa didn't lose no time humpin' up to the placed he'd noticed Devil limpin', and he posted his location notice on the Buckin' Bronco Mine. The lead was thar just in plain sight, he said. We all had been campin' on a regular mint of gold an' never knowed it. Leastways, that is what Hasayampa told us.

"Well, he took Black Devil down to the blacksmith at Dos Cabezas and hed some shoes made for him. He had quite an argument with the blacksmith to get him to make the shoes the way Hasayampa wanted 'em. He said that after they got through, the blacksmith did what Hasayampa told him."

Limber paused to light his cigarette, and philosophize, "It don't pay to argue, if you kin help it. Hurts the other party's feelin's when you get the best of him, an', Hasayampa had fists on him like cannon balls when he warmed up in a argument. All the same, you can't blame the blacksmith for callin' Hasayampa a 'locoed ijit' when you knowed the sort of hoss-shoes he ordered made."

"They was half-hollow, as if you dug a slot in 'em with a jack-knife. After Devil was shod, Hasayampa got some chamois skin, quick-silver and a small retort and went back to his claim.

"Now, here's what Hasayampa tol' us all for gospel truth, Doc. He put the quick-silver in the slots of them hoss-shoes, then jumped on Black Devil and let him buck up an' down that air claim. Hasayampa said it beat any four-stamp mill he ever seed. Then he got down and scraped the silver outen the hoofs, squoze it in the chamois bag and fired it in his retort to separate the gold. Hasayampa cleaned up a hundred dollars' wuth the fust day.

"It didn't take Black Devil long to understand his job o.k. That hoss would just wait for his shoes to be silvered, then go hisself and buck around, only stoppin' to come and git his shoes scraped and re-filled. Meanwhile Hasayampa, seem' Black Devil was handlin' his end of the partnership, put in all his own time runnin' the other end of the business, squozin' the quick-silver, firin' the gold and mouldin' it inter bricks.

"Hasayampa figured out jest how long it would take to make him a billionaire, and he'd a done it if it hadn't been for the earthquake in May '91. It did everlastingly shake up the country around here, and lots of permanent springs went plumb dry and never run again.

"Hasayampa had gone to Willcox to ship some bricks to the 'Frisco Mint, when he felt that earthquake, and he begun to worry about Devil, for he had turned him loose for a vacation. He humped back to the claim, and when he got thar he said he seen a white horse standin' with his head hangin' down like he was asleep; but never a sign of Black Devil nowhar.

"Whilst he was puzzling over what had became of Black Devil, he swars he seen that air white hoss raise his head, lift his hind foot, then begin buckin' in a dazed sorter way. It was Black Devil, and the shock hed turned his hair snow white.

"Hasayampa said the Buckin' Bronco Mine hed disappeared off'n the face of the yearth. He tried to make Black Devil understand that he warn't to blame for losin' the mine, but the hoss wouldn't eat nothin'. He'd just buck around, feeble-like, lift his leg and look at it, and then he laid down an' died."

Powell's laughter rang through the room. "What a pity such a genius as Hasayampa had to die," he finally gasped.

"Say, Doc," Limber spoke, "Hasayampa onct said that a man back east was willin' to pay for his yarns if he'd take time to write 'em down. He ast us what we thought about it, and we all tol' him that if any feller did say that, he was a bigger liar than Hasayampa and could write stories himself, an' Hasayampa said he guessed that was true. Do you, honestly, believe anyone would of paid for 'em?"

"I certainly do," was the positive answer. "Hasayampa deserves a monument to his memory! By the way, I never heard anyone tell how he died, but I'm pretty sure he did it in some original way."

Limber's face grew serious, and a lighted match in his hand flickered out. He watched it thoughtfully.

"Thar is a monument to Hasayampa," he said slowly. "'Tain't very big, nor very grand, and thar ain't many people knows whar it is, but it's a monument, all the same. Hasayampa never tol' this story, but the woman did tell it.

"She was jest a common sorter woman, not young, nor pretty, nor anything like that, an' it was out in the Yuma desert. Hasayampa was prospectin', and he rid along past the place where she was camped with her man. It's funny that a woman thet ain't married to a man will put up with heaps of abuse, but them women that hangs around mining camps seems to think it all goes in the game. So when she done somethin' that riled up the man, he up and busted her over the head with a stick of wood and she went down like she was dead.

"Hasayampa jumped off'n his hoss and lit into the man, and the feller knifed him, then run away, leavin' Hasayampa lyin' thar a dyin'.

"After awhile the woman come back to her senses, and she done all she knowed how; but he was too bad off. The feller that run was wanted for murder up in Montana, the woman said. He had took the two horses they had been ridin' and Hasayampa's pony, too; but what was wuss than everythin' else, he hed carted off all the water thar was in their canteens and left them without a drop.

"She said when she told Hasayampa that she wasn't a respectable woman-jest a camp-follower, an' no decent man had any call to fight for her, he jest looked at her an' smiled an' said, 'You're a woman. He hadn't no right to hit you.'

"He died that night in the dark, and she sat and helt his hand till sun-up, then she scraped a shallow grave with her bare hands and put him in an' covered him over the best she could. After that she started to hunt the trail. She walked around all day and was beginning to get desert-crazy when some men found her. It was too late. She died in a couple of hours, but she tol' about Hasayampa and ast if they'd bury her alongside of him, because it wouldn't seem so lonesome. An' they done it. So thar's a big cross over them both, with their names on it. Of course, we all knowed Hasayampa couldn't tell the truth if he tried, Doc, but when folks heerd about the way he died, everyone took off his hat to Hasayampa, you bet, for Hasayampa never done dirt to nobody."

"Did they catch the man?"

"Not that any one knowed of. That's one of the things that puzzles me. Why people what plays a square game is sometimes so out of luck. Seems as if they must of been put down with the grain of the table runnin' against 'em when they was started at the game, or else the Dealer stacked the cards. But, it 'tain't so mutch to a feller's credit holdin' a Royal Flush as it is to keep on playin' a square game to a finish when he ain't dealt nothin' but deuces and treys."

"You're right, Limber," said Powell, who was learning to find the gold beneath the surface.

He moved to the door, followed by Limber, and for a second they stood looking up into the deep blue of the sky where the countless stars, like clear-cut diamonds, trembled and blinked as though held on threads of silver by the mighty hand of the Creator.

"Come into my room," invited Powell, "I want to talk business with you, Limber."

The cowboy nodded, and when they were seated and the smoke of their cigars blended, Powell explained the plan of combining the work of the two ranges, adding as he finished; "I told Mr. Traynor that it is entirely up to you. I don't want you there unless you really would like to go. It would double your pay and make you range foreman of all of the ranches owned by Mr. Traynor and myself. I will have my hands full, getting the Sanitarium built, and we would leave the management of my cattle business absolutely to you. How does it strike you? Don't hesitate to speak plainly."

"So fur as I'm concerned, I'd ruther be over there. It's this way, Doc. Glendon ain't runnin' very straight, and nobody seems to give a damn exceptin' me. I'd like to do what I can for him, and though I don't know as I could do anythin'—you never can tell what'll turn up. 'Tain't right leavin' Donnie and Mrs. Glendon there by themselves the way he does. Glen told me he was goin' to quit as soon as he got a chanct; but if he stays here much longer he's bound to mix up in trouble. He's runnin' with a pretty bad bunch now. Another thing," the cowpuncher hesitated, "Thar's a Mexican girl named Panchita. I guess Mrs. Glendon is about the only one who don't know about her. Glen's plumb locoed over the girl and that's whar his money goes, when he gets hold of any."

Powell started angrily, "The cur! With such a wife and boy! Limber, sometimes I feel ashamed to call myself a man, when such creatures as Glendon are known as men."

"Mebbe Glen don't figger just what it is leadin' up to. He was a mighty different sorter person when he fust come here, and everyone liked him. He'd get full onct in a while, but he played white until this last couple of years. He's just the wrong kind of a man for Arizona. Take him some other place and mebbe he'd manage to average up pretty fair with the rest of the bunch; but he's sure goin' the wrong trail here."

The cowboy rose, and Powell held out his hand impulsively, saying, "All right, Limber. We pull together."

"So long as you want me, Doc."

Their hands gripped and as they looked into each other's eyes, both men recognized a bond that was stronger than blood-the brotherhood of real men.

After Limber had gone, Doctor Powell sat meditating over what the cowboy had told him concerning Glendon. The wreaths of smoke that rose from his cigar framed a shadowy vision of Katherine Glendon's face, and Powell wondered vaguely where he had seen her before they met in the cave near the Circle Cross. Memory refused to aid him.

# Chapter Seventeen

Powell and Chappo were alone in the new home at Hot Springs ranch. Limber had gone to the Diamond H in order to adjust the final details of the joint range work.

While the Mexican busied himself in the kitchen, Powell smoked contentedly in the living-room as he sat before the fire of blazing mesquite knots. He glanced about the home-like place, with its red-shaded lamp on a large table that was strewn with magazines. A desk occupied one end of the room and book shelves held well-worn volumes at the opposite end. The couch, which was covered with a glowing Indian blanket and mannish pillows, harmonized with the massive brown leather chairs and Navajo rugs on the floor. The pictures bore signatures of well-known artists.

"It's just what I've wanted all these years," said Powell aloud. The collie pup at his feet looked up with questioning eyes, then telegraphed reply with bushy tail. The man leaned over and patted the dog's head before selecting a magazine and settling down for the evening.

"Buenos noches, Señor," Chappo smiled politely, his shabby sombrero in hand.

"Buenos noches, Chappo," answered Powell, whose life for several years in a South American mining camp had familiarized him with the language and the type of people found in all Latin-American sections. A fortunate mining investment during those years had awakened a love of the untrammeled outdoors, and also made it possible for him to carry on his plans for a sanitarium.

After Chappo had departed for his bunk-room, the doctor became absorbed in his book. Three hours passed, then the drowsing collie started with a muffled growl and sharply cocked ears.

"What's the matter, old chap?"

The dog leaped up ran to the door whimpering, and Powell went on the front porch. It was too dark to discern anything and no unusual sounds reached the man, but the dog, with a hysterical yelp darted from the porch into the shadows. The short, sharp barks that broke the stillness were barks of welcome such as always greeted the doctor upon his return to the ranch.

A woman's voice spoke to the dog, and Powell ran quickly in the direction the collie had taken. The way led to the Circle Cross; the voice was that of Glendon's wife.

"Be quiet, Tatters," called Powell. As the noise abated, he reached Katherine Glendon's side, and in the faint light saw that she was carrying Donnie.

"Oh, I am so glad you are home!" she exclaimed. "Donnie is hurt, I don't know how badly—but his arm is broken."

Already the doctor had reached for the child.

"Let me have him. Don't try to explain anything now."

They hurried toward the house, entered the room and Powell laid the child on the couch. The doctor knelt down beside the almost unconscious boy, then with gentle touch felt the broken arm. Chappo came through the door, his faded brown eyes were full of pity as he watched the mother who stood with tightly gripped hands waiting the doctor's words.

Donnie looked at her, his quivering lips showed the effort to control his emotions when he tried to move his arm and saw that it was broken.

"It really don't hurt very much, Marmee," he said stoutly as Powell finished the examination and rose to his feet.

"We'll fix you up in no time," the doctor announced cheerily. "Nothing the matter with you except a broken bone, and that is in the very best place it could happen." He turned to Katherine and continued, "Don't worry, Mrs. Glendon. A healthy child's bones knit quickly and perfectly. It's a simple fracture, fortunately, and above the elbow, so only one bone to knit. He'll be playing around tomorrow."

Powell left her sitting by the couch, and Chappo listened carefully to the doctor's low-voiced instructions which were spoken in Spanish.

"I understand, Señor," nodded the Mexican. "Lots of times I have helped when there was no doctor. Horses, cows, dogs, and people, all bones are the same."

The books on the table were removed for rolls of bandages and surgical splints, then Powell turned briskly to Donnie and put his arm about the child's shoulder as he said, "Now, old man, Chappo and I will take care of that arm for you. It may hurt for a few seconds, but after that it won't bother you at all."

"Let him brace himself against you, Mrs. Glendon," continued the physician.

Chappo, at a nod from the doctor, grasped the boy's arm and pulled steadily. Donnie's face paled but not a sound escaped his tightly set lips. The doctor's fingers pressed the fractured bone and held it in place while the splints were adjusted. A sling in which the hand rested, finished the operation, then Powell arranged the pillows on the couch.

"Take it easy now, old man," he said. "You're the pluckiest boy I ever knew."

Donnie tried to smile, but tears filled his eyes and he held out his uninjured hand to his mother. She sat on the couch beside him smoothing his hair and talking in a low voice, until at last, with his right hand still clasped in hers, he fell asleep.

"All right now," Powell assured her, as he put away the articles on the table. "He is exhausted from the nerve shock, nothing more."

The doctor glanced at Katherine and exclaimed, "Bless my heart! You need attention almost as badly as Donnie."

He left the room and returned with a glass. "Just a little port wine. Drink every drop of it," he ordered.

Her hand shook as she lifted the glass to her white lips, then she held out the empty glass and sank into a chair that Powell rolled before the fireplace. Her eyes closed wearily. The doctor understood the over taxed nerves, and as he glanced from mother to child, a feeling of rage against Glendon consumed him. The only sound in the room was the sputter of the burning wood. Katherine looked anxiously at the sleeping child, then at the doctor.

"He's all right," Powell answered her unvoiced fear. "It had been a terrible strain on you both. The bone will begin to knit in a few days and Donnie will have nothing to remind him of the accident in a short time. It's part of a boy's life to have such things as broken legs and arms," he smiled.

"Please don't think I am ungrateful. There are some emotions one almost cannot express, because we feel them too deeply for words. I don't know how to thank you."

"How did it happen?" asked Powell, trying to divert her from any sense of obligation.

"It came so suddenly that it dazed me," she began. "Last summer the wall of the bedroom bulged and Juan made new adobes to fix it; but Mr. Glendon has been too busy to attend to it. We never thought of danger, for an adobe wall often stands for years with big cracks in it, you know. Donnie was sleeping next to the wall in my bed when the crash came. The wall fell outward, but part of the adobe struck his arm. It was dark. I spoke to him and he did not answer. I thought he was dead until I heard him moan." She stopped and bit her lip fiercely.

The doctor placed a fresh log on the fire, and while he prodded the embers, the woman gained control of her voice.

"I lit the candle, but when I looked at him he was unconscious. I lifted him and when the bed covers fell from his arm, I saw the bone had been broken. Then —I thought of you, and brought him here."

Powell knew that her fear that the child she carried might be dying in her arms, or that she might not find anyone but Chappo at the Springs, must have made the three-mile walk seem endless.

"Were you alone?"

"Yes. Juan is on the San Pedro for ten days and my husband went to Willcox yesterday morning. He does not expect to return home for a week. I had no horse or I could have ridden here."

"You and Donnie must go to bed now and rest," commanded the doctor, cutting short the words she was about to utter. "I have a guest room and Chappo sees to everything necessary, so you need not fear you are causing me the least inconvenience. Tomorrow we can drive down to your place and take inventory of the damage. Since Juan has the adobes ready to use, Chappo and I can fix up the wall. I learned all about adobes while I lived in South America eight years ago."

"That was the same year we came here," commented the woman.

Powell smothered an ejaculation of indignation and wonder at her endurance of such a life. "Yet," he mused, "a bruised flower becomes more fragrant." His elbow rested on the mantle and he looked down, studying her face line by line. Again that vague resemblance baffled him until he recalled a stream near his boyhood home, where a shallow current reached a bend and formed a deep pool. He had loved to sprawl on the bank and gaze into the wonderful, ever-changing reflections, where rough trees were softened, the sky became more blue and the many-hued flowers more beautiful. It was a magic pool to his boyish eyes; in later years be called it his Pool of Illusion.

Down in its mysterious depths lived a shadowy form. A woman's face with steadfast eyes looked back into his own, understanding his unspoken dreams, while her slender white hands were held out to him. The longing to touch them was actual physical pain, and often he dived into the water, but the vision vanished in the ripples. He had gone his way, looking into many women's faces in many lands, always hoping to find what he had seen in his Pool of Illusion, but the years of search had been fruitless.

Tonight the firelight from his hearth flickered across that dream face.

The dream and reality blended so perfectly that it startled him when Katherine rose from her chair and held out her hand, saying, "I do thank you with all my heart. I shall never forget what you have done for us. Maybe some day I can show my gratitude."

"Please don't speak of it again," he replied, and seeing Donnie on his feet, Powell added, "Good night, old man.

"It's lucky that adobe fell on the left hand, for it's much harder to learn to use it. My right arm was broken when I was your age. It's funny, though, how quickly my left hand learned to work like its twin brother. After my arm was well, I used my left hand much of the time."

Mother and child entered the cheerful guest room and for a while Powell heard their voices through the closed door. He sat by the dying embers of the fire. He had found the woman of the Pool. She was the wife of his neighbour Glendon. The realization of his dream was more unattainable than ever, but his bitterness held an undercurrent of happiness in knowing that he might be able to ease the burden she was bearing so bravely.

With a sudden movement he touched the chair where her head had rested. Then he turned out the lamp and went to his own room, but that night in his dreams he saw the Woman of the Pool sitting again before his fireplace, and a child leaned against her shoulder. As he drew nearer, her lips smiled and her eyes met his in perfect confidence and understanding.

He held out his arms to her and the child, for they were his own.

## Chapter Eighteen

The next morning when Powell entered the living room before breakfast, he found Katherine and Donnie already there. The child, though pale, smiled shyly at the Doctor.

"Hello! How's the arm this morning, Donnie?"

"It doesn't hurt at all," replied the child, while his mother held out her hand to her host and spoke, "He slept splendidly all night, so I know he did not suffer."

The doctor's answer was interrupted by Chappo at the door leading into the dining-room. The Mexican smiled mysteriously and beckoned Donnie, who glanced at his mother, then at her nod of acquiescence, the boy followed in Chappo's wake. The noise of sharp barks and childish ejaculation mingled with a stream of chatter in Spanish between the child and Mexican in the kitchen. The door closed, and Katherine and Powell were left alone.

Her eyes wandered to the sketches on the walls, and the doctor rose, saying, "My pictures and books have travelled with me to many strange lands, but this is the first time they have really seemed to be at home."

She followed him as he pointed out special pictures, and told some intimate detail of the artist's life, for the pictures had been gifts from their creators, his personal friends. Most of the signatures were world-known. Katherine turned to the rows of books, and recognizing many old friends whom she had not seen for years, she dropped impulsively on the floor and touched them with caressing fingers, her face alight with a radiant smile. Powell read the book-hunger, and begged her to select as many as she pleased.

"I love my books as few men love their friends," he said earnestly, standing above her and taking a rare first edition from its place. "They will be enhanced in value if you will only share them with me, so I can talk about them with you sometime."

Together they selected, while Katherine crouched on the floor read the titles, commenting and questioning, as they agreed or disagreed.

"It's like a child with a big box of candy," she laughed as she rose, assisted by Powell, who carried a number of chosen books and placed them upon the table. "I don't know what to start with."

She settled again in the chair before the fireplace, and the conversation slipped by degrees into the doctor's work in the east, and his plan to transform the Hot Springs ranch into a sanitarium for poor, tubercular children.

"My work in hospitals taught me the need of such a place. There are thousands of children who die each year because they lack the things Nature provides, pure air, nourishing food and an outdoor playground in this wonderful climate with its magical healing powers. I believe that environment can conquer heredity, in physical as well as moral conditions. You cannot realize what child-life means in the slums of our crowded cities of the east, Mrs. Glendon," he turned a face full of enthusiasm and her own glowed in response. "The first step was my good fortune in getting this place. It will take time, money and labour, but I know it is worth the effort."

"It will be wonderful to watch you develope your plans! Thank you for telling me about it all!"

Chappo appeared and announced breakfast, and Powell with Mrs. Glendon found Donnie already waiting them. The collie, Tatters, was beside the child, and it was evident a friendship had been cemented between the two.

The little Mexican cook beamed with pleasure as he installed Mrs. Glendon at the end of the table and placed the coffee-pot before her. Chappo and Juan were old friends, so Katherine and Donnie knew him well. His reputation as a cook was demonstrated in the meal he served, and he watched jealously that nothing was neglected. Donnie's attention was divided between his mother, the doctor and Tatters. The dog sat beside the boy's chair, occasionally poking his nose against Donnie's knee to remind him that he, too, liked butter muffins and tidbits of bacon.

Donnie patted him, but hesitated to respond to the dog's appeals, then as the child looked down and broke into a sudden burst of hearty laughter, Katherine was startled into the realization that it was the first time she had ever heard her boy laugh like other children.

"Look, Marmee!"

The dog, believing his wheedling ineffectual, was sitting on his haunches uncertainly, waving his paws frantically in efforts to keep balanced. It was hard work for a puppy, and his wildly rolling eyes made him more ridiculous. Even Chappo joined in the laughter with the doctor and Katherine. Tatters, understanding approval, barked and danced about them, until Powell tossed a piece of muffin which the dog caught and gulped down.

"I'm afraid I am not bringing him up properly," apologized the doctor, "but we are alone so much and he is such an intelligent, affectionate dog, that I spoil him. He thinks your breakfast must be better than mine, Donnie," he ended as the dog rejected a bit of muffin proffered by Powell and swallowed what Donnie held out.

At last breakfast was over, and the little party stood on the porch, prepared to start for the Circle Cross. Tatters yelped and begged to be included, but his special efforts were directed at Donnie.

"He seems to have adopted you, Donnie," the doctor laughed. "If your mother does not object, I think Tatters would be a fine friend for you."

"If he were a less valuable dog —" began Katherine, but Powell cut short her protests by his answer.

"It is natural for a boy to have a dog. A pup will desert a man anytime to respond to a boy's smile. If the dog will not cause you any annoyance, I'd be happy to know he was with Donnie. Tatters is unusually intelligent and affectionate, almost uncannily so at times. He would be a loyal friend."

Donnie watched with appealing eyes, and when his mother accepted the dog for him, the child's right arm went around Tatters' shaggy neck, and the dog, as though understanding, pledged his fealty with a quick touch of his pink tongue against the lad's cheek. Then Chappo drove the buggy from the stable and stood at the head of the team until Powell, Donnie and Katherine were seated and the reins in the doctor's hands.

The Mexican mounted a pony and loped ahead of the handsome span of fast trotters, while Tatters yelped before them, dashing away from the road into the brush to chase imaginary foes. They reached the Circle Cross and after an inspection of the broken wall, Chappo asserted he could fix it unassisted in a couple of days, since the adobe bricks were in good condition in the shed where Juan had stored them the previous summer. No damage had been done to the room inside, or the furniture.

"I think you and Donnie had better remain at the Springs until the place is fixed," suggested Powell. "The wall will be damp for a week, you know."

"If my bed is moved into the corner of the dining-room, Donnie and I can sleep there and get along splendidly;" was Katherine's answer. "The rest of the house is in good condition. The bedroom was the only room when we came here, and we built on the other three rooms. The old wall at the side of the house cracked last spring, and the rains weakened it, as the roof leaked badly. I noticed the crack widening several weeks ago, but you know, an adobe wall holds together when any other material would break away. We did not dream there was any immediate danger of its falling."

"I'll help Chappo," asserted Powell, despite her protest that the repairs could wait until Juan and her husband returned, and Powell and Chappo began their task.

Donnie and Tatters trotted to and fro, as Chappo wheeled the adobe bricks to Powell, who whistled cheerfully as he laid them accurately on top of each other between the soft layers of mud which he skillfully applied with a large trowel. The whistle was interrupted by snatches of conversation between Chappo the doctor and Donnie, partly in English and partly Spanish.

"Lunch is ready," called Katherine through the kitchen window.

"Fine!" answered Powell, "we're all good and hungry," then followed the sounds of splashing water, and in a few minutes Powell, with Donnie at his side, bustled into the dining room announcing they were ready to eat the dishes.

It was a merry meal, and afterwards while Chappo was eating his lunch, the doctor and Katherine sat on the porch talking. Donnie perched on the lower step, his eyes betraying his admiration for the man who was unlike any other man the child had ever known in his short life.

Work was resumed, and as it neared sunset, Powell said that he must tighten the bandages on Donnie's arm and the adjustment was completed with Katherine's aid. The splints had held in place, and the doctor announced everything satisfactory.

"I will be back early in the morning," said the man, clasping Katherine's extended hand. "Oh, by the way, we killed a calf a few days ago, so I will bring down a loin. Chappo and I are cultivating hearty appetites, you see!"

He was in the buggy before she could thank him, and the team whirled away in a cloud of dust.

Katherine watched the buggy until it disappeared, then Chappo and Donnie emerged from the stable and came toward her, talking volubly in Mexican-Spanish —which the boy had acquired from old Juan. Katherine had also fallen into the habit of using the same tongue when she and Donnie were alone with Juan, whose one symptom of allegiance to Mexico was his persistence in his native tongue, though he spoke English fluently.

"I will feed the chickens and bring wood and water, Señora," said Chappo; "then you can tell me what you want me to do. The cow is milked."

"There is nothing more, thank you, Chappo;" she replied. "You can go home now, for Donnie and I will manage nicely."

"I stay here teel Señor Glendon and Juan come home. El Doctor say 'stay.'"

"But, Chappo," she protested, "they may be away a week or more. You must go home and look out for the doctor."

"El Padrone say 'stay.' I must stay. He say, 'you come home too queek, I fire you;'" the Mexican smiled expansively, "Eet is all right, Señora. I stay!"

She realized that her objections were of no consequence to either the Mexican or the doctor, and a sudden wave of gratitude overwhelmed her. It was so new to have others think of her comfort or safety, to have the heavy burden lifted even for a few hours. What a difference it would have made in her life and Donnie's if Glendon were only a man like the doctor. Then there would have been no loneliness in the cañon, for the high walls could not have held her happiness. Her heart would have sent its message to every tree, bush, rock, bird and cloud, so that the very universe might share her joy.

Early the next morning Donnie was on the watch for his new friend, and his delight made him speechless when Powell told the boy that the pony tied to the back of the buggy was for him.

"He is too small to carry a man's weight," explained Powell, "but he is perfectly gentle, so you need have no fear."

"I can't let you do so much," faltered Katherine, "the dog was more than enough. You are heaping a debt of obligations that I cannot pay. Last night I tried to make Chappo go home, but he refused. He said you had ordered him to remain, and that you would discharge him if he disobeyed you. I know how many things need attention on a ranch and it worries me to cause you any further inconvenience. Donnie and I are used to being alone, you see, so there was no need of Chappo staying here all night."

"You must think I am a regular tenderfoot," retorted Powell, smiling. "I have roughed it under the most primitive conditions in South America, and am glad to do a bit of hustling to wear off the rust. Civilization makes many men helpless, you know."

"Then, let us compromise," she persisted. "Suppose you come down for your dinner each night while Chappo is here? I cannot consent to his remaining otherwise."

"Do you know," confessed Powell gaily, "that was what I was hoping you would say!"

So, each afternoon following, when the shadows lengthened in the cañon, Donnie, watching down the road would shout welcome, and Katherine coming on the porch, watched Doctor Powell pause at the bend of the road, waiting for the child, just as old Doctor King had formerly done, then Donnie, perched on the saddle before the doctor, rode in state to the front porch and his smiling mother.

On one of these rides, Donnie looked with serious eyes at the man, and said, "When I grow up, I'm going to be a doctor like you, and then, maybe, you'll let me come and help you. Marmee says that helping others is just the same as fighting in tour'ments or hunting the Sangreal!"

"Your mother is right, Donnie," was the grave reply. "Someday I want you to be my partner, and we'll work together. Now, remember, this is a contract between us, and I won't forget my promise."

After dinner had been eaten each evening, a romp with Donnie and Tatters, or teaching the dog a new trick, occupied Powell and the child, and later, Katherine and the doctor sat on the little porch and talked of the doctor's plans, while Donnie leaned against his mother's knees listening intently, for someday, he, too, would help in the doctor's work. The shadows in Katherine's eyes turned to laughter, her face became girlish in relief from constant worry, and Donnie watched her with adoring, wondering eyes.

"Marmee's lots prettier when she laughs, isn't she, Doctor?" asked the child suddenly one evening.

Katherine's eyes and Powell's met, and for the first time a feeling of awkwardness tinged their comradeship, but Powell relieved the situation with a laugh, as he said, "Little boys are lucky, because they can say just what they think, but grown-up people are not allowed to do it. How is Pet today?"

Donnie launched upon a report of the most wonderful pony in Arizona and the man kept plying him with questions until the strain of the situation had passed. But, Katherine was unusually silent for the rest of the evening, and the doctor rose early to say "Good night." He drove home slowly, thoughtful, troubled and yet glad. No matter what Fate might deny him in life, these wonderful days could never be filched from the treasure-house of Memory.

After Donnie had been tucked in bed, Katherine Glendon sat in silent self-examination. She realized the happiness of the last five days could not continue, but even though she could not have the kindly friendship of the doctor, it warmed her heart to know that for these few days they had walked side by side as comrades. It had imbued her with new hopes. Yet, she knew there was not the least tinge of disloyalty to her husband in any word, deed or thought. The pleasure she had experienced was as innocent as that which she felt when she and Donnie, walking in the cañon, found a new flower.

So, with untroubled eyes she knelt beside the bed where her boy lay sleeping, and prayed for the child, then her lips moved in a plea for the father of that child.

The following day Glendon returned home in a repentant mood, as was usual after a protracted carousal. He thanked Chappo effusively, and to show his gratitude, held out a whiskey bottle. But the little Mexican declined, "I promise El Doctor I would not drink again. Eef I do, maybe I die pretty queek, he say."

"Oh, a little whiskey once in a while won't hurt you," urged Glendon, who always liked company when he was drinking.

But Chappo was firm, though the battle was not won without a hard struggle when the pungent odour from the glass in Glendon's extended hand reached the dwarf's nostrils. Appreciating his own weakness, Chappo hastened to the barn and saddled his pony without loss of time.

Then he rode to the door where Katherine stood. "Adios, Señora. Yo me voy," (Good bye, Señora. I am going,) and he galloped away from temptation as fast as his pony could carry him.

Katherine told her husband of the kindness shown her and Donnie, and in response to her entreaties, he rode up to the Springs the following day.

Powell received him courteously and tried to evade the effusive thanks, but Glendon had reached a point of intoxication where he was garrulous.

"I want you to come down any time and make yourself entirely at home," he urged. "A man gets tired having no one but a woman to talk to, and Katherine's head is always in the clouds. The boy is getting just like her. When he's a little older though, I'm going to take him in hand myself. If Katherine hadn't been so high-headed with my folks things would be mighty different with me today. But here I am, stuck down in a God-forsaken cañon in Arizona and no prospects of ever getting out. If she had catered to my family we wouldn't be here, you bet. So, it's nothing more than she brought on herself, and I've got to take the medicine with her. The old man has plenty money, but it's doubtful if I smell a penny of it when he dies. If she'd come off her high-horse the old man might leave a wad to Donnie. Of course, I take a few drinks when I feel like it. Any man does. Once in a while it gets the upper hand of me, but I can stop when I want to, and I won't make any promises to any one to quit till I get good and ready."

Once started he rambled on. Powell gave up any attempt to check the half-drunken confidences, and sat silently smoking, trying to conceal his aversion. It was with a feeling of keen relief he saw Glendon rise and take leave. The heavy-set figure swayed uncertainly in the saddle. Then the memory of that man's wife, of the days they two had shared, swept over the doctor. The knowledge that Katherine was subject to contact of such a man as Glendon made his own loss more poignant. If he had found the woman of his dreams married to a man worthy of her, he knew he would have rejoiced at her happiness, though he went his own way alone through life.

"Poor little Lady of the Pool," he whispered, "I have found you only to lose you!"

He recalled a beautiful rose, frozen in a block of ice, which had been sent him by a grateful patient. He had longed to warm the cold petals and inhale their fragrance, but he knew that removing the icy barrier would mean destroying the flower. He left it undisturbed.

And the rose, in its loveliness passed its life; shut away from the caress of the summer breeze, from the kiss of the butterfly, from the quivering touch of the humming-bird's wings, and all the wonderful mysteries of life that throbbed around it.

# Chapter Nineteen

In May and June each year the Eastern and Northern cattle buyers flock into Arizona to procure "feeders" for their grass ranges in other sections. One, two and three-year old steers are then shipped to be held on pasture and finally "topped" on grain in some Eastern centre, to prepare the animals for the Kansas City, Denver, Omaha or Chicago stockyards.

A number of fine steers had been gathered on the Hot Springs range, and were being driven to Willcox to make part of a contract between a Montana buyer and the Diamond H and PL. The spring rains had been abundant. Wild grasses rose to the height of a pony's knees; sleek Hereford cattle browsed contentedly, while white-faced calves romped and raced between. Arizona was at its smiling best.

Powell, riding behind the herd while Limber directed a couple of Mexican vaqueros, was satisfied that he had made no mistake in identifying himself with this country. The plans for the Sanitarium were maturing perfectly. Letters with suggestions and experience culled from the best authorities all over the continent, as well as European health resorts, were in each mail. Architects had submitted drafts and plans, from which Powell was selecting the very best ideas.

Arrangements regarding the consolidation of the Diamond H work with the PL and Hot Springs herds had proven ideal, and the only unpleasant feature Powell had encountered was embodied in his neighbour, Glendon.

Though the man's antagonism to the doctor had now reached a point of open animosity, Powell ignored it. Limber went frequently to the Circle Cross, and old Chappo, making visits to Juan, managed to keep in touch with Katherine. They all knew they were unable to do more than this, unless she should allow it, or some dire necessity force her to call on them for help. Powell was compelled to keep entirely aloof from the Circle Cross, fearing to precipitate some disagreeable scene, should Glendon be in one of his aggressive moods. The doctor knew Glendon's type well enough to understand that the brunt of such situation would fall with its full weight on the woman. He hoped that she did not misinterpret his absence as due to indifference, since it was the only way he could help.

Limber dropped back of the herd and rode beside the doctor without speaking. There were long intervals when these two were together that neither spoke, yet each man knew the comradeship of the other. The cattle were plodding along steadily and in the distance could be seen the smoke of a train creeping like a rattlesnake across the flat between Cochise and Willcox.

The cowboy threw his leg across the horn of his saddle, sitting sidewise as he rolled a cigarette, which he proffered to Powell. Then making one for himself, the two men smoked as they rode.

"Juan told me last night that he had found another dead calf up the riverbed, and poisoned it," said Limber. "Thar was fresh lion tracks. He thinks it's the lion that was in the cave, but it ain't been thar since the day we found Mrs. Glendon and Donnie. It must of smelt our tracks and quit. Juan has been watchin' for it ever since I tole him about it."

"How much is the bounty?" asked Powell, puffing at his cigarette.

"Twenty-five dollars for a lion scalp," replied Limber. "I hope Juan gets it. We've been having lots of calves killed this year. Mr. Traynor figgers on puttin' a couple of men out trappin' and poisonin' them and the coyotes. It'll pay to do it. We had to shoot two horses not long ago, because their backs was broke."

"Do they fight at close quarters?" asked Powell. "The South American ones are nasty things."

"Well, sometimes they do and sometimes they don't. Say, did any one ever tell you about the time Hasayampa fit the mountain lion?"

"No, or I should not have forgotten it, I am sure," Powell smiled in anticipation.

Limber tossed away his dead cigarette, swung around in his saddle and began, "Hasayampa had a peculiar experience with a mountain-lion onct. You see, he was livin' in a one-room stone cabin down Aravaipa Cañon all alone by hisself, exceptin' for an ol' brindle dog named Killem. Hasayampa allowed that Killem was a canine orphun asylum, because he was related to near every dog between Willcox and the San Pedro. Killem's nose was bull-dog, his ears was collie, his tail looked something like a pug's the way it tried to curl up in a doughnut. He had a brindle coat of hair that was sprinkled with white patches and them mixed with black. He sure done his best to bear a resemblance to every one of his family connections. He had been a dandy scrapper when he was young, but he was so ol' he shed all his teeth, but his ki-yi was guaranteed indestructible. Hasayampa had trouble with a mountain-lion what wanted to make sociable calls, but was too bashful to come in daylight. It formed a strong attachment for some pigs Bill was raisin', an' that lion adopted 'em on the installment plan, an' the ol' sow took on somethin' dreadful. So between the pigs squealin' and Killem ki-yiing, he was pretty near crazy. Hasayampa said he couldn't stand the lady pig's grief, so he killed her and then he guv Killem a good kick to make him shet up, and went back to bed.

"The cabin had one door an' a little winder. Hasayampa was lyin' on his bunk with a candle stuck in a beer-bottle on a box longside him, right under the winder. Suddenly ol' Killem hopped right through the winder glass and landed plump on top of Hasayampa. He jumped up to kick Killem out, but before he done it, derned if that lion didn't come through the same way, but he knocked over the box and put out the candle. Then Killem and the lion started in for fust blood.

"Hasayampa's six-shooter had been knocked off'n the box and Hasayampa made a break fer the door-the room seemed a leetle bit crowded just then-but the door was locked and the key somewhar on the floor. He begun scratching for that key.

"Just about this time the stovepipe got knocked down. Thar warn't mutch fire, but plenty of smoke. Next thing they hit the table whar he had piled up all the tin plates, cups and pans that he washed on Sundays. Hasayampa said the noise was somethin' fierce, for Killem was yellin', 'Pen and ink,' the lion was screechin' its head off, and both of 'em kickin' tin things in every direction.

"All this time Hasayampa was havin' troubles of his own. He was clawin' the floor, lookin' for the key or his six-shooter. He didn't care which, but he wanted one of 'em and he wanted it in a hurry, which wasn't unreasonable noways, when you remember it was his own property he was huntin'. He finally got on his stomach and spun aroun' like a cartwheel and that was how he found his gun. Trustin' to luck he edged closer to the noise and put his gun against somethin' and fired. Thar was a yelp from Killem, a screech from the lion, then somethin' flopped around on the floor, but whether it was the lion or the dorg, was a conundrum Hasayampa wasn't prepared to answer off hand.

"Things got quiet. He crawled careful till he found the candle and lit it, holdin' his gun ready. Then he looked aroun'. Thar was Killem settin' scrintched up in one corner of the room, a bullet hole through one ear, but thar warn't no lion nowhar to be seen, and Hasayampa figgered he had shot Killem and the lion had gone out the winder, same route he took comin' in. Hasayampa did some tall cussin, and begun pickin' things up, when he seen the end of the lion's tail stickin' out under the bunk. He backed off without losin' no time and shot under the bunk. The lion never even kicked.

"After he'd waited to be sure it was dead, Hasayampa hauled it out by the tail, feelin' mighty big at such a shot in a dark room. Then he begun to hunt to see whar the bullet went in. Thar was just one bullet hole, and that was when he shot it under the bunk. He had missed it clar the fust time, but that lion was as dead as a door-nail when he fired the second shot, and Hasayampa knowed it."

Limber looked at Powell gravely, "Now don't that beat you?"

"But what happened?" demanded the Doctor. "Even Hasayampa must have had some theory about it."

"Well," drawled Limber, "ol' Injun George, wher he heerd about it said he had been puttin' pizen out, and findin' a half et pig had fixed up the carcass for the lion, and he allowed the one that visited Hasayampa had made a meal of that pig. But Hasayampa always stuck to it that the lion had naturally died of heart disease and nervous prostration brung on by the excitement. Anyway, that's how Hasayampa Bill won the lion record in Arizona."

"He proved his right to spell the word both ways," grinned the doctor as Limber reined Peanut toward the head of the herd.

They were approaching the outskirts of Willcox. Already their advent was being heralded by hysterical yelps from innumerable dogs belonging to the Mexican families who occupied shacks at the outskirts of the town. Each shack blazed with strings of dried, red chili peppers, while countless children grouped about each door, or the women gossiped volubly.

The cattle were driven into the shipping corrals a short distance from town. The gates secured, Limber and Powell rode side by side up the dusty street to the Cowboys' Rest and left their horses in charge of Buckboard.

Several other shipments were in town, being inspected according to rule of precedent. The railroad company was frequently short of engines to transport the heavy trains of cattle, and it often happened that a bunch of stock was delayed a week or longer before starting for its destination. In such event, the cattle were held on the range near town, or in some fenced pasture close at hand which was rented for the time necessary.

Limber had put in his order so as to insure the right of way when the cattle from the Hot Springs and Diamond H should arrive in town. He was anxious to ascertain whether they could load out that afternoon or not. The foreman and Doctor Powell walked up the main street together, stopping to speak to other cowmen, many of whom had not before met the new owner of the Hot Springs and PL ranches.

Bronco, Holy and Roarer spied and welcomed them vociferously, and Limber was informed that the Diamond H cattle were on a pasture, half a mile from town. The Inspector would be ready to handle their shipment right after lunch, as the cars and engine would be on time for them.

"I'll stop for the mail," suggested Powell as they passed the post-office, and suiting the action to the words he turned in the store, while the others continued their way to the Chinese restaurant.

They were about to enter, when Walton, carrying an old-fashioned carpet grip hurried through the door.

"Hello, Walton," was Limber's casual greeting.

Walton, seeing them, stopped short and regarded the group with an angry stare, then without replying, he rushed across the street to the railroad station, where the east-bound train was puffing.

"Seems in a hurry," commented Limber as they watched Walton climb aboard the train.

"Mebbe he's goin' to get married," grinned Bronco, "and he's scairt for fear somethin' will happen to them whiskers again."

Walton's face appeared at one of the windows of the day-coach. As the train puffed past the men, his eyes rested on them in mingled triumph and malice.

"Hump!" grunted Holy, "Looks like he'd just drawed four aces!"

"Well, I'm glad the country is shet of him," piped Roarer as they met Doctor Powell and imparted the item of news to him.

Powell handed a letter to Limber. The pencil writing was crude and the sheet of paper bore an enormous, brilliant red rose across one corner. The eyes of the other cowpunchers focused on that rose, as the letter had been folded backward.

"Looks like a love-letter," insinuated Bronco. "Say, Limber ain't that addressed to Holy? He's the only one of the outfit that writes letters to ladies, you know."

"It's been in the post-office a week," commented Limber, and they drew closer as he read aloud:

> *Dere Limber* —I seen Walton puttin' the Diamond H on a Lazy F calf and I give
> him a week to quit the country. He sold out to a fellow from Douglas, so I guess
> there won't be no more trouble from him. It wood be hard to make a case that
> would stick against him, because he wasn't branding the calves for himself. He's

a little off his cabazza, and them green whiskers stuck in his craw. My regards to the Boss and the boys.

Yours truly,

Billy Saunders.

Range Detective for the
Live Stock Sanitary Board.

"That's why he was in sech a hurry to get that train. He must of thought we knowed about it;" said Limber. "Well, he won't bother us no more." As they all entered the restaurant, Limber spoke to Powell, "The inspector'll be ready for us right after lunch."

They were shown a table near the front of the room, which was well-filled with a typical frontier mixture of humanity. Cowpunchers, miners, clerks and storekeepers, a couple of commercial travellers, and an Army officer in uniform, accompanied by his wife and two children, who had evidently just arrived on the train from California.

In a corner at the rear end of the room sat Glendon with a cowboy whose mutilated hand had won the name of Three-fingered Jack. They were talking earnestly in guarded tones. Glendon's back was toward the entrance of the place, but Jack, who was classed as a "gunman," because of his expert marksmanship, scrutinized the newcomers sharply.

"Who is that with the Diamond H outfit?" he asked.

Glendon twisted slightly, took a swift glance, scowled and leaned over to his companion.

"That's Powell, damn him! Bought the Hot Springs and PL herd and ranch and is going to put up a sanitarium for tubercular children. Limber stays with him most of the time, and puts in the rest of it at the Diamond H, so you never know when you're going to run into them. It's easy to pull the wool over a tenderfoot, but Limber is another proposition. If there's any trouble, the whole country will side with Limber. He's as sharp as they make em, and every one knows he's so damned straight that he leans backward. That doctor is no fool, either."

Three-fingered Jack shrugged his shoulders contemptuously and smiled into the other man's face. Both had been drinking heavily. The smile was a studied insult. Glendon did not notice it.

"Losing your nerve, Glen? I'll give that pill-pusher a little scare for you, and I bet when I get done with him he'll look like a cake of soap in a Chinese laundry after a big day's washing."

Glendon hesitated. "We'd better steer clear of them. It won't do to have any trouble now. It would ball things up for us."

"I'll keep away from Limber," promised Jack, now obsessed with one idea; "but it won't take anything except a good bluff for the tenderfoot."

"That Diamond II is mixing into everything," growled Glendon. "If it hadn't been for Traynor, King never would have patented that land and the will wouldn't have been worth the paper it was written on. I've hung out at the Circle Cross all these years expecting to get hold of the Hot Springs, but thanks to Traynor and Powell, I got left in the end. Bad enough when King was alive, shutting me off from the water, but now Powell is stocking up the range and it's going to knock me into a cocked hat. There's bound to be trouble between Powell and me before very long. I'm not going to put up with his prowling around watching things out there."

"What the devil do you care for the half a dozen calves he may keep you from rustling?" jeered Jack. "You've got a heap bigger thing ahead of you, if you just keep your shirt on a bit longer. Then you can quit the country for good. But, it won't be safe for us to come out there now, Glen. Better meet somewhere else."

"All right," assented Glendon, with a shrug. "You tell Panchita anytime you want me, and she'll get word to me."

They made their way rather unsteadily from the long room, unhitched their ponies and rode toward the corral conversing earnestly in low tones.

Half an hour later, Powell and the boys of the Diamond H reached the corrals where their entire shipment now was enclosed. Bronco remained down in the narrow chute, while the rest, after tying their ponies to the corral fence, climbed up and perched on the topmost rail.

Powell looked down on a mass of surging horns, his ears assaulted by deafening bellows. The inspector sat above a narrow passageway in which a draft of five cattle was driven, then the bar dropped and parted them from the other animals. As these five cows passed toward the car into which they were to be loaded, Bronco called the brand and ear-marks to the inspector, who recorded them. Then the cow was given a slight shove to accelerate its movements into the open door of the car. If it hesitated, it was not long, for only a creature of iron could withstand the fierce prodding in the ribs with sharp wooden poles, and the wild yells would make an Apache war-whoop sound a whisper of first love.

While the men worked, Limber, seated beside Powell explained the system of territorial inspection, and that at each shipping point an inspector was stationed to report officially on every brand and ear-mark of cattle offered for shipment. Each brand was registered with the Live Stock Sanitary Board at Phoenix, and reports forwarded immediately after any shipment, stating the owner of each animal, brand, ear-mark, shipper in charge, buyer, consigner and consignee. A certificate of health was also required, and without such official authority from the inspector no railroad company was permitted to move any live stock over its road. The shipper in charge, was also compelled to have copies. In addition to these duties, the inspector was authorized to collect and forward any amounts received for stray cattle, whose owners were not present or represented by an agent. Where a brand was found not officially registered, such animal was sold by the inspector and proceeds remitted to the board. This was given any claimant who could satisfactorily explain negligence to record the brand, and prove beyond doubt his ownership.

Limber, sitting beside Powell on the corral fence, explained these laws while they watched the inspection.

"Some of the brands are very indistinct," said Powell. "In case there is doubt, how is it decided?"

"Inspector clips the hair over the brand with horse-clippers, and if that don't settle it, he sells the animal to the local butcher. You see, when the hide is fresh from a cow, the first brand shows out the plainest, even if another is run over afterwards. Sometimes a brand is registered what gives a feller the chance to alter another. There was, one man ran O Bar O," Limber drew an imaginary brand on the palm of his left hand, O-O. "Afterward they found the Crooked H, Ɔ-C, the ⅃Ⴀ and the D O could be changed to the O-O and work the three biggest herds in the section. The fellow was honest, never aimed to do no dirty work, but the brand was stopped by order of the Live Stock Sanitary Board."

The fresh draft, headed by a large cow, was driven into the chute.

"This brand's been monkeyed with," Holy called up to the inspector, who sat on an elevated platform just above the chute.

There was craning of necks as each one studied the animal, for an altered brand was the business of every cowman in the Territory.

"What is it?" demanded the inspector.

"She looks more like an inspection certificate than a cow," was the answer. "Jumping Jehosaphat! Did you ever see such a mix-up? There's a B D looks like it's been changed from a P L; an' ol' Mule Shoe Quarter Circle on her side, one ear's slit an' the other's a jinglebob. Hold on, there's something on the other side."

Continuing his examination he moved around the animal and ejaculated in surprise; "Damned if here ain't a fresh Circle Cross. What d'ye know about that, Glendon?"

Every one looked at Glendon, who sat at Limber's left side on the railing. But before he could reply, Paddy Lafferty jumped into the corral chute and stooping down studied the cow's front legs, then he straightened up and spoke.

"Oi don't give a dum what brand she carries, that cow is moine. She runs over the Hot Springs range. Oi'd know the ould haythin anywheres becase she got cut by barbed-wire and

I docthered her, and she give me the divvle of a toime when I was doin' it, be jabers! There's the marks of the woire-cuts on her fore ankles. That brand's been burnt since I sold the PL herd to Doctor Powell."

"That's a lie!" shouted Glendon. "I bought her four months ago from a Mexican on the San Pedro. The B D is his brand. He had ten cows and sold them all to me before he went back to Mexico."

Paddy looked coolly into Glendon's bloodshot eyes. "Yez must hev laid awake noights fixin' up that loi," he sneered, keeping a close watch on Glendon's right hand. "Oi giss the inspecther hed betther take charge of her and sittle the matther. But it stroikes me that B D is a moighty quare brand for a Greaser to be running."

"As long as the cow has a P L," spoke Powell suddenly, "I suppose it gives me a voice in the matter also?"

The inspector nodded confirmation, and Powell went on, "Let the inspector take charge, as Paddy suggested. I don't want any animal on my range that carries a disputed brand. If the cow belongs to me, I want her shipped or slaughtered, and all possible disputes about her ended."

"Ship her," ordered the inspector. "I'll look up that B D brand, and if it is not registered the proceeds of sale will be forwarded to Doctor Powell. If it is registered, and the Greaser has left, as Glendon claims, it is up to Glendon to prove ownership by bill of sale from the Greaser."

"'Tain't the furst toime your brand has got on one of my cows, Glen;" asserted Paddy hotly. "Oi sold my brand and herd clane and straight to Docther Powell, and Oi'll sthand boy that sale to the last critter."

Glendon's hand slipped back a few inches, but Limber, sitting beside him, saw the movement and gripped his wrist in a steel clutch. It was done so quickly and quietly that no one but Paddy saw it, or heard Limber say, "Don't be such a fool, Glen. Killin' people don't change the laws of the Territory."

"If ever I catch that Greaser, I'll make him sweat blood," blustered Glendon.

Paddy mounted the fence, settled himself, then filled his corn-cob pipe, lighted it deliberately and took a deep puff before he remarked with a grim smile, "Oi'll hilp yez do it, Glendon-when yez catch him!"

His wrinkled, gnarled hand smoothed the leg of his overalls, which had originally been the orthodox blue of all self-respecting overalls, but long since had succumbed to Paddy's washtub and vigorous muscles. Below the edges of these anemic patched garments, loomed one old boot and one shoe, laced crookedly with a piece of rawhide.

The hand ceased its caressing movement, and Paddy squinted up again at Glendon, "Don't yez be afther fergittin', Glendon, whin yez catch him I'll take a hand at him-wid yez."

# Chapter Twenty

Limber unsaddled his pony in the Cowboys' Rest, after the trainload had pulled out. He found that the episode of the burnt cow was already being discussed openly.

"Glendon's goin' to get into heaps of trouble if he ain't more careful," stated Buckboard to Limber. "He's mixin' in with a mighty bad bunch."

Limber hung his saddle on a peg and stood rubbing Peanut's nose gently. "You're sure right, Buckboard," he replied slowly. "I'm derned sorry about it. I done all I knew how to pull him up, but 'tain't been no good, so fur's I can see. What stumps me is why a fellow what has so many chances to make good works as hard as Glen does a dodgin' 'em. He come here with plenty dinero, had heaps of friends and a rich father to back him. Then he was eddicated and has the dandiest wife that ever stepped on earth. Sometimes I think he's plumb locoed."

"Mrs. Glendon's got a good-sized bunch of trouble just now and more a comin', unless Glen wakes up and hits another trail pretty damn quick," growled Buckboard. "That Mexican woman is making a regular fool of him, and gets every cent that he handles. I've been wondering how much longer the stores will carry him. His herd don't amount to shucks any more."

"If I knowed a woman like Glendon's wife was waitin' for me at a ranch, I'd think I was the richest man in Arizona Territory, even if the ranch only had one room and I hadn't but five head of cows," Limber spoke earnestly, and old Buckboard, catching the look on the cowpuncher's face, paused a second before he answered.

"There's plenty good men that would be a heap better to her than Glendon, for all his fancy way of talking. But nobody can't do nothin' to help a woman like her when she's tied up to a skunk like Glendon. It's a damn shame, but a woman of her sort just goes along and plays out the game with a lone hand. But she plays it square."

"I know. That's what makes it hard. I try to do what I can to help Glen, just so's to ease the load on her, but he keep's pilin' it up more and more every day."

"When a feller like him catches on to other people letting him off easy on account of her, he'll work that game for all it's worth. Instead of tryin' to cover up his tracks, it'd be lots better to give him rope enough to hang himself. Then she could cut loose from him."

"No she wouldn't," contradicted Limber. "So long as Glendon is above ground she'll stick to him, no matter what he does. Glen knows that, too."

"Then, by God! I hope something will put him under ground before he breaks her heart," exploded Buckboard, giving a vicious slash with a tie-rope at a handy post which relieved his irritation, for he knew Limber had spoken the truth.

The conversation was interrupted by Bronco who hastened up to Limber.

"Guess there's goin' to be trouble in town," he announced.

"Glendon?" demanded Buckboard, hopefully.

"Nope. It's Three-fingered Jack this time," was the reply. "Alpaugh, the constable, is away at Tombstone, and Three-finger come in last night and has been tankin' up ever since, and by this time he figgers he's got the range to hisself."

"Whar's Peachy? Isn't he Deputy Constable?" asked Limber as they passed through the corral gate.

Bronco grunted. "Peachy? Whar's Peachy?" he paused to gather scorn. "Peachy's in hidin'. Jack shot out the lights in the corner saloon last night and every one ducked and stampeded, and that denied Deputy Constable dropped on all fours behind the bar and crawled outen the room jest like the yeller pup he is. All he needs is a few fleas to finish him! Then he lit out in the back yard and one feller told me he seen him jump over that ten-foot board fence back of the saloon, and he swars Peachy never teched it. He's some jack-rabbit when it comes to jumpin', and he's got as much nerve as one. Just because Jack's got the name of bein' a bad man and handy with his gun, he's got the whole town buffaloed. But the funny thing is, no one ever knowed who Jack has killed. He sure ain't done no gun-play here except plug tin cans to show off."

"He needs some one to take that freshness outen him;" Limber spoke quietly as though commenting on the weather. "If Peachy ain't handy, looks like it's up to us to see the Jedge and ask if he needs any deputy."

"That's why I was huntin' you," was Bronco's answer, but further conversation was interrupted by a fusilade of shots.

"I guess he's turned loose," Limber spoke as they ran toward the noises. "Thar ain't no time now to see the Jedge. It's up to us, Bronc. Come along."

They were joined by other men who ran from various directions and at a turn of the street they saw Three-fingered Jack standing in the roadway, close to the office of the Justice of the Peace, who represented the only judicial authority in Willcox. Jack's pistol was smoking. He regarded the assembled men insolently.

"I heerd there's some one who's going to serve a warrant on me," challenged Jack. "What I'm afraid of is that he won't know just where to find me."

He wheeled and sent several bullets against the large plate glass window of a corner store, accompanied by a hair-raising yell as the glass clattered to the ground in fragments.

Limber and Bronco reached the outer edge of the crowd and pushed through it, but stopped as they saw a man saunter nonchalantly around the corner from the Main street. He paused, regarded the crowd, then his eyes wandered interestedly to Jack, who was busy slipping fresh cartridges into his pistol.

As the gunman started to flourish his weapon, he became aware of the new-comer, who advanced toward him and said, "If I were you I would not shoot so promiscuously, my friend. You might accidentally hit something, you know."

"It's Doc," ejaculated Limber, "and he ain't got no gun!"

Jack evidently recognized Powell, for he swung and faced him demanding what he was talking about.

Powell held out a paper. "If you are Jack Dunlap, known as Three-fingered Jack, and supposed to be a gunman, I have a warrant for your arrest. I've just been made special Deputy Constable."

Jack regarded him with open contempt. "Oh, is that so?" he sneered. "Well, here I am! Come on and do your duty, Mr. Special Constable."

Limber pressed toward Powell, with Bronco at his side, and close behind them loomed Holy and Roarer, but Powell smiled at them and shook his head at the puzzled punchers of the Diamond H. Limber's finger rested lightly on the trigger of his pistol which apparently hung loosely in the hand at his side. His eyes glinted dangerously, his lips were tightened into a thin line. Bronco glanced at him, and knew Doctor Powell was safe. Only a few men were aware of the quickness with which Limber could draw and how accurately the apparently careless bullets were sent.

"I wonder what Doc is up to?" murmured Bronco, but none of them could solve the problem.

Powell moved deliberately toward Jack, who suddenly began firing his pistol at the ground close to Powell's feet, yelling, "Dance, you hyena tender-foot! Dance, damn you!"

The ground flew up and struck one of Powell's feet, but he only glanced at the place as though interested in Jack's marksmanship. "That isn't so bad," he smiled at the gunman.

Jack strode forward, cursing violently, but the doctor seemed oblivious to it, as he took a handsome cigarette case from his pocket, selected a cigarette with solicitous care and lighted it. Then he looked up at Jack.

The gun-man was nonplussed. He hesitated to attack an unarmed man, not because of moral scruples but the realization of the consequences to himself. Jack had not seen the men of the Diamond H who were grouped alertly back of him, each man's pistol ready.

Measuring the weight and height of Powell, Jack, who was much larger, shoved his pistol into the holster, saying, "I don't care to pot a jack-rabbit."

Powell made no move. Jack advanced in front of him, thrust his face against the doctor's and snarled, "Well, what are you going to do about that warrant, Mr. What-d'ye call 'em?"

"Oh, nothing except arrest you," was the calm reply as the doctor puffed a little volcano of cigarette smoke into Jack's face and looked him steadily in the eyes. "I am unarmed," said Powell loudly enough to be heard by all the bystanders, "but I believe you are too much of a coward to face any man without your gun, even though you know he is unarmed."

Goaded by the challenge, Jack ripped out an oath, unbuckled his pistol belt and handed it to a bystander, who accepted it with evident reluctance.

"Now, come along," yelled the gunman. "Come along and arrest me, if you can-but before you do it I'm going to take you across my knee and give you a regular spanking like your mother used to do, sonny."

He reached forward. Before any one knew what had happened, Three-fingered Jack was sprawling on the ground, while Powell sat quietly astride the man's chest, holding Jack's arms with his own knees. Jack writhed and struggled, but was unable to disturb the man who smiled down at him. As Jack's curses increased, Powell deliberately patted the outlaw's face gently, saying in soothing accents, "Don't let your temper rise, Jack! It isn't becoming in such a regular little Mama's darling like you!"

Howls of laughter roused Jack to the realization that his reputation was at stake. He broke into threats of dire revenge on Powell. The doctor paid no attention to the man who was helpless in the grip of steel, but merely asked, "Has any one here a rope that I could borrow a short time?"

Jack stopped cursing, and a disagreeable recollection intruded itself upon him. A man had asked for a rope in Wyoming. The crowd had cut Jack down before he was entirely unconscious, and Jack had emigrated to Arizona without delay.

Powell had no such intention. The rope was employed to truss the "gun" man from head to feet, like a fly wound in a spider's web. An involuntary murmur of approval passed among the men who had seen the episode, but at that moment Glendon staggered through the crowd and before any one could move, levelled a pistol at Powell.

"Take that rope off," he shouted with a volley of the foulest oaths at his command.

"Don't interfere," warned Powell, facing Glendon.

"You take that rope off or I'll put daylight through you, you white-livered sneak," screamed the other man.

His words died away in a thud, as Powell sprang at him like a wild-cat, clasping him about the arms and falling heavily to the ground with Glendon sprawled underneath. The pistol in Glendon's hand flew through the air, struck the ground and exploded harmlessly in the dust.

"I'll need another rope," apologized Powell in unruffled tones. "I'm sorry to trouble you again."

There was a laugh, and in less time than it takes to relate, Glendon was as helpless as Jack. The sight of them lying side by side was too much for the gravity of the crowd, and laughter was unrestrained. Powell looked down at Glendon, but there was no triumph in his heart. A woman's pleading face rose between him and the man at his feet who was voicing his vile thoughts and threats. Three-fingered Jack turned his head slightly and there was a twitch of the "gun" man's mouth, but he made no remark.

The driver of the one and only town truck was standing on the seat of his wagon surveying the captured men. Powell called to him, "How much will you charge to haul this load to the calaboose?"

"Do it for nothing," replied the driver promptly.

So he and Powell, assisted by many volunteers, lifted the mummy-like forms into the wagon, then the entire assemblage followed behind the vehicle as it moved slowly down the street.

"Gee!" laughed Holy, "That was the funniest sight I ever seed in my life."

"Looks like the funeral of a real, respectable citizen," squeaked Roarer.

"Well, it's Jack's funeral, sure enough," answered Limber. "He's a dead 'bad man' from now on, but the doctor has won his spurs, you bet!"

The wagon stopped in front of the little adobe building which was used as the town jail, and Powell assisted the driver to lift the prisoners bodily into the room which took the place of a cell. The ropes were removed. Jack and Glendon stood free in front of their captor. He eyed them in silence a few seconds, then said, "I want you both to understand that I had no personal feeling in anything I did. Law is law, whether in Arizona or any other place. Gun-play is for bullies, not men."

Neither replied. Powell picked up the two ropes and left the place. Outside he found Limber waiting, but there was no reference to what had just taken place. Powell handed the ropes to Limber and asked him to locate the owners, then the doctor continued down the street to the office of the Justice of Peace, who smiled at him cordially.

"It was just a simple trick of jiu-jitsu," explained Powell. "But now I want to know how much the fine will be for Jack and Glendon?"

"Thirty dollars, or thirty days in the Tombstone jail," answered the Justice.

Powell reached across the desk and appropriated a pen which he dipped into the ink-well. He drew out his check-book, saying, "I suppose this is permissable?" The Judge nodded.

"It may be a little hard on them to pay the fine," Powell spoke as he wrote. "I don't want them to know who did it. Keep the matter between ourselves. They have had a lesson, I think."

"The best in the world," responded the Judge, smiling at his recollection of the two trussed figures in the wagon.

It was only a short time later that Limber hunted up the Judge and volunteered to stand good for any fine imposed on Glendon. When he was told that another person had assumed the responsibility already, for both men, Limber left the office feeling pretty certain that Powell had anticipated his own intention. But neither of them ever spoke of the matter.

When the full moon peered over the horizon that night, it shone on two men who rode slowly toward the Hot Springs ranch, each of them glad to be back again in the peace of the mountains. And down in a cell, the moonlight flooded the floor criss-crossed with black bars from the window, and two men lay thinking in the silent hours of the night, but like the men who rode to the Springs, neither of them told his inmost thoughts to the other. Some thoughts are too holy to be spoken aloud; others too black.

The next morning Glendon and Jack, thoroughly sobered, were brought before the Judge for their hearing. After a sharp warning that a second offense would mean much heavier penalty, a fine of thirty dollars each was imposed. "I can't pay it, Judge," confessed Jack, frankly. "I'm broke, owe three months advance wages and have to find a job."

"Maybe Glendon can pay both fines until you are able to work it out," suggested the Judge amiably.

"I've got all I can do to pay my own," was the surly reply. "Unless Norton will advance it, I'm stuck."

"It seems too bad to have to send you both to the Tombstone jail for thirty days, boys," sympathized the Justice. "If the offense had not been so serious, I might have held you in the calaboose; but the charge was not only disturbing the peace, but also resisting an officer."

A grin spread over Jack's face. "Say, Judge, that's a real joke! Did you see how fur we resisted? Well, I guess we deserved it, and it's up to us to take our medicine like little men."

"I'm glad to hear you say that, Jack. Now, I want you both to give me your word of honour that you will not make any further disturbance in Willcox after this."

"All right," Jack answered readily, looking squarely into the Judge's face. "I don't hold any grudge against Powell. I own up he's a better man than I am."

"Glendon?"

"I wouldn't have made such an ass of myself if I had been sober," was Glendon's evasive answer, while he eyed a knot hole in the board at his feet.

"Both fines have been already paid."

They looked up amazed. "Who was it?" demanded Jack.

"I am not at liberty to tell," was the reply.

Jack stared a moment, then a smile spread over his face, "By Gosh! I bet it was that doctor!" he exclaimed. "Say, Judge if it was him, will you tell him I'm much obliged, and that he's a white man, and I'll lick the stuffing out of any one that picks on him, if he just lets me know anytime!"

Glendon made no comments as he left the office, but Jack turned back at the threshold to call, "I'm going to get out of town as fast as I can, Judge. I've got to hustle for a job so I can pay back that fine. I'll see that the money gets to you p. d. q. So long!"

"Good luck, boys," answered the Judge heartily. Then turned to his desk and papers, thinking that there was more manhood to the "gun man" than the one who accompanied him. The two walked side by side in apparent friendliness until Jack said, "Well, that was a surprise party all around, Glen. I bet I hit the bull's eye guessing it was the doctor."

Glendon's eyes glinted angrily at Jack's open praise of Powell. "He certainly made a laughing-stock of you," snarled Glendon. "Threw you down, trussed you up like a Christmas turkey, loaded you in the town truck, and now you are ready to lick his boots in gratitude after he puts the last insult on you by paying your fine. Pah! You make me sick!"

Jack gripped the other man's arm angrily. "See, here, Glen! I'm not such a mollycoddle that I won't fight you or any other man that talks that way to me." Jack stood glaring down at Glendon, who returned the angry stare. Then a grin started on Jack's face, and he drawled slowly, "Don't see that you've got any call over me, Glen. There was two Christmas turkeys, but you did the loudest gobbling. Don't you ever forget that!"

"I'm not apt to," retorted the other. "I never would have been mixed up in it if I hadn't been trying to help you out."

"And I wouldn't have started anything if it hadn't been for you egging me on. You said he was a tenderfoot. Tenderfoot! Wow! I'd like to know what kind of bad men they have where he came from, if he's a tenderfoot!" He paused to ponder over the possibilities of such an individual. "See, here, Glen, so long as Powell minds his business, I'll mind mine; and if you've got a grudge against him on account of his getting the Springs, you needn't try to get me to take it out on him for you."

Glendon's face was white with rage. "I suppose that means you are going to take backwater on everything and join some Church and shout 'Hallelujah! I'm saved!' Eh?"

"It means just what I said. If you've got any pick on Powell that is your own business. As far as the other plans go, the cards are dealt already, and I'll stand pat."

# Chapter Twenty-One

Three months after Glendon and Jack had encountered Doctor Powell in Willcox, Katherine was sitting on the porch of her home reading to Donnie. The noise of crunching wheels sounded far down the cañon long before a vehicle came into sight between the dense mesquite brush.

It was Doctor Powell who had returned from a trip to Willcox. Katherine watched her husband receive his mail, but she was not aware that the eyes of the two men met with unconcealed antagonism, and the conversation was as curt as possible.

No whisper of the affair in Willcox had reached the ears of Glendon's wife. She had no knowledge that her husband had borrowed money to send to the Judge without a word of thanks to his unknown benefactor. The money had been forwarded to Powell by the Judge. The other fine was sent the Judge by Three-fingered Jack, accompanied by a badly scrawled note of thanks addressed to the Justice of Peace and asking that the man who had paid the fine be told that it was appreciated, and that if he ever needed any help to call on Three-fingered Jack.

Aware of Glendon's dislike, Powell's visits to the Circle Cross had ceased some time previous to the Willcox trouble, but Katherine ascribed the doctor's aloofness to his knowledge of her husband's habits. Though she missed the infrequent visits, she did not resent it. She knew that the two men had nothing in common to make them congenial.

The doctor, seeing Katherine and Donnie on the porch, hesitated as he was about to drive away. He glanced at them, and with a touch of his hat in greeting, stepped into the buggy and went on his way. The happy light faded from Donnie's eyes, but without a word he slipped down again beside his mother, his arm about Tatters' neck.

Glendon came slowly to the porch with the canvas mail-pouch on his arm. He threw off his broad-brimmed Stetson, unbuckled his spurs and sat down to read his letters without vouchsafing a word to his wife.

"Is there nothing for me?" she asked finally, hesitating to take the sack from his lap and sort its contents.

"Only papers and some of your fool magazines," he snapped. "Seems to me you are old enough to get over reading sentimental trash."

Unmindful of his words she reached for the books he tossed angrily toward her. Books were the only antidote for the mental atrophy she dreaded. Rising, she picked them up, but paused as Glendon glanced impatiently from a letter in his hands.

"Wait, can't you? Or is the 'continued in our next' too important?" he demanded.

She did not reply, but seated herself quietly. Her eyes were unusually bright, for on a page of the magazine she held, she had seen a title. A thrill akin to that when she had first held Donnie in her arms, made her heart throb quickly.

Donnie had been flesh of her flesh, bone of her bone; but this, the first-born of her brain, had come through travail of her very soul. It was not necessary for her to read the eight lines of the poem; they were indelibly imprinted on her memory. A mother cannot forget the face of her child, and though it be commonplace and unattractive to all the world, in her eyes it is beautiful.

Glendon's voice brought her back from her world of dreams.

"I wish you'd stop sitting there staring like a locoed calf, and pay attention to what I have to say."

She turned her eyes on him. "I'm sorry, Jim. I didn't hear you speak."

"I didn't," he snapped. "No use talking when you have a mooning fit on."

"I am listening, dear. What is it?"

"Here's a letter from the old man. He wants Donald. You can see for yourself what he says."

Glendon handed her the letter, allowing it to drop from his fingers purposely, watching her as she reached down and picked it up.

As she read, a grey pallor spread over her face, making it look old and haggard.

J. M. Glendon, Jr.
Circle Cross Ranch, Arizona.


Dear Sir:


From reliable sources I have learned of your conduct since you went to Arizona, and understand that my ambition to see my son a man among men will never be gratified; nor will your influence or example make such a man of my grandson, Donald. The full realization of this has prompted me to break my determination never to communicate with you again on any subject.

Your wife is too egotistical and assertive, and her influence over the boy cannot fail to be detrimental. Women have no idea how to bring up a boy, especially college-bred women with their fads and theories. They have no judgment outside of flattery; they are all fools, —I do not care where you go, or who the woman may be, —and the man who tries to please a woman's whims is a fool.

My lawyer tells me that under the laws of Arizona you are absolute guardian of your child; so the decision as to my offer rests entirely with you. Your wife, legally, has no voice in the matter of selecting a school or any other arrangements you may see fit to make. It is time for you to assert yourself.

I will take Donald and educate him, provided he is given to me absolutely until he is of age, but I will not allow any interference with him or my plans for him. I will see that he does not grow up with any sickly, sentimental ideas, but to weigh his own interests first, without illusions about life or women. He will be taught that all women are inferior in intellect and reason, weak in moral force and must be treated accordingly. If he is sent to me, I will see that he is provided for during my lifetime, and at my death he will receive what you have forfeited by your own conduct.

I have selected a school for him which he can attend from my house, and where he will receive the training I consider necessary to make him the kind of man I desire. An immediate answer will oblige.

Yours truely,
J. M. Glendon, Sr.

The pages fluttered to the floor of the porch, and then Donnie looked up startled at the tone of his mother's voice, when she said, "Run away and play with Tatters, dear."

With a hasty caress, the boy, followed by the dog, moved slowly toward the front gate.

"Well," Glendon's irritable tones sounded in her ears, "how soon can you get him ready?"

"Let me keep him a little longer, Jim," pleaded the mother. "He's only a baby yet."

"He's going on seven," retorted Glendon. "You've always been harping on wanting him to have a good education. Now you've got your wish, I don't see what kick you've got coming. I'll never have money enough to send him away to school unless the old man helps me more than he has done the last five years."

Curbing her inclination to remind him bitterly that other men who were not drinking, but attending to their ranches and stock, were able to afford schools for their children, she said, "It has been my ambition ever since he was born, but there are other things more important to his character that I can teach him in the next two years."

Glendon lighted a cigarette and an ugly sneer distorted his lips, "Want to tie him to your apron-strings, the way you had me tied? Fine mess you've made of it for me! If you hadn't been so high-headed with my folks, I never would have left home to come to this God-forsaken hole and bury myself alive!"

"I hoped it would strengthen you, help you conquer yourself if we came away from companions who dominated you back there; but I was wrong. All your better instincts are dead and there is nothing left between us in common. Jim, if ever you had any love in your heart for me, don't send Donnie away just now. Have you forgotten that prisoners go mad from solitary confinement?"

"Your dramatics are wasted on me! I intend to be master in my own home. Father shall have the boy if he wishes, and I hope he will knock some of those fool ideas you have been putting into Donnie's head lately. They'll mould his character into something practical."

"They do not understand children," Katherine's voice trembled, "your father means well, but Donnie would learn to be a hypocrite through fear of him, or it would break the child's heart. When Donnie is older, he would understand better."

"Go ahead!" Glendon's lip lifted one side of his mouth and gave him the appearance of a dog snarling. His bloodshot eyes glared at his wife. "I say the boy shall go. That settles it!"

"You shall not take him from me," Katherine spoke passionately as she rose and faced her husband, who had also risen. "He is mine! For his sake I have endured the isolation of this place, the curses and abuse you have heaped upon me, the degradation that I saw facing you. I have not been blind to the class of men you associate with now, but I struggled to keep you from sinking lower, just because you were the father of my boy. The last eight years of my life have been continual mental starvation and moral crucifixion. Donnie has given me the strength to bear it, now he will give me the strength to keep you from robbing me of him!"

"You may as well stop your hysterical ranting," Glendon shouted furiously. "The law gives the boy to me, and I say he shall go to father next week."

"The law gives the child to the father," her voice quivered with indignation, "No matter what that father may be; while the mother, who goes down to death to give the child life, has no right! Oh, it is infamous! Why, even the wild animals recognize a mother's rights. Men who frame such a law and enforce it are worse than brutes!"

Glendon seized her arm roughly and glared into her white, defiant face, his own was livid with rage. "Nothing on God's earth can prevent Donnie from going."

"He shall not go!" her voice became suddenly quiet and determined, and her eyes met Glendon's without flinching. "You owe him to me in return for the things of which you have robbed us both. He has never had a father, never dared to laugh like other children do, because he was afraid of you. I will not never give him up to you or any one else. He is mine!"

Glendon thrust her away from him with such violence that she staggered. "I have the law back of me and I'll do what I say, if I have to walk over your dead body to do it!"

He flung himself into the house, knocking over a chair as he passed it; then a bottle clinked against a glass.

The leaves of the magazine at the woman's feet, fluttered in the breeze while she stared with despairing eyes at the grim mountains that walled her like a prison.

# Chapter Twenty-Two

The next morning was Wednesday, and Glendon announced that he would start East with Donnie on Saturday of the following week.

Katherine made no reply, uttered no protest. He supposed the silence of despair meant submission, as he and Juan started for Allan Flats, half way to Willcox, to be gone several days.

"I'll be home Sunday night," were his last words as he spurred his horse and headed it toward the road leading out of the cañon. Juan lingered a few seconds to say "Adios" to the mother and child. The old Mexican carried a heavy heart, for no one but the child was ignorant of the impending separation.

The day passed happily for Donnie, while his mother devoted her entire time to him. They strolled down the cañon, picking wild-flowers, then returning home, decorated the rooms and discovered that Juan had made a chocolate layer cake for their enjoyment. After supper they sat talking of the wonderful things Donnie was to do when he was grown. Then followed an hour in the dining-room with the beloved Galahad.

The next morning at breakfast, Donnie asked, "What are we going to do today, Marmee?"

"Just whatever you wish," she answered with smiling lips, but sad eyes.

"Can't we go on a picnic, Marmee?"

"Yes, dear," was her reply. "I'll fix a lunch and saddle the ponies and we'll be adventurers riding out to discover a new country, and we won't come home till the stars are out."

Donnie waited happily as his mother prepared the lunch. With practised fingers she saddled their ponies; on the boy's saddle, tied a canteen of water and the flour-sack containing lunch, while on her own was fastened a roll of Navajo blankets.

Katherine determined to snatch all the happiness possible for the child and herself during her husband's absence. Today she would forget that there must be a tomorrow; today the child was her own, despite his father, despite the laws of the Territory which said she had no right to her boy. So her smile met the child's laughter as they mounted their ponies and rode down the slope of the cañon to the place where the trail struck up the divide leading to Jackson Flats.

It was a tortuous trail. At times, going up the brushy mountain sides, where cat-claw, mesquite, cacti and mescal struggled between immense rocks. Disturbed quail, rabbits, an enormous lizard-the harmless brother of the poisonous Gila Monster-dashed across the trail. Each tiny incident was food for animated conversation between the two riders; a new flower, a change of view as they reached a certain point. In places there was hardly room for their sure-footed ponies to travel single file. One side of the trail was a high, rocky cliff, while the other side dropped a thousand feet below. A displaced rock clattered down the gully, startling a mountain-lion which leaped from a freshly killed calf and skulked away. A coyote appeared between boulders on the opposite side of the cañon, squatted down and watched the riders curiously.

Half way up the mountain they rode into a cave that was large enough to shelter twenty horses and men. The domed roof rose forty feet and the sides of the cave were painted with curious emblems of a dead and unknown people. The floor was strewn with bits of broken earthen pottery, decorated with the same characters as the walls. A few arrowheads of green and black flint were scattered among the fragments of pottery; all that was left to tell the history of those who had loved, hated, laughed and wept-then died.

It had been a favourite ride for the mother and child, and the relics had made foundation for many games and stories. So the boy gathered pieces of the pottery and amused himself trying to match them together, in emulation of his mother. As they worked she told him the history of those who had lived in this cave and fashioned the earthen jars. After a couple of hours the novelty wore off, and Donnie wanted to ride further.

"We can go to the top of the Box," said his mother. "You've never been there yet; but it will be a hard climb."

The child begged to try it, for she had told him that when they reached the top of the mountain they could see far across other hill-tops, beyond the San Pedro River-an unknown world to him.

After she had tightened the cinches of the saddles and they were mounted, she instructed the boy, "Lean well forward in your saddle and hold the horn tightly, dear. Give Pet a loose rein and you will not have any trouble at all. He will follow Fox. It is a hard climb, and if you jerk on the reins you will make Pet fall back."

The horses headed what appeared almost a perpendicular wall. Donnie saw Fox stretch his body like a greyhound and fairly hurl himself in leaps at the steep incline, scattering stones in every direction. Pet stood a moment, undecided, then with a shrill whinny started after Fox. Donnie grasped the horn of the saddle and clung to it desperately, leaning forward and shutting his eyes. His back jerked, his head wouldn't keep still, his heart beat violently.

"If Pet would only keep still a minute," thought the child. "Suppose Fox were to fall with Marmee, what would I do?"

He pulled on the reins, but Pet, watching Fox, fought the bit, and lunged ahead.

As if in answer to Donnie's thoughts, his mother's voice drifted cheerily back to him: "Almost there, dear.  Tired?"

"Just a little bit," he replied, trying to be brave, but wishing he could ride up beside her and hold her hand a minute. Then he remembered Galahad had ridden alone, and knights were not afraid of anything. He pretended that the trail led to the castle of an enemy and he was going to rescue those held prisoners, so with bolstered courage, he kept his eyes open and fixed on the horse ahead of him.

They reached a sharp knoll that formed the apex of the mountain; and after slipping from the ponies and tying them to a stunted bit of scrub oak, Katherine clasped Donnie's hand in her own, and together they approached the edge of the cliff, and peered cautiously over.

Two thousand feet below was the cañon, but where they gazed, four solid walls arose like a gigantic box without a cover. There was no entrance or exit. The Mexicans called the place El Cajon, or the Box. Grass, flowers, trees and a trickling stream from a spring lay at the bottom of the Box, but nothing living could reach there. The walls were as straight and sheer as the name of the place implied.

They drew back from inspecting it, and at Katherine's suggestion Donnie gathered wild flowers to decorate the table on which she spread the lunch. The mother made a pretense at eating, but the memory of the impending separation thrust itself on her despite her determination to forget it this one day. Neither she nor Glendon had told the child, so no shadow of tragedy spoiled his enjoyment.

The ride had tired him, and after lunch was over, she arranged the Navajo blankets. He stretched out lazily, watching his mother draw his favourite book from her saddlebag. Then he curled up with a sigh of ecstasy.

"Where shall I read?" she asked, smiling down at him.

"How Sir Galahad was made a knight," he answered, "and about the Siege Perilous."

So she read until the brown head nodded and the eyes closed slowly, then seeing the boy slept, she laid the book aside, sitting motionless and watching him with miserable eyes.

A white-winged butterfly flitted past her and hovered over the boy's hand, finally settling lightly on it then darting on its way. She recalled the story of the baby Galahad in his mother's arms and the white dove that had flown through the window, and the words of the maiden who bore the Sangreal, "And he shall be a much better knight than his father."

A mother-quail with her tiny brood slipped from the brush, peering about as she came forward. Fearing nothing from the sleeping child or the mother who did not move, the quail called her little ones about her and shared with them the discovery of some crumbs. Katherine watched them enviously; then her eyes strayed to the child. Rebellion against the law, against her husband, his father, and life itself, overwhelmed her. The quail had more right to its brood than she had to her child.

The shadows lengthened as she sat fighting her battle, all the training and beliefs of years falling from her.

What was the use of fighting any longer? She looked at the Box. It was so quiet down there; no one could take Donnie away from her. Just a step, and they would be safe together.

Her lips grew tense, and smoothing a piece of paper that had been wrapped about the lunch, she searched the saddle pocket until she found a stump of pencil, with which she wrote:

Jim:

I could not give up my boy to have him learn that money was the only thing worth-while —to be cruel and self-indulgent as your father wants him to be. I told you that you owed him to me in payment of your debt. The law refuses my child to me; you, too, would rob me of him, even though you know it will break his heart and mine.

I prayed God to aid me, and He will not answer my prayers. When you read this, Donnie and I will be together at the bottom of the Box. I did the best I could for you, and failed; but I will not fail with the boy.

Katherine.

Her hand was firm as she signed her name, and folding the paper, she tied it to a stone which she placed in the empty sack that had contained the lunch. The stone would attract attention when the sack was untied. Securing the sack to her side-saddle, she removed the halter-ropes from the ponies' necks; then slipping both bridles, she tied them to Donnie's saddle. If the horses did not go home at once, or should there be no one at the Circle Cross for a couple of days, she knew the animals could graze and water and would not suffer. They had left Tatters in the stables with water and food. She wished now that she had taken the dog back to its former master. It would miss them.

Heading the horses toward the Hot Springs trail, she slashed Fox across the flank with her whip. The animal gave a snort of surprise then dashed toward home, while Pet stumbled and tugged behind him down the narrow trail. She watched them disappear around the curve; but later she heard the tumbling of small rocks and knew her message was on its way to Glendon.

Walking to the edge of the Box she looked down unflinchingly. There was plenty time. When everything was dark and quiet, it would be easy to take the sleeping child in her arms; then neither man nor law could take him from her.

## Chapter Twenty-Three

Doctor Powell, lured by Chappo's description of the cave on Jackson trail, had reached the place an hour after Katherine and Donnie had started for the Box. It was while examining the designs on the various bits of pottery that he found fragments of broken geodes, and eagerly continued his search, which was rewarded with several specimens that were unbroken.

Powell, who was deeply interested in geology, knew there were few places where the curious white crystals were found, and his delight was augmented when he discovered two of them in which the water could be distinctly heard; moisture which had fallen on hot lava that had hardened too quickly to allow evaporation.

He was engaged in wrapping these rare specimens in his handkerchief, when he heard his horse whinny, and as he moved to the entrance of the cave, noticed Fox and Pet picking their way down the steep trail. He saw the saddles and that the ponies were tied together, so concluded the horses had broken away and were homeward bound, leaving Katherine and Donnie afoot higher up on the trail.

Powell waited until the ponies stood beside his horse. Then he moved quietly and secured them with his tie-rope, and mounted his horse to lead the strays up the trail. He had no thought of any danger to Katherine or Donnie, until a turn in the trail revealed the top of the climb and a woman standing perilously near the edge of the cliff. He dared not call out, for fear of startling her and precipitating a tragedy; but he dropped the rope of the two horses and urged his own forward.

Beads of perspiration stood on his forehead and his teeth bit into his lower lip. The horse puffed and stumbled, for the big Spanish spurs slashed its sides without mercy. Fox and Pet scrambled behind, the tie-ropes dragging on the ground.

He reached the summit and closed his eyes, fearing he was too late. With a throb of relief he saw Katherine still poised at the edge of the Box, while bits of decomposed earth crumbled unnoticed beneath her feet. He realized her danger. Chappo had spoken of the treacherous shale overhanging the Box.

So engrossed was the woman that she did not hear him slip from his horse and hasten noiselessly to her side; but, when his hand grasped her arm, gently, yet firmly, she turned in shrinking fear that changed to piteous appeal when she saw it was Powell, not Glendon, who stood beside her.

The man read the tragedy in her eyes. Slowly he drew her from the danger point, speaking quietly as he did so.

"This place is not safe, Mrs. Glendon. A moment's dizziness might seize anyone." The earth at the edge was crumbling as he spoke, a chunk of it crashed down into the cañon below, and Powell drew her further back. "That shale is rotten and liable to slide without an instant's warning. I was in an Indian cave when I saw the ponies had gotten away from you and Donnie."

She knew he was giving her a chance to evade explanations, but the woman had reached a point where she scorned further subterfuge. When one faces Eternity all else shrivels to insignificance. "I was not dizzy," she replied in a dull monotone. Then turning on him passionately, she cried, "Why did you come? Do you know Donnie is going away from me? In three days more my boy will be taken out of my life and given to strangers who care nothing for him? Why should we go on struggling? I am tired of it all!"

In a flash he understood her purpose, and knew the horses had not escaped accidentally.

"And you thought that you could keep him with you-down there?" Powell asked in a voice unsteady with emotion.

She looked at him defiantly. "Yes, you may call it a crime; but I am willing to bear the punishment if there is another world-if there is another world! It is a worse crime to take a child from its mother and give it to the father-no matter how unworthy he may be! I have borne everything for the boy's sake; I could go on-bearing everything the rest of my life-if I could only keep my boy!"

Her voice dropped. Powell saw that her hands and limbs were shaken with tremors. "I love him enough to give him up with a smile, if I could know that it was for his good. My only happiness lies in knowing I have done the best I could for him."

He silently waited the reaction that must come. Her hands covered her face; then a terrible sob shook her body. It was not the sharp cry of remorse; but the terrible soul-rending cry of a heart that is near to breaking, and the man beside her ached to take her in his arms and comfort her as he would a child.

"Tell me about it," he said at last, and she raised her tear-stained face.

Without reservation, she told the story of the long, bitter struggle to reform her husband; the hope that the child would bring compensation and finally the letter and her husband's decision which had driven her to desperation.

"Yet, when it came to the point, you never would have been cowardly enough to take your life and Donnie's," he asserted.

"I don't know," she faltered. "A swimmer who struggles against the tide reaches a moment when further efforts are impossible. I have struggled, prayed and fought until I am tired of it all. I want to stop thinking, stop fearing the future-and sleep. It is sometimes easier to die than to keep on living. Life is too hard, too bitter, too hopeless! You can't understand."

"But I do understand!" replied Powell earnestly. "Sometimes one reaches a stone wall where there is no way around, no way over it, yet, if we have the courage to hold on, the wall topples when we least expect it. What seems impossible today may be accomplished tomorrow. I am up against the hardest wall in my life, but I shall not give up. In the quest of the Grail there must be no faltering. We all see the vision once in life."

He laid his hands on hers, compelling her to look into his eyes. "I have heard a soldier whose bravery was beyond question, say that the impulse to seek a place of safety during a battle is almost overpowering. Many men have been unable to resist the temptation; and the pity is that often one deserts his colours just when victory is at hand. You are brave enough to face the bullets. Don't you know the man who deserts, influences many others to drop their colours too? Carry your colours bravely, comrade, that I may have the courage to go on with my fight-won't you?"

She turned impulsively and laid her two hands in his close grasp that imparted new courage. "I was a coward," she said, "but I promise I'll not give up again! You can't realize how much you have helped me! I will prove my gratitude by not running from the bullets."

The doctor smiled at her. "That's right," he said heartily; "but you overrate what I have done. You would have won the battle by yourself."

He turned then, to see Donnie looking at them from sleep-heavy eyes.

"Hello, Rip Van Winkle," called the doctor.

With a cry of delight the child leaped up and running to Powell, threw his arms about the man's neck. "Oh, you did come after all!" he cried triumphantly. Then Katherine and Powell understood how the child missed the man.

The boy's unrestrained gladness relieved the tension between his mother and the doctor. Finally Powell rose.

"Do you know, I forgot that Chappo fixed a lunch for me? Let's see what it is, Donnie. I'm getting hungry."

Katherine watched them make their way over the rough ground, the child's hand held by the man. The mingled voices happy with laughter, floated back to her from where the ponies were tied. There might be an occasional gleam of sunshine in life, if only the child were not taken from her, she thought hopefully. Then she saw them returning, carrying various articles which the doctor had extricated from his big saddle bags, and now deposited on the ground at her feet.

"Chappo knows I am a confirmed coffee-fiend," confessed Powell. "You gather some sticks, Donnie, and we'll pretend your mother is a captive queen whom we have rescued from the cannibals. I'm Crusoe and you're Friday."

"Friday was black," objected Donnie.

"Well, that was an island. This is a mountain, so you can be a white Friday here, you see."

When the fire crackled and the large cup which Chappo had provided for boiling coffee, sang merrily, the remnants of Katherine's lunch were added to what the Doctor had, so a plentiful meal was spread.

"The trail is rather bad," suggested Powell as they finished the impromptu feast, "so we had better start before it grows late."

He tightened the cinches of the three saddles and adjusted the bridles while Katherine and Donnie picked up the cups and spoons. She was replacing a few articles in a sack hanging on her saddle when she felt the rock and remembered the note she had written to her husband. Untying the sack, she tore the paper into fragments that were caught by the light evening breeze and tossed over the edge of the Box. She watched them, then with a smile turned to Powell, who waited to lift her to her pony's back. Donnie, already on his pony, followed his mother as Fox picked his way down the trail behind Powell's horse.

Six miles away the Rim Rock rose over two thousand feet or more, the massive, jagged sides reflecting a riotous confusion of colours from the setting sun, until its vivid beauty merged into a soft blue-grey, like the plumage on the breast of a wild dove.

Sometimes the boy and Powell talked together as they rode down the trail, or the mother joined in the conversation, but all the time she was conscious of a new strength, a sense of comradeship that she had never before known in her entire life. Her heart was lighter than it had been for many years when she, Powell and Donnie reached the gate of the Circle Cross. To her surprise, Glendon slouched on the porch.

It was only Thursday and Glendon had said he would be absent until Sunday night. She wondered what it meant.

Her eyes turned to the child and fear gripped her heart until it seemed as if she were suffocating. But Powell's words came back to her, "Carry your colours bravely, comrade" —She determined not to meet trouble prematurely. After all, there probably was a very natural explanation of the sudden return. Juan was coming up from the barn, carrying a pail of fresh milk. It was the usual routine of the ranch. She put her fears aside.

Powell opening the gate for Katherine and Donnie to ride through, raised his hat courteously and spoke to Glendon. It was the best way to aid Glendon's wife. The other man looked at him between half-closed eyes that were a studied insult, and made no reply. Neither did he make any effort to assist his wife.

The doctor helped her from her horse, then lifted Donnie to the ground, paying no heed to Glendon's attitude. With a few words to the woman and boy, Powell rode through the gate toward Hot Springs. His blood boiled, and it required all his will-power to avoid turning back and mauling Glendon as he deserved; but, he realized it would not help the woman.

Juan, having disposed of the milk-pail, hastened to lead the ponies to the stable. Knowing that Glendon was in one of his most surly moods, Katherine moved slowly up the steps of the porch, trying to choke back her terrible dread. "Carry your colours," she heard.

Something of the new-born hope and peace shone in her eyes as she faced her husband silently. He knew that she stood on heights he could not attain, and from which he was powerless to drag her to his own level. Enraged, he leaned closer. His unshaven face, bloodshot eyes, soiled shirt and hot breath redolent of liquor, struck her senses like a physical blow! With an effort she conquered the sickening repugnance, recalling her promise to Powell to carry her colours bravely. She smiled at her husband and was passing into the house, when he caught her arm in a brutal clutch, jerking her back so that his face was close to her own.

"Took you by surprise, coming back today, didn't I?" he said meaningly. The child stood with pale face and frightened eyes. "Thought I was out of the way, and you sneaked off to meet your affinity, using your child as a cloak! You can't fool me. If you and that dude think you are pulling the wool over my eyes, you'll find yourselves mistaken. You can tell him that, next time you and he arrange to meet each other. I thought you'd fall for the trap when I fixed it up yesterday morning."

Her face flushed deep red. She had borne every ignominy possible; but this accusation hurt like corroding acid. Her impulse to cry out in self-defense faded as she looked steadily into his wavering eyes. Like a whisper came the memory of Powell's words, "Carry your colours bravely." Quietly she answered, "Down in your heart, Jim, you don't believe what you say. Doctor Powell saved me and Donnie from death today. If he had not been riding on the Jackson trail and found us when he did, the boy and I would both have been lying at the bottom of the Box tonight."

"What were you doing up there?" he snarled, glaring at her. "More of your melodramatic drivel, as usual? Powell for an audience!"

"I wonder if it would make any difference to you if you knew the truth?" she said brokenly. "I am worn out struggling. The Box seemed the only way."

Dumbly, as though she had reached the limit of physical as well as mental endurance, she turned from him and entered the place she called home.

For a second Glendon hesitated; then with an oath he called after her: "You can't bluff me with threats of suicide. You haven't the nerve. I've said my last word about sending the boy to Father. I'm going on Monday, whether he's ready or not. I'll break your pride!"

Donnie's startled eyes widened and his face grew paler as he realized that he was to be parted from his mother. With a stifled sob the child stumbled blindly up the steps, past his father and threw himself into his mother's arms.

"Marmee! Marmee! Don't let me go!"

Katherine clasped the boy tightly, her eyes were dry, but it seemed as if her aching heart would burst with agony, knowing that she was helpless.

"Oh, God, give me the courage to live!" was her unuttered prayer.

# Chapter Twenty-Four

Limber and Powell were riding together in a deep cañon of the Galiuros. Neither had spoken for some time, for often they rode together without exchanging a word. Limber, who was slightly in advance of the doctor, stopped Peanut and leaned forward in his saddle. Then his quick glance brought Powell closer.

From the thick undergrowth ahead of them a tiny spiral of smoke rose faintly. Cautiously they urged their ponies; then through the brush, silently watched a man carrying a hot branding iron in his hand. A cow was roped and lying on the ground. The iron burned into the hide, the smell of singed hair, the bellows of pain told the story. The man's back had been toward them, but both Powell and Limber had recognized the figure and walk.

They waited. The man loosed the rope that bound the cow. It caught in a snarl, the cow struggled. With an oath, he jerked the rope, at the same time giving the animal a vicious kick on the head.

It staggered to its feet and stood dazed for a second, then darted into the brush; but not before Limber and Powell had seen the fresh brand. Limber leaned close to the doctor and whispered, "That's a PL cow and it's been changed to a BD."

The eyes of the two men met in understanding. Again they peered through the brush to see the other man rubbing the hot iron in the dirt to cool it. He turned to his horse, the iron in his hand.

An inspiration seized Powell.

"Quick! Let him know we saw him!"

Their ponies jumped forward under the spurs, but Glendon, busy tying the iron to his saddle, did not notice their presence until Peanut's hoof crackled on a loose branch. Glendon leaped to his horse, whirled it around and faced them with his hand resting on his pistol holster. It relaxed as he recognized them.

"Oh, hello!" he said affably, plainly speculating as to how long they had been watching him. Limber looked at him curiously. "Been brandin'?" he spoke in a casual voice.

"No:" answered Glendon. "I was just looking over the range. Glad we happened to meet."

Without comment, the cowpuncher rode to the still smouldering embers, slipped from his saddle, then kicked at the bits of charred and glowing wood. Before Glendon realized it, Limber reached out suddenly and touched the still hot iron fastened to Glendon's saddle.

Glendon glared at him as the cowboy said very quietly, "Looks as if your Greaser friend has come back from Mexico, Glendon. I jest seen another of them BD bunch you bought from him. It's got a fresh brand on it, too. You must of just bought it today."

Glendon's pony twisted toward Limber, Glendon's hand moved almost imperceptibly, but dropped quickly as Limber called, "Don't tech your gun, you idjit!"

The eyes of Glendon shifted cat like from Limber to Powell, then his hands rested lightly on the horn of his saddle and he leaned forward carelessly, saying, "Don't you think you two have carried your joke about far enough?"

"Joke!" vociferated the angry cowpuncher with an oath, "It means the Pen for you-if you call that a joke."

Glendon's eyes narrowed as they rested on Powell, and an expression of fury distorted his face.

"Oh, I see your little game now!" he snarled. "Going to try to railroad me to the Pen so Powell can make love to my wife. I'll see you both damned before you play your last card. I'll show both of you up-and Katherine, too!"

Two shots rang out together. The ponies reared as bullets pinged past, Powell, unarmed, looked at Limber, who stood with smoking pistol in his tense grip. The remnant of Glendon's six-shooter was lying on the ground some distance from his horse-knocked from his hand by the shot from Limber's gun. That shot had saved Powell's life.

Not one of the men spoke, but Powell who was unarmed, leaped from his horse. All the rage that had consumed him for months seethed over. He clutched at Glendon, dragged him, despite his struggles, from his horse, and then face to face they met. All the knowledge of the misery inflicted on Katherine by this man, lent additional strength to Powell's blows, while Glendon's hatred responded in full. It was caveman against caveman, with bare hands for weapons.

The fight was short but sharp. Though Glendon was a much larger man than Powell, and had once been able to hold his own with the gloves or at wrestling, years of dissipation told on him now. A crashing blow from the doctor stretched him on the ground motionless for several seconds; then his eyes opened and looked into the grim faces of the two men who stood watching him.

"Get up," ordered Powell.

Glendon dragged himself to his feet, swayed dizzily and passed his hand over his dazed eyes; slowly he moved to a fallen tree and dropped heavily on it.

"What are you going to do?" he asked sullenly. "Send me up? You won't get her that way. She'll stick to me."

Powell stepped to Glendon's side, his face white with fury, his hands clenched ominously. "Keep your wife's name off your dirty tongue," he commanded tensely, "or, by God! I'll kill you."

Glendon knew it was no idle threat, and his eyes sought the ground until he was roused by Powell handing him a note book and fountain pen.

"What's this for?" he demanded with an oath.

"Write what I dictate," Powell answered.

Glendon's head jerked angrily, "I will write nothing," he retorted.

"You have ten minutes to do as I say;" Powell's voice was like flint, and so were the angry eyes that regarded the man at his feet. "Write. 'This is to confess that John Burritt and Doctor Powell caught me changing a PL cow to a BD and marking it with the Circle Cross."

Glendon laughed contemptuously. "Do you think I'm such a fool as to sign a paper that will send me to the penitentiary?"

"It's the only way that you can keep from going there," was Powell's reply.

"Suppose I sign it?"

"Then, so long as you stop your crooked work and behave decently, no one will know of this episode except myself and Limber. In case you try to coerce your wife in any way, or take Donnie from her as you plan, this paper will be used by us to help her keep her boy. A woman has no legal right to her child in Arizona, but neither has the father if he is a convict. So it's up to you. I give you ten minutes."

The doctor seated himself on a boulder, holding his open watch in his hand, while Glendon sat staring at the ground in helpless fury.

"Time's up," announced Powell, snapping the cover of his watch and placing it in his pocket, "Well, what is your answer?"

"I'll write what you say," muttered Glendon, reaching out for the pen and notebook.

Powell repeated the words while Glendon with shaking hand signed his name to the confession. His face was white with rage as he returned the book to Powell.

"Sign as a witness, please, Limber;" and the cowpuncher signed his name, "John C. Burritt," beneath which was written, "Cuthbert Powell," and the date. Then the doctor pocketed the pen and book.

"You might as well know," commented Powell, "that this paper will be forwarded immediately to my attorneys in the East, with instructions how to act in event of any stray bullet or other mysterious accident happening to Limber or me. Our safety is your only protection. Now, I think we understand each other perfectly."

Glendon made no answer. The three men mounted their ponies, rode through the cañon, climbed the backbone of the mountain and worked down the narrow trail that merged into the road leading to the Hot Springs. None of them spoke. Each was busy with his own thoughts.

As they approached the Hot Springs ranch, Powell looked critically at Glendon's bruised eye and swollen hands. It was a purely professional survey, and Glendon recognized it as such when the doctor spoke.

"Come in," was the curt command. "You can't let your wife see you that way, unless you want me to tell her the whole truth."

Glendon hesitated, then reined his pony at the gate and dismounted painfully.

Though Powell's hands were deft and light, Glendon knew they were not ministering lovingly, while they bandaged the bruises they had inflicted. It goaded him to submit; but he had no alternative. Limber sat watching the two men. The room was silent save for the doctor's movements.

"That will do," he said at last, and Glendon rose from the chair, his hands bandaged and one eye covered with a patch. "Limber, you may ride down with him, and tell Mrs. Glendon that her husband met with an accident and we were lucky enough to be near; but there is nothing to cause her any anxiety so long as her husband is careful," he regarded Glendon steadily as he uttered these words.

Then without further addressing his patient, the doctor turned into his bedroom, carrying the bandages with him, and Glendon, with the suppressed fury of a volcano, followed the cowboy to the gate.

From a window, Powell watched them ride side by side down the road toward the Circle Cross. With grim satisfaction he recalled the fight in the cañon. He knew that Limber would deliver his message to Glendon's wife, and that Glendon would not contradict it.

When Limber returned, he reported to the doctor that Mrs. Glendon would care for the patient, and she sent her thanks to Doctor Powell. Limber's eyes had a lurking twinkle that was reflected in Powell's.

"It's plumb lucky you thought about fixin' things so's he can't take Donnie away from her," the cowpuncher spoke in admiration. "I'd a never thought of it."

For the first time the doctor told Limber of the desperation of the mother, and the narrow averting of a terrible tragedy in the Box. Limber's face was white and his grey eyes glazed.

"Doc, do you mean ter tell me that she ain't got no right to Donnie? An' Glen kin take him away anytime he wants to?"

"That is the way the law stands now, Limber. I looked up the matter through a lawyer in Tucson after I came to live at the Springs and saw the terrible struggle she was making. She does not believe in divorce, but even if she did, the law is on his side; so long as he keeps from being classed as a criminal. If she leaves Glendon, he can keep the child."

"If I'd knowed that," Limber spoke very quietly, "I wouldn't have been so careful aimin' at that pistol in his hand, when he pulled his gun on you and you wasn't armed."

"Well, it worked out still better," responded Powell, "We've got him just where we want him now, thank God!"

Limber stared at the cigarette rings above his head, and sat thinking for quite a while, before he said, "Some day somethin's goin' to bust them laws. It takes a heap to wake people up, but when they get woke up they'll be like the ol' white horse and the China pump at the Diamond H.

"You see, we uster work him at the big pond, and the water was pumped from the well with an' ol' fashioned pump called a China pump. That was before the Boss got gasoline engines. You may believe me, or not, Doc, but it was that ol' white horse that got the first engine on the ranch. For five years ol' Whitey was hitched up to the cross-bar and a blinder put across his eyes, then he was started, an' once he started, he jest kept on goin' round and round without nobody watching him and he never knowed the difference.

"But one day he stopped short, and of course, thar warn't no water pumpin', the troughs was dry and the cattle bawlin' their heads off. Me and the Boss rid near, and went over to see what was makin' the trouble. The cows was climbin' over each other's backs trying to get a drink. Well, we found ol' Whitey's blind had slid down so he could see outen one eye.

"I fixed it back and said, 'Gittap,' expectin' he would go long jest as he always done, but Whitey never moved a step.

"I touched him with my quirt, and then that ol' horse that was old enough to die three times over and had never done a mean thing in his life, turned loose and kicked the stuffin' outen the woodwork of that pump as far as he could reach."

Limber paused in retrospection, and Powell said, "What happened next?"

"Northin' happened. That was the trouble. They never could use him again on the pump; and every other horse we tried had to have a man stay with it, because Whitey was the only one that had worked without bein' watched, you see. So the Boss put in the gasoline engine down thar. When Whitey found he was bein' fooled into jest goin' around and around and never gettin' nowhar, he up and busted things good and plenty. An' that's the way with people when the blind slips off. Someday, some one's blind is goin' to slip down and then thar'll be Hell to pay with that law in Arizona!"

"If the men who frame the laws could see each individual affected unjustly by that law, standing before them and know how it could be twisted to injure a life, they would be more careful in enacting a law. Do you think for a minute, Limber, that any man, or body of men, who passed the law giving a father sole right to his children, would endorse that law today-if they knew what you and I know about Glendon and his wife?"

"No! You bet thar isn't a decent man in Arizona that would stand for it," Limber answered emphatically, "But it's thar, and we can't help it now. Only I wisht I knowed all this yesterday, that's all. Arizona's got some good laws. One of 'em is that the feller what draws on an unarmed man, ain't got no right to live hisself."

## Chapter Twenty-Five

Sunday morning Katherine woke in dread. Tomorrow, Donnie would leave her. The child now realized the truth and his grief had torn her heart. His eyes followed her in mute appeal.

Breakfast was eaten in silence. Afterward Glendon mounted his horse and rode from the ranch alone. He spoke not a word to Juan or Katherine, and Donnie watching furtively, kept out of his father's sight as much as possible.

Through a window Katherine watched her husband ride away. A look of determination shone in her eyes when she turned back to the work of clearing the dining-table. The look grew, while she washed the dishes and straightened the house. Juan was chopping wood and Donnie sat quietly on the steps of the front porch, his troubled eyes clouded with tears that he would not let his mother see.

"Juan," called Katherine suddenly from the kitchen window.

The Mexican let the ax fall from his hand and trotted to her, "Si, Señora," he smiled.

"I'm going to write a letter. Can I trust you with it?"

She did not need words to assure her of his faithfulness but he answered, as he made the Sign of the Cross, "On my heart I swear it, Señora!"

He went back to his wood-chopping, while Katherine seated herself at the dining-table and began writing. It was a desperate hope. Only the thought of her boy could have forced her to such a step.

When Katherine Courtney had been left an orphan at the age of ten, the only legacy had been unblemished reputations of her parents. An aunt of her mother's had come forward with an offer to educate the girl until she could support herself. It was distinctly stated that no further benefits were to be expected, and this was done only to prevent the possibility of even a remote family connection becoming a public charity charge, as was possible.

The sum allowed yearly did not tend to affluence or extravagance, and Katherine had felt the obligation from the very first day, she and "Aunt Jane Grimes" had an interview. The old lady's grim, aggressive manner had repressed the lonely child's inclination to fling herself upon the one human being who took any interest in her. Aunt Jane was wealthy, an old maid-and proud of it-energetic, economical to the verge of penuriousness, she recognized three great factors in the universe-her church, her country's flag and Prohibition.

The one meeting ended all communication between the child and old lady, until Katherine was graduated with the highest honours, and wrote Aunt Jane that she was now fitted to make her own way in the world as a teacher, and would soon begin paying back the heavy obligation of the years in school.

To her surprise, Aunt Jane invited her to come for a visit to the old-fashioned homestead in Maine. "I'd like to see what sort of a person I am responsible for," the old lady wrote. "Your reports from school regarding marks and deportment are satisfactory; but you can't wear these placarded on your breast for the rest of your life. So I'd like to have a look at you."

The inspection proved sufficient for the old lady to unbend and become almost human. Katherine's gratitude and her sincere desire to avoid being a burden, won Aunt Jane's silent approbation. After two weeks, when Katherine spoke again of plans to start earning her own living, the old lady had turned on her fiercely.

"Do you call that gratitude?" she demanded glaring through her steel-rimmed glasses. "Leaving me alone in this big house with only Ann, and she's a fool!"

Ann was the one maid employed, she refused to share her responsibilities with any other servant. Ann was a family heirloom, but despite her age she clung tenaciously to life. In fact, it had become a grim determination on the part of Ann, and likewise on the part of Aunt Jane, not to die first.

"Ann's just itching to see me buried," averred Aunt Jane, "and every morning when I go to breakfast she watches to see whether I eat all the boiled egg, or two full pieces of toast. I'm tired of being shut up alone with her all winter."

So Katherine remained, and for a wonder, Ann, too, approved.

"Miss Grimes is just waitin' for me to die," Ann grumbled, "but her Paw's will says I'm to have a home here as long as I live. And I'll be here long after I hear 'em singing over her coffin. I'm glad you're going to stay here. The winters are terrible when we're snowed in so long, just her and me, and she's awful old and crotchetty."

Companion, housekeeper, peacemaker between the two old women; nurse to each in turn; secretary for Aunt Jane's large business correspondence and charities, Katherine paid her debt cheerfully for three years, and nothing broke the monotony of her life.

During the winter months the seaside village hibernated, but in the summer it woke as a resort for wealthy society people who wished to avoid what they termed "the rabble." It was only for a short period; and during that time, Aunt Jane shut her front blinds tightly, and with Katherine and various old-fashioned trunks containing her feather bed and own linen, hied to a still more remote farm inland; only returning when the gay, social whirl was a thing of the past.

But, the third summer, Aunt Jane succumbed to a touch, of gout, and had not the courage to go away from the old doctor who had attended her family for two generations. He had presided at the advent of Aunt Jane into this world of troubles. "I don't mind his seeing my bare foot and ankle," she announced, "but I'm not going around showing it to any strange man at my age, even if he is a doctor."

So the trunks and feather mattress were not disturbed, the green blinds were not fastened, and the wide porch become a place of habitation after Katherine had installed chairs, a couch, books, and at last a tiny table which was used in the afternoons for a cup of tea out of the old-fashioned blue and white china-the pride of Aunt Jane's heart. Ann's austere face relaxed, and on one memorable occasion, Katherine found the erstwhile foes, laughing together over long-forgotten jokes.

Then, the unexpected happened. While in a store, a former classmate recognized Katherine, and insisted on calling. Aunt Jane succumbed to the wiles of the newcomer, whose sympathy at Katherine's isolation resulted in various invitations to a "bite of lunch with just me, alone." Thus it was that Jim Glendon saw her one day, obtained an introduction and lost no time in his determination to marry her.

Aunt Jane, when the young man called, listened grimly to his family social assets and financial standing, then she looked him up and down appraisingly, and announced calmly, "I don't like you. There's your hat."

Glendon retreated in confusion to report to Katherine and her chum. Between his insistence and the urging of the girl friend, the affair terminated in a hasty marriage. When Katherine broke the news to her aunt, she was informed that Katherine Courtney was dead. "I've never been acquainted with any one named Katherine Glendon, and I don't care to meet such a person," was Aunt Jane's ultimatum.

Each month, for several years, Katherine had written her aunt, but none of the letters had been answered. Then she wrote to Ann, and received the letter endorsed, DEAD! The writing was that of Aunt Jane, and Katherine had shed bitter tears; for she now understood that these two old women had given her their affection, and shown it in the only way they knew how.

Today she wrote again to Aunt Jane. The letter told without reserve or palliation, the conditions at the Circle Cross, the plan of Glendon to rob her of Donnie, and that the law gave men such rights. She reminded Aunt Jane of their last interview, "You said then, 'When you wish the shelter of my home from the man you have married, you will be welcome-but not till then!' I beg sanctuary for my boy and myself. I will work till the flesh wears from my fingers, if you will try to help me someway now. I cannot give him up. If you ever loved any one in your entire life, Aunt Jane, try to remember it now, for my boy is the only thing that makes me try to live."

The letter was splashed with tears. It was her last hope.

She gave it to Juan; "Take it to the Hot Springs and ask them to please send it to town by the first person who goes from there." Juan's eyes looked into hers, "Si, Señora, I understand." He tucked the letter into his shirt, mounted his waiting pony and loped down the cañon.

He did understand, and what he told Doctor Powell and Limber caused the cowpuncher to saddle Peanut, take the letter and ride to Willcox at once. Juan went back to the Circle Cross and reported, "Leember, he was ready to start to Weelcox, so he took the letter with heem, Señora."

Juan knew that the Priest told him it was a mortal sin to lie; but he did not count this any lie-Limber had taken the letter to Willcox.

Katherine wondered at herself, planning surreptitiously to oppose her husband for the first time in the years of their married life; but, when her eyes went to the boy, she felt she had done right. Aunt Jane, if favourably disposed, would use all her wits to circumvent Glendon, whom she hated. If Glendon knew that Aunt Jane was ready to take her part and the boy's, he probably would not press the matter of sending Donnie away. Glendon's father had refused further financial aid, or to even communicate with his son, and Aunt Jane was wealthy. This might influence Glendon.

In her anxiety to get the letter off, Katherine had omitted mentioning her complete isolation from all mail facilities. Even, now she forgot it.

Night fell. Two hours after dark Glendon reached home. The horse from which he dismounted was worn and weary; the hair was stiff with dried sweat and lather, its flanks drawn.

Without a word, Glendon ate the belated supper. Donnie watched him with frightened eyes. Juan hovered in the kitchen on various excuses, until Glendon went to bed.

Monday morning broke. Breakfast was a silent meal. Katherine's face was pallid, deep circles of black lay under her eyes, her lips quivered. The morning passed. Glendon loafed about the ranch all day, coming into the house at frequent intervals. Each time he did so, his wife started nervously, and Donnie's breath came more quickly. Glendon scrutinized them with a malignant smile. He knew they were both suffering with dread, but was determined he would not relieve their fears. He gloated at their mental torture.

When a boy, Glendon had revelled in tearing the wings from butterflies, so that their delicate flight in the sunshine must end in creeping mutilated upon the ground. Though his wife was not responsible for his thwarted plans, still he gloried in his power to torture her for his humiliation by Powell and Limber.

Monday passed, and Tuesday followed. She dared not hope, for she did not know what hour Glendon might decide to start. She feared to ask any question that might precipitate the crisis she dreaded. She felt like a prisoner condemned to death who is kept in ignorance of the day or hour of his execution, and each passing moment, dies a new death.

Glendon studied the dumb agony in her face. It gave a new zest to his life. He knew that neither Powell nor Limber would tell her of the paper he had signed, so long as Donnie was not sent away; but, neither Powell nor Limber had thought they were giving him a weapon to use upon her-the torture of uncertainty that drives to madness.

So the days passed into weeks, but not once did Glendon allow her a glimmer of hope. All the while she waited for an answer to the letter she had written Aunt Jane. But, at last she gave that up in despair.

For three months the situation remained unchanged. Katherine grew haggard, her movements listless, and Donnie still watched his father's goings and comings with frightened eyes and beating heart.

The drouth was telling on Glendon's small herd, but he had more important things to think about now. His trips to Willcox were frequent; his periods in town stretched over many days. Katherine might have wondered, had she not been occupied with her own anxiety-Donnie.

Each time Glendon made preparations to drive to Willcox, she waited the command that would tear the boy from her. When trip after trip was made without the ordeal, her heart began to take courage.

# Chapter Twenty-Six

Arizona, like a pouting child, was indulging in one of her periodic drouths, and cattle were slowly succumbing to starvation. The winter snows and rains had been insufficient to start the Spring grass, and though it was now late in August and the summer rains usually began in June, not a drop had fallen.

Most of the water-holes were dry, and water in the wells of ranches sank further from the surface each day. Many springs considered permanent, degenerated into mere mudholes where cattle bawled and crowded one another into the bogs till the weakest fell and were suffocated or trampled to death. The country was not only devoid of green grass, but what dry feed was left contained no nutriment whatever.

Ranchers fortunate enough to own permanent springs, or wells that were not yet dry, guarded the water jealously, notifying neighbours to come and care for the stray cattle that lingered bellowing around the closed watering places, or walked aimlessly for miles beside the barbed wire fences that kept them from the water they could smell. Tiny calves trailed weakly behind skeleton cows; other cows abandoned their young; and all added hysterically to the din of constant bellowing wherever there was a pool of water to lure them.

Sulphur Springs Valley was over a hundred miles long. It spread twenty miles across from the Grahams to the Galiuros, and was broken by groups of cottonwood trees clustering about small ponds of water supplied by windmills. Ordinarily these ponds were open to all stock, but now the gates were closed. Unless the water were used economically there would soon be none in reserve, as a few days without wind would cut off the daily supply from the windmills, and dry up the ponds.

Each day at ten o'clock the gates were opened. Cowboys stood guard, allowing the cattle bearing the ranch brands to enter the water-corrals, all other stock being "cut" away from water. The owners of these strays, having been notified, sent men to drive their own cattle home; but the animals would not remain away. Accustomed to ranging and watering in a certain locality, they would return and stand dumbly watching other cattle drink, waiting patiently for their own turn. When night fell, they lay down by the fence, lowing pitifully until morning, when they would again stagger to their feet. Sometimes, in frenzy, an animal tried to break through the wire fence, cutting itself on the barbs and growing steadily weaker hour by hour, till at last there was another carcass to be hauled away from the fence about the water corrals.

The August heat was intensified by the drouth, and a discussion in the corrals had annoyed Traynor. With the mood still on him, he entered the living-room of the Diamond H, where his wife was sitting beside a couch on which Jamie was sleeping. The boy had grown listless of late, and Nell tried to deceive herself by blaming the weather. Doctor Powell had been with them almost constantly, battling with all his skill for the waning life.

Traynor stooped over the child, then paced restlessly up and down the room. "I wish I could see a way to get you and the boy off to California, Nell, until this drouth is over. You both need the change. You have been a plucky little woman, never making a single complaint; yet I know how much the boy means to you. He is as dear as an own son to me, and it is maddening to be tied hand and foot, so that I cannot help you. I was a fool that I did not accept the offer of that Eastern syndicate last Fall-but cattlemen are all fools! None of us will sell during a good year. When the drouth hits us we curse ourselves for letting a sale slip. Drouth or no drouth, the men have to be paid; grain bought for the horses and provisions for us all. Where the money is coming from, the Lord only knows —I don't."

He flung himself moodily into a chair. Rising swiftly, Nell went to his side and slipped her arm about his neck, looking down into his face as he tried to smile up at her.

"Can't you pay the men with checks on the stores as you have always done?" she asked. "You told me once the stores carried all bills for five or six months, and accounts were settled when cattle were sold at the regular shipping season."

"That would be all right, ordinarily; but unfortunately the stores don't see it that way just now. They not only refuse further credit for cash or merchandise, but are asking settlements of all accounts in full, saying they are being pressed by their own creditors. Of course, one cannot very well blame them. They have to 'save their own bacon;' as the boys say."

"Is there any chance of getting money from the Tuscon bank?" asked his wife, hopefully. "When Mr. Eisenbart was here he said this ranch was the finest piece of property-not only in the Territory-but in the entire west."

"That did not cost him anything," retorted Traynor bitterly. "You see, like most cattlemen, I have never established a credit at any bank, being satisfied to do all my business through the stores which cash my checks. Consequently, now that the stores are closing down on me, I have no other place to turn!" He paced the floor restlessly and Nell watched him with troubled eyes, realizing how little she could help.

"I should have opened an account with some California bank long ago," he continued. "However, there's no use crying over spilled milk. I did not fully understand how critical my position was until I wrote to Eisenbart two weeks ago. I offered a mortgage on the ranches and all the stock, at twelve per cent. for a five thousand dollar loan! Why, this place is worth five hundred thousand dollars! He answered they were not making any new loans and were calling in all outstanding notes. No one wants a mortgage on dead or dying cattle, but the land would have been ample security for ten times what I needed."

Traynor stood by the window, staring out at the sky. He turned and resumed his restless walking to and fro, "God! If it would only rain! It's not just myself, but you and Jamie, and I want to get you two away to the Coast for a while. Then I got Powell into the mess, too. This drouth hits his plans pretty hard. All his money is now tied up in the Springs and the PL herd that he bought from Paddy!"

"But the Springs are not affected?" said Nell, "Limber told me that nothing can influence that water supply."

"No; there is that much to be thankful for, at least," he admitted wearily, sinking down into a chair, and letting his head drop into his hands. Nell crossed softly, and her hand caressed the bowed head, until Traynor's face looked up at her. The haggard, drawn lines about eyes and mouth, distinct in the glaring light from the window, smote her heart with pity and longing to comfort him.

"Dearest, I don't care how poor we are, so long as I have you and Jamie;" she was looking into his eyes bravely. "You did not marry a rich girl; but one who knew what poverty meant, and poverty where there was no one to speak an encouraging word. We have a roof that is our own. Even if the cattle die, the drouth cannot last for ever. When the rains come again we can mortgage the land, and get-why we can get a few chickens and a milk-cow, maybe," she laughed. "I have learned to make dandy butter, so we can sell butter and eggs if we can't get money enough to buy a bunch of cattle. We won't stay down, if we do get bowled over!"

"Nell! Bless your heart, you'd help any man get on his feet. Someday, please God, I will be able to give you everything money can buy."

"Nothing you could buy would make me as happy as knowing I am able to help you," she smiled through a mist of tears.

"I must go out and see what the boys are doing," and with head erect Allan Traynor passed through the door. Soon Nell heard his whistle-the first time for many days.

The regular round-up had been deferred until Fall, as the cattle were too weak to be handled and branded. The Diamond H men were kept busy, however, working the cattle at the watering places or riding the range where the weakest stock was "cut out" and driven slowly to the ranch and fed at the big stacks of native hay, or in the pastures that Traynor's foresight had reserved for such an emergency. Other ranchers, who had been amused at his idea of fencing pastures when the whole country was an open range, now saw his plans had been good judgment, and looked with chagrin at their own dying cattle which might have been saved by such measures.

One afternoon near sunset, Paddy Lafferty appeared at the Diamond H stables. Tying his dejected, flea-bitten grey horse in a stall, he unbuckled his rusty spurs and hung them over the horn of his saddle.

"Whar's Limber?" he asked Bronco, who passed the door of the building.

"Hot Springs," Bronco returned, in gasps of lighting a cigarette. "Doc's at-Tucson."

"Whar's the bye?"

"Inside the house."

Paddy waited no longer, but stalked through the Court and knocked at the door of the sitting-room.

Nell met him and her eyes lighted with pleasure, for his quaint, Irish humour was never tiresome to her. Then, too, she saw the sincerity under the surface. Paddy stepped with awkward care across the room and seated himself on the edge of a chair.

"How do he bye a doin'?" he asked in his customary hoarse whisper, jerking his head toward the lounge where Jamie lay in uneasy sleep.

"Not as well as usual, Paddy. He tires easily," she answered sadly, knowing only too well that the little life was slipping away hour by hour, though she had kept the thought to herself, believing that Traynor was still blind to the truth and not wishing to add to his many anxieties. She was unaware that Powell and Traynor had warned the boys not to speak to her of the child's serious condition.

Paddy had also been told of the deception, and had given his word to Traynor. He sat looking at Nell intently, knitting his shaggy eye-brows, and trying to think what to say without betraying his knowledge.

"Mebbe it's the weather do be a doin' it. Misthress Thraynor. Whin the rain comes he will be afther falin' betther."

"Oh, if we could only get rain!" she cried. "Do you think the cattle blame us for their suffering when they look at us with their pitiful, patient eyes? I want to tell them we are suffering, too. Yesterday I watched a cow, standing by her dying calf, licking its face. It was like something human. After it died the mother stood there-and this morning she would not leave it until I asked Bronco to take it away from her. I couldn't stand it. Please don't think I am crazy, Paddy, but it seemed so cruel that a tiny, helpless creature should come into the world for a few weeks, only to suffer and die."

"Yez ain't the only wan that do be a worritin' over the sayson, Misthress Thraynor," rejoined Paddy, who had found conversational bearings at last. "Paple passes on the road widout savin' ache ither, becoz they're all so busy lookin' up at the sky —" he was trying hard to tide her over the danger point. "They're all a boyin' linnyments to rub their necks, becoz of the kinks from lookin' for the clouds." Nodding approval at a faint smile he had evoked, he went on: "Yez was talkin' about cattle havin' rayson, Misthress Thraynor. Did yez be afther knowin' whin ould cows on the range have young calves too wake to walk fur, they all put their heads together and talk it over, loike a lot of women-folks does, an' thin wan of thim cows sthays and takes care of four or foive calves, whilst the ither cows goes off to wather, mebbe tin miles away. Thin she takes her turn whin the ithers comes back. Now, if that ain't rayson, be jabers, phwat is it?"

"I believe all animals have some reason, Paddy. It is human beings who do not understand them. We call them dumb brutes, because we lack the patience or intelligence to comprehend. I have learned a great deal since coming here to live."

"Did yez iver say a cow funeral, Misthress Thraynor?" asked Paddy.

"No, but I have heard the boys speak of them," she answered.

"It's a funny thing," went on Paddy. "Sometoimes a critter's been killed a wake or two, and no soign of it to be seen. Thin an ould cow will come along wid her nose to the ground, loike a dog on a trail, shniffin', and suddenly she raises up her head and lits out a yell loike an Apache Injun. As soon as she does thot all the cattle that are nigh enough to hear comes a runnin' to beat the divvle, an' yellin' as loud as they can. Thin they all sthand around ashniffin' and bawlin' and pawin' up the ground to beat the band. They don't seem to moind if a cow dies natural, but when wan of thim is killed so its blood touches the ground, it upsets the bunch of thim as soon as they find out about it. There was a tinder-foot that committed suicide three years ago, when he laughed at one of the Erie outfit that was tellin' about a cow funeral. The Erie boys had things pretty much their own way, them days."

"Suicide?" asked Nell, wonderingly.

"Well, it figured out that way. He killed hisself by bein' too slow drawin' his gun."

"How much longer do you think the cattle will hold out, Paddy?" she asked anxiously.

"Oi belave the strongest wans kin hould out six wakes, but the poorest wans can't last over two. Yez say, afther the rains comes it beats down the dry fade that is lift, and there won't be any strength to the new fade for siveral wakes, so thot makes it harder for a whoile afther the rains stharts. Thin's the toime cattle gives up." Paddy paused and smoked reflectively, while Nell rocked slowly, immersed in anxious thoughts. Paddy squinted at her from under his heavy eyebrows, then broke the silence, saying, "Did yez iver say ould man Brandther?"

Nell shook her head.

"Will," resumed Paddy, "he's the only wan in Arizony I'm not sorry for. He's gittin' it in the nick, now, an' Oi'm dumned glad of it! Oi till yez, he's a genywine hypercrit! Always says grace at male toimes; and whin he gits out of bed mornin's he goes on his knaze wid his noight-shirt a floppin' around his shanks and t'umps his craw and tills the Good Lard what a fine man ould Brandther is! Thin, he goes on the range and swoipes a couple of calves; and when noight comes, he gits on his knaze agin an t'umps his craw, and t'anks the Good Lard for all the marcies He has besthowed that day."

Despite her heavy heart, Nell's eye twinkled, her mouth twitched and a dimple began to show. The dimple had been hidden away for many days. Paddy saw and approved it.

"He sthayed to my place wan noight the last toime he come to his ranch, and thot's how I know about his religious belafes of hisself. Afther he had lift, Oi flopped on my knaze and t'anked the Saints and the Good Lard that thar wasn't but wan real good and holy man in Arizony so long as I was in the cattle raising business."

In spite of her anxiety, Nell's laughter rang through the room, as she pictured the pompous Mr. Brander thumping his "craw." The man was very wealthy, and only visited his ranch at intervals, but was so rabidly anti-Catholic that he never missed any opportunity to harangue on the topic, and he allowed no Mexicans employed on his ranch, because of their religion.

"It seems pitiful that we need rains so badly here, while the farmers in the East are complaining of too much," Nell said, unable to avoid the topic that was so vital to them all.

"Oi'm siventy-foive years ould, Misthress Thraynor, and Oi've found things ginerally works that way. Boy-the-boy, have yez iver been to Nye Yark?"

"I was born there and lived there with my parents till they died, then the money went and I worked, Paddy. I had to earn enough for Jamie and myself, you see. There was no one to help us. You get frightened when you know you are only one in the four millions people around you."

"The nixt toime yez go to Nye Yark," said Paddy, "there's a little restyrant yez want to be afther thryin'. Oi disremember the name of the strate yez sthart from, but ony way, yez go tin strates to the roight, thin thray strates to the lift, and thin yez kape straight on till yez say the place, and there yez are. Yez can't miss it. Yez can git the best male yez iver ate in your loife," he leaned over and dropped his voice more confidentially, "and they only charge tin cints!"

In order to hide the twitching corners of her mouth, as she conjured up a vision of turning cannibal and devouring "the best male yez iver ate in your loife," Nell moved to the window and stood picking dead leaves from a common geranium growing in a crude window box on the inner ledge formed by the thick adobe walls of the house.

"It's growing beautifully, Paddy," she said to the old man, "and Jamie and I love to watch it. Only, I hate to have you give it up yourself after you have had it so long. It's a beautiful geranium."

"Oh, well," Paddy replied carelessly, waving his hand with the pipe, "I was away from the house so much that half the toime I'd fergit to wather it. It's a long ways betther since you took care of it. Only, yez remimber, yez mustn't give it away to anybody ilse. Yez see, it belonged to the ould Dootch woman I married, and she thought a lot of it. Oi wouldn't give it to any wan ilse but you and Jamie."

Nell's face was sympathetic. She had heard of the strange wife of old Paddy, who spoke only Holland Dutch, while Paddy spoke not one word of the language; but they had managed to get along together till she passed away. Paddy had never called her anything except "The ould Dootch woman."

"It needs water now," Nell spoke after prodding in the earth. "I'll get some from the well."

When she left the room, Paddy laid his beloved pipe aside, then drew his chair near the sleeping boy. As he watched the pale, parted lips, the faint breath, the dark rings under the half-closed eyes, something warm and moist slipped down the old man' cheek and dropped upon his wrinkled, calloused hand. "Lard," he whispered hoarsely, "I can't see why yez let an ould useless bag o' bones like me kape on livin' and take the little lad that iverywan wants and loves. Can't ye swap us?"

Then Nell returned, and Paddy straightened up. "He never even peeped," he announced, turning to watch her water the plants. There was a peculiar expression on his face as he walked slowly over to where Nell let the water flow gently on the dry soil, then taking a pair of scissors from her work-box she pruned the plants carefully, saying, "Jamie usually takes care of them himself, but the last week I have done it for him. He is so easily tired. Did you ever think that life is just like a plant, Paddy? It starts out so bravely, sending its roots deep into the soil, and spreading its tender leaves to the sunshine-Happy, just because it is alive. Then the Gardener comes and prunes the stalks, and the plant does not understand why it is treated so cruelly. Sometimes it seems as though the leaves would never start again, but after a while the blossoms are more beautiful than ever, for pruning makes it stronger." She paused, looking down at the plants, then her voice trembled a little, "I am trying so hard, Paddy, to believe that the Gardener knows what is best."

He knew she was thinking of the child on the couch, and he held out his rough hand; "Oi giss yez are roight, Misthress Thraynor. Things wurrk out in the ind, if we do be doin' the bist we know how. Oi've lived among the cattle so long that I don't know anything ilse but cows and cow-talk, but if iver yez nade a frind, jist yez remimber ould Paddy."

# Part Three

# Chapter Twenty-Seven

Glendon, just back from one of his numerous trips to town, tossed a letter to his wife without a word. It fell to the floor, but she reached for it quickly, her heart beating fast at the thought it might be a reply from her Aunt Jane.

There had been no further discussion between herself and her husband about Donnie going away, but she did not know at what hour the ordeal might face her. Even if Aunt Jane declined to advise her in this matter, or aid in any way, Katherine wished that the strained relations between herself and the only one belonging to her by ties of blood, might be more kindly. She had come to understand Aunt Jane's attitude and to acknowledge that the old lady had read Glendon's character better than the girl who married him.

Looking back, Katherine saw all too clearly, that what she had mistaken for love, had been reaction against the dull monotony of her life with Ann and Aunt Jane, and a longing for some outlet for her repressed emotions. This very knowledge made her more staunch in her attitude to Glendon, fearing that her own lack of deep affection made her more alive to his shortcomings.

Her husband stood watching her, and she knew that whatever might be the contents of that letter, he would demand the right to see it. She had no friends who wrote her. If Aunt Jane mentioned receiving any letter, or referred to the appeal, Glendon would at once understand that his wife had written without his knowledge and this very fact would precipitate the catastrophe she had hoped to avert.

The letter was lying face down between them on the floor. Hiding the nauseating fear, she picked it up and turned it over. The engraved address of a firm of lawyers met her eyes. Her name, the ranch, typed.

Puzzled, she tore open the long envelope and started to read. Then she looked up at Glendon, her eyes full of tears, her lips trembling, as she said brokenly, "Aunt Jane is dead!"

"Well, what of it?" he demanded. "Do you expect me to howl with grief? You've not heard from her for years. Can't see that it makes much difference to you whether she's dead or alive. The old cat!"

Her eyes went back to the pages in her hand. They were typed and lengthy. She read them through, then, without comment handed them to Glendon.

"It's a legacy," she said simply.

He sat down and began perusing the contents of the communication, his brows knitting angrily as he grasped the purport.

Dear Madam:

Miss Jane Grimes, whose will has been left in our hands, has made you and your son, Donald, beneficiaries subject to certain conditions.

A sufficient sum to educate your son is set aside, all bills to be rendered to the Trust Company and paid by them. Your desires to be considered in the selection of proper school, but one which must be approved by the Trust Company.

Twelve hundred dollars annuity to be paid to you after the death of your husband, James W. Glendon. Until demise of James W. Glendon, the twelve hundred dollars per annum and accruing interest shall be held by the Trust Company.

In event of failure to agree to the terms set forth in the will, copy of which is herewith enclosed, the entire estate is to revert to the Prohibition Society of America. Otherwise, the estate will pass to your son on his thirtieth birthday.

Kindly communicate with us at your earliest convenience, and oblige, Yours very respectfully,

Goodrich Trust Company.

P. S. Letter enclosed from Miss Grimes.

The other letter read,

Dear Katherine:

You have had time now to realize that my estimate of James Glendon's character was correct. I have been at some pains and expense during the last seven years, since you moved to Arizona, to keep myself informed as to your husband's actions. I feel that I was justified, and it impels me to do all I am able to assist you after I am gone, without being of any comfort or benefit to a man whom I despise.

You are to confer with the Trust Company regarding a school for Donnie. It must be a school where self-respect and honour are taught; in fact, an old-fashioned school where boys are trained in the almost forgotten standards of an old-fashioned gentleman.

The annuity of twelve hundred dollars a year will be paid you at the death of your husband, for I know your inflexible principles and that you will never invoke the aid of the law to protect you by a divorce. It is because I, myself, am opposed to the wide-spread evil of divorce, that I am trying my best to aid you without aiding your husband financially. I wish to prevent him from benefitting in any way. I am confident that you will sorely need enough to provide a roof and food in event of his death, and should I make any other provisions for you and your child, I do not believe either of you would benefit one cent by my legacy.

He is the type of man who has no sense of moral obligation, but I want you to understand that you have my sympathy, and that you always had my love.

Affectionately,
Aunt Jane Grimes.

Glendon finished the two letters, returned them to his wife with a shrug of his shoulders, saying, "Sweet old cat! She certainly had it in for me from the very first day we met!"

Katherine waited for a violent tirade, but Glendon turned on his heel and left the room. It was a relief to her, but the uncertainty was not dispelled.

Four days went by, and then Katherine broached the topic.

"Jim, I've got to answer that letter."

He was sitting on the porch step smoking, his thoughts evidently far-afield.

"What letter?"

"About the legacy and sending Donnie to school," was the woman's reply. She knew that the future of the child depended on the answer she waited from the child's father. Her hands lay in her lap, gripped tensely, her eyes looked pleadingly at the face of the man.

"Do as you please about it," the words were indifferent. "I haven't any time to waste talking over these things. This drouth will about wind up my remnant of credit in Arizona. It won't make any difference to you, for you're heeled for life, if I am out of the way."

She tried to tell him her appreciation, "Jim! I will stand by you, no matter what comes! With Donnie's education provided for, we can surely win out together!" she moved impulsively to his side, laid her hand on his shoulder and stooped over to kiss him, but Glendon's shoulder jerked away roughly, as he answered, "Oh, for God's sake, Katherine, stop your melodramatics and let me alone!"

Despite the rebuff, her heart was singing with joy as she hurried to write the Trust Company, and stated that she could have Donnie ready to start East in two weeks; but that she had not the money, nor could she come with him on that account. The drouth in Arizona had stagnated all cattle business temporarily.

Katherine explained to the child that his going away was with her full consent, and that it did not mean he was to stay away, except during the school term. They could be together for the summer vacations. She also told him of the strange old aunt who had cared for her own education, and who, though dead, now made it possible for him to go to a good school, such as his father could not afford. She made him understand, too, that his father had given consent, and without such consent, no one could have done anything.

The reply from the Trust Company informed her that one of the members of the firm would meet the child at Willcox on a date specified. That business matters had made a trip to California imperative, and the return trip would be arranged via Willcox, if the child were there at the time.

Katherine timidly told this to her husband, but met with no opposition. His acquiescence surprised and touched her. She ascribed it to his desire to make amends, and her gratitude was pathetic. Yet, knowing his vacillating character, she hastened to perfect arrangements. Not until she saw the child in charge of the man who met them at Willcox, and accompanied them to the depot platform, did she feel safe. She clasped the boy in a last, close embrace and watched him wave from the window of the train. The "stone wall had toppled over," and the hideous fear of losing her boy completely was laid to rest.

Aunt Jane had not answered her letter but now Katherine knew that the old lady had understood the situation and set her wits to work to aid the niece she really loved.

Before the train pulled out Doctor Powell crossed the street, and stood talking with Donnie, thus helping both in their battle to be brave. Then, Katherine and Powell stood side by side, watching the train pull away until it disappeared in the gap between the Graham and Dos Cabezas ranges. But, long before the crags intervened, it had vanished from the mother's eyes in a blur of tears.

"Tell me," Powell spoke, "Is Donnie going to his grandfather?" He was thinking of the paper that reposed in the hands of his lawyers, and wondered if Glendon had dared defy him.

"No," Katherine smiled happily, "Jim gave up that intention some time ago. It was a legacy from an aunt of mine, which provides for Donnie's education. So, you see, you were right. The stone wall has toppled over!"

Powell's hand gripped hers, "I'm glad for your sake and for Donnie's!"

# Chapter Twenty-Eight

Another month passed and the drouth was still unbroken. Stores were threatened with bankruptcy and cattlemen saw vast herds, accumulated through years of hard toil, dwindle to one-fourth the original number, and faced the possibility of losing that also.

The Arizona ranges for years had been badly overstocked; but each rancher waited for his neighbour to get rid of the surplus cattle, hoping thereby to benefit his own herd. Over-crowding ranges resulted in the tramping out of the roots, and what was more serious, grass was cropped so closely that there was no opportunity for seed to mature and fall to the ground and germinate for another year. In former times a drouth would not have been so disastrous as under the existing conditions of the ranges.

Having done all in his power to mitigate the situation, Traynor fought a despondency that was entirely foreign to his nature. It was augmented by his desire to conceal the facts from his wife, and to this was added his knowledge that Jamie was continually growing weaker. He had called the men into the office and told them frankly that he would not be able to keep them much longer, as he was straining every financial possibility.

The result of that conference was a surprise that unmanned him. Limber, Bronco, Holy and Roarer declined to be "fired," stating they would work for "chuck" until the drouth was over, and when he remonstrated, the four of them stalked out of the room, as Limber remarked, "We've got business to attend to outside-instead of talking foolishness inside."

"If I could manage to get a few thousands," said Traynor to Nell as they left the breakfast table one morning, "I would not hesitate to round up all the weakest cattle and ship at once to Colorado, leaving the stronger ones take their chances here on the range. However, I might as well wish for rain; that would be less improbable than obtaining the money. The most aggravating thing is knowing that I could save the greater part of the herd if I could only ship them. Native grass is plentiful and pasturage cheap in Colorado this year; once I had the cattle there I could easily raise money at one of the Colorado banks on the stock, and so relieve the tension here as well as there. If I pull through this year, I will keep money in readiness for such an emergency, hereafter. It's been a good lesson; but a mighty expensive one."

As he walked slowly to the barn, he passed Paddy with a large parcel coming into the courtyard.

"Oi've got somethings for the bye and the misthress," he explained, and Traynor told him they were in the living-room.

"Hello, ould Sphort!" Paddy said to the boy, who was standing by his sister, watching her water the geraniums.

"There's a new bunch of buds Paddy;" the child announced and Paddy examined the plants critically.

"Yez can't giss what Oi brought wid me for yez;" he said. "A babby deer. Oi caught it at Mud Springs an' brung It in fer yez."

"Oh, Paddy!" Jamie's face glowed with delight. "How did you catch it? Where is it?"

"From the looks of it, its mother has been dead for a couple of days. Giss the coyotes or a lion got her, and the little fellow was mighty wake, and was willin' to make friends. Oi carried him twelve moiles in me arrums on the ould grey horse. He's out in the stables now, and the byes says for yez to come out and get introjuiced to him. They're goin' to give him milk from a bottle till it gits big enough to ate ither things."

The child's eyes were bright with excitement as he made his way to the barn, where Bronco and the other boys surrounded a small fawn. Holy was holding a bottle of milk to its mouth, while Bronco stroked the throat to help it swallow, for the fawn was very weak. "Gee! he was hungry!" said Holy to Jamie. "We have to learn him to take the milk this way, and when he gets a little stronger he can take it from a pan. Isn't he pretty? He is such a dark brown on the back, and just look how plain his spots is. Funny they lose 'em when they're yearlings!"

"What you goin' to name it, Kid?" asked Bronco.

"Patsy," replied Jamie promptly, as he knelt and stroked the soft fur with his thin hand. The fawn turned its head and licked his hand, then gazed at the child with its beautiful eyes. The thin arms went about the fawn's neck gently.

"He knows you won't hurt him, Kid;" spoke Holy, then turned away quickly, swearing to himself. "They're both about all in, an' nobody can't do nothin'."

After Jamie left the room, Paddy untied the string that held a flour-sack in an unsightly bundle. He tiptoed over to the table and laid the parcel beside Mrs. Traynor's work-basket.

"Oi just got this from the stage dhriver, Yez mabbe afther hearin' Oi niver knowed how to rade an' write, Misthress Thraynor?"

She nodded her head, and Paddy, finding the string obdurate, produced a gigantic pocket-knife, such as is used by cattlemen in ear-marking calves.

"Will, Oi hed an agrayment wid ould man Sullivan that he was to rade the poipers fer me, an' would yez belave it, the dummed ould skoonk was afther thryin' to make me pay him for radin' thim. He says, says he, 'Oi've been to the throuble of radin' thim for wan year, an' be jabers, Oi desarve cumpinsation.' An Oi says to him, says Oi, 'Ahl roight, Sullivan. Phwat's the damidge?' 'Foive dollars,' says he as bould as brass. 'Ahl roight,' says Oi. 'Oi'll pay yez foive dollars fer radin' thim poipers, Misther Sullivan, and yez are goin' to pay me tin dollars for the use of thim.' He jumped up and roared at me, 'Thim poipers only cost foive dollars for wan year.' 'Thrue for yez,' says Oi; 'and yez nadent git hot in the collar about it, at all, at all. Oi'm only charging yez fer takin' up my toime whilst Oi was waitin' fer yez to spill out the big wurrds!'" Paddy smiled grimly as he crowded some fresh tobacco into his pipe, and after taking a few preliminary puffs, he continued. "Will, Sullivan niver collected thot foive dollars. Oi thought Oi would be afthar bringin' thim poipers here, so you can rade thim and till me the news forinst Oi come again."

As he spoke, he shook the sack, and a solitary paper fell on the table —*The Tombstone Epitaph* —which was published weekly at the County seat. It consisted of one page of local gossip, two pages of pictured cattle, bearing various hieroglyphics, which to the initiated represented brands and ear-marks, while the fourth page was filled with advertising matter of the local stores. A similar paper was published weekly at Willcox. "Oi loike the *Epitaph* and the Willcox poiper," explained Paddy with twinkling eyes, "becaze Oi can look at the cows and tell which ind of the poiper goes bottom side up. Here's a book the stage dhriver got fer me. He says it's foine; and yez can rade it to yourself, then tell me about it, sometoime. It's called 'The Revenge of Bloody Dick.'"

A final shake of the sack and "Bloody Dick" appeared, followed by several magazines of fashions, and a couple of home periodicals, containing carefully censored stories for women and children, which huddled together limply like shocked old maids surprised in questionable company.

Nell struggled with a hysterical desire to laugh, as she glanced from the strangely garbed figure of the old man to the conventional fashion-plates; but, appreciating the rough chivalry that had inspired the act, a lump grew in her throat, and dropping her head on the table the sobs came unchecked.

Paddy moved to her side and stroked her hair gently, speaking as though to an injured child.

"Shure, Oi didn't mane to make yez fale bad, at all, at all, little gurrl. Oi thuoght if yez was radin' yez wouldn't be worritin' so much about the cattle."

"It is Jamie, too," she sobbed. "I know he is growing weaker; but Allan does not know it, yet. I've been keeping it from him, for he has so much worry now. If he could ship the cattle to Colorado and save them, he said he could get money there to carry us through."

Paddy listened thoughtfully. "He's roight about that," said the old man. "It would save the wakest wans, and lave more fade for the sthrong wans. Don't be afther sayin' anythin' to the Boss, Misthress Thraynor, but yez know Oi have some money put away handy, and if the Boss wants to borry it to hilp ship his cattle, Oi'll lind it to him. Oi've got the money from the sale of the PL Ranch, and there's a few more dollars ilsewhere that I can get widout trouble. The Diamond H is good property whin the drouth is done, and Oi'm not afraid of losin' the principal wid the Boss. Oi niver thrust any banks becoz they moight go boosted any toime." Paddy crammed fresh tobacco in his pipe. "Oi kin let the Boss have twenty-foive thousand dollars in gold if he wants it. Now moind, don't yez till him onything, but lit me fix it up my own way wid him. Oi'm goin' to Willcox airly in the marnin', Misthress Thraynor, an' whin Oi come back Oi'll talk wid the Boss, and foind out whin he wants the money ready."

Nell started up, but Paddy waved her back. "Don't yez begin a thankin' me," he commanded fiercely, "or ilse Oi won't lit him have a dummed cent! It's jist a matter of business, an' Oi'll charge him intherest, all roight. Oi moight as well be makin' intherest on my money as to be lavin' it buried in the ground."

He held out a grimy, calloused hand, saying, "Good noight, Misthree Thraynor. Git a good noight's slape and don't worrit ony more. Oi'll say that the Boss has what money he nades, and a little over, so that you and the bye can go to Californy for a while, until this dry spell is over. Thin whin the rains comes, the little chap will be afther comin' back with chakes as rid as thim posies;" and he disappeared through the door, leaving Nell feeling he had carried her troubles with him.

A couple of hours after sunrise the next morning, Paddy riding leisurely along the road from the Diamond H to Willcox, encountered Limber a few miles out of town. Limber had ridden from the Hot Springs.

After the usual salutation, Paddy reined his grey, gaunt horse close to Peanut's side, leaned over, held his hand cupped about his mouth and with a glance at the miles of prairie that sheltered no eavesdropper, the old Irishman whispered, "Say, Limber, thar's somewan sleeperin'. Warkin' on the PL and Diamond H. Oi tould the Boss and he's goin' to warn the byes to look out. Oi mebbe misthaken, but Oi've got an idee that Glendon's at the bottom of it. 'Twon't hurt to kape an oye on him over at the Springs. Goin' back soon?"

"I have some thing to attend to for the doctor. He's up to Tucson this week," Limber answered as they unsaddled their ponies at the Rest. "I'm goin' to the Diamond H tonight, after sundown. It'll be cooler then and give Peanut a good rest."

"Oi'll see yez before yez start." Paddy had reached the gate but turned back, "Say, Limber, Oi want yez to pick out a noice little collar. I found a fawn and packed it in for the bye, so long as you're goin' to the Diamond H, yez can take it along. I've got to go to the San Pethro for a few days."

He held out a twenty-dollar gold piece, which Limber slipped into his pocket.

"Say, Paddy, if I was you I'd put my dinero in a bank. You take lots of chances," remonstrated Limber seriously. "Someday you'll go to your cache and find your money's been dug up."

"They'll have a dummed hard toime a foindin' it," retorted Paddy cunningly, "and a dummed harder toime gettin' away wid it, for Oi kape a close watch on it. Oi'm figgerin' on makin' a loan to the Boss, so's to help him ship cattle. Oi got thirty-five thousand dollars put away. Oi ain't no Rockyfeller, but Oi've got enough for salt pork and frijoles for the nixt tin years, an' Oi don't belave Oi'll be in urgent nade of thim afther that toime. If the Good Lard thinks Oi'll pass the Inspection Chute, Oi'll be fading on milk an' honey widout payin' fer it. Oi'm siventy-six, come my nixt birthday."

"Well, your money will be safer if the Boss has it," Limber finished the conversation as he turned into the store, while Paddy walked up the street, stopping to speak to people he knew. Every one liked the old fellow, who was noted for his sobriety and honesty as much for his peculiarities. He was passing the swinging door of a saloon which had none too savory a reputation, when Alpaugh, the Constable of Willcox, who was also the Deputy Sheriff of Cochise County, called to him.

"Hello, Paddy! Come in and have a drink," he invited cordially slapping the old man's shoulder.

"Ahl roight, Dick," was the reply, "Oi'm goin' to git somethin' to ate, and it will be an appytizer. I rid from the Diamond H this marnin', but it was too airly for breakfast whin I started out."

The bar-tender mixed the concoctions ordered and set two glasses on the bar, then saying, "I'll be back in a minute," he left the room in response to a call, leaving Paddy and Alpaugh alone, except for a man sprawled across a table at the end of the room.

Paddy looked at the man. "That Glendon is always dhrunk," he remarked in disgust. "Pity his woife don't loight out and lave him." He moved, nearer, "Say, Dick," he whispered, though his voice carried distinctly, "Oi think yez had betther kape an oye on Thray-fingered Jack, Glendon, Bentz and Burks. Oi run into them last wake nigh Glendon's place, and they was squattin' on the ground drawin' loines. They didn't say me, but they was talkin' about the Express car to the Jumpin' Frog Moines. Oi don't loike the looks of it."

Alpaugh glanced at him sharply. "Much obliged, Paddy;" he replied. "Did you speak of it to any one else?"

"Nary a sould," responded Paddy.

"Don't tell any one else," cautioned Alpaugh.

"Ahl roight, Dick;" answered Paddy, lifting the glass to his lips. "Here's lookin' at yez."

A shot pinged through the air, and the glass fell from Paddy's fingers as he tumbled in a grotesque heap on the floor. Glendon, holding the still smoking pistol, sprang to Paddy's side and emptied four more cartridges into the motionless figure.

Alpaugh stooped quickly, breaking the buckskin thong around the trigger of Paddy's pistol, and threw the gun beside the dead man.

"He didn't know you and Bentz saw him out there. Stick to self-defence," said Alpaugh. "Dead men tell no tales, and the damn fool knew too much."

A crowd of excited men filled the place when Limber came running in. "Who done it?" he demanded, looking around.

"I did," replied Glendon, facing him; and Limber stepped back as though menaced with a blow.

"You —"

"Yes! Alpaugh was drinking with Paddy when he turned on me without any warning, and I shot in self-defence. The old man's been nutty for some time, and had it in for me ever since we had trouble at the corral over that cow. If you don't believe me, you can ask Alpaugh. He saw it all."

Alpaugh looked at the faces of the crowd, and knew he must keep his head level, for Glendon was not popular, and Paddy had many friends.

"I saw Paddy going past, and asked him in to have a drink with me," said the constable with apparent frankness. "Otto mixed the drinks and went back to the end of the room, and Paddy was talking to me. Glendon was at the other end of the room, but got up and started to walk over to us, and I was going to ask him to have something with us, when Paddy saw him and reached for his gun. Glendon had to shoot quick or be shot himself. The trigger of Paddy's gun caught in the buckskin loop of his holster, or else he'd got Glendon first. That's all there is about it. Paddy's been itchy against Glendon for some time. Every one knows that."

He turned to Glendon, "I've got to arrest you, Jim, until after the inquest."

"That's all right," answered Glendon, then he saw Limber scrutinizing him sharply. "Say, Limber, will you tell my wife? She's expecting me home tonight."

Limber's eyes were riveted on Glendon, as though trying to read the man's thoughts. "Yes," he replied curtly, turning on his heel and walking out the room without another word.

"There's something crooked in back of it," he muttered to himself, as he reached the Cowboys' Rest and picked up his saddle. Then he remembered Paddy's promised assistance for Traynor. "No one knows where Paddy hid his money, and that settles the Boss," he stopped to pet the nose of Paddy's gaunt, old, flea-bitten grey horse, which had been a joke with every one, then Limber flung his saddle on Peanut and mounted. "Sometimes it looks like it don't pay to be square, Peanut," he said as the little pinto pony headed for the road leading to the Circle Cross Ranch.

# Chapter Twenty-Nine

Katherine sat on the porch of her home, watching the road that led to town. It was long after six o'clock and Glendon had promised faithfully he would return early in the afternoon. The Circle Cross herd which had not been large enough to pay its owner's debts under the most favourable circumstances, had dwindled through the drouth until Glendon refused to try to save what was left. Juan rode out alone each day, doing the best he was able, while Glendon puttered about the house and corral, or stretched in a half-drunken stupor on the couch in the tiny living-room. Katherine was spared the knowledge that Alpaugh held a note worth more than the remnant of their cattle and that the money had been used by Glendon to pay several gambling debts, as well as to keep Panchita in a good humour.

Her meditations were interrupted as Tatters came to the porch steps and thrust his moist nose into her hand.

"What do you think is wrong this time, Tatters?" she asked, looking down at the dog's intelligent eyes. Since Donnie had left, the woman and dog had been drawn together by their mutual longing for the boy, and Katherine had fallen unconsciously into the habit of talking to the collie.

She slipped an arm about the shaggy neck, and silently watched the twilight deepen into darkness. Juan hovered anxiously in the doorway, and tried to persuade her to eat supper; but she put him off, saying she would come soon. A foreboding clutched her; she had no desire for food. Shaking his head dolefully, the Mexican retreated to the kitchen.

Suddenly the dog stiffened, sniffed the air and gave a low growl. Then he sprang from the steps and ran to the gate, where he squatted down, and stared sharply at the road.

Katherine heard the faint sounds of hoof beats, and confident that it was her husband returning, she hastened to see if the belated supper was beyond hope.

There was a knock at the door. Surprised, she turned to open it, when she heard a man's voice speaking.

"Don't be frightened, Mrs. Glendon. It's only Limber, I brung a message for you from Glendon."

He entered the room, and blinked in the lamplight, but Katherine, seeing the expression on his face, was not deceived.

"What's the matter?" she asked quickly.

Limber hesitated, cleared his throat and wondered how it would be best to tell his message. All the way he had been puzzling what to say. If it had been a man, or any other woman, it would have been easier; but the cowpuncher shrank from adding to the troubles of the woman. It was like striking her.

"Why-it's —just-don't be frightened, Mrs. Glendon," floundered Limber, and cursed himself for making matters worse. "It's not so serious —"

She clutched the back of a chair; her face was white, but her voice steady. "Tell me, just as you would another man, Limber. I won't break down. Is he dead?"

"Not a bit of it," replied Limber in relieved tones. "He's all right-well as I am. But thar's been trouble in town and Glen shot Paddy Lafferty. Dick Alpaugh seen it and says it was self-defence. So Glen will be acquitted all right; but he's under arrest till the inquest. He wanted me to come and tell you."

Limber repeated the meager details, avoiding her eyes as much as possible, and watching Tatters, whose head he was stroking as he talked. The silence became oppressive after he ceased speaking, and Limber lifted his eyes.

Katherine, apparently forgetful of his presence, sat staring at the wall, her hands twitching nervously at her kitchen apron. Her face was deathly white. Limber wished she would cry, though he dreaded a woman's tears.

"Don't take it so hard, Mrs. Glendon. It's just a matter of form, him bein' held. Glendon will be home tomorrow night."

"Did you see him kill Paddy?" her eyes searched Limber's, forcing the reluctant truth from his lips and telling him plainly that she doubted the story as he had told it.

"No, Mrs. Glendon. I got thar afterwards. I heard Alpaugh say what happened. He was there. Then Glendon ast me to come and tell you. That's all I know."

She rose. "Thank you, Limber. I understand. It was good of you to come the thirty-five miles. After you have supper I will be ready to go back with you, if your pony can stand the trip. Fox is the only horse I have here, Jim took the team to town."

"Peanut is good for the trip," asserted Limber, "but it is a mean ride at night till we strike the flats. Mebbe you'd better wait till mornin' if you think you'd oughter go."

"I must go tonight;" she replied and Limber made no further protest. He knew the tension under which she laboured.

Juan insisted that she make an effort to eat, while Limber swallowed a cup of coffee, then necessary articles in a small bundle were tied to her saddle as Fox and Peanut rubbed friendly noses.

The old Mexican's heart was heavy as he watched them ride away, and the dog's ears drooped dejectedly. Out on the long night ride the ponies swung into a steady lope. The soft breeze fanned the cheeks of the riders like a cool spray. A young moon slipped coyly over the horizon. The air was heavy with the perfume of Yucca that even the drouth could not kill, while faint and sweet came the lilt of a mocking-bird.

Katherine could not make herself believe that out of the beauty and peace of the night she would find the man she had sworn to 'love, honour and obey' with human blood on his hands—the murderer of an old, defenceless man who had done many an act of kindness for her and her boy.

Once she turned and spoke. "Where is he?"

"In the hotel;" answered Limber. "Alpaugh has charge of him till the inquest is over."

They rode again in silence, each absorbed in thought until, after weary hours, the lights of the town grew visible. At last the ponies stopped in front of the Willcox Hotel. A few men loitering about, stared curiously as Limber helped Katherine from her saddle. It was after two in the morning. The by-standers who recognized Mrs. Glendon, lifted their hats respectfully. One of them spoke her name. She turned her dull eyes on him. Her lips moved but there was no sound. The man understood, and choked an oath.

Limber untied the bundle from her saddle, and she followed him stiffly into the hotel, shrinking in the narrow, dimly lighted hallway while the cowboy made arrangements with the sleepy nightman.

"I'll take you up to the room," said Limber. She nodded silently.

On the second floor the cowboy paused at the door and knocked.

"Come in!" called Glendon's voice.

Limber smiled reassuringly to Katherine; then he turned and left her. She stood biting her lips, trying to control her emotion, and holding the doorknob in a nerveless hand that was trembling with exhaustion.

"What the blazes is the matter? Come in, I say!"

The door was jerked open violently and Glendon stood staring at his wife. An oath rose to his lips.

"What brought you here?" he demanded roughly.

She passed into the room, turned and held out her hands to him, saying simply, "Where else should I be, Jim, when you are in trouble? I thought you wanted me to come."

"Well, I didn't. I might have known you'd not be able to resist an opportunity to twit and remind me how you've begged me to stay away from town, and all that rot! I only asked Limber to go and tell you what had happened, and as usual, you go to extremes and come hiking in here in the middle of the night. You're making a mountain out of a mole hill. I'd been home by this evening. There was not the least excuse for your coming here."

Obeying an impulse, she moved near and laid her hand on his shoulder. He shook it off roughly and started from the chair into which he had slumped.

"For God's sake, Katherine, cut out that rot! I'm sick of your saintly pose, and I don't want any preaching or praying. I had to shoot Lafferty or be shot myself."

"Was it self-defence, Jim?"

He noted the undercurrent of doubt and ripped out an oath.

"I told you once, and I'm not going to keep jabbering about it the rest of the night. You go to the inquest and hear Alpaugh's testimony, as long as you don't believe me."

He strode across the room to the table and poured out a generous glass of raw whiskey, which he followed by a second, then a third, and at last threw himself on the bed. In a few minutes the room was heavy with the fumes of liquor and noisy with snores of the drunken sleeper.

Softly Katherine lifted the little window, and let the clean pure air blow across her face. Somewhere a clock struck three. The woman, sitting in the darkness, stared with dry aching eyes, thinking of the past, wondering what the future held. It was like looking into a chasm.

When grey dawn, like a feeble, sick thing, crept through the window, Glendon woke refreshed and buoyant; but his wife was haggered and worn, with great dark rings under her eyes. Her husband looked at her critically, contrasting her with the flamboyant attractions of Panchita.

"Can't you fix yourself up a bit?" he demanded in aggrieved tones. "You're losing your good looks completely. Anyone would take you for twice your age. Lot of good you do me, coming here with your glum face!"

She made no reply, which added to the anger he vented by kicking a chair out of his way. Glendon's hand shook as he poured out a drink of liquor to steady his nerves, while Katherine opened the parcel she had brought with her, laying out his razor, a clean shirt and collar. His clothes were creased and rumpled, as he had slept all night in them. Then she picked up a small pitcher and went in search of hot water. She finally obtained it from the Chinese cook in the kitchen, for the hotel bragged no bell-boys or bells.

The inquisitive glance of the Chinaman and a Mexican whom she passed at the kitchen door, brought to her the full realization of the ordeal she was facing. If she could only believe that her husband had acted in self-defence, she would stand unshaken beside him, defying the entire world; but she could not make herself credit his story. Always when he had tried to deceive her, some subtle instinct betrayed him to her. Through the night she had reiterated again and again, "It was self-defence," but louder and louder a chorus of voices kept whispering in her ears, "He is lying! It was murder!"

She seized the pitcher of water from the Chinaman's hand and hurried up stairs to her room. Glendon accepted her services as a matter of course, proffering no word of thanks.

Half an hour later Alpaugh knocked, and the three went to the hotel dining-room for breakfast. Glendon's appetite was excellent. Alpaugh and he talked casually, occasionally interjecting a joke; but the food choked Glendon's wife, and with a feeling of relief she rose and returned to the bedroom followed by her husband. Alpaugh, as a matter of form, hovered at the entrance of the hotel.

"The inquest is at nine," said Glendon as they entered their room. "It's half-past eight now," he consulted his watch.

"Jim," she hesitated, "I think I will stay here in the room. I'm not feeling quite well this morning."

He looked at her and a sullen rage consumed him. He realized that she was not deceived by his story.

"Going to shirk it, eh?" he asked sneeringly, "Well, you will have to come, that's all there is to it. Look fine for me when everyone knows you rode here last night and then hid away just at the time when you, or any decent wife, should stand by a man. That would be enough to condemn any one in my fix."

It was not that he desired her company; but he was aware that her presence would have its influence, in case anything should upset Alpaugh's testimony. The bartender might have seen more then they thought; besides there was no telling what unexpected snag might be struck during the inquest. Paddy had many staunch friends.

As these thoughts beset him, Glendon looked at his wife. "Well, are you going to stand by me, or not?"

Her reply was to pick up her hat which she adjusted. As he opened the door, she said imploringly, "It was self-defence, wasn't it, Jim?"

"Good God, Katherine, you will drive me mad! I said it once. Now you can listen to Alpaugh and make up your mind about it as you please. Stop nagging me."

Without further conversation, husband and wife accompanied Alpaugh to the little office of the Justice of Peace, where the inquest was to be held. A group of men at the entrance, glanced peculiarly at Glendon; then their expressions changed as they saw the woman at his side. Glendon was quick to notice this and congratulated himself that Katherine was with him. With assumed solicitude he led her to a chair and stood silently beside her, his eyes on her bowed head, until the proceedings began.

The inquest fully exonerated Glendon, as the bar-tender had not seen what occurred and Alpaugh was the only actual witness. The broken buckskin thong was admitted as proof that Paddy had drawn his gun, thus making it impossible for any jury to bring in a verdict against Glendon. There were many witnesses to the quarrel at the shipping-corral, when Paddy had refused to shake hands with Glendon after the latter had apologized to him; and as no one had heard Glendon utter any threats against Paddy, there was apparently no motive except that of self-defence. On the other hand, the old Irishman had often expressed his dislike for Glendon.

As soon as the verdict was rendered, Glendon was surrounded and congratulated by Bentz, Three-fingered Jack, Burks and Alpaugh. With smiles and light words he shook their hands; but other men exchanged glances and left the room, talking in subdued voices.

Katherine saw the doubt in many faces, and shrank at the reflection of the fear in her own heart. Glendon's callous indifference, his careless air, revealed her husband in a new and hideous light.

With trembling limbs she made her way to his side, placing her hand on his arm. He looked down in surprise, and an expression of annoyance crossed his face. He had completely forgotten his wife's presence and had been about to suggest to the crowd that drinks were in order at the most convenient place.

She realized it all, and wished that she had remained at the ranch. "Jim —I don't feel very well. Will you take me to the hotel?"

He shrugged his shoulders, but remembering others were watching, answered, "Yes." Husband and wife moved side by side toward the door.

"See you later, Glen," said Three-fingered Jack, and Alpaugh added: "You're not going out today, are you?"

Katherine looked up. Glendon, with a sudden sense of shame, replied; "I'll go back with my wife this afternoon when it gets cooler, but I'll see you both before I leave town."

Her eyes were grateful. Glendon, conscious of a halo of self-importance and good intentions, walked down the street, speaking to passers-by, though many of them responded only in deference to the woman at his side.

As they passed along the street, several men standing in front of the post office, watched them disappear into the hotel.

"Glen's turned over a new leaf," observed one of them.

"'Twon't last very long. New leaves are awful tender. They get torn mighty quick," laughed another.

"It'd been all-fired excitin' if Panchita had been in town. There'd been fur flyin', and I bet Glendon would have vamoosed and let 'em fight it out to a finish. You can get a rise outen Panchita any time you speak about Mrs. Glendon."

"If it ever comes to a show down between 'em I bet on the Mexican girl for a winner. She's got the inside track sure. Glen's wife is too high-headed to win the race."

None of them noticed Limber pausing close by as he heard Mrs. Glendon's name. The cowboy's eyes glinted, his lips were compressed and his hands clenched.

"I ain't so sure about Mrs. Glendon losing the race," retorted the first speaker. "I noticed that Glen quit prancing mighty quick when his wife slipped the halter over his head and led him off to the home pasture!"

The burst of laughter that greeted this witticism was hushed suddenly, as Limber broke through the group and faced them with blazing eyes.

"You are a fine bunch of things to call yourselves men! You fellers ain't fit to wipe the dust off'n Mrs. Glendon's shoes, let alone takin' her name on your dirty tongues. The feller what makes any more remarks about her has got me to fight just as soon as I hear his name. If there's any one here that don't like what I say, he knows what he kin do."

Limber waited a reply, but the thoroughly abashed men were silent, and the cowboy stalked away.

When he was well out of hearing, one of the men, a recent arrival in Arizona, uttered an oath, "I ain't goin' to stand for that sass from nobody," he blustered.

Another man grabbed his arm. "Look here! You ain't been very long in this section and you won't be here very long if you think you can put it over Limber. He's the best pistol shot in the Territory."

"And you'd have as much chance against him," warned another bystander, "as a jackrabbit would have, if it smelt the cork of a whiskey bottle and then got brash and slapped a bull-dog in the jaw."

"Go ahead and try it, if you want to," commented the third man, "We haven't had a funeral 'round here for some time now. It'd liven things up a bit for all of us-except yourself."

The new-comer looked after Limber's figure with respectful eyes.

## Chapter Thirty

When Nell heard the news of Paddy's death she felt she had lost a sincere friend. As her eyes rested on the door she seemed to see the wrinkled face with a strangely softened look, and hear his voice saying, "Good noight, Misthress Thraynor. Git a good noight's rist and don't worrit any more." Poor old Paddy! How little they dreamed of the long rest he would find the next night.

She was glad that she had obeyed his injunction not to let her husband know anything of the promised loan until Paddy himself should speak of it. Her silence had saved Allan from indulging in plans that could not now be carried out. Everything seemed more hopeless than ever.

Doctor Powell had been trying to secure a loan through friends in the east, in order to assist Traynor to ship some of his stock; but his efforts had been fruitless, so far, and a letter told them that he was going to Los Angeles to see if anything could be done there.

The stage-driver who delivered Powell's letter, brought the little collar that Paddy had commissioned Limber to buy for the fawn. The cowboy had scribbled a few words explaining that the gift came from Paddy. Jamie was delighted. They did not tell him that his old friend was dead.

A week after Paddy's death, Nell stood picking a few withered leaves from the geranium in the window, and her tears fell on the brilliant red flowers. She stared out the window, wondering why those who tried to do right, found life the hardest.

A gaunt calf stumbled weakly and fell near the fence, making no effort to rise, as though understanding the futility of struggling any longer.

"Oh, it is horrible!" she cried, turning away that she might not see the dying convulsions of the animal.

She felt the drouth was a living, relentless thing, wrapping its coils about them all, men and brutes alike, choking and crushing the very heart of the universe. Unnerved by constant anxiety over the sick child, the worry of the drouth, and the shock of Paddy's death, she fell sobbing to her knees beside the couch where the boy lay asleep, breathing heavily, his cheeks burning with fever.

In the distance a strange haze had formed. It moved slowly and majestically nearer, gradually growing thicker-first a misty grey, then changing to a black velvety curtain, dropping straight down from sky to earth. Creeping stealthily, it turned to a brilliant red hue that looked as if it were dripping with fresh blood, a colour that stung the eyeballs until one put up a hand to shut out the grewsome sight. Its hot breath crawled into the lungs and stifled one; licked the face and fanned the hair. Then with diabolic menace the colour changed to an inky blackness, while high above rose the edge of the pall. Tipped with grey and white it bellied out like the crest of an enormous black wave that seemed to poise a second before hurling itself to the earth. Cattle bellowed and tramped frantically beside the fences, trying to escape the dry scorching air, as with a great swirl and deep suction, like a mighty sob, the dust storm enveloped the ranch.

Although it was three o'clock in the afternoon the rooms were dark enough to need lights. The rays from the jets filtering through the misty, moving clouds of dust, looked weird and uncanny. Every window was tightly closed; the air was stifling. Jamie moaned and moved his head restlessly as Nell sat fanning him. Slowly the dust sifted through the windows and under the doors, settling on every thing, until the pillow under the child's head became grey and finally brown. For two terrible hours the storm lasted in all its fury, then a faint gleam of light slowly turned from grey to liquid gold, and Nell ran to raise the windows and let in the fresh air.

The window sash was warped and stubborn; the woman excited, and in her anxiety something caught on the flower-box. With an impatient exclamation she hauled the heavy box nearer the edge of the wide window-sill, and then leaning forward, she forced up the sash.

A wave of fresh, pure air, tinged with a peculiar odour, filled the room. As Nell, panting from her exertion, leaned against the ledge, there was a sudden crash, and the box of geraniums lay wrecked at her feet. Something else lay there. Shining gold in twenty dollar pieces-Paddy's legacy to Jamie.

She stared stupidly a moment, then clutched at the gold pieces. They showered from her hands as she lifted and kissed the coins passionately. This would mean life and happiness for Allan and Jamie.

A strange rumble startled her. Then came the sound of a frightful crash, the rush of hurrying feet, and the door was flung open as Traynor clashed in.

"Look-look, Nell! Rain! Rain! Rain! Thank God! We are saved!"

The deafening roar of the storm almost drowned his voice as the rain beat on the corrugated iron roof and flooded the court.

Then he saw the box and the scattered gold. While the storm shrieked and flooded the country, making great running streams of the dry prairie, Nell told her husband of the secret she had held with Paddy.

She slipped down on the floor, lifting the coins into her lap, and counted them slowly. "Twenty-five thousand dollars!" she exclaimed, and the last gold piece fell with a tinkle like laughter, as though old Paddy, standing by, invisible, were chuckling at his joke.

"Poor old Paddy!" said Traynor, "We none of us understood the old chap except you and Jamie. You've been a plucky little woman, and now the rains, and this legacy of Paddy's, everything is coming out right!" Nell picked up the broken geranium and held it against her lips. "God bless you, Paddy!" she said.

She rose to her feet and her husband slipped an arm around her waist as they stood together at the long, French window, looking out at the glorious rain, while Paddy's gold lay shining at their feet.

All night the rain fell in torrents, and then for the following weeks, each day brought its storm, filling the ditches and watering places in the flats and mountains, while the cattle scattered over the ranges instead of crowding in the few spots where there was water.

The worst drouth in the history of Arizona was over.

# Chapter Thirty-One

Doctor Powell, who had returned from Los Angeles a few days previously, was following Chappo about the garden after supper, praising the flowers the little Mexican had planted and cultivated with such success. Limber, coming from the stable after a final visit to see that the horses were all right for the night, noticed a rider on the road from the Circle Cross.

"Juan is coming," announced the cowpuncher.

Powell turned quickly. "I hope nothing is wrong."

They walked toward the gate. Juan dismounted, slipped the reins over his pony's head and held a note to Powell, saying, "From La Señora. El Señor Glendon is seek."

The doctor hastened into the house, lighted a lamp and read;

Dear Doctor:

Will you come back with Juan? My husband is ill. He had a severe chill, but is now in a stupor and I cannot rouse him. I do not know what is the matter. Please hurry, for I am much alarmed.

Sincerely yours,
Katherine Glendon.

Powell returned to the porch and questioned Juan, who told him Glendon had not been well for a couple of days and had refused to allow his wife to consult the doctor as she had wished to do.

Hurriedly packing what medicines he thought might be necessary, while Chappo saddled a horse, Powell explained the situation briefly to Limber and set out, Juan at his side, for the Glendon ranch.

Katherine was at the door when he dismounted and handed the reins of his horse to Juan.

"Oh, I am so glad you have come!" she exclaimed. "I don't know what is the matter. I have never seen him this way before. Usually I know what to do for him."

She led the way into the bedroom, as she spoke, and Powell noted the unconscious revelation in her words. Glendon lay on the bed, his red congested face and relaxed sensual lips adding to a bestial appearance. The doctor drew a chair to the bedside and lifted the limp, heavy hand from the coverlet, then he leaned down and placed his ear against Glendon's chest. Slowly the seconds ticked away. The doctor leaned back and studied the dissipated countenance, while Katherine waited at the foot of the bed.

"Is it serious?" she asked anxiously.

"Pneumonia," replied Powell gravely. "I will have to be frank, Mrs. Glendon. He has wrecked a fine constitution. The heart is in bad condition from drinking. Alcoholism and pneumonia combined leave very slight chance for recovery in this altitude."

"I understand that," answered Glendon's wife, "but there is a fighting chance, isn't there?"

"Yes—a fighting chance, nothing more. His heart is weak. When the crisis comes it may stop, or it may respond to treatment and rally sufficiently to go on. That is the one chance for him to pull through."

As Powell turned again to his patient, she asked very quietly, "Is there anything I can do?"

"Bring a spoon, glass of fresh water, and some strips of flannel, if you have them?"

She hurried away, and returned in a few minutes.

"That's good," approved the doctor, as she laid the neatly rolled flannel bandages on the table beside him and arranged the tumbler, spoon and pitcher of water where he could reach them conveniently. "Heat that camphorated oil, please."

She followed his instructions and watched him saturate the flannel, which he slipped around Glendon's chest and across his back with the deftness and gentleness of a woman. Then he drew the coverlet smoothly and looked at Katherine's pale face.

"You had better get a little rest," he said. "I will stay here until the crisis is past. Take this," he commanded, preparing a mixture in the glass and holding it out to her.

Katherine swallowed the contents of the tumbler, while Powell added, "You have a couch in the other room? I'll call when it's necessary. There is nothing you can do now, and you must save your strength all you can."

The reaction from three days of anxiety and responsibility aided the sedative in bringing sorely needed mental and physical relaxation. The door leading into the sitting-room was open, and after a short interval the doctor moved softly to satisfy himself that she was sleeping. A chill was creeping through the house. He went to the bedroom and lifted an extra coverlet from the foot-board of the bed, and carried it to the other room. The light from the bed-room fell upon her face and throat, and as the doctor carefully placed the coverlet over her, he saw dark bruises against the pallor of the skin. In repose, the lines of suffering were revealed plainly, and the pathetic droop of the mouth like that of a sorrowing child. Through her half-parted lips he heard the quivering sound of a suppressed sob. He gazed at her, a world of love and pity in his eye, then he glanced through the open door at the man who lay on the bed.

Slowly the doctor returned to the chair at the bedside, he leaned over and looked at Glendon intently. The crisis was not very far off. Powell studied the heart action, took count of the pulse, then his eyes went to the medicine on the table. No sound except the ticking of the clock and the stentorian breathing of Glendon broke the silence. In the other room Katherine slept quietly. The doctor's eyes did not move now from the face of the man on the bed. The pulse beats were growing weaker. Powell's hand reached toward the medicine, paused a second, then withdrew and fell heavily in his lap. Moments went by, and still the woman in the other room rested quietly; the man on the bed drifted more closely to the whirlpool of Eternity, and the man beside the bed, with white face, tightly set mouth and eyes like smouldering flame, sat waiting. Once the doctor rose and walked softly back and forth across the room, the hands clasped behind him were bruised by the nails that cut into the flesh. On the mantel of the living room was a picture of Donnie. The child's eyes looked into his own, they followed him as he moved about.

Powell returned to the bed and sank into the chair, then his face was buried in his hands. With a quick movement he roused himself and watched Glendon steadily. At last he turned slowly to the table and grasped the vial. He held it before him and looked once again at Glendon, but this time the doctor's eyes were untroubled.

Slowly and carefully he poured a few drops of the fluid that would drive the sluggish blood to the heart that had almost ceased to beat. Slowly it responded. Then, in the silence of the night Powell began his battle to save Katherine Glendon's husband. Dawn like a shadowy grey wolf, crawled over the tops of the Galiuros and slipped down into the Hot Springs Cañon. The cragged peaks were bathed in sunlight as Powell looked at them, his face drawn and haggard, his eyes weary, but in his heart a prayer of thanksgiving and a plea for strength to carry on his battle without faltering.

A slight noise at the door caused him to turn. Katherine came swiftly to his side.

"How is he?" she asked eagerly.

"Rallying perfectly. The crisis is past for the present. Unless something unexpected occurs, we shall pull him through."

"Why didn't you call me?" asked Katherine.

"You needed the rest," he replied. "Though the danger point is almost over, you will have a long siege of nursing that will tax your utmost strength. I shall remain here until I am reasonably sure he is safe, and then, you can take charge. Do you know how to use a thermometer or take a pulse?"

"Yes. Doctor King taught me that."

"Then you can manage as well as though you had a trained nurse here. But, remember! You must conserve your strength. That is rule number one for a nurse. It is inflexible. Understand?"

"I promise to do exactly what you say," she replied. "Now I am going to get your breakfast and a good strong cup of coffee will be ready very soon."

Glendon continued to improve during the day, and Powell's vigilance never relaxed. Katherine relieved the doctor for a few hours at a time. When a week had elapsed without developing unfavourable symptoms, Glendon was pronounced practically out of danger. The doctor knew his own weakness now, and with his patient on the road to recovery, Powell's antagonism to the man returned with greater intensity. Yet, as the doctor rode home he determined that as soon as Glendon was well enough, he would try to awaken any shred of decency that might be dormant in the husband of Katherine Glendon, the woman whom Powell loved.

The professional calls continued several weeks, but Powell and Katherine only met in the room where Glendon lay weak and thoroughly frightened, for Powell impressed upon Glendon the seriousness of his physical condition and the inevitable result of continuous drinking, which had weakened his heart. Glendon's promises to reform were genuine. Another month went past. An awkward restraint had grown gradually between Katherine and the doctor, and though he flayed his conscience, he could find no reason for it. As days went by, it became unbearable torture for him to see her in her home with Glendon, and yet, it was still harder to resist the temptation to go there. Finally Powell determined to leave the Springs, and Chappo a week later carried a note to Katherine.

Dear Mrs. Glendon:


I shall be at the Diamond H ranch for a month, after which time I am leaving Arizona for an indefinite period, on business pertaining to the plans for the Sanitarium. Limber and Chappo will be at the Springs all the time, so do not hesitate to call on them should you require assistance at any time or in any way.

With my sincere regards for your husband and yourself,

Most cordially yours,
Cuthbert Powell


Katherine read the note in her room. Her eyes blurred with sudden tears. Now that Powell had gone out of her life, thoughts that she had held in restraint, rushed across her like angry animals breaking their leashes. She saw with unblinded eyes the hideousness of her life, the hopelessness of the future, for during the past few days Glendon had started again to drink.

The note trembled in her fingers, a tear dropped on it and her heart was sick with despair. She understood at last the meaning of the courage, the peace that had come into her life, and she knew that she could go on to the end that she might purify her love for Powell, by the flame of sacrifice.

As the note blazed up in the fireplace, then died to a quivering grey mass, she lifted her face to the tall peaks that bent over the cañon, and their strength seemed to reach out to her.

# Chapter Thirty-Two

With the breaking of the drouth, Jamie seemed to acquire fresh vitality, and by the time the grass covered the valley he was able to take short rides on his pony, carefully guarded from over-exertion by Limber and Doctor Powell. Under their united care the little patient gained additional strength. They all hoped that the crisis might be successfully tided over.

One day when Limber and Jamie had returned from their ride, the cowpuncher accosted Traynor in the stable, while unsaddling the ponies.

"Thar's goin' to be a sale of Government horses at Port Grant tomorrow, and maybe I'd better go an' look 'em over."

"Good idea," assented the Boss. "Better get over early and size them up before the bidding commences."

Early the next morning Limber reached the garrison and made his way to the Quartermaster's Corral where the horses destined for sale were tethered. Frequently good horses could be gotten cheaply at such sales, because of blemishes that rendered them unfit for Cavalry use, yet did not interfere with other work. Only a perfect horse was reckoned a match for the ponies of the Apaches.

Limber selected two animals, then stood watching the sales. He noticed with surprise that no one was bidding on a big, handsome sorrel with cream mane and tail and eyes that were alight with intelligence. The slender legs and tapering ears showed heritage of racing blood.

The cowboy examined the animal, but there was no sign of blemish. Puzzled, he watched inferior horses put up and sold after lively bidding; but no one made an offer on the sorrel, that watched the other horses with evident interest that was almost amused curiosity. Limber liked the horse, somehow.

"What's he condemned for?" asked Limber of a soldier who stood near him.

"Unmanageable. Breaks rank, won't face with the other horses, dances when he ought to stand still, and runs like the Devil, everytime they line up in parade. He's racing stock. A dandy horse, alright, but too high-lived for Cavalry work, and they can't break him in to it. He's got more sense than any other horse in the troop, but after they punished him a few times, he got to fighting every time a saddle was put on his back."

Limber remembered several excellent horses at the Diamond H that had been more un-promising material. When he went back to the ranch after the sale, he led the big sorrel horse, intending to handle it himself.

Jamie was in the stable when Limber arrived, and the horse leaned out its graceful neck until its nose touched the child's shoulder. A sudden thought struck Limber. The horse had been used to children, evidently, at some period of its life.

"Go get some sugar," said Limber to Bronco, and when he returned, Limber handed a lump of sugar to the child. "See if he will take it from you." Jamie held out the sugar, and Gov'ner, with a little nicker, took it carefully from the boy's hand. After repeating the operation several times, the boy moved slowly away, holding out his hand, and the horse followed him, threading gingerly between the buggies, around the men, and receiving his reward.

Traynor and Nell came out to watch them, and Gov'ner condescended to make friends with the woman, also, but flatly refused to accept sugar from any of the men. He plainly showed his preference for the child, and Traynor laughed as he said,

"He has no use for any one but you, Jamie. He's your horse from now on; but you must not ride him until Limber says that it will be all right."

So for days Gov'ner was educated, gently and kindly, and always with the child near by. At first the boy was placed on the animal's back, while it was led about the barn. After that, Limber, mounted on Peanut, led Gov'ner on the road at a walk, while Jamie talked to the horse or patted the shining neck. Not once was there any indication of fractiousness on the part of Gov'ner. A child's love and kindness had conquered where discipline had failed.

Mornings, when the day's work on the range was light, Gov'ner would be led out and the miniature cowboy saddle placed on his back. Neatly coiled and tied to the saddle was a beautifully made riata, the gift of Bronco, who was noted for his skill in making these ropes. When the childish figure appeared, equipped with leather leggings and tiny spurs, there would be a sharp, joyous yelp from Dash, the leader of the greyhound pack, and an answering call as Killem, Catchem, Scrub and Beauty came leaping in delight, knowing there were rabbits and coyotes to chase.

Fong shuffled out with a lard-pail slipped into a flour sack, which he carefully tied to the little saddle, with the smiling information, "Clake and clookies." Then Nell kissed the boy good-bye, saying, "Take good care of him, Limber;" and the man, turning in his saddle would reply, "Don't you fret, Mrs. Traynor. We all look out for the Kid."

In the evening, the cowpuncher, dwindling to a tiny white-robed figure, crawled into Nell's arms as she sat in front of the big, "comfy" fire-place, to tell her about the baby calves, and how many rabbits had been chased. Once, with shining eyes and flushed cheeks, how "Me and Limber roped a coyote-but we let it go home again to its fambly —'cause I told Limber I knew they would be waiting for it to come."

One day Jamie did not come out to Gov'ner's stall, and the horse whinnied in vain. The men went around speaking softly, taking off their spurs to avoid any possible noise on the board floor of the stable, and Doctor Powell never left the bedside of the darkened, quiet room, where he battled for the life of the child they loved so deeply.

"You had better take him and Mrs. Traynor to Los Angeles," the doctor advised Traynor. "She is breaking down under the long strain, and in her condition needs care as much as the boy. I will go with you and stay as long as I can be of any assistance."

"Do you think there is any hope for him?" asked Traynor.

"A child's life is a bit of delicate mechanism," answered Powell, "even when all hope was lost, I have seen wonderful rallies. Not through the skill of a physician, but through some peculiar recuperative power we don't understand, as yet."

Traynor wrung the doctor's hand silently.

Arrangements for the trip were completed, the trunks and luggage loaded on the heavy wagon had already started for Willcox. As Traynor assisted Nell into the carriage, Gov'ner, poking his head from the box stall, wondering what it was all about, saw Limber carry a limp little figure from the courtyard into the stable. The horse recognized the boy and whinnied joyously. Jamie lifted his head and spoke to Limber, who carried him over to the horse. Gov'ner's nose reached out and the thin little hand stroked it weakly.

"Good-bye, Gov'ner," came the faint voice. "Limber will be good to you till I come home. Won't you, Limber?"

Limber's face twitched as he answered, "No one shall ride Gov'ner whilst you are gone, Kid."

After the carriage disappeared and the men had gone about the various duties of the day, Fong shuffled into the barn and looked around cautiously. Seeing no one, he sneaked into the saddle room and picked up a shiny little lard pail, that had once been used to hold cookies. Clutching it tightly the Chinaman ran swiftly across to the kitchen, and shut the door with a bang.

Limber, who had been saddling Peanut, unobserved by Fong, witnessed the incident, and when evening came, the cowboy knew it was not opium that caused the Chinaman's red-rimmed eyelids.

Gov'ner was very lonely in the stables and pastures all day when the other horses were busy, and at first he called incessantly. Then finding that it brought no response from the child he loved, he stood patiently watching the door that led into the court.

Letters came from Traynor saying that they were winning the battle, and that Jamie would come back to them better than ever before in his life. Then came another letter which Limber read with a choking voice, for Traynor told the boys of the Diamond H that they now had a new Boss, and that the little mother was well, happy, and sent her love to them all. That she said they were "all her boys," and she would not be satisfied until she got back home again and showed them the wonderful baby. Traynor added that Doctor Powell would be home that week, but the rest of them would not return for another month.

Fong, on a hunt for eggs, passed through the stable as the letter was finished, and Limber called him to tell him the news. The old Chinaman's eyes filled up with tears that streamed down his face. "Klid he comme home all light; new blaby clommee allee samee. When he clome? I blake a cake!"

That night the Mail Order catalogue was the centre of attraction in the bunk-house, and for hours the index and illustrations were scanned in search of a suitable gift for the new Boss. Saddles, spurs, chaps were debated as not quite fit articles for immediate use, as the recipient would be about two months old when he reached the Diamond H. In a quandary they hunted up Fong.

The old Chinaman bristled with importance and put on the horn spectacles that made him resemble a reincarnated Confucius. Slowly and critically he squinted at the catalogue, then a "smile that was child-like and bland" expanded his face, while his long-nailed finger pointed triumphantly.

"You clatchee him. He all light for blaby."

They stared at the illustration, gazed blankly at Fong and then looked again at the book.

"What's it for?" demanded Bronco.

"No savey? Blimeby-blaby clatchee teeth!" Fong gave a vivid impersonation by chewing the end of a fork which he seized.

"I guess that's o.k. so far as it goes," Roarer endorsed, "but we've got to get somethin' else. That's too durned measly."

Once again they studied, suggested, rejected, and finally, in the hours approaching dawn, the order sheet was filled out. The articles enumerated ranged from the teething-ring and rattle, a baby buggy, a high chair, silver mug, one pair silver-mounted spurs, one silver-mounted bit, a small-sized saddle, bridle and a gold bracelet "for a lady" that was to be inscribed "from the boys of the Diamond H." A letter explained the circumstances and eventful arrival, and asked if the head of the store would take special care with the order, and pick out a nice bracelet, as they were all cowpunchers and didn't know anything but cows, —perhaps the store-keeper might get his wife to pick out the right sort of bracelet.

Two weeks later they received word that their order had been carefully filled, and a handsome, plain gold bracelet inscribed as desired had been forwarded, together with the other articles in their esteemed order.

# Chapter Thirty-Three

The morning that Traynor was due at the ranch with his family, the men and Fong were up long before daybreak. Inside and out, the ranch had been scrutinized mercilessly, to see if everything was in perfect order. Fong's pigtail jerked like an expiring rattlesnake, as he rushed here and there, putting the final touches to a meal which was to be the culinary achievement of his life.

When the carriage was finally driven into the stable, the men crowded around, talking and laughing, asking questions but not waiting replies, until Traynor piloted his wife and baby into the house; Jamie lingered with his friends.

There was a joyful reunion between the child and the greyhounds which had been shut in the corral. Then, surrounded by the leaping, yelping pack, Jamie and the men turned to Gov'ner's stall. The door was opened by Limber, and they all stood waiting till Jamie called to the horse, "Gov'ner! I'm back home again!"

Gov'ner's head flung up alertly, his nostrils distended, his eyes shone; then as he saw the little chap outside the stall the horse whinnied, tossed his head and pranced through the door. The proud head lowered as the horse reached the child, and the lips nipped playfully at Jamie's coat, while the boy laughed in delight, petting the satiny neck, as he said triumphantly, "You see, he didn't forget me while I was away."

It was a new Jamie that had come back to them. For sometime Powell had been studying the cause of the boy's retarded recovery, and had finally concluded it was due to other reasons than the tubercular tendency. He had not suggested this to Traynor until consultation with two noted specialists, had confirmed his diagnosis. After the operation which was found necessary, the lad's improvement was astonishing; so when he reached the Diamond H, nothing more was necessary than outdoor life in the high, dry climate and plenty of nourishing food, to make him a normally healthy boy.

Traynor joined the boys as they watched the reunion of Gov'ner and the child. Then he asked, "Don't you boys intend to come in and meet the new Boss and his mother? They're expecting you."

Without hesitation the men followed him into the living room where the young mother, with the baby on her lap, waited the homage she knew would be accorded freely by these loyal friends.

Cautiously they all approached and regarded the small atom of humanity that gazed back at them with serene eyes.

"Feel how heavy he is," offered Nell, holding the infant toward them. Each one shrunk back a bit and their eyes shifted to each other.

"Take him, Bronco. He won't bite;" laughed Nell.

Bronco edged back of Limber, as he replied, "Limber's the foreman. He's got the first throw!"

Limber's arms went out, and the little mother laid the child carefully upon them, fussing with the dainty white dress, and smiling down into the baby face against the blue flannel shirt. As she stepped back, she caught a passing expression on Limber's face, and her eyes grew misty. Though he did not know it, she glimpsed Limber's soul in that moment.

The baby blinked up, then a quivering, uncertain little smile touched his lips.

"Gee! Look at him," ejaculated Bronco. "Say, he's made friends with Limber already. Isn't he the smart little geezer, though?"

Gaining courage the rest of the men pressed closer, and Bronco put out a horny finger to touch the pink palm. Like the leaves of a sensitive plant, the fingers curled tightly around the cowboy's digit, then pulled determinedly toward a puckering mouth, while Bronco's eyes opened in consternation.

"Say, you don't want to eat me, do you? That ain't a stick of candy!" he pulled gently but firmly until he managed to rescue the threatened finger, and the other men chuckled in unison.

"Ain't he got a dandy grip! He'll be able to hang onto a steer when he gets it roped, you bet!" Roarer's squeak asserted.

"Smartest baby I ever seen," Holy pronounced oracularly, ignoring the fact that it was the first time in his life he had ever been near a young baby.

Fong hovered in the doorway, and as they looked up they saw a cake with gorgeous white icing. It was Fong's only way of expressing his fealty and congratulations. He deposited the cake on the table, and Nell beamed on him.

"We'll make baby cut his own cake, Fong!" Then she turned, "Limber, won't you call Allan?"

Traynor joined them, and the entire outfit stood in admiration, while Nell held the tiny hand about the big butcher knife and thrust it into the heart of the lacy design of icing. Fong's eyes blinked rapidly, and he kept saying, over and over, "Velly fline blaby! Him velly fline bloy!"

Once again Traynor brought champagne, and the glasses were lifted as he gave the toast, "To the Boss of the Diamond H and his mother. God bless them both!"

After that Nell got the teething-ring, and when the child grasped and thrust it into its open mouth, the men all grinned. "He sure knows what that is made for," chortled Bronco, "an' that's more'n we knowed till Fong tol' us."

They bombarded Nell with questions regarding his weight, how soon he would acquire real teeth, and how long before he would be wearing trousers. They were thirsting for information regarding infantile development, and when Roarer, in an off-hand manner, referred to his "sister's twins in Texas," they looked at him with envious eyes. Roarer did not disclose that said twins were almost as old as himself. He dilated on various events in their careers, which he remembered hearing the aforesaid twins relate themselves. He cudgeled his brain for historic data.

The boys were feeling very much at home, when the baby began to squirm uneasily in its mother's arms. Its face screwed up, its eyes squinted and disappeared entirely, and the boys looked anxiously at Nell.

"Does he have fits?" inquired Bronco solicitously. "I know its all right for puppies to have 'em, but does babies?"

The infant answered for himself with a sneeze, and Nell looked around at the open window. This gave the men an excuse to plead work, and tiptoe from the room.

Once in the stable they halted, and Bronco, still seeking information, faced Roarer. "Say, Roarer, did your sister's twins in Texas have fits?"

"Sure," answered Roarer cheerfully. "They was so uster havin' 'em that we never paid no attention at all when one come on. It's just like puppies, you know. 'Twouldn't be noways natural if thar wasn't fits-an' fleas. Don't do no hurt. Jest look at all the people that lives to grow up, anyways!"

But that night Roarer borrowed the big book, telling "How to be Your Own Doctor," which was the Court of Final Appeal for everything from cooking recipes to getting rid of bedbugs, lawsuits and other worries, together with a complete list of the "ills to which the human flesh is heir," and infallible remedies for all.

The men did not know that he was studying assiduously every bit of data obtainable regarding the diseases of infants. They wondered afterwards at Roarer's unfailing supply of information about babies, well or ill; but he ascribed his knowledge entirely to his associations with the Texas Twins.

Once more the interrupted routine of ranch life was resumed and Limber divided his time between the Diamond H and the Hot Springs. Though the cowpuncher passed the Circle Cross at intervals he never dismounted. Chappo and Juan kept in touch with each other, and through them Limber and Powell knew that Glendon's wife found life more bearable since the anxiety about Donnie had been removed. Yet she never suspected the part that Doctor Powell and Limber had taken in forcing Glendon's acquiescence to her wishes and plans for the boy.

# Chapter Thirty-Four

Unlike most ranches in Arizona, the Diamond H cultivated a number of its fenced fields. Millet, sorghum and other cattle feed was stacked for use of the horses and the thoroughbred bulls during winter, thus insuring first-class condition of this particular stock when the grass started and they were turned out on the open range. This system of Traynor's avoided losing time that would be otherwise required to put his bulls in good breeding condition each spring.

During the plowing season, the blacksmith at the Diamond H suddenly decided to leave for parts unknown, between sunset and sunrise. The cowboys were all able to shoe their own ponies, but tires had to be set, tools sharpened, plowpoints kept in shape, pumping machinery needed constant repairing, and a first-class blacksmith was a necessity on the Diamond H. Willcox could not fill the vacancy, and advertisements in Tucson and even Los Angeles papers brought no response. Each of the men on the ranch had done the best he could to fill the void, but all acknowledged ruefully, "it's a durn sight different from jest shoein' a pony."

In this emergency Loco, the Mexican who had obtained work at the Diamond H after leaving Walton, announced that he had been a blacksmith in Mexico.

"Well, he can't do no worse than the rest of us," Bronco decided, but one day's trial proved Loco was first-class in that work, and so he was transferred from range work to the blacksmith shop with increased pay and additional respect.

He was pounding a red-hot iron on the anvil one day, when Traynor sauntering to the entrance of the shop, stood watching him.

"How soon will you be ready to start, Loco?" he asked.

"In a few minutes I will finish, Señor."

"What is it?" Traynor asked idly.

Without looking up the Mexican replied; "It is a branding iron, Señor."

He skillfully bent the end of the iron, thrust it into a tub of water for a couple of seconds, then withdrew and examined it critically, after which he heated it again. It was a peculiarly shaped iron, and Traynor dropped on a box and looked with interest, as Loco pressed it on a board, leaving a mark covering a space four inches each way.

"That's an odd brand," said Traynor, picking up the burnt board and scrutinizing it, while the Mexican regarded him closely.

"It is my horse brand," explained Loco. "Apache is leg weary and I am going to turn him on the range a while. I bought another horse."

"There are plenty good horses in the herd without using your pony, Loco."

The Mexican shook his head; "Many thanks, Señor, but I can do better work with my own horse."

"Well suit yourself;" Traynor agreed carelessly. "I want you to go with me this morning to Mud Springs, so I can show you where I want the ditch dug and the mill put up."

Loco was studying the iron with the smile of an artisan who recognizes a satisfactory piece of work. "I will get the horses, Señor;" he said, and turned to the stable carrying the branding iron in his hand.

If Apache, Loco's pony, was leg-weary, it was not very evident as it pranced and danced along the road beside gay little Chinati, whose swift movements had earned his name, "Blackbird."

Mud Springs lay twelve miles away from the Diamond H, in the Galiuros toward Hot Springs. The trail through Mud Springs was not often used, as the Box Springs trail, a few miles further north, was more direct and also much easier. It was a wild, desolate place and the spring in a narrow, rocky cañon, so cattle preferred the valley during the grass season. This spring was of great value to the Diamond H and PL ranges, however, giving cattle access to feed in the mountains that otherwise would be too far from water. Traynor, having learned wisdom from the drouth, had decided to build a huge reservoir at the mouth of this cañon for the storage of water that would otherwise be wasted by spreading.

He explained the details carefully to Loco, pointing out where the ditch was to be dug to conduct the water to the reservoir site.

"I want the wind-mill put up beside the reservoir, like the one at the house. I'll get the boys at work next week; but you can go on with the mill work before then. I am going over to Hot Springs for a few days."

"How long did you live in Mexico, Señor?" asked Loco.

"I have never been there," answered Traynor, wondering at the question.

"Only Americanos who have lived in Mexico speak as you do," persisted Loco.

"I learned Spanish at college," replied Traynor. "By Jove! What a shot! It's too far for a pistol!"

He was gazing up at a magnificent blacktail deer which stood like a statue on a ledge six hundred feet above them. Its head was thrown back, nostrils dilated, the slender legs were tense and ready for flight as it sniffed the wind. Then with a snort, it whirled and vanished.

Traynor had been so absorbed in admiration of the buck that he had momentarily forgotten Loco's presence. The Mexican, fifteen feet in the rear of Traynor had untied the riata which hung on his saddle and coiled it cautiously, watching the other man sharply. With a swift movement he flung the rope about Traynor's body, pinioning his arms firmly. Chinati, feeling the jerk on his bridle, leaped forward and Traynor fell helpless to the ground.

The sun was setting when Traynor again became conscious of his surroundings and saw Loco standing over him.

"What happened, Loco?" he asked stupidly. "Was I thrown?"

Loco made no reply, and as Traynor still dazed from a deep gash on his head, tried to rise, he realized that he was securely bound, hand and foot. The loss of blood made him faint and sick, and his brain seemed incapable of lucid ideas. He had struck his head on a sharp rock in falling from his horse.

For a while he lay with closed eyes, then he looked up and saw Loco a short distance away, gathering pieces of dead wood, which he heaped systematically into a pile. Traynor recalled the Mexican's peculiar ways and wondered if the man had suddenly become insane. He knew that if such were the case, the best plan would be to avoid irritating him.

Traynor turned his head. The hope that Chinati had gotten away and might give the alarm by returning to the ranch riderless died, when he saw his own pony standing quietly beside Loco's. Then he noticed his pistol glistening a few feet from him, and wondered if he could worm his way to it without attracting Loco's attention. Keeping close watch upon the Mexican, Traynor slowly writhed toward the firearm until he was within a foot of it. By half turning he believed he could grasp the pistol as his hands were tied in front of him. Loco lit the fire, and with a fiendish grin untied the branding iron from his saddle and laid it on the flame.

A thrill of sickening fear shot through Traynor as he strained at the rope binding him. One more effort and he would be able to touch the pistol. The Mexican calmly arranged the wood which had fallen, then walked over to Traynor, who closed his eyes, hoping to throw the man off his guard; but Loco, with a malicious leer, picked up the pistol and seated himself on the ground beside his captive.

"I saw you, Señor;" he chuckled.

"What are you going to do, Loco?" asked Traynor, trying to appear unconcerned. He now understood that he was at the mercy of a maniac, and thought what a fool he had been to forget the many irrational actions of the man, whose name, Loco, should have been warning enough in itself. The loco weed of Arizona and Mexico effects the brains of horses, causing even the most reliable and well-broken animal to develop sudden fits of viciousness. Loco's moodiness, his outbursts of anger, had fastened the nickname on him while he worked for Walton.

Loco rolled a cigarette, which he lighted deliberately.

"So! You have not been in Mexico, Señor?" he drawled sarcastically.

"Never! I have no object in lying typo about it;" said Traynor earnestly. "Why should I deny it?"

"Oh, no, Señor! You never knew Ramoncita?"

"I never heard of her." Then catching sight of a small crucifix that hung against Loco's breast where the blue flannel shirt fell apart, Traynor looked the man steadily in the eyes, and said slowly, "Hold that crucifix before me, Loco, and I will swear that. I am telling you the truth."

The man wavered a second, then laughed cunningly, "A crucifix means nothing to a Gringo, and fear makes liars of all men."

"Let me go, and I will give you money to make life easy for you, Loco. You can go back to Mexico to your friends and be happy."

The words roused the man to frenzy. He leaped to his feet, murder and insanity stamped on his distorted features.

"Go back to Mexico, you Gringo dog? Do you know when I will go back there? When I have killed you, as I swore. You stole her from me. You rode away laughing, and that night she killed herself!" He jerked the crucifix from his breast, and shook it in front of Traynor's face. "You would swear it? On this —? You did not know that I took this Cross from her dead heart! And I swore on it as I knelt beside her coffin, that I would leave my country, my friends, and never rest or return until I had found you, who had made her an outcast. Every one turned from her while she was alive, and when she killed herself, the Church turned from her, and she was buried in unconsecrated ground just outside the Church fence. The Padre said that the Saints and the Holy Angels turn away because she took her own life."

His voice rose more shrilly, "You did not think I could find you, but Walton knew you. He saw you with her in Mexico while I was away. Walton knew you, you Gringo dog! You killed her body! You killed her soul! You thought you were safe, but Walton knew you!"

"Walton lied to you," Traynor answered furiously, recalling rumours of Walton's threats of retaliation on the Diamond H owner and cowboys. The Mexican, Loco, had been Walton's catspaw. Traynor subsided, groping for some plan to influence the Mexican.

"You cannot escape this time!" gloated Loco, circling about Traynor as buzzards circle about their prey. "I swore you should pay."

He went to the fire and tested his iron. Then, seeing it was not yet hot enough, he came back and leaned over the prostrate man.

"They are waiting patiently, Señor! As patiently as I have waited seven long years."

A number of crows rose from the bushes with discordant caws as he waved his arms wildly in the air and cried, "Look!" They soon settled down again, to watch the two men. Higher in the air circled a couple of buzzards, and the faint, quivering yelp of a coyote disturbed the silence.

"I shall not kill you, for I want you to live long enough to suffer. I will leave my brand on your face and shall cut your ears as they do the calves. Then I will go back to Mexico to my amigos and say, 'I have kept my oath!' The buzzards and coyotes will keep you company after I have gone, Señor!"

With a half-suppressed groan, Traynor thought of his wife. He had told her he would remain a few days at Hot Springs, so there would be no alarm at his absence. Later, when they missed him, a few tattered shreds of clothing and fleshless, scattered bones would tell where the buzzards and coyotes had feasted.

Muttering, the Mexican brought the white hot iron from the embers and knelt by Traynor's side. He pulled the crucifix from his bosom, kissed it reverently and replaced it; then he made the sign of the Cross in the air above Traynor's face. His eyes gleamed exultingly as he clutched Traynor's hair and brought the hot iron closer and closer.

Traynor could smell and feel the heat, and great beads of anguish broke out as he made a last convulsive effort to free himself of his bonds. It was useless! His muscles relaxed, he closed his eyes, clenched his teeth and waited.

Loco was too intent upon his revenge to notice a cowboy racing toward them down the side of the cañon, until a wild yell woke the echo of the rocky walls. The Mexican looked up and recognized Limber. Fearful of being thwarted in his revenge, Loco stooped quickly over Traynor and lowered the iron deliberately while a fiendish smile distorted his face, and a sibilant hiss, like a rattlesnake about to strike, sounded between the gleaming teeth.

Traynor, too, had heard the yell, but he had no hope that Limber would reach him in time. His eyes looked into Loco's. The iron almost touched Traynor's flesh, the grip of the Mexican's hand that clutched his victim's hair, was so tense that Traynor could feel the quivering nerves.

A shot rang out. A look of surprise flashed over Loco's face, the iron slid from his hand, but Traynor jerked suddenly so that it fell against the ground, while Loco crumpled slowly across the body of the other man. Weak with reaction Traynor became unconscious once more, and when he opened his eyes, Limber had slipped his arms under Traynor's shoulders and held a flask to the white lips of the rancher.

"Drink it," commanded the cowpuncher, who was now, trembling with nervousness. "That was a mighty close call. Did he hurt you any?"

"I'll be all right in a few minutes," answered Traynor, as Limber cut the rope and assisted him to his feet. The tight coils had made his body numb and the cut on his head was an ugly one. Traynor was no coward, but he felt a spasm of nausea as he looked at the iron which was now turning from white heat to dull red.

"Better let me fix that cut," suggested Limber.

He helped Traynor to the spring, and washed the ugly wound as tenderly as a woman, then he bound it with Traynor's white silk handkerchief as he listened to the explanation of what happened.

"It's a lucky thing for Walton he ain't in the Territory," said the cowboy tersely. "You can't blame the Greaser for believin' Walton's lies. He's been off his cabeza a long time and everybody knowed it; but Loco wouldn't of hurt nobody if Walton hadn't put him up to it. We wondered why Walton was so all-fired rushed to catch that train, and had figgered out it was because Billy Saunders ordered him to quit the country. It's Walton oughter be layin' there instead of Loco."

The two men moved to the side of the dead Mexican, and as they stood looking down at him, Traynor recalled Loco's words, "and she was buried in unconsecrated ground, just outside the Church fence, and the Padre said the Saints and Holy Angels turn away because she took her own life."

The little crucifix dangling from the cord on Loco's neck had slipped from the half-open shirt. Traynor knelt down and placed it on the dead man's breast, then lifted the limp hands and laid them above the crucifix. Limber took off his coat and covered the Mexican's face.

"I'll send a wagon from the ranch," said Traynor. "It's a mighty lucky thing for me that you happened across here today. I was on my way to the Springs to see you about a letter I had from Doctor Powell."

"I was workin' on the Divide, when I seen you and Loco comin' this way; but I was busy with some cattle and didn't pay much attention. When I got through and rid up on the Divide I seen Loco with the two horses and you layin' on the ground. I thought mebbe you'd been throwed till I got near enough to see what he was up to. I had to shoot him. Thar wasn't nothin' else to do."

Traynor laid his hand on the cowboy's shoulder, looking at him earnestly, "I owe you a debt that can never be paid, Limber."

The cowboy flushed with embarrassment. "You ain't got no call to thank me, Mr. Traynor. Peanut done it, not me. He just busted hisself gettin' here in time. I never seen him run so fast. Looked like he knowed it was up to him and he done it."

"Peanut can't have all the credit," responded Traynor. Then he drew a letter from his pocket. "Doctor Powell has written me that he would like to make you his partner in the P L ranch and cattle, provided it would not interfere with my plans."

Limber looked up in open surprise. "I ain't got enough to pay for 'em" he said. "I only saved up nine hundred dollars, all told."

"Well, Powell says if you won't accept half interest, he will close out his cattle entirely. The Sanitarium will take all his time and attention, and he wanted you to handle the stock for him. I wrote him I would be glad to see you two in partnership."

The cowboy stared at the ground. "I don't say that I wouldn't be glad to take the chanct, because I've been savin' up hopin' some day I could buy a bunch of stock; but I can't let him give it to me. I can't owe no man, Mr. Traynor."

"Neither can I, Limber," was the quick retort. "The debt I owe you can never be paid; but I can pay part of the interest due on it. Let me buy the half-interest for you from Powell."

Limber shook his head slowly. "I don't want you to think I'm mulish, or that I don't appreciate what you and Doctor Powell is offerin' me, but I just can't do it."

"Then, let me make it a straight business deal, as if we were all strangers. Give me your note and pay when you feel able. Surely you can't make any objection to that?"

Limber took the proffered hand, "If you make the note out reg'lar, just as if it was some one else," he stipulated.

Traynor smiled broadly, "All right, Limber. That's a go. I'll write Powell about it. Now, I'll hurry down to the ranch and send one of the boys with the wagon."

Peanut looked up as Chinati galloped away with Traynor, but seeing Loco's horse, Apache, tethered to a bush, and that Limber was sitting quietly not far away, the gallant little pony fell contentedly to cropping the grass.

Limber rose, loosened the cinch and removed the saddle and blanket from Peanut's lathered back which he rubbed with a wisp of grass. He stroked the pony's nose absently and looked with pity at the dead Mexican.

"Dern that Walton! The cards was sure stacked against you, Loco. I'm sorry I had to do it."

# Chapter Thirty-Five

In spite of the general impression of frontier lawlessness that prevailed during the 'eighties', Arizona had probably as clean a moral standard as many of the Eastern States which considered themselves far in advance of the unsettled country. Though men 'packed' guns, and personal affronts were settled out of Court, Arizona could brag that any good woman was protected by every man in the Territory.

So, when the Southern Pacific train was held up west of Willcox, the community was as much surprised and shocked as any more conventional town might be. Seventy thousand dollars were taken from the express car by the robbers, and no definite clue to their identity or whereabouts could be discovered.

The railroad people, believing the first success would encourage others, secretly armed all express messengers with sawed-off shotguns, heavily loaded with buckshot, the most deadly weapon known for short-range work.

These precautions were justified six months later, when the regular west-bound train was nearing Cochise, a little place twelve miles west of Willcox. The engineer, observing a danger signal, slowed down and finally stopped. As the track was treacherous at that point during rainy weather, he had no suspicions. Frequent washouts occurred in the sandy roadbed. The track-walker approached, swinging his lighted lantern.

"What's the trouble?" asked the engineer, as he and the fireman leaned over the side of the engine, staring through the darkness.

"Track's soft. You'll have to go slow for about a quarter of a mile," was the reply. "They wired to Willcox from Cochise but you had left on time. Hold on a minute and I'll ride back with you."

"All right," answered the engineer, then as the man swung on the cab, "You're a new man?"

"Yes. Just went to work this week. I was on the Santa Fe before I came down here," he drew a pipe from his pocket, filled and lighted it as the engineer turned to start the engine.

The fireman had returned to the rear of the cab and set to work shovelling coal.

"Hands up!"

Two armed, masked men confronted the engineer and the fireman faced three others. There was no alternative except to obey. The train was made up of an engine, express car, three Pullmans and two day coaches; the express, as usual, being directly back of the engine and coal car. Three of the bandits guarded the fireman and engineer, the other two running back a short distance. As the brakeman approached to ascertain the trouble, he was met and commanded to uncouple the express car and engine from the rest of the train. Then, having complied under protest, he was compelled to join the other two men who were under guard.

"Pull ahead till we tell you to stop," was the order, and the engine puffed on its way, leaving the passengers and conductors to discover their predicament later.

Four miles from Cochise, in a spot where there was no human habitation, the engineer was forced to halt. Three robbers remained on guard while the other two went to the express car and knocked sharply on the door.

"What is it?" the messenger demanded.

"Open the door!"

There was no reply.

"Open the door, and we won't hurt you;" called the robber a second time.

Again there was absolute silence.

"We'll give you one minute to open that door, or we'll blow you and the car to Hell!"

The man inside the car knew there was nothing to be gained by delay.

"All right," he called. "I'll open it, boys."

There was slipping of bolts and creaking of wood. The door opened slowly about two inches. Three-fingered Jack standing close to it, jumped backward and thrust the barrel of his pistol through the aperture. A flash, a scream of agony, and the door closed with a bang. The messenger stood with blood streaming from his right arm, the sawed-off shot gun smoking at his feet; but as he slipped unconscious to the floor, he knew one of the robbers was badly hurt.

Outside, the men surrounded Three-fingered Jack, who had torn the red handkerchief from his face. Blood poured from a gaping wound in his side. His comrades eased him to the ground, then turned their attention to the express car. This time it would be short work-dynamite.

"Hurry!" urged the leader.

They moved to obey; but stopped with oaths. Down the track from Cochise shone the headlight of an engine. They knew there was no other passenger train due either way at that hour; but they could not count on freights or specials. The railroad officials had given instructions that each train-despatcher keep close watch on the time between stations, and if any train were late to wire at once to the last station; then, unless satisfied, rush out an extra engine, or pusher, with armed men.

These men, seeing the headlight of the stalled engine, were ready for action as the 'pusher' raced forward at full speed. The robbers, realizing that flight was imperative, ran to the horses they had left tied in the brush, only pausing long enough to seize their wounded comrade. They boosted him roughly to a pony, leading it by the reins while Jack clung moaning to the horn of the saddle. Each movement was excruciating agony, as they rode madly through the mesquite brush in the darkness.

The rescue party found the unconscious messenger, and the kidnapped engine and express car were backed to the rest of the train, while the pusher raced to Cochise for a posse and horses to trail the robbers.

It did not take very long to load armed men and saddled ponies into an empty box-car at Cochise, and in record-breaking time the little special again reached the hold-up. While they were unloading their ponies, the belated passenger train, carrying its excited passengers, its untouched express car and the wounded man, rattled past the posse. The engineer leaned from his cab, waved a grimy hand and sounded a long-drawn whistle. Out in the darkness, the fleeing outlaws heard and knew what it meant. Their progress had been impeded by the condition of Jack, and each movement of his pony brought groans and curses.

The leader halted.

"It's him, or all of us," he said, and the rest agreed.

"We're sorry. Jack, but it can't be helped. We've got to leave you behind."

The wounded man cursed them for cowards and traitors; but fell limp as they helped him to the ground and made him as comfortable as possible. Then they rode away, carrying his pistol with them, for they would need it worse than Jack. His curses followed them.

The darkness made it impossible for the posse to strike the trail until dawn, but no time was lost after that. Whether the robbers had some definite plan, or had become too demoralized at their surprise, puzzled the trailers; for the riders had kept together instead of scattering in order to make pursuit more difficult. The work of following was made easy by the softened condition of the country from recent rain, and occasionally a splatter of blood on a stone proved that the messenger was justified in his assertion that he had wounded one of the outlaws.

Five miles from the railroad track they found Three-fingered Jack at the point of death. He lay gasping, and watched them approach until they stood looking down on him. A sardonic smile twisted his features. He would have his revenge on the men who had deserted him. With curses and vituperation he told the names of those who had fled to save themselves-then added names of others in the band. Several names mentioned were not unexpected, as they were men known to be ready for any crime; but no one was prepared to hear him accuse Jim Glendon and Alpaugh, who was the constable of Willcox and Deputy Sheriff of Cochise County.

Tom Graham, the constable of Cochise and leader of the posse, leaned down and said, "What was that? Did you say Alpaugh and Glendon?"

Jack saw the incredulity on the faces above him. Quietly, but with rasping voice, he replied, "I said Glendon and Alpaugh. I'm making this statement before I die, and I want you all to witness what I say. They didn't play square with me;—they even took my pistol so I couldn't shoot myself. Glen and Alpaugh were staying home to prove an alibi-We were to go to Glendon's after the job was done-give the money-to him-till row was over." His eyes closed. The men thought he was dead, but he gathered his ebbing strength once more. "We were to share-and-quit the country —" Blood choked his utterance; his head sank back and the jaws relaxed.

The group looked at him, then glanced at each other dubiously. The accusation against Alpaugh astonished them. He was acknowledged a good officer, sober, fearless and apparently worthy of the confidence the community placed in him while Glendon, though known to drink heavily and be aggressive in his cups, had never been considered criminal in his tendencies. But, Jack's statement, made in full consciousness that he was dying, and with apparently clear mind, was damning evidence.

Slowly the posse returned to the track, carrying the dead man across a saddle-horse, while the original rider sat behind, balancing the limp form. When they reached the railroad the body was placed on the floor of the caboose and the engine started to Willcox.

Rumours of the hold-up drew a curious crowd to the depot and questions were asked eagerly; but no information was vouchsafed for fear of alarming those implicated.

Limber was crossing the street of Willcox when Graham saw him, and taking him aside, said, "I want to swear you in as deputy, Limber, and may need you several days. I want men who can hold their tongues and be relied upon. We're up against a well-organized bunch."

The cowboy listened to Graham's concise statement of the hold-up and Three-fingered Jack's death; but was not told of the accusation regarding Alpaugh and Glendon.

"I'm ready any time you want me," was Limber's assertion.

"Might as well come with me now."

"Which way you goin' first?"

"Alpaugh's house."

Believing that the constable of Cochise intended to co-operate with Alpaugh, the Willcox constable, Limber strode beside big Tom Graham, though neither of them again spoke. When they reached the neat little cottage where Alpaugh and his wife resided, the constable was sitting on the porch smoking, and came down the steps to meet them.

"Hear you had a lively time out your way last night, Tom," he commented. "I was ready to go out and join the chase but as it was in your section and you did not wire for help, supposed you did not need me. Catch your men?"

"One of 'em. The others had a good start; but a strong posse with relay horses is trailing them. Three-fingered Jack is dead." Graham watched the effect of his information.

Alpaugh started, but recovered himself. "Dead? Was he one of them? Well, you know he's always had a fishy reputation."

"He was wounded by the express messenger. Lived long enough to make a full confession."

"Who?" asked Alpaugh, trying to appear unconcerned.

"Hold up your hands, Dick. Don't make trouble. I've got to arrest you."

Limber controlled his amazement, and in obedience to a nod from Graham, removed the pistol from Alpaugh's hip pocket. Then Graham told his prisoner he might put down his hands.

The constable laughed in amusement. "Well, I might get mad if it wasn't all so darned foolish. I can't figure out whether you are off your cabeza, Tom, or if it was Three-fingered Jack trying to get back at me because I arrested him once." His voice dropped and his face grew serious. "I don't want my wife to know this. It's all a big mistake and you'll find it out later on; but I don't want her to worry. You've got to do your duty, Tom, so I haven't any hard feelings against you or Limber. I'd like to make an excuse to Jennie about going away, if you don't mind."

"All right. Don't stir up trouble, Dick; that's all," warned Graham.

"It's too silly to make any row over," Alpaugh answered with open contempt as he walked to the hall door and called to his wife, "I've got to go out of town at once, Jennie. Graham wants me. There's been a hold-up near Cochise. Don't get worried if I'm gone several days. I won't need any war-bag. Be back as soon as I can make it."

Mrs. Alpaugh was a plump, quick body, with brown eyes, brown skin, smooth brown hair and alert way of cocking her head on one side, much like an impudent sparrow. She came on the porch and smiled at them.

"I might as well be an old maid," she pouted. "Dick is away nearly all the time, lately."

"Good-bye, Jennie," interrupted her husband, fearing she might innocently complicate matters.

"Don't let the train-robbers catch you all," she laughed as they headed across the street, where Alpaugh was taken to a room in the hotel, to be held in custody until the Sheriff from Tombstone, the County seat, should arrive.

Limber and Graham walked together from the hotel. "Got to get our horses," said the officer.

At the Cowboy's Rest they were joined by other men who were waiting. Limber flung the saddle on Peanut, adjusted the headstall of the bridle and mounted.

Out on the street Graham rode up to him, and Limber's eyes met his. "Who else, Tom?"

"Glendon," was the reply.

The cowboy twisted quickly in his saddle, his face filled with consternation. "How did he get in?"

"Don't ask me," was the moody answer. "Three-fingered Jack made a dying statement and accused them both; so I've got to arrest him. 'Tain't a pleasant job when you've known the men for years and have slept with them, shared chuck and worked together. It's bad enough mess when there ain't any women, but Alpaugh and Glendon have decent wives. What business has a man with a family getting into such a mess, anyhow?" he growled, voicing the thoughts of the man who rode beside him.

Limber wished heartily that Powell were home at the Springs, now. In imagination he pictured Glendon's wife alone at the Circle Cross with only Juan and the dog to sympathize with her in this new trial; he regretted that Graham had selected him as one of the posse, but it could not be helped now.

It was a very quiet quartette which rode up to the gate of the Circle Cross. Glendon came down the front walk.

"Hello, boys! Off on a hunting trip?" he asked affably. "Get down and have a drink."

"We're after you, Jim," said Graham bluntly. "Three-fingered Jack split on the gang."

Glendon started in surprise. "What the Dickens are you talking about. What have I to do with Three-fingered Jack? You must be joking!" He regarded them so frankly that they wondered uncomfortably whether the dead man had told the tale in spite, as Glendon hastened to suggest.

"I had trouble with Jack over two months ago, and I suppose this is his way of getting even with me."

"He said you were with them on the first hold-up, and that they were to bring the loot to you this time for you to take care of for them. I guess it's up to you to go quietly, Jim. We don't go much on what he said, but we can't help ourselves."

"It's a fine proposition when a man stays home and minds his own business, then finds he's accused of being mixed in a thing like this," Glendon spoke indignantly. "I bet Three-fingered Jack won't repeat that story to my face."

"No he won't, Jim;" returned Graham quietly. "He's dead. He made his statement when he knew he was dying, and called the posse to witness what he said. He shot the express messenger; —got a load of buckshot himself."

Glendon shrugged his shoulders impatiently. "Oh, well, I suppose I've got to go, but you're on the wrong trail this time, boys. I haven't been away from home for over a month, as my wife can tell you."

He turned toward the house as though to call for corroboration.

"No use dragging Mrs. Glendon into it," said Limber, quickly. "I guess you can get other witnesses outside of her, if you need 'em Jim. It ain't the sort of thing for any woman to be mixed up in, and we don't want to make it harder for her than we have to."

The others nodded approvingly; but Glendon's eyes narrowed and he faced Limber in sudden fury.

"Look here, Limber, you're an old friend, but don't presume too far. I'm not as big a fool as you think I am. You mind your own business, damn you! What's my wife to you anyhow? You and Powell have butted in a good bit in my family affairs!"

Limber's face was white; his right hand flashed to his pistol, then fell away. His eyes stared in dumb misery toward the house. The other men saw Katherine Glendon standing in the doorway. Every head was bared instantly. She understood that something was wrong, and an expression of dread darkened her eyes as she moved to her husband's side.

"What is it, Jim?" she asked.

Glendon kicked the gravel but no one answered. Then as her eyes moved from face to face, she recognized Limber.

"What is wrong, Limber?"

The cowpuncher kept his eyes on the horn of his saddle. He would have shot Glendon for the insult passed, but he could not force himself to tell Glendon's wife their mission.

Graham cursed inwardly. Glendon's lips wore an ugly smile, and he refused to speak.

"The train was robbed again last night, Mrs. Glendon," explained Graham, at last. "Three-fingered Jack was killed. He made a statement accusing Glendon and Alpaugh. We're all friends of Glendon's and don't believe the story was true; but we have to take him back with us. We can't help ourselves."

Katherine held tightly to the picket fence while the man was speaking.

"You are making a terrible mistake," she cried in relief. "He has not been away from home for over a month."

"He told us that," was the answer, "and we're glad of it, too."

She turned to her husband, her hand rested on his arm. "Jim, tell me you are innocent, and I will believe in you in spite of everything," she implored.

He glanced suspiciously at the men. "You forget, Katherine, these men will be witnesses to every word I speak."

"We will ride off a bit, Glendon, but we've got to watch you," replied Graham. Following the constable, the rest rode out of earshot, leaving husband and wife practically alone.

"Are you mixed up in it, Jim?"

"No;" he replied boldly, trying to look her in the eyes. As his glance wavered, she knew that he was lying, and he knew that she read his guilt. The knowledge roused his resentment.

"Jim, be honest with me," she begged earnestly. "Trust me. No matter what has happened—what you may have done, you are my husband and I will stand by you. Tell me the truth."

"There is nothing to go into hysterics over," he retorted. "You know as much about the affair as I do. You know I have not been away from home for a month. If you want to help me, as you pretend you do, that statement from you will counteract anything Jack may have said. I don't know whether your testimony would even be admitted as evidence."

"I could say that truthfully," she answered; "and, oh, Jim! I am so thankful."

"I know you have already accused, tried and sentenced me as guilty," he shrugged his shoulders and walked over to the men. "I'll be ready as soon as I can saddle up."

Katherine stood by the gate, numb with the shock, and as the men rode past, they touched their hats. She only saw the careless nod that her husband gave her, and he rode away, chatting with the men.

Motionless Glendon's wife watched the last trace of the dust-cloud from the horses' hoofs, then, she turned with dragging steps into the house.

A few days later, she learned through Juan, who had been to see Chappo, that the posse had caught up with the fleeing bandits near the Mexican border. Their surrender was effected after the ponies of the outlaws had been shot from under them.

Downing, Burks, Wentz and two brothers, named Rowan, constituted the remainder of the band. They, together with Alpaugh and Glendon, were taken to the County jail at Tombstone to await their trial.

Then a note from Glendon reached Katherine. He wanted her to come to Tombstone at once and stay there until the trial was over. So, leaving Juan in full charge, she obeyed the wishes of the man she had married.

# Chapter Thirty-Six

When the trial took place, the fact that Alpaugh and Glendon had been in their homes, and there being no proof of their actual connection with the attempted robbery, merely the unsupported statement of Three-fingered Jack, augured their complete vindication.

As the case was about to be closed, a bomb was thrown by the prosecuting attorney, who asked to have Wentz put on the stand as a witness for the Prosecution. Alpaugh and Glendon, with their attorneys were not prepared for Wentz' evidence which corroborated the story of Three-fingered Jack. Assured of a very light sentence, or possible freedom, as result of his turning State's evidence, Wentz made a complete confession of his part in the matter, and the convincing details remained unshaken by the most severe cross-examination by the lawyers for the defence.

Alpaugh and Glendon, as the testimony progressed exchanged glances of consternation, and the confusion of their attorneys was apparent not only to Judge and jury, but also to casual spectators who had no knowledge of the twists of legal procedure. The jury was out but a short time, and the verdict of "Guilty" was no surprise to any one who was in the Court room. A few days later Glendon and Alpaugh, together with all the others implicated, were sentenced to ten years in the Yuma Penitentiary. Public sentiment approved of the verdict, but many sympathizing eyes turned on Katherine Glendon, who sat white-faced, at the back of the Court room.

She had remained in Tombstone during the entire time of the trial, and like many others, believed Glendon and Alpaugh the victims of spite on the part of Three-fingered Jack. To her, the unexpected development was crushing. In her heart she felt it was the truth, although her husband persisted in declaring his and the constable's innocence. Her own testimony had been brief and convincing, but in no way conflicted with the minute circumstances stated by Wentz regarding Glendon's activities. In fact, it only served to prove that Glendon had planned a perfect alibi with his wife as an innocent accomplice.

Immediately after the conviction, Wentz was given his liberty as promised. With his first appearance a few hours later on the streets of Tombstone, the open threats of friends of the convicted men, caused him to hasten back to the County jail and ask its protection until he could arrange to get away from Arizona safely.

The warden allowed him the privilege, but was not enthusiastic over it, as he said, "Well, Wentz, you're in a fine mess, now. I wouldn't change places with you for a lot! You're out a job, busted, got no friends and have to quit the country. Derned if I haven't got more respect for those fellows in the cells!"

Wentz made no reply, but slumped down in a chair, trying to figure some way out of his dilemma, and the warden, lighting a cigar, continued grimly, "You're in the same fix as the feller that sawed the limb off the tree, while he was sitting on the end of the limb."

The other man scowled, but held his tongue. This was his only place of refuge at present. Even those who had no sympathy for the outlaws had still less use for the man who had betrayed them. The warden rose with a smile as Katherine Glendon entered the room. She had come to see her husband. Wentz' head dropped until he heard their retreating steps in the corridor.

"Is there anything I can do?" Katherine asked almost hopelessly, as she sat in the cell talking to Glendon when they were alone.

"Go home," commanded Glendon. "There's no use hanging around here any more. Forbes, our lawyer, says that the railroad company stretched a point in having the indictment read 'interfering with the United States mail.' No one touched the mail car. The railroad company never could have won, and that's why they made it a Federal case. It was a put up job all around, and Wentz stood in with the railroad people to get us."

"Why should Three-fingered Jack have accused you?" she uttered a thought that had puzzled her.

"Well, you see I had a row with him in Willcox the last time I was in there," Glendon replied glibly, then hurried to add, "Now, see here, Katherine, you've got a chance to help me, and no one else can do it. Will you stand by me? I swear that if I get out of this trouble you will have no further cause to reproach me. I have done a few decent things since I married you. Not many, but can't you remember that I let you keep Donnie instead of sending him to father, as I had a legal right to do?"

"Yes, Jim! I will never forget it! But even without that, I would do my utmost to help you, because you are the father of my boy."

"You're a brick, Katherine! Now, see here, I want you to circulate a petition for my pardon, after the first excitement has died down and I have shown myself a model prisoner. You will have to get a certain number of names, as the petition has to go to Washington, because it was a Federal case. The Governor of the Territory has no jurisdiction over it. You won't refuse to do this for me, will you? Every one is against me now, and if you fail me, I shall take advantage of the first opportunity to kill myself."

"Jim, have I ever failed you yet?" she asked simply.

"No; you've been a long way too good for me," he answered, "and if I can get this squared, I'll show you how I appreciate you and what you have done."

Despite his promises, she left the jail with a heavy heart, knowing his weak and vacillating character, and feeling that his protestations were not to be reckoned seriously. But, she also knew that when the time came, she would help in any way she was able. So husband and wife parted, and the woman returned to the Circle Cross ranch the following day.

Juan and Tatters met her with delight. The old Mexican hovered about her in dumb sympathy. A letter from Donnie was full of his childish interests. The touch of the badly scrawled pages comforted her as though the child's hands were laid on her own. A feeling of thanksgiving surged over her, that the boy was away where no knowledge of the shadow in their home could cloud his eyes.

When the Mexican stood in the door of the kitchen, saying in his liquid, native tongue, "Buenos noches, Señora" (Good night), she remembered that she could not keep the man, there was so little money left now.

Gently she explained the situation to Juan. The bewildered expression on his face suddenly changed to eagerness.

"Señora, I have saved up money. Eet is for both of us. Some day-mañana-you pay me back."

"I cannot use your money, Juan." Her voice told how the offer touched her. "I must look out for the cattle myself, there is not enough to pay you wages."

"You have frijoles, no?" demanded Juan. "Eet is enough. I stay!"

The matter was ended by Juan hurrying from the room before she could protest further. Each time during the following days when Katherine broached the subject, Juan evaded the issue by having important work, and Katherine unable to do otherwise, let their lives settle in a routine that promised to stretch into years.

She made one more trip to Tombstone after the sentence had been passed. Glendon instructed her about circulating the petition, but bade her wait until four or five months after he had begun serving his term. She left him in his cell, carrying with her an undefinable impression of a man whom she did not know; for already she sensed a subtle change.

The day before the convicted men were to be transported to the penitentiary, Glendon lay on his bunk in his cell, wondering whether his plans would fail or succeed. He was playing for high stakes; to lose meant forfeiting his life.

Panchita had called at the jail several times since the trial, ostensibly to sell tamales to the prisoners and their guards. In no way had the Mexican girl been identified with the train-robbers, so her actions created no suspicion. She managed to let Glendon understand that she was ready to co-operate in any plans he might make.

He had given up his original idea of hoping to win a pardon, which if obtained, would only mean being financially penniless, and branded as a felon. The more he thought of the alternative, the more alluring it became.

Panchita had told him that the money from the first train hold-up, was safely sewn in a bustle made of newspapers which she wore constantly. She had whispered this while he pretended to joke and dicker for tamales. Tonight, there would be little steel saw-blades in the tamales she was to bring for his supper. In order to disarm any suspicion, she had laughingly promised to bring tamales for all of them, because they were going on their long journey the next morning. The warden had given consent, especially as she had promised double allowance for him so that he could take them home to his wife.

Glendon knew that once he possessed those tiny saws, he could cut the bars of his cell before morning. Panchita would be waiting with a pony, and later she would follow to Mexico where they would meet. He had no fear of her failing him, knowing her insane jealousy of his wife.

He rose and paced the floor nervously, as the afternoon waned. Five o'clock passed-half-past five-then the clock in the sheriff's room struck six. The jailer passed the barred door.

"Say," called Glendon, "hasn't that tamale girl been around yet? She promised to give us all a tamale supper tonight, you know. Celebrating our journey."

"She's dead," answered the jailer, stopping at the door. "The place where she was staying caught fire last night. It was a frame shack, and the rest all got out except her. She wasn't burnt but smothered in the smoke."

"That's tough luck," said Glendon, trying to appear careless. "Was it much of a fire?"

"No, they got it out in half an hour."

"Was she living with her folks?" Glendon was striving not to betray his disappointment and anxiety, but he felt like springing at the jailer and choking the truth from his lips. Panchita was dead-but where was the money?

"She boarded with a Mexican family, and they didn't know anything except she came here lately and sold tamales. She was making tamales last night just before they all went to bed."

"Who takes charge of the body and property in such cases?"

"Oh, the County buries them and burns up their old duds. These Mex women never have nothing! Funny thing, though, about that," he paused to coax a cigar that failed to draw properly. "Gosh! That's a rank cigar!" he ejaculated taking it from his mouth and regarding it in disgust, while Glendon's fingers twitched. "I gave two bits for it, too."

"You were saying something about the tamale girl's duds. What was the joke?"

"Oh, yes"; the jailer resumed, laughing. "You see, there is a Mexican woman that lives in the same shack and she works for my wife. Does washing. She had some of our clothes there and so came up to explain that she couldn't get them done up on time. She told my wife all about the fire, and that the girl had only an old dress and a black shawl, but a fine pair of high-heeled slippers and silk stockings, and-ha! ha! ha! a bustle made out of newspapers. Can you beat that? Got to be in style, someway."

Glendon's eyes flickered and he caught his breath quickly.

"Funny combination, wasn't it? But all women folks are alike. If one of them rigs up so she has a hump on her back like a camel, all the others break their necks fixing up humps. If they were born that way, it would keep the doctors busy operating to get rid of 'em."

Glendon stretched his face in an effort to smile, but the muscles were almost rigid.

"Well," continued the narrator, enjoying his own story, "after the body was taken away, this old washwoman and another one started to clean up the place, and picking around they found the things. They got to scrapping over the stockings and shoes, that was too small for either of them to wear. But they never let up till they had 'em tore to pieces. The old woman was crying when she told about it. My wife almost had hysterics when she told me the story."

Glendon pretended to enjoy the joke hugely. Then after a short period, he asked, "But what did they do with the bustle? Who got that souvenir?"

"Oh, they burnt that up. It was just old newspapers. Nobody wanted that. My wife asked about it, because she thought the old woman might be wearing it herself. So that's why none of us got our tamales tonight!" the man concluded as he moved away from the cell door.

Glendon threw himself on the bunk, cursing his ill-luck.

"Seventy thousand gone up in smoke!" he muttered, never giving a thought to the girl who had risked everything for his sake. His only regret was that her inopportune death interfered with his plans for escape. His former passion for the woman turned to resentment.

"Paddy's money is safe," he meditated as he lay staring at the wall. "If I could only get out!"

His last hope lay in the slim possibility that Katherine might be able to obtain a pardon for him, then he could get Paddy's money and go to South America. But such a pardon would take months to accomplish. Glendon got up and walked the length of his cell, kicking the wall when he reached the end of the room. Curses rose to his lips. The wall in front of him reminded him of the grim grey walls of the Arizona Penitentiary, and he felt that if he could only get Wentz by the throat and choke him slowly to death, he would be willing to go to the Penitentiary for life. But-Wentz was free.

# Chapter Thirty-Seven

Wentz, hovering in the corridor of the Tombstone jail, had overheard the conversation between the jailer and Glendon. With knowledge of Panchita's death, Wentz realized that his own plans were in chaos. Glendon's nonchalant attitude at the news confirmed Wentz's belief that Glendon knew where the money had been concealed by the Mexican girl.

"If Glendon were free," Wentz muttered, "he would probably get the money at the first opportunity. There may be a chance after all."

Deep in thought, he returned to the room where the jailer waited for the deputy to relieve him that he might go home to supper. Wentz picked up a newspaper and began to read. The deputy entered the room, and nodded to the jailer, who exchanged a few casual words with him and departed. Wentz had greeted the new-comer, but a curt nod had been the only response.

The curse of Judas was upon Wentz. Since the trial none of the men he had betrayed would speak to him, and their eyes were threatening. Other men in the jail, officials as well as prisoners, held him in open contempt. Outside were those who made dire threats of vengeance. Wentz envied his former comrades and began to feel that he would rather share their punishment than face his own black future. He was without money. No place in Arizona would harbour a traitor; no man would trust him or hold out a hand in comradeship. The railroad would give him work, so he would not starve, but life would be unbearable. If he made his way to another section, it would mean without a cent in his pocket, no credit, no work. If he could only find where that undivided money from the first hold-up had been hidden, then he could laugh at them all.

The deputy had picked up a book. Yawning and stretching, Wentz dropped his paper, then rising slowly walked along the corridor. He reached Glendon's cell, paused and called, "Hello, Glen!"

The figure on the bunk turned heavily, and Glendon's bloodshot eyes glared in fury at his former comrade. He uttered no word. With a peculiar expression Wentz returned to the office.

The deputy glanced up carelessly, and resumed his reading. Wentz passed back of him and, with a swift movement, snatched the man's pistol from the holster that hung on his hip, and struck him a stunning blow on the head. The deputy dropped to the floor. Tying and gagging him, Wentz secured the keys, then ran rapidly along the corridor, unlocking the door of each cell until he reached Glendon's.

"Get up, Glen! Hurry!"

Already the escaping prisoners, including Alpaugh and the other train-robbers, were rushing past. Glendon leaped to his feet bewildered. "You —"

"Don't waste time, you fool! Some one may come!" said Wentz, pulling Glendon through the door and keeping close at his heels as they reached the street, having stopped only to pick up guns and cartridges in the room where the deputy, now conscious but helpless, watched the procession of escaping prisoners.

A number of cowponies were tied to the hitching posts in the streets, as is usual, while their owners were about town, or eating supper. These were hastily mounted by the outlaws. The presence of a number of horsemen galloping through the streets of Tombstone was too common a sight at the County seat to cause curiosity or comment. The escaping prisoners broke into small groups and left town in different directions, to avoid any suspicion.

The fugitives had another advantage in the unusual darkness, not only because of the hour, but, also, of the gathering black clouds that presaged a storm at any moment. So, even those who might have recognized the men in the daytime, would be apt to pass them without a second glance in the dim light.

When the jailer returned from supper an hour later and discovered what had happened, a posse was formed without delay. It divided into several parties, that all roads might be covered as soon as possible; otherwise the darkness and approaching storm would make pursuit practically impossible until morning. By that time any trail made by the horses of the fleeing men, would be completely obliterated, should it rain.

The band headed by the furious deputy who had been the victim of the treachery, finally caught sight of Wentz and Glendon, who were keeping together; and a rapid-fire duel began between the pursuers and prisoners. The gait of the horses, the uncertain light, and the intervening rocks about the outlying district of Tombstone, all favoured the fugitives. A bullet brought down the horse Wentz was riding, pinning the man under it as it fell. He struggled desperately to free himself. Seeing capture was inevitable, the traitor lifted his pistol to his own head-and the posse saw a flash.

Glendon, in advance of Wentz, heard the shot and looked back. Then something struck his leg and he felt the blood oozing down into his boot. Rather than give up now, he determined to follow Wentz' example and use a bullet on himself.

Ahead of him rose huge boulders, looming like gigantic tombstones. Once he could attain their shelter, it would be almost impossible for the posse to catch him, or to take accurate aim. The horse he was riding responded to the hammering of the man's heels-he had no whip or spurs.

At last he reached the shelter of the rocks and darted in circles from one to the other, keeping them between himself and any chance bullets. By degrees, the sounds of shots died away, the voices of his pursuers ceased. He knew he had outwitted them for the night; but there was no time to lose before dawn.

When he had pressed on a couple of miles, he pulled up his horse and slipped to the ground, laying his ear against the wet earth while he listened intently. But the only sound he heard was the rumble of distant thunder growing louder and louder. Back of him the sky was inky black, punctured at short intervals with zigzag streaks of dazzling light. The storm was already upon the town from which he had escaped.

With a sigh of relief, he examined the wound in his leg. It was superficial. Glendon tore a sleeve from his shirt and bandaged the wound. Then, mounting the panting horse, he doubled back on his trail for a mile and made a cut across the mountains at a point where no one but an Apache had ever dared to cross, except in daylight.

This trail had not been used for a long time. Glendon knew the danger of it; but death in the mountains at the bottom of a gully, was preferable to the Yuma Penitentiary for ten years, or longer.

By morning the rain would have completely obliterated his tracks, and the posse would, no doubt, continue their search in the direction they had last seen him following. He realized there was another danger. He was trying to reach the Circle Cross. The authorities would probably telegraph to Willcox and a posse be started from that point to Hot Springs. He must reach the Circle Cross, get clothes, food and a fresh horse before any one else could make that ranch. But first, there was something else to do.

His thoughts were interrupted by the storm breaking over his head. The reverberating thunder, incessant flashes of lightning and shrieking wind sounded as though all the fiends of the netherworld were keeping pace with him, rejoicing at his escape and conspiring to aid him. Across the backbone of the range he urged his frightened, stumbling horse. Five miles from the Circle Cross, Glendon halted and sat peering in all directions when a flash illuminated the brush and trees. He had no fear of pursuers now, but he was searching for one particular tree, and it was hard to identify in the fitful glare.

At last he found it, dismounted and tied his horse. Then from the underbrush Glendon dragged a rusty shovel and began to dig. The ground was soft from recent rains, but he paused frequently to wipe the beads of perspiration that mingled with the rain dashing into his eyes.

"I didn't put it so deep," he muttered, plying the shovel more rapidly. "I wonder if some one else has found it!"

A rustling in the trees caused him to straighten up suddenly and with a startled jump he glared about on all sides. The lightning showed only the waving branches, the pouring rain and the wind-whipped bushes.

His tongue licked his lips. "God! I wish I had a drink! My nerve's all shot to pieces!" He dug furiously. "It's lucky I caught old Paddy burying this money. That gave me a chance to get the old fool out of the way without suspicion. Even Alpaugh was in the dark about that. He's as big a fool as the rest. Damn 'em. Why didn't they blow out Three-fingered Jack's brains before they left him there!"

Still he dug, and the rain hammered down while the wind whistled and screamed around him. The shovel struck a deep root of the tree. Something brushed against Glendon's face. With a scream of fright he dropped the shovel and ran to the snorting horse. Glendon's eyes staring into the darkness pictured Paddy's sardonic face in the bushes, and back of Paddy was old Doctor King, looking at him with infinite pity. Glendon's arm went across his face as though shielding himself, and his foot was thrust into the stirrup of his saddle. The horse moved a few paces, then Glendon looked back, and jerked violently on the reins. He lifted his fist and shook it at the gloom, shouting wildly, "Damn you! You can't frighten me away! I'll have it in spite of you and Heaven and Hell!"

He leaped from his saddle and grabbed the shovel, cursing as he resumed his work until he found the canvass bags with the buried money. Unable to cram the sacks into the saddle pouches, he tore off the strings of the bags and poured the gold into the leather saddle pouches on either side of the horse. Once more he mounted, but as he faced the trail to the Circle Cross he shouted at the nickering shadows, "Damn you! I've got it!" Then he rode on his way.

"It'll take four hours yet for any posse to reach the Circle Cross from Willcox," he said, leaning low on the saddle to avoid the lash of the wind and the rain. "There'll be a big flood at Hot Springs. I'll have to leave this gold with Katherine. It's too heavy to pack and too big a risk. I'll take a couple of hours to rest and get ready. Then I can hit the trail for the border. Easy to do after I get away from here and across the Willcox flats. I'll take Fox. He has no brands on him. My saddle's at the ranch, too-That'll get rid of this horse and saddle-They'll all be looking for this outfit now. With Fox and some money—I can make my way without any trouble, once I get clear of the flats. I must cross before dawn-or hide in the mountains till tomorrow night, then cross. Sixty miles to the border-then I am safe!"

A thought of his wife intruded. "I suppose she will balk at keeping the gold," he muttered, "but she will have to do it! There is no one else I can trust with it. I won't stand any nonsense now. She'll have to do what I tell her, by God!"

He had no fear of Juan, knowing the Mexican's dog-like devotion to Katherine. Beside, the Mexican could not reach any place to give an alarm until after Glendon was well upon his way. Katherine's exaggerated sense of duty would keep her silent, no matter what might transpire. Everything was propitious.

His hand went back and patted the wet leather of the saddle-bags that held ten thousand dollars in gold, and his lips twisted in a sneer, "You old fool, Paddy! You thought it was safe!"

# Chapter Thirty-Eight

Limber, who had been across the Galiuros riding the Sulphur Springs Valley for a couple of days, decided to go home by the way of Willcox instead of cutting over the mountain trail, as he was anxious to hear from Doctor Powell to whom he had written about the hold-up and trial. Powell was in New York intending to sail for Europe within a few days.

As the cowboy came out of the Chinese restaurant, after having eaten supper, Jack Green, the station agent, hailed him.

"Hello, Limber! There's been a telegram at the office two days for you, but I hadn't any chance to send it out your way. I guess it'll be like the Irishman's letter, for it was to let you know that the doctor was coming. He arrived this afternoon, and I told him."

"Is he here?" asked Limber eagerly.

"No. He got a horse at the corral and went right out to Hot Springs. Said he wanted to see you as soon as possible."

"Sorry I missed him. I came in thinkin' I'd hear from him. So I'll get out as soon as Peanut's had a couple hours' rest."

They walked across the street together. As Green opened the door of the station, he heard the telegraph instrument calling insistently.

"Just a minute, till I take this call," he said, seating himself at the table. As the message began coming in rapidly, Green's face was startled. He jumped up as he closed the message, turning to Limber.

"The whole bunch of train-robbers and all the other prisoners in the Tombstone jail are loose. Wentz did it. They want a posse to start at once for Hot Springs."

He and Limber started rapidly. "They think Glendon will try to reach the Circle Cross, and probably others will be with him. I've got to see the constable and Judge at once."

Green darted down the street. Limber hurried to the Cowboy's Rest and saddled Peanut.

"Goin' to be a big storm," said Buckboard. "Why don't you lay over till mornin', Limber?"

"I been at the Diamond H," Limber replied as he slipped the headstall over Peanut's ears. "I missed Doctor Powell and want to get out to the ranch tonight."

He led his pony from the stall as he spoke.

"Wait a minute and I'll lend you a slicker," offered Buckboard, disappearing in his sleeping quarters and returning with the unwieldy, yellow, water-proof coat.

"Won't you need it, yourself?"

"I got another in the bunkhouse. You can send it back when it's handy."

Limber thanked him and tied it across the back of his saddle, glancing up at the threatening sky. "Guess I'll need it before long," he said, riding to the gate. "Much obliged. So long!"

He turned Peanut's head to the Point of the Mountains, northwest of town, passing the O T ranch five miles out. Then he struck the road to Hot Springs, which lay thirty-five miles north of Willcox on a road that was totally invisible, now. Limber did not hesitate to urge his pony into a swift gallop, for he knew he could rely on Peanut's wonderful instinct to carry his rider safely.

"If we kin reach the Springs before Glendon does," the cowboy spoke to his pony, and the tapering ears went back at the sound of the voice Peanut knew and loved, "We kin warn Glen the posse's comin' so's he kin git away in time. She'd had enough troubles without being thar to see him get killed or kill somebody else, Peanut. Thar's goin' to be shootin' if they find Glen!"

Steadily the pony swung along, and the storm beat down on them mercilessly. The constant flashes of lightning revealed a stream of running water where the road bed, worn deeply by wagon wheels and hoofs of teams, left a high ridge in the centre. Peanut, with goat-like agility kept on the top of this ridge. It was the only solid ground visible. All else was a swamp.

The road had never seemed so long to Limber as when at last, the pony slipped down into the mouth of the Hot Springs Cañon.

"Seven miles more, Peanut!"

It was the only way to reach the Springs or Circle Cross. During the dry season, there was no water in the bed of the creek, as the Hot Springs Creek seeped into the ground a short distance from the ranch house, and the little stream was usually only two or three feet wide and a few inches deep. Owing to the immense watershed of the cañon, a rain of short duration often made crossing impossible. The banks of the creek rose fifteen feet, or more, perpendicularly from constant floods, and often these banks were over-running.

This knowledge was the basis of Limber's hope as well as his anxiety. If he could cross the creek before the flood, that very thing might prove an obstacle to the posse, and give Glendon a chance to get a good start. If the flood was ahead of him, the cowboy knew he would have to wait and lose any opportunity of seeing Glendon first. Then the other men would be there with him.

He listened intently. As the sound he feared —a smothered roar-reached his ears, he leaned forward in his saddle, and Peanut started with a snort at the unusual touch of the sharp spurs.

It was a race for life now. Limber knew he must reach the one spot in the cañon where his pony could scramble up the sheer embankment to the upper road before the flood could catch them. Stumbling, panting, the pony tore over the rocks and fallen trees that had been washed down in previous floods, and crashed among dead limbs in the darkness. Peanut fell heavily to his knees, but struggled up instantly, while Limber spurred and called, "Yip! Yip! Yip! Peanut! Go on, you rascal!"

The pony's ears were flattened back. He knew the danger, now. The noise of approaching water grew louder. Watching for the next flash of lightning, Limber's eyes measured the distance between himself and the point where the road struck sharply up the steep incline that led to safety. With the same glance, he saw the wall of seething water tumbling close to the crossing. Could they reach it in time?

The sounds became a deafening roar, and Peanut flagged. Limber leaned over his shoulder and spoke to him, and at the sound of the loved voice, the little pony made another effort. With a convulsive leap he reached the slope of the road and scrambled wildly to safety, then stopped with low drooping head and quivering limbs. Limber jumped from the saddle and went to the pony's head, putting his arm over the rain-soaked neck, the cowboy stroked the mane and forelock. They could rest now. No living thing could cross that cañon until the storm ceased and the flood subsided.

As the lightning flashed, Limber watched the flood sweep below, carrying great cottonwood trees like straws, and over-turning immense boulders as if they were marbles.

Man and pony had ridden against Death that night, and Peanut had won the race.

# Chapter Thirty-Nine

Katherine was looking out the window at the storm-swept cañon. Juan had ridden to the San Pedro that morning. He figured that he might work up a trade of two unbroken colts for a gentle workhorse. Then when he was compelled to make a trip to town with the team, Katherine could use her own pony, Fox, to care for the cattle on the range.

As the fury of the storm increased, she closed the heavy shutters to protect the glass windows from the branches that were broken and flung violently against the little house. The storm on the outside seemed emblematic of her life. Yet she remembered that it would pass and the sun creep gently into the places where the bruised things had been beaten down, and by degrees the beauty would be restored.

Lighting the lamp, she seated herself at the table and drew a letter toward her. In the stress of events following her husband's illness and Paddy's subsequent murder, the publication of her verses had passed from her memory. Many months had elapsed before Katherine happened to pick up the magazine in which her poem was printed. Like a seed that had lain dormant, waiting the proper season to germinate, rose an impulse to tell the thoughts that surged within her. In this mood she had written a story of the little ranch in the lonely cañon, and the things that made life for the woman living there with the old Mexican, the dog and the mountains.

Hesitatingly, she had sent the story to a magazine; it had been accepted and the editor had written a pleasant note to her, asking for more of her work. The letter opened a world of possibilities. Not that she dreamed of leaping into fame and fortune as a writer; but because it gave her empty life an object. In grasping at a straw, she had found a friendly hand that dragged her from the black waves of despair and pointed a beacon light, encouraging her to struggle on. The way was no longer lonely; it was peopled by unknown friends with whom she could share thoughts which had been suppressed for years.

The legacy received from her aunt would amply provide for Donnie's education until he was able to assist himself; she could remain on the ranch with old Juan, caring for the remnant of the Circle Cross herd, which would furnish what they needed, with the help of the garden-patch, chickens and a cow. If she could sell a few stories, Donnie could spend his summer vacations with her.

"Ten years," she thought, ashamed of the knowledge that it meant peace unspeakable. "Ten years-and then?"

Forcing the thought from her, she took the second letter from its envelope. It was from Glendon's father, reiterating his offer to take the boy and educate him. The tone of the letter was the same as the first one he had written his son about Donnie. It was a grim, hard letter. Katherine, reading between the lines, felt no resentment; she realized the old man's keen disappointment in his only son, and her heart cried out in sympathy.

So she wrote, thanking her husband's father explaining courteously about the legacy providing for the boy's education, and stating that she would remain at the ranch until such time as her husband returned to it.

Having sealed the letter, she sat idly listening to the storm, when a knock on the door startled her. She thought there was no one in the neighbourhood except herself and old Chappo at the Hot Springs ranch, and she wondered what could have brought him out in such a night. A second knock sounded before she opened the door, holding it with difficulty against the wind, her eyes blinded by the darkness of the night, and the rain beating across the threshold.

"Is that you, Chappo?" she called above the noise of the storm.

"Katherine!"

Her eyes became tragic and her face white as Powell entered the room.

"You?" she whispered doubtingly and yet with a little thrill of gladness in her voice.

He grasped her cold hands, looking eagerly into her face.

"You poor child!" Only three words, but they seemed to cover her with warmth and protection. Then she remembered, and drawing her hands from his, sank trembling into a chair, while Powell stood by her side. A great happiness illumined his face, for he had caught the look in her eyes and had heard the note in her voice.

"I tried to stay away," he said at last. "I thought I could blot you out of my life, but I could not. I was in New York when Limber's letter reached me, telling about the hold-up, trial and conviction. I took the first train home. If the letter had been a day later, I should have been on my way to Europe. You will never know what it meant, picturing you alone here with this new trouble to bear."

"Don't!" pleaded Katherine. "Do you realize what has happened?"

"I know that the law has taken it course justly," replied Powell. "Glendon's conviction is sufficient to justify your appeal for a divorce. No further sacrifice is necessary on your part. Surely you will not hesitate, now?"

"He has no one else," she answered slowly, "Therefore my obligation is the heavier."

"No obligation is due a man like him. He has heaped indignity and suffering on you and Donnie. You cannot point one redeeming trait in his character."

"He is my husband. Only death can cancel that obligation."

"He is a curse to humanity," Powell's voice vibrated with emotion. "Even should you remain here until he serves his time, it will a mean a more hideous life after he returns. Either Donnie will succumb to his father's influence, and you will have two brutes to cope with, or the boy will hate his father, and someday Glendon will kill Donnie or Donnie will kill his father. You have no right to force such a situation on the boy, to face such a future for yourself."

Katherine stood before him, her hands tightly locked together to control the trembling, she did not answer, but the look in her eyes told that she realized the truth of his words. Powell was overcome with compunction and tenderness. His hands were laid gently on hers.

"Please forgive me," he begged. "It maddens me to see you in such trouble and know I am powerless to help you. The only gift I crave of life is the privilege to serve and protect you and Donnie."

She lifted her eyes to the hands that were reaching out to her, then her gaze rested on his face.

"Can you understand," she said, "how a hungry beggar feels outside in the storm and cold, looking into a warm room where a banquet of rich food and wine is spread before his eyes? I am starving for a crumb of your love; yet I must turn away hungry."

He started toward her with a cry of joy, but she moved farther from him.

"Do you think I would have told you, if I had not believed I had the strength to turn away?" she asked in a dull voice. "It is my atonement. I tried so hard to be true to him, in spite of everything; but at night you came to me in my dreams, and I lived in another world, till dawn brought me back here again. Oh, why does God let us make such terrible mistakes when He knows we have only one little life to live? I am tired-so tired of struggling!"

Powell knew that it was her moment of weakness, and the temptation was strong upon him to urge her; but he also knew that no happiness would be lasting unless she came to him without a shadow of the past falling across their lives.

"You are right, Katherine," he said, gravely. "I shall not worry you any more. All I ask is that you will remember I am waiting, to help you when you need me." He lifted her hand to his lips and then she watched him pass out into the storm.

# Chapter Forty

The wind beat the windows and screamed like a living thing in maniacal rage; it struck the door and whipped the trees, tearing away branches and throwing them down the cañon. One crash barely died in the distant rumble when another crash succeeded. A cloud-burst added to the wildness of the scene.

The flashes that lit the huge cliffs about the Circle Cross, revealed a rain-sodden figure mounted on an exhausted, stumbling horse back of the little ranch-house. The horse picked its way uncertainly until it reached the shelter of the stable shed. Glendon slipped stiffly from its back and opening the door, led the animal into an empty stall. The horse stumbled and Glendon gave it a vicious kick as he cursed it.

Fox stopped munching his hay to poke an inquisitive nose across at the stranger, while Glendon started to unbuckle the saddle-bags. As he lifted them, he saw a saddled horse in the stall on the opposite side of Fox. Cursing his luck, the man tossed the saddle-bags back on the horse he had ridden, and adjusted them hastily. Then he reached up behind the hay at the end of the stable and extracted a bottle of whiskey which he had put there just before his arrest. After taking a couple of copious drinks, he thrust the bottle into his coat pocket and mounted the horse whose stiffened movements told that it was badly foundered. Glendon dug his heels into the heaving sides, and the animal with low hanging head, stumbled wearily through the trees directly back of the house.

Glendon checked the horse at a point where the dense undergrowth protected him, yet allowed a view of the house and stables in the flashes of lightning. He wondered who could be there at that hour, unless Chappo were visiting old Juan. Had the unknown rider intended to remain all night, the strange horse would have been unsaddled. Glendon sat shivering until overcome with curiosity and the knowledge that each moment's delay was dangerous, he dismounted, tied his horse and crept cautiously to the side of the house where he peered through the crevice of a broken window shutter. Possibly some one had already reached the Circle Cross from Willcox, and was now waiting to catch him if he appeared.

Through the shutter he saw Powell and Katherine. The noise of the storm deafened their voices, but the man outside read the story in their faces. He saw Powell lift Katherine's hand to his lips.

Glendon started in fury. He reached for the pistol he had taken from the jail; but remembering that he needed his wife's assistance, decided that his vengeance could wait. He would let the man go, but the woman should pay for both. Later Powell should know of it. Glendon's lips twisted in a vicious smile.

When Powell started toward the door, Glendon shrank against the adobe wall where the chimney jutted out. The doctor passed him, entered the stable, then Glendon watched him ride swiftly toward the Hot Springs. Feeling secure from other intruders, Glendon returned to the horse and led it to the stable where he unsaddled it. He made his plans. Fox had never been branded, so would not be easily identified, and with his own saddle he would be fairly safe, once he reached the Mexican border.

No one would ever suspect Katherine of having the gold, and when he felt safe, she could come to him with it. It was a good thing Panchita was out of the way, now.

He grasped the heavy saddlebags and staggered to the dark and silent house. Tatters, hearing the approaching steps, barked fiercely. Glendon twisted the knob, but the door was locked. He knocked sharply.

"One minute," he heard Katherine call. "Is that you, Juan?"

Glendon did not reply. Then the door opened and Katherine, with a bathrobe over her thin white gown and her bare feet thrust into a pair of shabby little kid slippers, saw her husband, dripping from the rain, brush past her into the room. Tatters ran up but received a kick, while Glendon dropped the gold-laden bags with a dull thud on the floor.

"Damn that brute!" he snarled. "Make him quit his noise and keep out of my way if you don't want him killed!"

The collie crept under the bed and Glendon threw off his streaming coat.

"God! What a night!"

Katherine stared at him, dazed and uncomprehending. He regarded her with a nasty smile.

"Well, you don't seem overjoyed to see me," he sneered. "Nice wifely reception I get. Thought I was locked up for good, I suppose. Didn't expect any visitors tonight, eh?"

The significance of his remark did not penetrate her thoughts. She stood silently looking at him, trying to understand how he was here, waiting his explanation.

Glendon turned in rage. "What do you mean standing there staring like an idiot?" he demanded. "This is no time to waste. Get a move on you. I want some grub and dry clothes."

Mechanically, dumbly, she hastened to obey him. Glendon ate the food that she set before him, then he finished with several drinks from the bottle in his pocket. The warmth of the room began to effect his head, after drinking; it loosened his tongue. The woman who watched him with dead eyes, made no comment.

"Wentz knocked the deputy over and tied him and opened the jail doors," he bragged as he ate. "They didn't find it out for some time, and when they saw us it was so dark they could not keep track of me among the rocks. They shot Wentz's horse and he killed himself. Damn him! It served him right. If he had held his tongue at the trial, Alpaugh and I would have escaped conviction. Then we could have helped them all as we promised to do. Alpaugh and Bravo Juan kept together. I've got to keep moving. They got me in the leg, it's only a scratch."

He limped across the room and dragged the saddlebags to the table. With trembling hands he unfastened the straps and let the gold flow out in a dull, glowing stream, fingering it caressingly. "Take care of this money until I write to or send word where you can join me with it;" he ordered. "I'm going to cut across to the Mexican border; then work my way down to South America. Any man speaking Spanish can get along there. It's a country where they don't ask too many questions. There's ten thousand dollars," he ran his hands over the coins. "That will give me a good start down there. I'll write you under the name of Reese, but not for five or six months. I'll have to cover my tracks pretty well, or the Federal officers will locate me. I'll take Fox and my own saddle. I don't want Juan to know I'm here tonight; but after I leave, you must start him out to the Rim Rock with the horse I rode tonight. Tell him to hide the saddle and shoot the horse and skin it, and bury the hide. He'll do anything that you ask him, and won't talk."

"Juan sold your saddle after the trial. We needed money so badly," said the woman slowly.

"Then I'll take Juan's. I dare not risk using the one I rode tonight, nor the horse, either."

"Juan is riding his own saddle. He won't be back for several days. He is trying to trade some colts."

Glendon paced the room cursing his ill-luck as he saw his carefully formed plans disintegrate. He bit his knuckles nervously as he tried to decide what to do. Katherine leaned across the table as Glendon paused and once more ran his fingers through the coins. She looked up and his eyes met hers.

"Where did you get that gold, Jim?" she asked quietly.

"None of your business," he retorted, deceived by her even tones. "It's mine-do you hear? Mine! No one else can claim it!"

"No one else can claim it," she echoed. Then her eyes widened. "It is Paddy's money!" she cried.

Glendon shrugged his shoulders. "What of it? He buried his money and every one knew it. He had no one belonging to him. It is Paddy's money! Now, what have you got to say about it?"

"You found that money first and killed him afterwards," she said tensely. "Oh! I knew there was something wrong when you killed him." She recoiled in horror.

"I was acquitted," he faced her like a trapped coyote. "No one can prove it wasn't self-defence! You're my wife and you've got to hold your tongue!"

Possibly the repugnance in her face stung, for he reeled to her side with an oath. She looked at him unafraid and the knowledge that he had no more power over her goaded him to frenzy.

His clenched fist was lifted and brought down with a crashing blow in her face. She fell against the sharp edge of the window-ledge, clinging blindly as she struggled to her feet, but he knew she was unconquered. Dragging the pistol from his belt, he hurled the loaded weapon at her. It struck the window casing a few inches above her head, then dropped to the floor, the black composition handle shattered, leaving only the steel rim, but the cartridges failed to explode.

Glendon glared at her as she stood panting against the wall, her white face contrasting vividly with the blood that oozed from cuts on cheek and lip-the eyes that regarded him held no fear. She knew that death was standing beside her, but it seemed a welcome friend, with outstretched, sheltering arms.

"I'll make you understand that you are my wife," the man started threateningly toward her, his hand reaching down to pick up the pistol on the floor. Neither of them saw the dog which had been watching from beneath the bed, and now was dragging itself stealthily forth, its lips twitching, its eyes blazing in fury. With a sudden spring, it caught Glendon's hand in its strong, gleaming teeth.

The man's curses mingled with deep-throated growls, and as they fought, the woman stood dumb, unable to move. The blood on her face dripped slowly on the white gown. There was a shot, and Glendon rose to his feet, kicking the dog that lay dying on the floor.

With a cry of pity, Katherine stooped, and the brute that had given its life in an effort to protect her, lifted its head feebly and licked her hand. Then with its eyes on her face, it gave a convulsive shudder. With quivering lips and trembling hand she laid it down on the floor, rose and faced her husband.

"Will you do what I tell you?" he demanded.

"No! You can kill me as you have killed Tatters, but I will not touch that money!"

He leaped at her, caught her by the throat and flung her violently to the floor. Weak, voiceless, still unconquered, he watched her drag herself again to her feet. He levelled the pistol at her head. She did not flinch as she faced it.

Glendon thrust it back into the holster. "Damn you! I'll get along without you; but I won't kill you. I'm going to kill that dude doctor and see how you like that to remember me by!"

He poured more liquor, then bending under the weight of the saddle bags, he strode through the door.

Katherine stood dazed, staring down at the dead dog on the floor, as though her brain had ceased working. Outside, in a lull of the storm, sounded the sharp beat of hoofs. Glendon was riding past the house.

"He is taking the road to the Springs, Tatters," she said slowly, her eyes on the dead dog as she spoke to it. There were chains on her brain; —it could not think; chains on her hands and feet-she could not move.

A tiny red stream was creeping over the wooden floor toward her and she wondered what she would do when it reached her. Fascinated she watched it, then when it touched the hem of her gown making a stain like those above it, she woke in a wild frenzy of despair.

"No! No!" she cried flinging the door open. "I will do anything you wish, Jim! Come back! Come back!"

But Glendon was gone. The wind tore and lashed the curtains with the gay cretonne bands. It blew out the flame of the lamp and the rain beat down on the bright Navajo rugs and the dead dog lying on the floor.

The woman ran to the stable. The heavy door banged on broken hinges. She clung to the empty stall and thought she saw her husband riding up to the Hot Springs Ranch. She saw him jump from his horse and knock at the door-Saw Powell open that door, and then-she saw a tiny red stream trickling across the wooden floor.

Without stopping to reason that she had no chance against a man on a horse, she turned and faced the storm. The wind whipped her long, dark hair across her face and tore the robe back from the thin white gown. Her slippers, rain-soaked, dropped from her bare feet, and the sharp stones cut the tender flesh. She ran on, unconscious of everything except the knowledge that Powell-the man she loved-was in danger.

Slowly and more slowly she ran, her breath coming in sharp little gasps that hurt. She staggered a few more feet, then with a tired sigh, sank to the ground, trying with her last conscious thought to remember whether it was Tatters or Doctor Powell lying dead, where the little scarlet thread kept creeping-creeping-creeping —.

# Chapter Forty-One

"Only a little way further, Peanut, old boy," Limber encouraged the pony, patting its neck as he swung once more to its back; and Peanut, knowing the distance home, started willingly on his way through the storm.

They were on the main road which led directly to the Hot Springs ranch, but a few feet from the creek-crossing it forked to the Circle Cross. As they neared this Y, the pony jumped and stopped, snorting. Limber leaped from his saddle and sheltered by Peanut's body, crouched low, holding his pistol ready. When the next flash came, illuminating the landscape as brilliantly as though it were midday, he slipped the pistol quickly into the holster at his hip and ran to a white heap huddled in the road.

Limber stooped at the woman's side and held his shaking hand against her heart; then he opened his flask and forced whiskey between the closed teeth, and chafed the cold hands. There was no response. Hurriedly, he unfastened the yellow slicker he was wearing, and gently wrapped it about the unconscious form. Then, lifting her in his arms, the cowboy mounted his pony, thankful that Doctor Powell was so near.

The wind blew the woman's hair across his lips, and a wonderful sense of happiness thrilled him. In the flashes he could see her pale face lying against his wet coat, and his heart throbbed with love and tender pity.

Doctor Powell opened the door in response to Limber's call. A vivid flash showed Peanut with Limber on his back holding Katherine in his arms.

"What's the matter, Limber?"

"I found her at the forks of the road on the ground. She's just fainted, I think," explained the cowboy as he placed the unconscious form in the doctor's arms.

Chappo ran from the house and took the reins from Limber, leading Peanut to the stable while the two men entered the house. The doctor laid Katherine on the couch and brought restoratives. Limber knelt beside her and gently chafed the cold hands.

"Glendon's broke jail at Tombstone with the rest of the bunch. There's a posse, comin' from Willcox. I was comin' out to let you know; but they can't cross the Creek now. It's runnin' from bank to bank. Peanut just made it by a scratch."

The light from the lamp fell across the cut and bruised face, and Limber's eyes turned to Powell.

"Do you think she done that fallin' in the road?" he asked significantly.

"No," was the positive reply, as Powell studied her face. "It looks like a blow; besides, those are finger marks on her throat. I saw her two hours ago-she was all right then-Juan is away —I left her there alone."

Limber rose from the side of the couch and looked into Powell's eyes. "Nobody would lay a hand on her exceptin' Glendon."

Powell uttered no sound, but his face was pale with emotion as the cowboy went on speaking in low, tense voice.

"They got away at six o'clock, and if Glendon had a good mountain pony and took the old Indian trail, he could've got to the Circle Cross before now. If I knowed he'd hit her, I'd kill him on sight! She's the nerviest woman I have ever seen-and the finest."

Doctor Powell held out his hand and gripped Limber's.

"You've been a loyal friend to her, Limber."

"Thar ain't nothin' I wouldn't do for her," said the cowpuncher, simply. "Thar's lines that is drawed between humans, jest as in animals. Glendon wasn't meant for her, noway."

Understanding each other thoroughly, the two men who loved her sat watching the unconscious woman until her eyes opened slowly, resting curiously on Limber; then as she saw the other man, her expression turned to one of terror. With a cry, she tried to rise, but Powell's hand restrained her.

"Lie still," he said quietly. "You are safe."

She looked up wildly. "Bar the door! Quick!" she cried. "He is coming to kill you!"

Their first impression that she did not realize what she was saying, vanished as they listened to her story. She did not speak of the blow, nor her refusal to hide away the money, but told them that Glendon had seen the doctor talking with her, and left the house with the avowed intention of killing him.

"Thar's been plenty time for him to get here ahead of you, Mrs. Glendon," Limber assured her. "He'd a been here long before I found you at the forks of the road, if he was comin'. I guess he was just bluffin' you, and when he found it didn't work he lit out with the two horses."

Powell agreed heartily with Limber, but to calm her fears, the cowboy barred the door. Katherine, succumbing to the sedative the doctor administered, relaxed gradually. Her lids closed wearily, but her lips moved, and in half-broken sentences she went over the terrible scene; pleading with her husband for Powell's life, or talking to the dead dog, begging it not to let the little scarlet thread reach her; then she sank into silence, unconscious of all that she had revealed.

The men's eyes met. They read each other's thoughts. Limber's face was set and white, as, with a nod to the doctor, he rose and tiptoed from the room into the kitchen where Chappo was sitting near the stove.

The cowboy took his pistol from the holster at his hip, and looked at the cylinder. Twisting it between his fingers he slipped the cartridges from it. They were wet from the rain.

"Got some lard?" he asked Chappo, and when the Mexican brought it, Limber greased the cartridges and put them back into the cylinder, then dropped the pistol into the holster of his cartridge belt. A Winchester rifle hung in a leather scabbard on the kitchen wall, and Limber lifted it down.

Chappo watched him examine the magazine of the gun.

"Eet is all right," he said. "Eet shoots good." The Mexican's eyes met Limber's. "You go hunting, Leember? Take heem."

"Yes. Give me some jerky, Chappo. I may not get any game for a couple of days."

Chappo understood, and hastened to get the stiff strips of sun-dried meat which he put in a small cotton sack and handed to the cowboy, saying, "Good luck, Leember! Shoot straight!"

With a grim smile the Mexican saw the cowboy and gun disappear.

Peanut looked up in surprised reproach as his master reached for the saddle hung on a peg. The pony knew he had well-earned his blanket and bin of oats that night.

"We've got some more work to do, Peanut," said Limber, throwing the saddle across the pony's back, and Peanut, with a final bite at the oats, turned again to face the storm with his master. The cowboy was sure that Glendon had pushed on toward the border, and not knowing about the gold he was carrying with him, supposed he had taken Fox as a relay horse. This would give Glendon the advantage should the chase be protracted; but, Limber knew that Peanut's nervous energy and staying qualities in the mountains made him equal to any two ordinary horses.

"We'll follow him till Hell freezes over, Peanut, and we'll sure get him in the end," said the cowpuncher as he rode into the night.

He did not try to justify himself by recalling that Glendon was an outlaw, whose capture or death was demanded by the law of the country; he did not remind himself that Glendon had killed old Paddy and had broken the unwritten law of fair play. It was the recollection of the woman with the cut face and finger-marked throat that sent Limber out into the storm. The woman Glendon had tried to drag into the mire of his own infamy as a reward for nine years of loyal devotion; the woman whom Limber had held in his heart and worshipped reverently.

Peanut slipped on the rain-sodden earth, and Limber, leaning forward in his saddle, kept his Winchester ready as he listened for the faintest indication of Glendon's presence. Limber did not believe that Glendon had carried out his assertion that he would go to the Hot Springs. Otherwise, he would have been there long before. It was more possible that he had doubled back on his tracks, and struck out through the mountains toward the south, heading for the border, in order to cover his trail as much as he could by dawn. He would have to keep well-hidden in the day time.

Suddenly, from the darkness sounded the shrill neigh of a horse. Limber threw himself on Peanut's neck and reached down, grasping the pony's nose firmly to prevent him from answering. Still keeping a grip on Peanut's nostrils, the cowboy dropped to the ground, and stood back of the pony's shoulder, believing that Glendon had seen him and was creeping on him in the dark. The flashes of lightning were less frequent. The rain and wind raged more furiously.

Then from the gloom trotted a riderless pony, calling again and again as it approached them. A flash enabled Limber's keen eyes to recognize Fox. With a little nicker of delight, it trotted to Peanut's side and stood rubbing its nose against the other pony's shoulder. Limber saw a weather-beaten saddle and new saddlebags on Fox's back, while a broken halter-rope dangled from the animal's neck. He knew the horse had broken away from Glendon, and was probably making its way back to the Circle Cross, the only home it had ever known. If so, Glendon would follow until he caught it, for he would need the extra horse in his long flight.

Limber hastily tied the broken halter-rope to the horn of Peanut's saddle, and left the two animals standing in the centre of the road as a decoy, while he crawled to a projecting clump of brush and slowly wormed his way parallel to the road. He was following Apache tactics, now. A prolonged flash of quivering, dazzling light, and Limber's half-blinded eyes scanned the brush and trees. Then the rifle leaped to his shoulder and his finger rested on the trigger.

Down the road he had seen Glendon. At the same time he knew that Glendon had seen him. Back into the brush he slipped lying flat on his face and writhing cautiously forward. There would be no time for a second shot-Glendon was waiting, too. How close was he, now? Inch by inch Limber dragged himself. Somewhere in the night, another man was crawling toward him, gun in hand-The man who had left the marks of his fingers on a woman's throat. God! Would there be no flash of lightning now that he needed just one more.

It came, as though in answer to his prayer. Dazzling, blinding and with frightful crash as though the whole world had fallen into space and crushed another world to atoms. A sharp tingling pain shot through Limber's muscles, his gun dropped from his hand and exploded; he wondered if Glendon had hit him, but it was rain, not blood that soaked his sleeve.

He gripped his gun and threw another cartridge into place. Once more he began creeping and waiting. When another flash came, the cowboy lowered his gun, and rose to his feet. At the side of the road ahead of him was an uprooted cottonwood tree. Under it lay a horse and a man.

Uncertain whether the man was dead or merely stunned, Limber crouched warily in the brush, waiting a tell-tale movement. But the horse and man did not stir.

Then the cowboy approached and looked down in the fitful glare of the flashes, and saw an immovable figure-face distorted with agony-open eyes staring unseeing into the storm-clothes across a charred breast-an odour of burnt flesh and singed hair-the body of a dead horse.

Limber gazed down at the man, his mind filled with conflicting emotions. He had intended killing Glendon as he would have killed a mad coyote or a rattlesnake, and he would have felt no regret; but, now —

He raised the dripping hat from his head. Not because of the broken thing that lay at his feet, but in recognition of something higher and more incomprehensible which rules the Universe-with its three unfathomable mysteries, Life, Death and Eternity.

Replacing his hat, Limber made his way back to the horses and slipped the Winchester into the scabbard which hung from Peanut's saddle.

"It's worked out all right, Peanut," said the cowboy as he mounted the pony and faced the Hot Springs ranch. "I'm glad I didn't have to kill him. Just the same I'd a done it ruther than let him drag her through Hell another hour. He can't bother her no more, now."

He stabled Fox and Peanut, then went to the kitchen where Chappo, like a faithful old watchdog, was dozing beside the stove. He started to his feet as Limber entered, but asked no questions when the cowboy, without a word, hung the Winchester on the pegs where he had found it.

Powell, sitting by the couch in the front room, heard Limber's steps. With a glance at the sleeping woman, he rose softly and went to the door that led into the kitchen. He closed the door and his eyes met Limber's.

"He's dead," said the cowboy. Then, reading the unspoken question in the doctor's eyes, he added, "No. It was the lightning done it. A tree fell on him and his horse."

"Thank God!" said Powell, but his tone was reverent, not jubilant.

"Is she all right?" asked Limber anxiously.

"Resting quietly. We'll take her over to Mrs. Traynor in the morning, Limber. She needs a woman friend, now."

"The Little Lady will look out for her," said the cowboy. Then he glanced at Chappo, and after a slight hesitation continued, "I wish you'd come out and take a look at Peanut's ankle, Doc."

Powell, catching the peculiar tone, nodded and followed to the barn where the ponies stood contentedly in their stalls. Limber closed the stable door and spoke in a low voice.

"Glendon was ridin' the horse and saddle he stole in Tombstone. It's a Lazy F pony. The lead-rope on Fox was busted."

"All right. I'll notify the Lazy F people," Powell replied wondering why Limber thought secrecy necessary.

"That ain't what's troublin' me. You see when Glen was arrested he rid his own saddle to town with the posse. I was with 'em, and I knowed his saddle. Besides, I bought it from Juan afterwards, when they was hard up for dinero. Mrs. Glendon didn't know I bought it. That saddle's over to the Diamond H and been thar for two months."

He walked to the corner of the barn and pointed at the saddle he had taken from Fox.

"That's the saddle that was on Fox," he said slowly. "It belonged to old Doctor King-we all thought the Apaches got it."

Powell grasped Limber's arm. "You don't think Glendon killed King, do you?"

"Thar ain't no way I can see to think he didn't," responded the cowpuncher. "From all we could find out, King and Glendon rid to the forks together and separated. King was goin' down the San Pedro and Glendon to Jackson's Flats. You can see how easy Glendon could of shot from the upper trail. The bullet went into King's head above the left temple and came out behind the right ear. You seen that yourself. I thought it was kinder queer when I heard Mrs. Glendon say the Apaches didn't reach the Circle Cross till noon and you said King had been dead over night. But then I figgered the Indians was snoopin' round that part for a couple of days."

"What object would Glendon have had?"

"He'd pick a fight with any one when he was tanked up a bit. You know he always wanted the Hot Springs, and King wouldn't sell it to him. He didn't know the land was patented, and mebbe he figgered that if King was dead it would be easy to jump the Springs. Of course, he didn't know about King makin' any Will, nor that you and the Boss was workin' up a deal with King. That's why Glendon's had it in for the Diamond H and for you ever since."

The chain of circumstantial evidence seemed conclusive as forgotten details were recalled.

"Thar's a heap of gold coins in the saddle bags that was on Fox," Limber went on. "Looks like it was Paddy's money that every one was hunting for. We all knowed that he had thirty-five thousand dollars in gold buried some place around. Thar was twenty-five thousand in that flower-box he guv to Jamie and the Little Lady; and this makes ten more. Paddy scattered it around."

"I wonder how Glendon happened to locate it?" mused the doctor.

Limber whirled about. "He located that money before he killed old Paddy! That's why he done it, and Alpaugh stood in with him! Glendon was too much of a coward to do anythin' exceptin' shoot old men and bully his wife. He was too rotten to live and too damn rotten to die! But, now what I want to know, Doc, is what are we goin' to do about that saddle and money? The posse will be here soon as the creek falls."

"Suppose I take charge of it and consult an attorney," suggested Powell after a few minutes' thought. "We have no absolute proof that it belonged to Paddy. As he had no heirs I am rather at sea about the proper procedure."

"All right. I'm goin' to take that saddle of King's and bury it," asserted Limber. "Thar ain't no use shoutin' about it now. Glen's dead and 'twon't do King no good, and Mrs. Glendon's got enough trouble to pack without havin' this extra bunch."

Powell returned to the house and told Chappo to go to bed. Out where the brush grew most thickly, Limber dug a deep hole like a small grave, and Doctor King's saddle was covered, while the steadily pouring rain obliterated all tell-tale marks of disturbed earth.

As the hours passed, the thunder grew faint and fainter; the lightning ceased; the rain fell in a soft patter, like children's voices whispering in the night. A dim, grey light mingled with the darkness of the sky, sleepy chirps and twitters sounded from rain-soaked nests, the pink fingers of Morning reached out and caressed the tips of the mountains.

Down the cañon near the crossing a man stood waiting to guard the woman he loved from knowledge of what had happened in the night. The rushing torrent was fast subsiding.

He lifted his head at the sound of galloping hoofs and men's voices, then he turned and looked down at the posse from Willcox. They reached the opposite bank of the stream and let the reins fall loosely on their ponies' necks as they recognized Limber.

"Hello, Limber! You was lucky to get here last night," called the leader. "We all were stuck at the mouth of the cañon till this morning. Seen any signs of Glendon?"

Limber was among them now. "Yep. He's on the road between here and the Circle Cross," was the answer.

"All right. Much obliged. Hurry up boys;" but Limber's upheld hand made them pause.

"You all don't need to hurry. Glen's dead. Lightnin' hit him and his horse. Mrs. Glendon's up here. She's sick and don't know nothin' about it yet. Doctor Powell is goin' to take her over to the Diamond H Ranch this mornin' to Mrs. Traynor."

"Gosh! It's sure tough on her anyway you put it."

"Is there anything we can do for her?" asked the leader of the posse.

"Jest don't let her know you're here, and try to manage so's to get Glendon away without her seein' him. That's all."

"We'll sure do that, Limber. She's a fine woman and we're glad to do anything we can for her. Glendon was no good to any one. Not even to himself."

"Juan is away with the Circle Cross team, but I'll send Chappo down with the wagon," were Limber's last words as the posse rode slowly down the cañon.

# Chapter Forty-Two

A year and a half passed by. Katherine sitting in her room at the Diamond H Ranch, was thinking of the many changes that had come into her life. Doctor Powell and Limber had brought her to Mrs. Traynor, and for long weeks afterward they had battled untiringly to save the life that threatened to slip away. With tender, encouraging words they fought the reaction of despair; but it was Nell who suggested sending for Donnie; Nell, who laid her baby boy in Katherine's arms; Nell, whose constant watchfulness and loving little caresses, finally brought answering smiles to Katherine's pale lips.

Donnie and Jamie at once struck up a friendship akin to David and Jonathan, and when the two lads would wake the ranch with their happy laughter-it was tonic to Katherine's bruised and aching heart.

For a long time she had believed that Glendon had escaped to Mexico; but at last Nell told her the truth. Donnie knew only that his father had been killed by lightning in a storm. Over at the Hot Springs, work was being pushed rapidly on the Sanitarium, and Limber and Powell divided their time between the two places.

There had been a "surprise party" as Bronco called it, when a couple of weeks previously, Traynor and Powell had called the four cowboys into the office, and handed each one an official envelope addressed by name. Upon opening it, they discovered that the Hot Springs, PL, Diamond H and Circle Cross ranches had been incorporated into the "Galiuro Cattle Corporation," Traynor as president; Powell, secretary and treasurer; and Limber, general manager. Bronco, Roarer and Holy were astounded to receive stock to the value of five thousand dollars; but Limber's envelope held, not only the five thousand dollars worth of stock, like the other boys; but also his note which he had given Traynor in return for the half interest in the PL herd. Limber looked at it puzzled, then he saw across the face of the note, the endorsement, "Paid in full with compound interest in loyalty and devotion." Beneath these words were the signatures of Allan Traynor, Nell Traynor and Cuthbert Powell.

The cowpuncher tried to speak, but was unable to utter a word. In silence he gripped Traynor's hand.

That was an uproarious evening on the Diamond H. The boys and old Fong surrounded the foreman in the bunkhouse after dinner. Fong, once again, had fashioned a huge cake. When it was set down on the wooden table, the Chinaman lifted the tissue paper that veiled it, and the boys let out a wild whoop. A five-strand fence bounded the edge of the cake; a small white cabin loomed in the centre, with a desperate attempt at a cow in icing beside it. A naturalist might have scorned the cow, but there was no mistaking the Diamond H brand in red icing that was the finishing touch on the animal's hip.

The boys clapped Fong on the back till his pigtail squirmed like an eel, and his grin threatened to split the lower part of his face.

Traynor standing outside watched the proceeding, then went over to tell Nell and Katherine.

"Poor Limber had to make a speech," he chuckled. "Fong joined with the rest, and they kept at him till he had to say something to get peace. Say, Nell, I wish you could have seen him! He stood up, looked at them, got red in the face, opened his mouth, shut it, then burst out, 'You're the orneriest bunch of boys in Arizona Territory, and if you don't quit pesterin' me, I'm goin' to fire the whole outfit the very first thing I do!'"

"Poor Limber!" laughed Nell, but the laugh was very tender. "They do worry him; but he knows they would give their lives for him!"

Like a panorama, these memories flitted swiftly before the eyes of Katherine Glendon, obliterating the darker days of her life. There was no bitterness now. Like the terrible storm of the cañon, they had passed away forever, and over the broken places bloomed beautiful flowers; a message of forgiveness.

The bit of lace she was sewing on a dress for Nell's baby, slipped from her hands, and her eyes wandered through the open door to the snow-cap of Mt. Graham across the Valley.

At first, Powell had hesitated to allow her return to the Hot Springs to live, dreading the effect of those terrible memories upon their happiness. When he told her of this, and that he would find a partner to live at the place, she had convinced him that her happiness lay helping him with his work at the Springs; so it had been decided. Now, that the project was nearing completion, Powell received offers from many sources, so that he might carry out the plans on the most extensive scale. The money found in the saddle-bags the night Glendon died, had been also added to the funds, after communication and consultation with proper legal authority. This provided for the maintenance of additional children.

All the plans had been discussed between Powell, Traynor, Nell and Katherine, and the two women had made many suggestions the men overlooked. There were even toys, games, books with wonderful fairy tales, already unpacked at the Springs.

Two weeks had been passed there happily, arranging, sorting and working together. Donnie and Jamie, with their ponies and Juan and Chappo as guides, had explored trails and planned many future adventures. The two old Mexicans were as happy as children, and at night, when they related tales of Mexico, or Chappo told of his captivity among the Apaches, the boys felt that life could hold no more fascinating experiences.

Katherine's thoughts were interrupted by the sound of steps. She rose quickly and turned to the open door. A pink Rambler rose in full bloom twined above the porch, and a puff of wind caught the blossoms and showered the fragrant petals over her as she held out her hands to welcome the man she loved. He looked at her with happy eyes and saw-no longer a vague dream —a living, glorious reality, smiling with no shadow on her beautiful face, his Lady of the Pool.

The rose leaves fell softly, about them. "See, dearest," he said, "it is a symbol of our future. The roses are shedding their petals on your path, so that not even the tiniest pebble shall bruise your feet!"

She smiled at him, her eyes misty with happiness, then together they entered the room, to discuss their plans.

"I've got to have a talk with Donnie today," said Powell. "I hope he will understand."

They heard the noise of ponies dashing into the stable, the laughter of happy voices. Like a small cyclone, Donnie rushed into the room and faced Powell in boyish delight.

"Is the Sanitarium almost done?" he asked breathlessly.

"Finished, at last!" Powell's arm was across the lad's shoulder. He smiled into the glowing, upturned face, thankful that it bore no resemblance to Glendon. Donnie was his mother in every feature. "The first children will be here next month!"

"I bet they'll get good and well after we have them awhile," prophesied Donnie. "You know, you promised I could be your partner."

"Yes, old man! I want you to study so that when you grow up you can work with me. I'm going to take you over to the Springs so you can start your studies very soon. How will that suit you?"

The boy's face clouded. He glanced from Powell to his mother.

"I can't leave Marmee alone. I'm her Knight, and the only one she's got to look out for her, now."

"How about taking her over with us?" suggested Powell.

"Oh, will you?" Donnie's face glowed with delight. "Marmee, you will go, won't you?"

The doctor laid his hands on the boy's shoulders and looked at him seriously. "Donnie, would you let me be your father, so that I can take care of your mother and you, and we all be partners as long as we live?"

The child's startled eyes wandered from the man to the woman. For a brief space he made no reply. Then flinging his arms about his mother's neck, he clung to her in the first pang of renunciation. The eyes that looked at him were very tender.

With a strange little dignity, he drew himself up and held out his hand to the doctor, saying, "I'm awful glad she likes you." The voice trembled, the lips were uncertain, a lump hurt in his throat. Donnie was afraid that he was going to cry. He was too big to cry now-his shoulders squared. Quickly, he turned and left the room. The man and woman watched the pathetic little figure, with drooping head, pass the window.

"He will understand soon that I am not going to take you away from him," Powell's voice was gentle, "but I know how it hurts at first."

Drawing some letters from his pocket, he seated himself beside Katherine on the couch. "These are from the children and the matron who will travel with them and help care for them at the Springs," he explained.

Together they read misspelled words scrawled in crude characters. One child wanted to know if he could have a real, live chicken; another asked nothing but a chance to see trees and places where 'the cops don't make you keep off;' a third begged permission to bring his cat, Nigger, "becoz Nigger ain't got no one to luv him but me-becoz he has got a crooked tail and one eye's gone, but I luv him and he luvs me and he'll be lonesome after I go way."

Katherine remembered the dog that had been her sole companion so many hours-the dog that Limber had buried in a little grave at the Circle Cross.

"Of course, Nigger is coming?" she laughed with a catch in her voice.

"A special invitation has already gone for him, and the matron is authorized to buy a basket for Nigger's comfort;" was the answer.

Katherine was silent for a moment, and Powell leaned toward her. His hand lifted her face gently, "Sweetheart, what are your thoughts?"

Her eyes were dim and her voice trembled, "'And a Knight shall come that shall have a head of gold, the look of a lion, a heart of steel, conditions without weakness, the valour of a man, and faith and belief in God. And he shall be the best Knight in the world.'"

Powell's arms slipped about her and he drew her close. "May I prove worthy to be your Knight for all the days of my life, dear Lady of the Pool!"

# Chapter Forty-Three

Only the Galiuros knew that a pinto pony had trodden unbroken trails through the night, until it reached a spot where the tangled growth of brush thinned and ended on a high ledge overlooking the undulating flat of the Sulphur Springs range.

The mysterious beauty of coming dawn merged with dying starlight, where faint shadows outlined the rugged peaks of the Grahams across the broad Valley. Above them all Mt. Graham lifted its glorious, snow-capped head. Unconquered, unscathed by the storms of centuries past, it gazed steadfastly at the sky above it, while the world slept at its feet.

Limber sat on the back of the pinto pony. His grey eyes shone with a wonderful light, for the strength of his loved mountains had crept into his heart during the long hours of his silent battle. Out of the storm and turmoil, the trail had led to peace.

A faint rustling sounded sibilantly. It was a vagrant, gossiping breeze telling the leaves and grasses that a new day had been born.

Yesterday, with its joys and sorrows, its ambitions and disappointments, was dead. Its ghost floated into the clear blue sky that smiled down between the drifting clouds.

Today came laughing over the mountains. Her gold-shod feet twinkled as she ran. The sunbeam in her hand gleamed like a magic wand, transmuting each thing to dazzling beauty. It reached a little pinto pony standing on an overhanging ledge. Like the flash of a golden lance, the sunbeam rested on the shoulder of the man, who craved no greater privilege than to give all, and ask nothing in return.

His head was bare. The sunlight touched his upturned face and the tender smile on his lips.

"God bless her, and make her happy," he whispered softly.